STAY
AWAKE

STAY AWAKE

MEGAN GOLDIN

ST. MARTIN'S PRESS
NEW YORK

First published in the United States by St. Martin's Press, an imprint of St. Martin's Publishing Group

STAY AWAKE. Copyright © 2022 by Megan Goldin. All rights reserved. Printed in the United States of America. For information, address St. Martin's Publishing Group, 120 Broadway, New York, NY 10271.

www.stmartins.com

Designed by Michelle McMillian

Library of Congress Cataloging-in-Publication Data

Names: Goldin, Megan, author.
Title: Stay awake / Megan Goldin.
Description: First edition. | New York : St. Martin's Press, 2022.
Identifiers: LCCN 2022005929 | ISBN 9781250280664 (hardcover) |
    ISBN 9781250283962 (Canadian) | ISBN 9781250280671 (ebook)
Subjects: LCGFT: Novels.
Classification: LCC PR9619.4.G654 S73 2022 | DDC 823/.92—dc23/
    eng/20220225
LC record available at https://lccn.loc.gov/2022005929

Our books may be purchased in bulk for promotional, educational, or business use. Please contact your local bookseller or the Macmillan Corporate and Premium Sales Department at 1-800-221-7945, extension 5442, or by email at MacmillanSpecialMarkets@macmillan.com.

First U.S. Edition: 2022
First Canadian Edition: 2022

10 9 8 7 6 5 4 3 2 1

To "TLEA." With love . . .

Just because you're paranoid doesn't mean they aren't after you.
—Joseph Heller, *Catch-22*

STAY
AWAKE

Chapter
One

Wednesday 2:42 A.M.

Starbursts blink from streetlights like they're sharing a secret as I wake to find myself slumped in the back of a cab, without any recollection of how I got here, or where I'm going.

I stare hypnotically out the window as city lights streak by against a blanket of darkness, lulled by the pensive hum of the car radio.

"Not much longer," the driver murmurs, braking suddenly at a red traffic light.

Our eyes lock in the rearview mirror until the traffic light changes and the city slides away in a swirl of neon.

"This tune is for all the insomniacs out there, looking for sleep like it's a star-crossed lover." The DJ's laconic voice disappears under the strum of an acoustic guitar.

We cross the Brooklyn Bridge listening to Paul Simon sing about the moon's desolate eyes. I look up, above the jagged skyline of the city's silhouette. There's no moon in the murky sky tonight. A siren wails ominously in the distance as we cruise through a maze of sleepy streets.

"We've arrived." The driver's voice breaks through the jumble of my drowsy thoughts.

I pay with a crumpled fifty-dollar bill clutched in my fist and cross the one-way street to the apartment I share with Amy. It's on the second floor of an old brownstone that's been transformed into a modern apartment block with a sundeck on the roof.

When I'm at the street door, I realize I don't have my keys or purse. I rest my forehead wearily against the rough brick wall next to the entrance and reluctantly press the intercom buzzer to wake Amy.

"Come on, Amy. Please be home."

Leaves fall from half-naked trees like autumnal rain. I do a double take. The leaves are not just an anomaly. They're an impossibility. Who ever heard of fall leaves in midsummer?

Watching the leaves float ethereally onto the sidewalk deepens the disquiet I've felt since waking in the cab. The last thing I remember before opening my eyes was working at my sun-drenched desk by the office window until I was startled by the sudden ring of my desk phone.

"This is Liv," I said into the receiver as I looked out at a magnificent summer sky.

Everything after that is a blank, until now.

My breath hovers in the frigid air like a restless ghost. Summer, I realize with a shiver, has disappeared like a wrinkle in time.

I press the intercom buzzer again, and again. Each time, I keep my finger on the button for a little longer until eventually the kitchen lights turn on, illuminating the stoop. I hear a clatter of footsteps on the stairs.

"Amy, I am so sorry . . ." I begin as the building door swings open.

It's not Amy standing on the threshold. It's two strangers. The woman is tall with straight hair. Salon gold. She wears pajamas with a blue bunny print. Her pedicured feet are bare. Next to her is a tall, athletic man with tousled blond hair and matching stubble. He wears gray sweatpants and a white top that he lifts to scratch his taut belly.

"What the hell are you thinking, ringing our doorbell in the middle of the night?" It's the woman who chews me out.

"I didn't know that Amy had friends staying tonight," I stammer, taken aback by the bite of her tone.

This is not the first time I've returned home to find strangers staying at my apartment. Amy is a brilliant doctor who graduated at the top of her class. I love her to death, but she can be scatterbrained about updating me on what she considers mundane things, such as friends from back home camping out on our living room floor for a couple of weeks.

"I'm Liv," I introduce myself. "I'm so sorry I woke you. I forgot my house keys. Again." I roll my eyes self-deprecatingly.

The woman's humorless gaze remains fixed on me.

"That's why I rang the doorbell. . . ." My voice fades out.

Neither of them moves out of the way. Their blank expressions unnerve me.

"Well, I guess I'd better go upstairs and get some sleep. It's been a long day." I step forward, eager to get into the warmth of my apartment and, hopefully soon, the comfort of my bed. As I move across the threshold, the woman slams the door shut to try to keep me out.

"Ouch." I wince when the door hits my foot.

Despite the pain, I don't move my foot out of the way.

"You need to go," she tells me.

"That's my apartment." I point to the top of the landing.

"That's where we live," says the man. "You've made a mistake."

I almost believe him until I catch a glimpse of the distinctive tiled hallway floor and the dark timber staircase banister with its curved edge. They're unique period features preserved to maintain the building's heritage character.

"I've lived upstairs with Amy for years."

Recognition flashes across his face at my mention of Amy. I exhale in relief. We're no longer talking at cross-purposes.

"Amy Decker?" he asks.

"Yes!"

"That's the doctor whose junk mail we get," he tells his girlfriend, as if I'm not here.

I want to tell him that Amy still lives here. As do I. I bite my tongue, aware they have the upper hand. After all, I'm the one standing out in the cold.

Soft warm light beckons from the partly open apartment door upstairs. I ache with a crushing longing to go up there and resume my life. The only way to do that is to convince them to let me in.

"I'm so sorry for the mix-up," I grovel. "It's been one of those nights! I've lost my purse and my phone." I shiver in the cold. "Can I at least use your phone to call my boyfriend, Marco, to come and get me? It's freezing out here."

The woman gives me a death stare. I could die of hypothermia on the doorstep for all she cares. Her boyfriend is more sympathetic.

I look up at him, my eyes wide and pleading. He hesitates and then pushes open the street door to let me in. His girlfriend stares daggers at him for caving in. Her feet stomp angrily all the way up to the landing.

Chapter
Two

All my certainty disappears like a popped bubble when I'm inside. I've made an embarrassing blunder. It isn't my apartment. Sure, the layout is the same. But the decor is entirely different.

The apartment looks like the cover of an Ikea catalogue, its interior designed to an inch of its life in a mélange of whites and natural accents. Even the kitchen cabinets are new.

My seasoned teak dinner table, my tattered Persian rug, and my colorful artisan bookshelf filled with my eclectic collection of books and magazines have all been replaced with minimalist designer chic.

I'm about to make my apologies and leave when I catch a glimpse of brightly painted flower boxes in the apartment window across the way. I've stared at that view for years. This is definitely my apartment.

My head spins with questions. Who are these people? Where's my stuff? Most importantly, though I can hardly bear to dwell on it, why have I forgotten that I don't live here anymore?

"Where's Shawna?" I ask, sticking to practicalities.

"Who?"

"My cat!"

"There was a one-eyed ginger cat that kept sneaking in last winter. We took it to the shelter."

"You had my cat killed?" I'm horrified they'd be so callous.

"We didn't have her killed. We gave her to the animal shelter."

"What do you think they do to half-blind cats?"

"Look," the woman cuts in impatiently, handing me a phone. "We need to get back to sleep. We both have work meetings first thing in the morning. Call your boyfriend, and then go down and wait for him on the street."

I wander through an open doorway, barely hearing her as I enter my bedroom.

"Hey, you can't go in there!" she yells, coming after me.

The ultramodern platform bed with rumpled bamboo-cotton sheets is not mine. Neither is the metal floor lamp, or the abstract zebra print on the wall. I pick up a photo frame from next to the bed. Everyone in the picture is a stranger.

"Don't touch that!" She snatches the frame from me.

I'm vaguely aware that her face is too close to mine. Her skin is mottled red, draining all her natural beauty. Her yelling is drowned out by a crackling sound inside my head. It gets faster and faster until it sounds like a Geiger counter hitting a radiation contamination site.

"Grant, call the cops," she orders.

The noise in my head stops abruptly. The last thing I want right now is a confrontation with the police. I'm acutely aware the police won't take my side. Even in my confusion, I know it looks bad for me. I can hardly explain myself to the police when I don't have the faintest idea what's happening.

"Wait!" I say, louder than necessary. "I'll leave."

I hold the staircase handrail tightly so that my legs don't buckle under me as I walk down to the street entrance.

"Don't come back. If I ever see you here again, then we *will* call the cops," the woman calls from the landing. I open the building door and step out into the cold.

Lowering myself to the top stair of the stoop, I lean weakly against the brick wall under the intercom as I try to think of somewhere to go. I've been cast out of my home into the cold in the middle of the night. I remind myself that it's not my home anymore. The couple upstairs have clearly been living there for some time.

My head throbs with confusion. I pat down my pockets on the off-chance that I have my phone tucked away somewhere. In the front pocket of my jeans I find a wad of cash. There's an object wrapped in a T-shirt in the pocket of my long cardigan.

I prop the T-shirt on my lap and carefully unwrap it. Inside is a stainless steel knife streaked with blood so fresh I can smell it. I flinch instinctively, repulsed by the thought that this was in my pocket. The knife tumbles onto a step, hitting the concrete with a metallic clatter.

I'm reluctant to touch the blade. After a moment of hesitation, I pick it up with the T-shirt and toss both the knife and the shirt into a trash can set against a brick wall. As I close the lid, I hear car doors slam farther up the street. It's a cab dropping off passengers. I stand in the middle of the street and wave down the cab as it drives toward me, its headlights shining on the wet street ahead.

"Where to?" the driver asks once I'm inside.

I give him Marco's address even though I don't know how Marco will react when I turn up at his place in the middle of the night. Our relationship has clear boundaries. One of them is that we don't drop in on each other without calling first. We don't even have keys to each other's apartments. I reassure myself that Marco wouldn't want me wandering in the dark with nowhere to go.

City lights pulsate in the distance as the cab weaves through thinly trafficked streets to mournful notes of Billy Joel singing good night to his angel on the radio. As we pass a streetlight, I notice writing on the backs of my hands. I look like a human graffiti board.

A few messages are legible. Most are so washed out that they're virtually indecipherable in the streetlights strobing intermittently across me.

Above my knuckles are letters written in black ballpoint pen. I put both fists together. The letters spell out the words STAY AWAKE. Above my right wrist I've written the name and address of a place called Nocturnal.

I lean forward and tell the driver to take me there instead.

Chapter
Three

Wednesday 3:44 A.M.

There's nothing familiar about Nocturnal when I press my face to the stippled glass door of the bar entrance. Smudges of color move behind the thick art deco glass like an impressionist painting coming to life.

The roar of the bar spills into the street when the doors open. The blur of colors I saw through the mottled glass turn into people in long overcoats, arranging scarves around their necks. Their inebriated eyes scan for passing cabs as they talk loudly among themselves in voices not yet modulated for the quiet of the street.

Once they pass, I grab the door before it shuts and enter a cavernous room filled with moody lighting and a deafening hum of laughter and clinking glasses.

"We're closing soon," an attendant tells me as if she knows me.

She disconnects a velvet red cord. It flops behind me as I walk inside. To my right is a closed-off section with empty restaurant tables. A cleaner in a white uniform silently mops the floor as if he is slow-dancing in his sleep.

I go down two steps into the busy bar area, where I get tangled in a party of eight rising from their table. They scrape their chairs against the floor as they get to their feet and drunkenly stumble toward the entrance. They take the bulk of the noise with them.

A few hard-core drinkers remain, swilling their drinks as they perch on stools. None of them talk to each other. They keep their eyes firmly on their liquor glasses as if that's their only source of solace. Behind the bar is a 1930s-era triple-paneled mirror.

It feels as if I'm looking at a distorted version of myself in a carnival mirror. My hair is very long and much darker than my natural honey-brown shade. It's the color of coffee: Americano. I plait it to get it out of the way, surprised at how practiced I am at a skill I don't remember learning.

A bartender with a dark goatee and white shirtsleeves rolled to his elbows to reveal a tattoo pours a drink for a man slouched on a barstool. The bartender looks directly at me, flashing a broad smile filled with warm recognition.

"Liv!"

I'm so surprised this stranger knows my name that I instinctively glance behind me to see if some other woman with the same name happens to be in the vicinity.

"I knew you'd come back before we closed." It's as if he's picking up the thread of a previous conversation.

"What can I get you, Liv? It's on the house."

"Thanks, but all I want is water," I tell him as I squirm onto a vacant barstool. "I'm not drinking tonight."

"That's not what you told me a few hours ago," he chuckles, handing me a glass of ice water.

"I was here earlier?"

The bartender's eyes dance in delight at my brain freeze. "Sure. At around ten. You had a few drinks and then you left."

"Alone?"

"You were with a dude, Liv," he says, watching me carefully. "You don't remember?"

My chest tightens with unease. The bartender clearly knows more about me than I do right now.

I must have been here with Marco. Maybe we were drinking. That would explain the out-of-body sensation I've felt since I woke in the cab.

"Everything's fuzzy right now," I explain. "What did he look like, the guy I was with?"

"I only saw the back of your heads as you left. The place was jam-packed. You know what it's like when we have a live band playing."

I smile knowingly, even though I don't remember anything. Not the bartender. Not this bar. Not the man I left with last night. I change the subject and ask whether I left my purse or my cell phone when I was here earlier. They both appear to be missing.

"Not that I've seen, but I'll ask the staff once we close and let you know when you come in tomorrow." He pours liquor into a cocktail shaker.

I'm so focused on trying to reconstruct last night from the tiny scraps of information he's given me that I jump when he puts a cocktail glass in front of me and asks me what I think.

"It's a new take on a gin and tonic. I use ginger ale instead of tonic. Try it."

I shudder as the liquor hits my throat.

"You don't like it?"

"It's pretty good, actually. It's just that I'm not in the mood for alcohol tonight."

I stifle an exhausted yawn. The brass clock on the wall says it's close to four in the morning. "I should go. It's way past my bedtime," I joke.

"You're never in bed at this time," he assures me.

"Then where am I?"

"Here. Drinking. Talking to me. Taste-testing my new cocktails. Anywhere but in bed."

"Why?"

"You hate sleeping. Especially at night."

The manager announces the bar is closing in five minutes. As if in unison, all the stragglers sitting along the bar swallow what's left of their drinks and trail out of the main doors to the street. I hang around talking to the bartender as the staff pile chairs on tables.

"How do you know so much about me?"

"You tell me all your secrets," he teases.

"What secrets?"

In answer, he gestures toward the ballpoint letters above my knuckles that spell out the words STAY AWAKE. I snatch my hands away in embarrassment.

"I sometimes write reminders to myself," I explain, self-consciously. "It's a bad habit. From when I was a kid."

"You do it so you don't forget stuff. Like this." He points to writing on my hand that says: DON'T SLEEP! Below it, partly hidden by my sleeve, it says: WAKE UP.

"What do I have against sleep?"

"You're afraid of what you do in your sleep." He flips a white cloth off his shoulder and wipes a beer glass dry as his words sink in. "At least, that's what you told me the other night."

"What could I possibly do in my sleep?" I ask.

Then I remember the bloodied knife.

Chapter
Four

Darcy Halliday pushed through the crowd pressed against police barricades outside the entrance of an apartment building. A television crew was setting up a camera and sound equipment near a patrol car with its siren lights whirring. A reporter in pancake makeup paced nearby, rehearsing her lines.

Nobody paid much attention to Halliday as she moved toward the police tape. She wore navy running shorts and a pink Lycra tank top. Flushed and sweaty from her morning run, she looked like any other curious jogger stopping to find out what was going on.

"Move along. There's nothing to see here," ordered a cop manning a police barricade outside the building. Halliday pushed through a gap in the crowd and ducked under the police tape.

"Miss, I need you to step back," the cop barked. He was about to block her way when he noticed the detective shield she held out.

She stepped around him and took the steps to the lobby. She'd been on her morning run to the precinct when a message popped up on the precinct group chat about a homicide on East Fifty-Third. The captain had asked if any of his detectives were in the vicinity.

"I'm a block away," she'd messaged back, even though she was more like three blocks away.

Still, that put her closer than anyone else. She sprinted past gridlocked traffic with the certainty she'd be the first investigator at the scene.

In the two months since Halliday moved to homicide on a six-month temporary transfer, she hadn't once worked her own case. She didn't even have a regular partner. She was the extra pair of hands assigned to help other detectives with their investigations. She knew the drill. It was all about paying dues. Two months into the job, she was done proving herself. As far as she was concerned, she'd already paid every due she ever owed. With interest.

Halliday had served in the military for six years with distinction, during which time she'd done multiple tours in Iraq and Afghanistan. She joined the NYPD after her discharge. Her first two years were spent as a patrol cop, with occasional stints in vice, dressing as a hooker to act as bait. Halliday did a stint in forensics after she aced the detective's exam and then five months in Major Case while she waited for an opening in homicide. It came in the form of a temporary position to replace a detective who'd gone on long-term sick leave.

Halliday had more than earned her badge. Yet her time in homicide felt like her first year as a beat cop, where she was treated as a wet-behind-the-ears rookie despite her military service and combat experience. So when she saw that she was in the vicinity of a homicide, she jumped at the chance to get in early on the case.

"What floor?" she asked the doorman, flashing her badge.

"Sixth."

Halliday jogged up the stairs to avoid waiting for the elevators. On the sixth-floor landing, she unzipped her runner's pouch and took out an NYPD zipped top and blue nylon warm-up pants that she kept for such emergencies.

She put them on and brushed her shoulder-length chestnut hair with her fingers before swinging the stairwell door open, coming out into a corridor where a cop was questioning a red-haired woman near an apartment sealed off with crime scene tape.

The woman spoke in broken English with a strong Eastern European accent. Halliday assumed she was the person who'd alerted 9–1–1 after finding the body.

"The cleaner's name is Olga Kuznetsov," the patrol officer told Halliday when she took him aside for a quick update. He mispronounced the name. "She says she arrived to clean just after seven. Found a dead man in the bed. Apparently, she cleans the apartment a couple of times a week. The owner stays some nights. The rest of the time he puts the apartment up on Airbnb or some other website."

Halliday turned to the cleaner. "Is the dead man the owner?"

"I never seen owner before. He always at work when I clean. Doorman give me key. I give key back after I finish," Olga explained in halting English.

Next to her was a cleaning trolley. Olga told them that she worked for a company that provided maid service for short-term apartment rentals.

"Olga, did you take anything out of the apartment? Towels, bedding, garbage, anything at all?" Halliday asked.

"I throw out one bag from kitchen." She pointed at a garbage chute near the elevator.

The police officer who'd been questioning her groaned softly. He knew what that meant. He'd have to take Olga down to the garbage room to identify the trash bag she tossed down the chute.

Halliday took crime scene gloves out of her runner's pack and put them on, along with shoe covers. Another cop stood guard outside the apartment's front door, which was crisscrossed with crime scene tape.

"Any other detectives arrive yet?" Halliday asked, taking a clipboard and signing in.

"You're the first," he answered.

Halliday held out her phone to film her movements as she ducked under the crime scene tape and entered the apartment. It stunk of ammonia. The faux marble tiles by the entrance were damp from fresh mopping. Streaks of cleaning fluid were drying on the mirrored living room walls.

"Looks like Olga cleaned the place before she found the body," she called out to the cop by the doorway.

"She cleaned the living room and kitchen before she went into the bedroom. That's where she found the stiff. In bed with a hole in his chest. Push open the bedroom door and you'll see him."

The apartment was the size of a hotel room and just as impersonal. It had a compact kitchen and living area. There was a gray leather L-shaped sofa and a round coffee table with a freshly vacuumed shag rug underneath. On the wall was a large-screen television. The kitchen counter had two metal barstools for meals. The apartment was too small for a dinner table.

Halliday filmed the living room and kitchen area before opening the stainless steel fridge. Inside were shelves of deli containers of salads and cut-up fruit from Whole Foods, an assortment of yogurts and a half-drunk bottle of orange juice.

Next to the sink were two tall drinking glasses that had been cleaned and left to dry. More evidence washed away. "Damn. We really can't get a break," Halliday muttered.

She popped a piece of mint gum into her mouth and cracked it as she pushed open the bedroom door, holding out her phone to record her entry into the room where the murder had taken place. Halliday felt a rush of cold air from a rotating ceiling fan as she stepped inside.

She didn't turn off the fan. Nor did she turn on the bedroom light.

Nothing could be tampered with until the forensic team officially photographed everything exactly the way it was found.

The bedroom was semidark. The lights were off and the window shades were pulled down. Halliday could see enough to determine the victim was male, likely in his thirties.

The wildly rotating ceiling fan tousled his hair as it spun, making it look as if he was still alive. Halliday squatted down to get a closer look at him. The indents in his square-jawed cheeks suggested he had dimples when he smiled. He looked like a man who smiled a lot. His jaw was square. His nose was aquiline. His lips were decidedly blue.

He was naked except for black boxer shorts. His clothes were in a pile on the carpet. An ugly gash under his rib cage suggested the murder weapon was a sharp object of some sort, probably a knife. Halliday hadn't seen a knife lying around during her cursory inspection of the scene. She wondered if the killer had taken it.

She guessed the victim died instantly. It explained the lack of any notable blood splatter at the scene. It did not explain the serene set of his mouth. Nobody looked that relaxed while being stabbed to death.

She saw nothing lying around to help identify the victim. There was no wallet on the bedside table. No cell phone. The bedside drawers were all empty.

"How did you get here so quickly? Traffic's backed up for miles this morning."

Halliday spun around to see Dr. Franklin, the medical examiner, entering the bedroom.

"I was on my morning run to work when the call came in," Halliday said. She knew Franklin from her time in forensics.

"You're still running?" he asked.

"Six miles a day. Five times a week. What about you?"

"Gave it up after my knee surgery."

Dr. Franklin's narrow face was pursed in concentration as he checked the room temperature from three different locations. He was close to retirement and had given up any pretense of adhering to dress code conventions. These days he tended to wear polo shirts and chinos rather than suits and ties. It gave the impression he'd abandoned a golf game to come to the murder scene.

"I assume the ceiling fan was on when the victim was found?" he asked. "It might affect my calculations on the time of death."

"I believe so. We'll double-check with the cleaner," said Halliday, poking her head into the en suite bathroom while Franklin examined the victim.

Splashed water on the floor suggested someone washed up in the preceding hours. A long strand of dark hair was balanced on the sink. The forensics team would collect it when they processed the scene.

"Any idea of how long ago he died?" Halliday opened the bathroom cupboard.

"The ceiling fan would have kept things cooler in here and slowed down decomposition. So I'd guess he's been dead for between six and nine hours. I'll do a more exact calculation later. Cause of death appears to be from a stab wound to the heart. That's why there's not much blood. His heart would have stopped midbeat."

"Does anything about the vic strike you as strange?" Halliday asked cryptically.

"Other than the gaping hole in his chest?" he asked flippantly, before realizing Halliday was serious. "What's troubling you, Detective?"

"Looks to me like he slept through his own murder."

"You think he was drugged?"

"I'd say it's a distinct possibility. There's no bruises or scratches on his body. No sign of a struggle. The victim was at least six foot tall. He was in good physical shape. A man that strong would have fought like a demon."

Halliday squatted next to the victim and examined his hands and nails with the flashlight of her phone. There were no obvious defense wounds.

"I don't see abrasions or trauma to his nails or fists. I'm betting he never put up a fight." She stood up and took a step back, bumping into what felt like a brick wall.

Chapter
Five

It wasn't a brick wall. It was Detective Jack Lavelle. He was surveying the crime scene with the jaded gaze of a homicide cop who'd seen too many murders to count over his fifteen years on the job. He wore jeans and a brown leather bomber jacket. He, too, had been heading to the precinct to start his shift when the call came through.

Halliday gritted her teeth as she prepared to fight her corner. There was no way she was going to get bumped off this case just because the hotshot detective decided to mosey on over and steal her case.

"Detective Lavelle," she said sweetly. "I guess you stopped by to see if I need a hand. I don't."

"I can see that, Detective," he said, making no effort to move.

"Good. I presume you're heading back to the precinct."

"I can't."

"Why not?"

"The captain wants me to work with you on this case," Lavelle responded. "As partners," he added, when he saw Halliday's eyes flash angrily.

"I thought you don't work with partners."

"I don't," he said, squatting on his haunches to take a closer look at the victim. "But I don't always get what I want. Catch me up here. Any ID for the victim?"

"Nothing so far," Halliday said after a frustrated pause. "No wallet that I could find. No cell phone. The body was found by the cleaner. We believe the victim rented the apartment on Airbnb or something similar," she said. "The cleaner doesn't usually clean on days when the apartment is rented out. Apparently, the owner forgot to cancel the cleaning service this morning."

"Anything else?" he asked.

Halliday moved to the other side of the bed and shone the flashlight on the pillow next to the dead man. "My guess is that he wasn't here alone," she said, fixing the beam on an indent in the pillow. "Someone was lying in bed next to him. Most likely a woman."

"Why a woman?"

Using the flashlight beam, she traced a single long hair on the pillow. The forensics team would bag it when they arrived.

A half-empty bottle of wine was on the table next to the bed. "There are no glasses. I'm guessing they drank straight from the bottle."

"We'll get the lab to do a rush job on the bottle. I'll tell them to check for fingerprints and DNA. Maybe there's saliva on the rim."

"We'll need toxicology as well," Halliday added.

"Why toxicology?"

"I think the victim was sedated. That would explain the absence of defense wounds. We'll need to get the apartment owner's name and find out who booked it," Halliday said. "We'll also need to rustle up some extra hands to see if the murder weapon was discarded in a Dumpster nearby, and collect and run through security footage. I'm sure this building has plenty of surveillance cameras."

"I took down the owner's name and details from the doorman on my way up here," Lavelle said. "The owner's on a flight to Hong Kong.

Business trip. I've arranged for a team of uniforms to help with the grunt work."

A sudden racket outside the apartment announced the arrival of the forensics team. Halliday and Lavelle waited in the living room while the crime scene photographer filmed the bedroom. The rest of the crime scene team arranged their equipment in the hallway by the elevators.

"Detective Halliday," someone called from the doorway.

Halliday headed over to the threshold where a patrol cop who'd gone down to the trash room with the cleaner swung a white garbage bag in his gloved hand.

"How do we know this is the trash the cleaner threw out?" Halliday asked, unknotting the handles of the garbage bag and peering inside.

"Olga's one hundred percent certain. She'll put it in her statement. She says there wasn't much trash in the bag. This was the only bag that fitted her description."

Halliday rifled through the trash inside the bag with her gloved hands. There was an apple core and an empty yogurt container, the same brand as the ones in the fridge. At the bottom were yellow Post-it notes crumpled into balls of paper. One note, written in black marker, said: STAY AWAKE. The others had messages that were no less weird. DON'T OPEN THE DOOR. DON'T ANSWER THE PHONE.

"Detective Halliday, you'd better come over here," Lavelle called. "You're going to want to see this."

She handed the trash bag to a crime scene technician to collect as evidence and joined Lavelle in the bedroom. While she'd been going through the trash, the crime scene photographer had ripped off the bedsheet to continue photographing the victim. With the top sheet gone, the soles of the victim's feet were visible. They were cut up and drenched in blood.

"There are multiple slashes to his feet," Lavelle said.

"Strange. Why go to the trouble of shredding the victim's feet when there's only one stab wound in his torso?" Halliday squatted down at the end of the bed to take a close look at the gashes. "It's as if the killer couldn't decide whether to be frenzied or restrained."

"Maybe the killer had a foot fetish," said Lavelle. "Why else cut his feet to ribbons?"

"For the blood." Halliday rose. Her eyes scanned the bedroom. "The killer needed his blood."

"Why would the killer need his blood?" the crime scene photographer asked. He bent down and twisted his camera lens to take a close-up of the victim's feet.

Halliday ran her flashlight around the bed looking for the answer. The beam hit a tiny drop of blood on the plush gray carpet. And then another, and another. The trail led to the window shades. Halliday pulled at a toggle and lifted the shades to expose an expansive floor-to-ceiling window.

Written across a glass pane in blood was a message: *!PU EKAW*. A camera flash lit up the room as the crime scene photographer took a photo.

"It looks like gibberish," he said.

"It's sign writing. It was written backward so it can be read properly from the outside," said Halliday.

"What does it say?" the photographer asked, taking a burst of photos.

"It says: *WAKE UP!*"

Chapter
Six

Pigeons warble by my feet as I doze on a park bench. My body sways like a pendulum, moving left to right as I drift to sleep, snap awake, and then do it all over again. All the while, I'm riddled with a nagging feeling that something is wrong.

The urgent siren of a fire truck startles me. I open my eyes only to be blinded by the sun. Shielding my face with my arm, I blink rapidly as my eyes adjust to the explosion of light. My disorientation disappears like a burst bubble when a shape emerges from the blinding light and morphs into an arch.

I'm at Washington Square Park. The arch reassures me. I often come here in the summer to drink coffee in the sunshine before heading to the madhouse that's my office a block away.

On my lap is a paper bag with the remnants of an orange poppy seed muffin and an empty coffee cup with dried milk froth on the lid. It's my standard take-out breakfast. All that's missing is my phone, which I usually leave at my desk before heading out here so I can chill before being bombarded by work calls for the rest of the day.

Now that my eyes have adjusted to the light, I notice there's not a scrap of blue in the gunmetal sky. As I look around, I absorb other incongruencies.

People crisscross the pathways of the park in buttoned-up coats and scarves, or sweaters in bleak colors that match their somber faces. There's no lush summery foliage on the trees. Quite the opposite. The dogwoods and elms are a mass of brittle branches in the final throes of fall. Piles of dead leaves scatter across the pathway, blown by a wind infused with the unmistakable chill of approaching winter.

I'm baffled as to how it could almost be winter when my last memory before waking on this bench was sitting at my sun-streaked desk by the office window, typing on my laptop on a perfectly beautiful summer day.

My desk phone had rung abruptly. "This is Liv," I said into the receiver.

Next thing, I woke up here, on this bench.

I blink to clear away the cobwebs of sleep that must be to blame for my confusion. My hands feel numb from cold. I open and close them into fists to get the blood circulation back. As I do, I notice they're covered with writing.

I used to write on my hands as a kid until Mom married husband number two. Unlike me, Randal's daughter from his first marriage, Stacy, always came home from school pristine. Stacy never jotted messages or scrawled pictures on the back of her hands. Her ponytail was never askew.

"Why can't you be like Stacy?" Mom would say, sending me to the bathroom to wash my hands clean. "Try not to write on your hands again, Liv. It's unladylike," she'd tell me in the Southern accent she'd affected so she'd fit in with Randal's snooty country club set.

It was a far cry from her previous life as a single mom waiting tables at a Jersey restaurant that claimed to serve the best steaks on the Eastern Seaboard. That was where Mom and Randal met. He came to the steak house for a meal during a business trip. Mom served his table. Three weeks later they were married. I was the flower girl. I was the flower girl at all her weddings.

Despite Mom's efforts to cure my tendency to doodle on my hands, I've apparently returned to the habit. I stare at the swirls of blue-and-black ballpoint writing decorating my skin. The writing goes all the way under the sleeves of my sweater. There are letters written under each knuckle that form the words: S-T-A-Y A-W-A-K-E.

Near my wrist it says: DON'T SLEEP! I FORGET EVERYTHING WHEN I FALL ASLEEP.

I've underlined it twice for emphasis. I fell asleep right here on this park bench. I can't help but wonder what I've forgotten.

A rustle in the bushes sends pigeons squawking into the air in a tumult of flapping wings and falling feathers. Amid the fracas, I feel someone is watching me with a frightening intensity. Whoever's there has vanished by the time the birds have flown away. I'm in danger. I feel it in my bones.

I get up and rush out of the park, stopping only when I'm on the sidewalk outside the entrance of my office building. I pause to watch people rotate like spinning tops through the revolving glass lobby door. I don't join them. I'm reluctant to go up to the office feeling so dazed.

Down the street is the café where I often buy lunch. I decide to get a coffee to calm my nerves. When I reach the corner, I find the café is closed down. Its windows are boarded up.

Next door is my hair salon. I drift inside, drawn by an inexplicable desire to see a familiar face.

"Can I help you?" asks a woman with blue-tipped hair, folding salon towels behind the counter.

"Is Stevie here?"

"Stevie moved to Miami after the wedding."

"Stevie got married?" I ask, surprised. I consider Stevie a friend as well as my hairdresser. "Stevie never mentioned anything about getting married the last time she cut my hair."

"That must have been some time ago," she says.

"Why?"

"Because it looks like it's been a while since you had a haircut."

My eyes drift toward a long-haired woman standing behind the hairdresser. For a split second, I'm shocked at this woman's sudden appearance, seemingly out of nowhere. Then it hits me that this woman is me. I barely recognize myself. I've lost weight. My hair is very long and shades darker than my natural color. I run my fingers through it uncertainly.

The hairdresser misinterprets the gesture. "I have an opening now if you want a cut."

I like the idea. Maybe if I go back to looking like me, it will pop the surreal bubble that has enveloped me since I woke in the park.

She leads me to a chair by a salon sink where she pulls back my head and turns on the water with a hiss. Geometric patterns from an overhanging chandelier flit across the ceiling, mesmerizing me while she rubs shampoo into my wet scalp with long nails. I close my eyes and try to relax to the gentle splash of water.

"We're done," she announces, turning off the faucet.

She rubs my hair dry with a black towel and wraps another around my head like a turban before escorting me to the closest chair.

"You have gorgeous hair," she enthuses, running her fingers through my wet strands. She asks how I want my hair cut.

I describe my usual style. For years, I've worn it in a short chic cut that brings out the green in my hazel eyes and accentuates my wide cheekbones.

The first clump of hair drops to the floor with a snip of her scissors. More hair follows, until the white floor tiles by my feet are covered and the hair dryer roars in my ears.

I panic at the cash register when I realize I don't have my credit card on me. Fortunately, I find a roll of money in my pocket so I pay with cash.

As I open the glass door to leave the salon, I almost collide with a man in a charcoal suit striding along the sidewalk like he's in a rush. My heart skips a beat. He looks like Marco. He has a chiseled face and jet-black hair, and he walks with the same cocky self-assurance.

"Sorry," he says, stepping around me.

He's not Marco. For a moment I can't breathe as sadness crushes me.

Chapter
Seven

"Liv. Liv. Wake up."

I wake, blinking blindly until the fuzzy blur leaning over me morphs into Marco. His chocolate eyes look down at my sleepy face as he gently shakes my shoulders. I stare up at him; too paralyzed to say a word. My eyes are open. The rest of me is fast asleep.

"Liv. It's time to get up," Marco tells me. I nod and drift off for a second before forcing myself to wake.

"What's the time?" I mutter sleepily.

"It's just after eleven."

"You have to be kidding!" I pull myself up and lean groggily against a pillow behind me. "Marco, you were supposed to wake me an hour ago."

"I tried. Believe me. I've never seen anyone so exhausted before in my life."

Marco opens the window shades with a long tug of a cord. I cover my face with my arm as sunshine streams into the bedroom.

"Marco, close the shades. The sun is killing me." I throw the covers over my head to block the blinding light.

In response, Marco disappears into the kitchen. He returns with a steaming mug of extra-strong coffee. I drink it and sink back onto the pillow, immune to the caffeine surging through my body as I drift off again.

There's no pick-me-up on this planet that could possibly wake me. Not after the party that Marco threw for me last night. I haven't stayed up this late since college. Nor have I drunk this much champagne since I drowned my sorrows at my mother's third wedding when I was seventeen. It must have been a portent of what was to come. She was killed a couple of years later when the bastard she married drove into a semitrailer while he was blind drunk.

Maybe that's why I hate drinking champagne, although I didn't tell Marco that last night when he produced a bottle of Bollinger. We were celebrating my promotion to senior staff writer at the magazine. I'll be writing features and other assignments, but mostly I'll be writing about food. My editor says that food is the new pop culture.

My promotion was a long time coming. I've been working at *Cultura Magazine* for six years. I joined the magazine right after I left teaching after a year of hell at my first school. I was lucky to get a temporary job at *Cultura* editing copy. Over the past six years, the temp job became permanent. Now, I've finally been promoted. I savor my new title. It might not sound like much, but I've worked my ass off to get it. I drift off, vaguely aware of a violent crash of water as Marco showers in the en suite.

"You still haven't gotten up!" His amused comment jolts me awake.

I open my eyes to see Marco walking across the bedroom with a white bath towel slung around his waist. He puts on blue chinos and a fitted casual shirt with gray hexagons, which he buttons up before disappearing into the bathroom again. When he comes out, his jet-black hair is neatly brushed. His cologne smells like ocean spray.

"Looks like you're getting ready for a hot date!" I joke.

"I'm off the dating scene. I have a girlfriend."

"Really? Do I know her?"

He leans in to kiss me. I try to unbalance him so that he'll fall on top of me, my fingers working at his top button. "God, I wish we could, but I'm going to need to take a rain check." He gently removes my hands from his shirt.

Marco and I have been dating for almost three months. He's different from my other boyfriends. Maybe it's because he's European in nationality and sensibility. He has a way of making me feel cared for that I haven't experienced before. I can't remember when I've been this in love. The downside is that I'm not sure if Marco feels the same way. I think he does, but I sure as heck am not going to ask him. I've learned from experience that asking too many questions is the perfect way to ruin a relationship.

Marco's a very compartmentalized person. We see each other two to three nights a week when he's not traveling for work, which he does a lot. Marco left a job in finance to set up a technology start-up. It's something to do with advertising software. He's on the road a fair bit, raising capital and doing deals.

"Where are you going?" I prop myself up against a large pillow.

"I'm meeting an investor for lunch. Remember? You said last night that you'd join us. That's why I woke you. Otherwise I'd have let you sleep longer."

"I totally forgot!" I groan.

That's not technically true. I have a vague memory of a drunken promise to join him. It was quickly followed by regret. Being an appendage at a working lunch while Marco charms an investor is hardly my idea of a fun-filled Sunday with my boyfriend. Marco's so driven, but I wish he'd give his wheeling and dealing a break on weekends.

"I'm a mess. There isn't enough time for me to get ready." I run my hand through my disheveled hair.

"There's plenty of time for you to get ready." He puts on his watch.

I make a comical face in the mirror on the wall, amused at how my hair sticks out in a dozen different directions. I look like an ingenue with hair this short. It makes my eyes bigger and my face pointier and uncertain. I look much younger than a woman who's just hit the big thirty.

"Marco. Will you hate me if I skip the lunch?"

Disappointment shifts across his face so quickly that I wonder if I imagined it. "You don't have to come, Liv. It's up to you. Dean's bringing Emily, but I never told him that you were definitely joining us." He shrugs, leaving the rest unsaid.

I like that Marco doesn't push me. I've always had a tendency to date overbearing boyfriends who expect me to be at their beck and call. Marco's not like that at all. He's easygoing. It makes me want to please him.

"On second thought, I'll go. It'll be fun," I say, with forced enthusiasm.

"Great! You'll love Emily." I suspect he knew all along that I'd agree. Am I that predictable?

"What does Emily do?" I ask a few minutes later after I've showered. I take out linen pants and a navy off-the-shoulder top from Marco's closet. I keep a few outfits at his apartment. Sometimes I go straight to work when I stay overnight because he lives a few blocks from my office near Washington Square Park.

"She's a designer. Handbags and accessories. She's very talented. Dean tells me it's a tough industry to break into."

I hear that a lot. The market is flooded with designers trying to get discovered. It's the Project Runway effect. Some of the designers are amazing and yet they struggle to survive in a saturated market. These days, it's not how good you are as a designer but who you know, or how many Instagram followers you have. Celebrity is what sells. I tell Marco some version of this as I get dressed.

"If you like Emily's collection, then maybe you could get *Cultura* to do a write-up."

He says it nonchalantly, but I sense his expectation. My eyes flick to his face in the mirror while I apply lipstick. He sits on the edge of his bed putting on his socks, his face inscrutable.

"It's not my beat, although I can always ask the style team if they're interested," I offer.

I'm starting to suspect the real reason that Marco wants me at this lunch is so I'll meet Emily and get roped into arranging free publicity at my magazine for her label. I immediately feel bad about my uncharitable thoughts. Marco is not manipulative. If he wanted me to help his investor's wife with free publicity, then he'd have come right out and asked. On the other hand, he doesn't usually take meetings on a Sunday.

I'm uncharacteristically quiet as we leave the apartment.

Marco senses my disquiet. He puts his arm around me when we're out on the street. "How about we go on a bike ride after lunch?"

Marco has a set of road bikes. I've always presumed he keeps the smaller road bike for his girlfriend of the moment to join him on weekend bike rides.

Until I met Marco, I hadn't been on a bike since I was a kid. My dad taught me to ride during a visit to see his family in England when I was five. It's my last vivid memory of him before he walked out on Mom the following year.

Marco's an avid cyclist. After our second date, I borrowed a friend's bike and went riding by myself until I felt confident enough to join him on his weekend treks. I'm starting to get the bug, too. In fact, we're talking about doing a cycling trip in France in October.

"I'd love to, but I arranged to go to a kickboxing class with Amy this afternoon. She's already signed us up."

"I thought you hated kickboxing."

"It's growing on me. The instructor says I have potential."

"What does he mean by 'potential'?"

"He says I have great technique, but I'm too timid with my punches. Why don't you come over tonight instead?" I suggest to Marco. "I'll cook. Name any cuisine and I'll make you a feast."

Marco looks tempted. He knows I'm a great cook. My love affair with cooking began after Mom was killed in the crash. Cooking became my therapy. I studied *cordon bleu* cooking part-time as a hobby. I even thought about working in the industry until I decided I preferred writing about food to working in the restaurant business. I like nothing better than to spoil my friends with a restaurant-quality meal at home. Surprisingly, instead of jumping at my invitation, Marco suggests we go out to eat.

"How about I ask Amy and Brett to join us?"

Marco's frown is immediate.

"Come on, Marco! A double date. It will be fun."

"With Brett?" he mocks. "Dr. God Complex? All he talks about is his patient list and how he's single-handedly saving humanity. He has zero interest in discussing anything that isn't about him. As for Amy, every time we meet up, we argue over politics. It totally kills the vibe."

"There won't be arguments," I say, not particularly convincingly, because their political discussions can get heated. "I'll ask Amy to tone it down." We both know that's unlikely to happen.

"Liv, you're going to have to get used to the idea that Amy and I don't get along. I know she's your best friend and you want us to like each other, but the two of us are like oil and water. We don't mix."

Chapter
Eight

Wednesday 9:56 A.M.

Natalie with her singsong "good morning" greeting isn't at the reception desk as I come out of the elevator and head into the office. Instead, a receptionist with blond-tipped bangs is taking a call on her headset.

"*Cultura Magazine.* How can I connect your call?"

The receptionist looks up as I pass her desk. I flash a confused smile. She doesn't smile back. Instead she asks briskly who I'm here to see.

"I'm not here to see anyone. I work here. Where's Natalie?" My tone comes out more rudely than intended. An accusation more than a question. Natalie's been *Cultura*'s receptionist for so long that it feels wrong for anyone else to be behind the reception desk.

She looks at me blankly. "Who?"

"Natalie." My voice drops off as I realize she must be a temp. Maybe Natalie is on sick leave. "Never mind."

I walk past the reception desk toward the main office, where I beeline to my cubicle, pausing at the expansive window by my desk to take in the familiar view of the street.

As I turn to sit on my black swivel chair, a leggy young woman with long red hair tosses a jacket over the back of the seat. She's dressed like a runway model in a tartan miniskirt with thigh-high boots and a black cropped sweater. She drops her purse on the desk and leans forward to plug in a laptop.

My gaze shifts from her to a photo montage pinned to a corkboard on the cubicle wall. The strangers' faces in the photos blur into a kaleidoscope of colors as my head spins. I put my hand on the back of the chair to stop myself from losing my balance.

"Who are you?" I think she asks me. Maybe it's me who asked her.

"I'm Liv. Liv Reese."

Her mouth widens into a beaming smile of recognition. "Liv! I'm Josie." She talks as if I should know her. She opens her arms and gives me a hug. "I am thrilled to meet you. Finally."

"It's wonderful to meet you, too," I respond out of politeness rather than recognition. I try to place her but I can't. There's nobody called Josie at the magazine.

"It's so great to see you back at *Cultura*," she gushes.

I want to tell her that I never left, that I've been here all along, when I look around and realize the office looks different. It's had a radical makeover.

The carpet used to be dark blue. Now it's a textured concrete gray decorated with splotches of lime and electric blue that look faintly like hopscotch markings.

Desks are arranged in little island hubs across the open-plan floor space. Scattered under pillars are sitting areas of backless round sofas also in lime and electric blue. Jeans-clad people slouch about on the sofas like teenagers in their bedrooms, typing rapidly on their laptops as they sip from mugs of coffee.

The office is too fluorescent. Too pulsating. Too hard on the eyes. It's alien, and yet familiar. *Cultura* is written on the office wall in giant three-dimensional reflective silver letters in the same archetypal font used on the cover of the magazine. I'm definitely in the right place.

Farther along is a wall covered with glass-framed *Cultura Magazine* covers going back years. I've worked on every issue of the magazine since I started working here. I know all of the covers like the back of my hand, but I don't recognize any of the most recent ones.

Everything is out of sync. I need to figure out why. I glance at the writing on my wrist. DON'T SLEEP! I FORGET EVERYTHING WHEN I FALL ASLEEP. I fell asleep on the park bench. What did I forget?

Josie's chatter washes over me as I try to remember. She talks about the magazine's new direction as she shepherds me around the office. My unease turns into near panic as I realize I don't recognize anyone. Everyone at the office is a stranger. I feel as if I'm in a parallel universe.

My eyes dart toward the entrance. I want to make an excuse and get out of here, but Josie is already introducing me to the team. Everyone is superfriendly, getting up from their desks to greet me with a succession of warm hugs. They treat me like I'm the prodigal daughter returning to the fold.

"You look wonderful, Liv."

They all give me different versions of the same compliments in saccharine voices that are too chipper to be authentic. They're being too nice. That bothers me more than the hopscotch carpet.

A woman rushes toward me and embraces me as if I'm a long-lost sister. I hug her back, thinking that I don't know who the hell she is.

"Liv, I wish we'd known that you were coming today. We'd have arranged a lunch to welcome you. It can't be easy. . . ."

"What can't be easy?" I ask.

"Coming back here after all this time . . ."

I stare at her uncomprehendingly. Her cheeks flush. She looks away, squirming with discomfort.

She changes the subject.

"I'd love to hear about your life in London."

I'm lost for words. I don't know what she's talking about. I've never lived in London. Without pausing for breath, she inundates me with questions. What part of London did I live in? Did I do a lot of traveling around the UK?

I want to tell her that she's mixing me up with someone else. The only time I've spent in Europe was a six-week backpacking trip with friends after college. I certainly have never lived there.

"You must be very jet-lagged," she says. "It always takes me a day or two to adjust when I fly back from Europe."

Jet lag? Maybe that's why I feel so numb.

Josie sweeps me away toward the office pantry area. It's been remodeled into an open-plan lifestyle area with an assortment of white-and-lime tables and chairs. A giant white shelf of bright green ferns in white pots serves as a natural divider with the rest of the office. She prepares us coffees on a shiny new coffee machine as she jabbers on about *Cultura*.

She talks as if I'm aware of all the changes at the magazine. I'm not. If anything, I'm shocked by what she tells me.

It turns out that it's not just the office decor that has changed. The magazine was taken over by a European magazine publisher. There's been a radical change of strategy. Now there's an emphasis on a younger, millennial audience. The online and social channels get as much attention as the magazine. There's talk of turning the hard-copy magazine into a quarterly.

"I barely recognize anyone here. The staff is completely different."

"It's the restructure. They let a lot of people go," Josie explains.

I'm shocked to hear that Frank, my editor, and Sonya, the style editor, were retrenched along with Natalie and many others. Poor Natalie. She's a single mom. She really needed the money, and she loved working here.

"We're going for edgy. That's why they hired Niko to be the executive editor and why the editorial team has changed. It's a younger team to reflect the demographic of our new readership. Ted, as you know," she pauses meaningfully, "transferred here a few months ago to run the commercial side of the business. Neither of them is here today."

"Where are they?" I ask, largely because it seems expected that I show interest.

"Nico is at a cover shoot in L.A. Ted is home sick. It's bad timing. They would have loved to have been here to welcome you."

Josie prattles on at a mile a minute while I try to make sense of all these changes at the magazine. Everything is off-kilter. I need to get back in control. To do that, I need a laptop so I can check my emails and refresh my memory. It's not possible that I've blanked out for what seems like years.

"Actually," I pipe up. "Ted asked me to come in . . . to work on a project." I become more confident as I lie. "He was supposed to organize a loaner laptop for me, and somewhere to work. I hope he didn't forget."

"Ted gets more forgetful the closer he gets to his wedding day." She bites her lip and flushes as if she's said something out-of-line. I have no idea what she's talking about, or why I'd care.

"It's so great that you two are still . . ." she starts to say, and stops when she notices my frozen expression. "I'll find you a spare laptop."

Josie escorts me to a small glass-walled meeting room overlooking the lunch area. She tells me she'll be back in a minute with the computer.

While I wait, I stare at the morning news on a large TV screen. The footage cuts to police officers standing behind crime scene tape at the entrance of an apartment building. A graphic at the bottom of the screen says: MURDERER WRITES MESSAGE IN VICTIM'S BLOOD.

The camera crash zooms from street level to an apartment window. Painted on the window in red letters are the words

WAKE UP!

I've seen that message before. I push up my sleeve. The same words are scribbled just below my wrist bone.

Chapter
Nine

The laptop Josie brings me is a clunky old beast with a sticky space bar. While she sets it up for me, I stand by the meeting room's internal window and scan the office looking for my missing handbag. I assumed I'd left it on my desk, along with my phone, when I went out to get breakfast and take a breather at the park.

I now know that my handbag's not here since I clearly haven't been in the office for some time. My desk isn't even mine anymore. It belongs to Josie.

"Is there something wrong?" Josie asks as she rises from the floor after bending to plug in the laptop charger.

"I think I've lost my purse," I tell her, without revealing that I'm more concerned that I might have lost my mind. How could I have forgotten that I don't work here anymore?

"Let's check with the police lost property," she suggests. "Maybe someone turned it in."

Before I can protest, she looks up a phone number for the local police precinct on the loaner laptop and dials it on the desk phone.

"I'll take it from here," I tell her, as the line rings. "I don't want to hold you up from your work."

She hands me the receiver and heads for her desk. I feel uncomfortable about involving the police. I have a deep distrust of cops, dating back to when I was briefly put in child protection after Mom was arrested for a DUI during her acrimonious divorce from Randal.

While I navigate the computerized phone system, pressing the various number options to get to the police lost and found department, I read the spidery ballpoint messages on my hands. STAY AWAKE, it says under my knuckles.

"I'd like to report a lost or stolen handbag," I tell a curt duty officer when my call is answered.

"Which is it?" she demands.

"What do you mean?"

She sighs impatiently. "Was it lost or stolen?"

"I'm not sure. I fell asleep on a bench at Washington Square Park. When I woke, it was gone."

"You fell asleep? And your handbag was gone?" she says with disbelief. "Okaaaay. . . ." She drags out the word. I feel like an idiot.

"Can you describe your handbag and tell me anything about the brand and color?"

Since I don't remember which purse I had with me today, I describe the three handbags that I use interchangeably. I sense her impatience.

"You just described three different purses," she snaps in exasperation. "Are you missing one or three?"

"One."

"So which one are you missing?" She barely conceals her impatience.

"I don't know. I can't remember which I took today," I stutter.

"Let me get this straight," she says. "You fell asleep on a park bench. When you woke, your handbag was gone. You don't know if someone stole it while you slept or if you lost it. And you don't remember what color it was, or the brand." She pauses for breath. "Listen, lady, I have a suggestion for you."

"What is it?"

"Why don't you call us back when you remember," she says in an angry staccato.

The phone disconnects with a click. I'm so annoyed by the woman's rudeness that I take a pen from a container on the table and I write on my hand: DON'T TALK TO THE COPS <u>EVER</u>!!

It's a childish gesture, but it makes me feel better. That police officer treated me as if I was nuts. I'm not. I'm certain there's a perfectly reasonable explanation for my confusion. Perhaps I'm feeling the aftereffects of a sedative that's left me in a zombie state. Or maybe I really am jet-lagged. That might explain why everything feels as if it's happening to someone else.

I put my head in my hands and try to focus on what to do next. If I've lost my purse then someone may have my credit cards. I need to cancel them.

I pick up the phone again and call my bank. After I've worked my way through the self-serve system, twice, my call is answered by "Brad" from customer service.

I tell Brad that my wallet is missing and that I'd like to block all my credit cards and access to my bank account. We go through a verification process of my name, social security number, and all the rest.

Brad puts me on hold while he checks my details. The tinny hold music rubs my nerves so raw that I breathe an audible sigh of relief when his officious voice returns on the line.

"Ma'am, there must be a mistake. You don't have an account with this bank." His tone is patronizing.

"You are Chase Bank?"

"Yes."

"Then I definitely have an account with you. I've been banking with you since high school."

"Ma'am, our records show that your account was closed more than two years ago."

"Who closed the account?"

"You did."

"That's not possible."

"There's no mistake, ma'am. Perhaps you've forgotten? I suggest you go to a branch with your ID. Someone will help you further."

"But I don't have my ID. It's in my handbag. The one that's missing. That's the reason for my call; to cancel my credit cards."

"You definitely don't have any cards or bank accounts with us anymore so there's nothing to cancel," he says.

I hang up the phone feeling physically sick as I consider the possibility that my bank accounts have disappeared, which means I have no money. In a panic, I take out the wad of cash I found in my pocket at the hairdresser. I count the money, note by note, making a pile on my lap. There's over a thousand dollars in crisp notes.

My eyes well with tears. Everything has felt inside-out since I woke on the bench at Washington Square Park. My bank account at Chase has been closed, apparently for years. My desk at work has been taken over by bubbly Josie with her tartan skirt and legs that seem to go on forever. The office has changed almost beyond recognition. Almost everyone here is a stranger to me. They all think that I've been living in London, which is patently ridiculous. Who forgets relocating to a foreign city?

I look again at the message written on my hand. DON'T SLEEP! I FORGET EVERYTHING WHEN I FALL ASLEEP.

The sentence reverberates in my head. What else have I forgotten? I sense it's something important. No matter how much I try, I can't think of what it might be. The only thing I know for sure is that time has skipped ahead without me noticing.

"What's today's date?" I type into the search bar on Google.

"November 2," says the search result.

That surprises me. My last memory is from July 31. I distinctly remember seeing the day marked on the calendar pinned to my cubicle wall when I reached across my desk to answer the phone.

Three months have passed.

No, not three months, I correct myself. I focus on the date on the computer screen.

Two years have passed, and I remember none of it. It feels as if I've been catapulted into the future.

Chapter
Ten

Two Years Earlier

Lunch is a disaster. Marco's investor, Dean Walker, is a cradle-snatching misogamist who makes it clear he expects me to use my contacts at *Cultura* to get free publicity for his young wife's fledgling design business.

It puts me in an awkward bind. Apparently, Marco's other funding options have fallen through. Marco tried to sound blasé about the whole thing, but he obviously has a lot riding on this pending deal with Dean.

Emily's in her midtwenties, a handful of years younger than me. She has coltish legs and long hair that's more strawberry than blond. Her bust, if real, would be a wonder of the modern world.

Dean's in his midsixties with dyed hair plugs and a face so Botoxed that he looks like a lecherous gargoyle. An ex-investment banker who runs a private equity fund, he met Emily at a green energy conference in Vegas. "The rest," he says, waving his hand dramatically in the air, "is history."

When we've settled at our window table, Dean and Marco jump

straight into a discussion about their prospective business venture. I ask Emily about herself.

"I'm a dancer but my real love is fashion. I especially adore accessories," Emily enthuses. "They can make or break an outfit. That's why I designed my own handbag collection."

She confesses that she has no design background and no experience in the fashion industry. "Dean says all I need is good publicity and my designs will be snapped up. Plus, I have my Instagram account."

Her label is called Embr. "It's the first two letters of my first and last name. The name was Dean's idea."

Emily takes out her phone and scrolls through to show me her handbags and accessories designs on her Instagram feed.

It's obvious she's here to pitch to me and I give the appropriate encouraging responses.

Emily asks me about *Cultura*. "It must be amazing to work at such a prestigious magazine."

"Oh, it is," I respond. "I'm very lucky."

I try to move the conversation in another direction. Every time I do, she brings the discussion back to the magazine. Eventually, she gets to the point.

"So how does *Cultura* choose the fashion items it features in its hot new trends column," she asks.

Getting a spot in the *Cultura* design column is very sought-after since it is closely followed by fashion aficionados and department store buyers.

"To tell you the truth, I don't deal with the style side of the magazine. I generally write features and do interviews."

"Really? On what?"

Dean has apparently been listening to our conversation while talking to Marco and he intervenes to ask me bluntly whether I can arrange for Emily to be featured in the magazine.

"I was just telling Emily that it's the style editor who decides. Of course, I'm always happy to put in a good word for talented designers," I say, as diplomatically as possible.

His eyes get narrow and mean. He's about to say something when the waiter arrives with our meals artfully arranged on oversized white plates. The waiter moves around the table putting our orders in front of us, while telling us the names of the dishes and the key ingredients. When he reaches Emily, she asks whether the homemade aioli in her Caesar salad is vegan.

The waiter seems lost for words. Judging by the unease in his pale eyes, I can tell that he's wondering whether he should point out that a Caesar salad is a decidedly non-vegan menu choice regardless of whether the aioli has eggs in it or not. Eventually, he says in a masterfully polite tone that he'll check with the chef. He heads to the kitchen and returns a minute later.

"I'm afraid the aioli is not vegan. The chef tells me that since there are eggs, anchovies, and Parmesan cheese in the salad, he uses a traditional aioli. However, he can remake the salad for you with vegan mayonnaise if you prefer. Or if you prefer a vegan meal then you could choose one of the vegan items listed on the menu. They're all marked 'Vegan.'"

I admire the lack of irony in his voice.

"How long will it take to make her salad from scratch?" Dean snaps.

"About ten minutes," the waiter says.

"So we're all supposed to wait?" says Dean, staring him down.

The waiter holds his stare for a fraction of a second before his face goes blank and a servile expression magically appears. I sense it's far from sincere. Who could blame him? Dean's rudeness makes me blush.

"It doesn't matter. I'll keep the salad," says Emily, staring at the ground as if she wished it would swallow her up.

"No, you won't, honey," Dean tells her. "Choose something else. The chef will expedite your order. Right?" he challenges the server.

"We'll do our best."

She chooses a Greek salad instead.

"The Greek salad contains feta cheese, which is a dairy item," the waiter says haltingly. "Is that an issue?"

"Get her what she wants," Dean snaps. "Hurry up. We've been kept waiting long enough."

When he's gone, Emily takes out a designer shopping bag with her logo and presents it to me as a gift. Inside is a bright-yellow handbag with a tassel and a matching purse.

I'm about to refuse it as nicely as possible when Marco gives the slightest shake of his head. He's worried I might offend them.

The plea in Marco's eyes wins out. I thank Emily and gush over how much I love her bags, even though they're flashy and not at all to my taste.

Emily's salad arrives. The chef has cleverly put the cheese in its own container on the side. The rest of the meal goes in a blur of desserts and coffees. Dean uses every opportunity to get a gibe in at the waiter, who ever since the Caesar salad showdown can apparently do nothing right as far as Dean is concerned.

I look at Marco and silently beg him to say something. He gives an imperceptible shake of his head as if to indicate that he's powerless. I suppose he is if he wants Dean's money.

When the waiter brings the bill, Dean insists on paying. "Marco, you got it last time." They argue the point. Dean wins by snatching the bill and waving it in the air along with his credit card.

The three of us chat as the server processes the credit card and brings it to Dean to sign. I'm vaguely aware of Dean taking out his wallet and leaving cash before we rise from the table.

It's only as we're walking out of the café that I hear Dean whisper to Emily that the waiter will regret his rudeness and terrible service when he sees his tip.

When we're on the street, I turn and glance through the window of the café just as the server picks up Dean's measly ten-dollar tip, all in single bills. It was left under the salt shaker on our table. The waiter should have been tipped at least four times that amount based on my rough estimate of our bill.

The waiter looks up and sees me watching. I'm absolutely mortified. Dean and Emily get into a cab, while Marco kisses me goodbye and heads back to his apartment. I've already told him I'll go straight home from the café since there's a subway station at the end of the block.

When Marco's out of sight, I go back into the restaurant. Our table is already being set for the next customer and the waiter is taking orders at another table. I approach him during a brief lull.

"I'm sorry my, er, friends were rude," I tell him. Scrambling in my purse, I hand over forty dollars, which is by my reckoning the balance of the tip he was shortchanged on.

"You don't need to do that."

"You should have been tipped properly to begin with . . . Kevin." I read his name off his name badge. "I served tables when I was in college. I know this is your income."

"Thank you," he says, putting the cash into his pocket. As I turn to leave, he says: "By the way, I'm a big fan of your columns in *Cultura Magazine*."

"Thanks."

In truth, it creeps me out that he'd been listening so intently to our conversation while he served us that he knows who I am and the magazine I write for.

Chapter
Eleven

Detective Darcy Halliday flicked through photos of the crime scene she'd taken on her phone as Jack Lavelle steered the navy Ford through heavy traffic on their way to the city morgue. Those photos were all they'd have until they received the official crime scene images sometime in the afternoon.

The crime scene photographer had still been snapping away at the scene when they'd left, accompanying the victim's body, which had been zipped into a black body bag and taken on a stretcher down to a morgue van on the street. Halliday and Lavelle had studiously ignored the reporters calling out questions from behind a police barricade as they exited the building.

"Our biggest problem right now is that we have no ID for the victim," Lavelle told Halliday as he drove. "Homicide investigations are exponentially harder when the identity of the victim is unknown."

The owner of the apartment wasn't due to land in Hong Kong until late afternoon New York time. Lavelle hoped the owner would be able to tell them who had rented the apartment for the night. That individual was most likely the victim, or possibly the killer.

In every other respect, the investigation was looking good, even though it was early days. The forensics team had found fingerprints all over the bedroom and the bathroom.

In fact, the embarrassment of riches of trace evidence found at the scene was something of a headache in disguise. They'd be lucky if they received the fingerprint results by the weekend. Hundreds of prints would have to be cross-referenced and collated before being run through the system. The lab had to exclude the victim's prints and the prints of everyone who'd been at the scene, including Olga, the cleaner. She'd be asked to provide her fingerprints and samples of her hair when she came to the precinct later to sign her statement.

At the morgue, Halliday and Lavelle waited at the entrance of the autopsy room while the pathologist finished a Y-incision on a morbidly obese middle-aged man who lay with his lifeless head hyperextended on the slab and a sheet pulled down to his waist.

The chief pathologist was a sixty-year-old doctor with a semicircle of white hair on an otherwise hairless pate. He had the somewhat apt name of Dr. Cutter, although he generally went by his first name, Richard.

"Can I help you, Detectives?" Dr. Cutter asked, looking up from the metal autopsy table once he'd completed the incision.

"Any chance you can expedite the autopsy of the stiff that's just checked into cabin twenty-four?" asked Lavelle. "So far we're stumped on the ID. We haven't found anything at the scene that so much as tells us his first name."

"There's a backlog of bodies waiting for autopsy, and I have two staff members out sick," said Dr. Cutter. "But we can definitely get dental impressions done today, even if the autopsy has to wait a few days."

"Whatever you can do, Doc," Lavelle said. "There was no murder weapon at the scene so we're keen to find out what sort of implement was used to stab the vic. By the way, this is my partner, Detective Darcy Halliday."

The pathologist picked up a round electric blade for cutting through the rib cage. "Detective Halliday, I don't know what you did to draw the short straw and get Jack as your partner. But either way, you have my deepest commiserations." He turned on the electrical cutter and began working the round blade into the body on the slab.

"And that," whispered Lavelle ironically to Halliday as they turned to leave, "is why no male detective ever likes to stand too close to Dr. Richard Cutter when he's doing an autopsy."

After their fleeting visit to the morgue, Lavelle did a quick detour to the forensics lab. He double-parked while Halliday ran out to drop off several pieces of evidence they wanted fast-tracked. Among them was an evidence bag with the wine bottle Halliday had found next to the bed. She hoped it would turn out to be the holy grail of evidence. There was as good a chance as any that the bottle contained the killer's fingerprints, and perhaps even saliva so they could extract the killer's DNA.

"We'll head back to the precinct," Lavelle said when Halliday returned to the car. "The first batch of security camera footage should be there soon. I'm expecting we'll get hundreds of hours of CCTV footage to trawl through."

Halliday glanced sideways at Lavelle. She wondered whether he'd try to put her in charge of reviewing all the security camera footage. That was the sort of desk jockey work she'd been assigned since she'd been transferred over to homicide. As if reading her thoughts, Lavelle told her he'd rustled up two detectives and a few uniformed cops to go through the video footage.

"We both need to be out in the field. Not chained to a desk," he said.

A small team of rookie cops had been assigned to search for the murder weapon in trash cans and drains in the vicinity of the building where the murder had taken place. Another team had fanned out across the neighborhood, knocking on doors to collect security camera footage and checking whether anyone had witnessed anything suspicious overnight. They were in the process of collecting surveillance footage from city CCTV cameras, as well as private security cameras in shops and buildings in the vicinity of the murder scene.

The only lead Halliday and Lavelle had to work with, at least until the security camera footage arrived, was the writing on the bedroom window. Halliday zoomed in and out of the photo she'd taken of the words WAKE UP! written in the victim's blood.

"Ever seen writing in blood at a crime scene?" she asked Lavelle.

"A few times," he conceded. "Usually when the killer was drugged out of his mind, or going through a psychotic episode. In those cases, they write lots of crazy stuff, sometimes in blood or feces. Usually whatever they write is rambling garbage."

"That's not the case here," Halliday said, staring at the two succinct words on her photo of the crime scene window. "The killer was making a point. The question is what point, and why go to the trouble of writing WAKE UP! in blood on the window?"

Even though Halliday had been assigned to Lavelle's precinct for a couple of months already, the two hours they'd worked together on the homicide was the longest she'd ever spent in his company.

They knew each other in passing. She'd nodded to him a few times when she'd seen him lifting weights at the fitness center near the precinct where she also worked out. They'd shared elevators and rubbed shoulders making coffee in the kitchenette by the Detective Bureau. They'd attended plenty of team meetings at the precinct. Their casual interactions had never gone beyond the most basic niceties, and they'd never worked together on a case.

Halliday had been in the unit long enough to get the impression that Lavelle rarely socialized with the rest of the team. Despite that, the other detectives treated Lavelle with the same deference they gave to the captain.

"What did the neighbors tell you when you interviewed them earlier?" Lavelle asked, making a left turn near the precinct.

"The teenage son of the neighbor who lives at the end of the hall said he was binge-watching a TV series in bed when he thought he heard a door slam. He thinks it happened at around two in the morning."

"How can he be so sure of the time?" Lavelle asked.

"It was near the end of his episode. He set his alarm and went to sleep as soon as it finished. It's possible the noise he heard was the killer leaving the apartment."

"Did you talk to anyone else?"

"The woman who lives diagonally opposite the apartment didn't hear or see anything last night. However, she did see a couple coming out of the elevator yesterday morning around ten, when she was waiting to take it down to get to work. She said the man looked like Ryan Reynolds. That's why she remembered him. The woman accompanying him had dark hair. Very long."

"Did the couple go into the apartment where the murder took place?"

"She didn't see where they went because she stepped into the elevator and the doors shut behind her. She did say that she'd never seen them before. That might not mean much. Two apartments on that floor are regularly rented on short-stay websites. There are always new faces around. My hunch is that the couple did go in there."

"What makes you think that?"

"The long dark hairs I found on the pillow and in the bathroom fit the neighbor's description of a woman with extremely long hair."

"So you think our killer was a woman."

"It's certainly possible. It explains why she drugged him. So he wouldn't put up a fight."

While they waited at a traffic light, Lavelle called the security company responsible for the CCTV cameras in the apartment building to find out when copies of the footage would be ready for collection. The supervisor said it might take a few more hours.

"I have a bad feeling about this," murmured Lavelle, hanging up before stepping on the gas when the light turned green.

"We really need that footage," said Halliday. "The CCTV video must have visuals of the killer."

"I agree. Unless, of course, the killer had wings and flew out of the sixth-floor window, in which case we really are screwed," remarked Lavelle.

"What did the doorman tell you when you spoke with him?" Halliday asked.

"He didn't see anyone or anything suspicious. Having said that, he only started his shift at six A.M., an hour before the cleaner found the body. He said we should talk to the overnight doorman. I called a couple of times, but his phone is off. I'm guessing he's asleep."

Lavelle glanced at Halliday as he pulled the car into the parking lot next to the precinct. She was relatively young for a detective. He figured her for late twenties. He hadn't had any personal dealings with her since she'd moved to the unit on a temporary transfer. He'd heard she'd received the highest marks in the detective's exam in seven years and that she'd done a standout job at Major Case. He happened to have seen her at the firing range the previous week and had been impressed at how she handled a weapon. She was an incredible shot. He'd heard she'd been a sharpshooter in the military. He also knew she was very fit because he often saw her running to work.

"You're a serious runner," he said.

"I run for fun, mostly. Although right now I am in training for an ultramarathon next spring in Arizona."

"What distance?"

"Fifty miles. Through the desert. We run at night."

"With the coyotes and the rattlesnakes?"

"Something like that," she laughed.

"Why would you put yourself through that hell?"

"For the challenge. And to raise money."

"Any particular cause?" he asked.

"An old friend from the military, Lieutenant Antonio Lopez. Lost a leg in a roadside blast near Mosul. It was on Tony's bucket list to run this ultramarathon. I'm doing it on his behalf. The money I raise will go to his baby daughter and to help other wounded veterans adjust to civilian life."

"That's very generous of him, and you. But he's also a wounded veteran. He doesn't need the help?" Lavelle asked.

"Well, that's a sad story," Halliday said, not saying anything for a long moment as she looked out the car window, blinking furiously. "It just so happens," she said finally, a crack in her voice, "that Tony took his own life earlier this year."

Chapter
Twelve

Now that I know it's two years in the future, I quickly scroll news headlines on my loaner laptop, looking for something to jog my memory. A headline from this morning catches my attention.

"Killer Wrote Message with Victim's Blood on Bedroom Window."

When I click on the headline, an article opens up.

"Police believe a murderer wrote the message—*WAKE UP!*—on the window of an apartment after killing an unknown man," the article says. "The body of the man was found in bed this morning in a midtown apartment. NYPD detectives are investigating."

Below the article is a photo of police wearing navy CSI jackets going up the stairs into the lobby of an apartment building. The article provides no information about the dead man. No name. No details of his identity.

There's a suggestion the man might have been killed during a robbery. The article quotes a resident of the apartment building where the man was murdered as saying there had been several incidents of petty theft and a home burglary in the complex in the past month alone.

Near the bottom of the article is the building's location. I give up on reading the news and open my personal email account in the hope that my emails will lift the fog that's surrounded me since I woke on the park bench.

The system rejects my password. A security notification tells me that "unusual activity was noticed in your account." It says a code has been texted to my cell phone to restore my account. The problem is that I don't have my phone.

When I try to access my social media accounts, the same thing happens. After three passwords guesses are rejected, I get locked out of my social accounts as well as my email. I've been electronically cut off from my life.

The meeting room phone rings suddenly, startling me with its insistent peal.

"Hello?"

"Liv, this is Dee from reception. I have a call for you. Please hold while I transfer it through."

There's a single beep followed by a man's voice. "Liv?"

Something about the muffled voice makes the hairs prickle on the back of my neck.

"Yes?" My throat is tight. I can barely raise my voice above a whisper.

"Where did you put it?"

"Put what?"

"The knife," he hisses. "What did you do with the damn knife, Liv? You took the goddamn knife when I was in the bathroom, and you walked off with it."

"I don't know what you're talking about. This must be a wrong number." I resist the urge to hang up the phone. I feel compelled to know more.

"Don't tell me you fell asleep and forgot everything again?" he says.

He frightens me with the accuracy of his comment. "How do you know I woke up with no memory?"

"Because you lose your goddamn memory every time you fall asleep. Listen, here's what I want you to do . . ."

The door opens with a rattle. I put my hand over the receiver as Josie pops her head through the doorway.

"The spring issue planning meeting is about to start," she says. "We'd love for you to join. As the guest of honor. Everyone's waiting for you."

"Okay. Um, sure. That would be great. I'll be there as soon as I'm done with this call," I tell her.

"Sure," Josie says, still hovering.

I hold the phone against my chest until Josie's left the room.

"Who are you?" I whisper into the phone once she's closed the door behind her.

There's nobody on the line. All I hear is an engaged signal.

I put down the receiver with a click. A sickening dread creeps through me. Something terrible is going on and I don't have the faintest idea what it is.

Chapter
Thirteen

Two Years Earlier

We spend the better part of an hour passing around mood boards and swatches of colors as we discuss plans for the December issue of *Cultura*. December is almost six months away, but the Christmas issue is always a blowout, which means months of extra planning, pages of extra content, and pullouts with glossy advertising.

After canvassing our opinions on the design colors and cover proposals, Frank, our editor, assigns us the articles he wants us to write in addition to our usual beats. For me, that's food. For obvious reasons, food is always a big deal in the December issue. The other highlight is *Cultura*'s signature year-end articles.

"I always like our end-of-year features to have a fresh perspective," Frank reminds everyone. Naomi, who likes to think of herself as our resident arts writer, is visibly furious when Frank assigns me to write on the arts scene.

Naomi's never liked me anyway, not since I complained about George, a photographer she was dating, who put his hand on my thigh and propositioned me while we drove to cover a music festival. He was subsequently fired after it turned out that was his go-to move with young reporters. Naomi's pretty much hated my guts since.

When the meeting ends, Frank leaps out of his seat and rushes to his office so he doesn't have to hear everyone's complaints about their assignments. I go after him.

"Frank, you have writers here who are far more knowledgeable than me about the art world." Like Naomi, I think, who studied fine arts and considers anyone writing about the arts at *Cultura* to be not just stepping on her toes, but squashing them to smithereens.

"That's exactly why I want you to do it, Liv," he says. We walk past the wall of framed historic *Cultura Magazine* covers and enter his office.

"The last time I wrote a review on the Milo Zee exhibition, he sued me and the magazine. Do you really want to take the risk again?"

"It was all for publicity. He dropped the lawsuit," he says, dismissively. "Your article cut right through all his bullshit. It skewered him. The rest of the media took off their gloves after your piece came out."

Frank doesn't mention that the media frenzy led to Zee being accused of beating his girlfriend and ultimately being "canceled."

"It was just a review. I didn't intend to destroy his career."

"You have nothing to feel bad about, Liv. You were doing your job: giving a brutally honest review of his art show. I loved it, and so did our readers. It's why you were promoted."

He pulls last year's November issue from a shelf behind his desk and reads my review in a toneless voice.

> *No wilting wallflower, Milo Zee describes himself as the ultimate bad boy artist and founder of his own school of millennial nihilism art. Zee has near-guru status among his more than one million Instagram followers who hail him as a #Zeenius.*
>
> *Zee's exhibition* Sum of Us *features enormous canvases created with paint made from his own bodily fluids. Zee says*

he slashed his wrist to produce the blood for the largest canvas, titled Deathwish2. *He claims he almost died in the making of that curiously bland painting.*

The New York exhibit contains new works produced by Zee since his sellout shows in London. Among them are an actual #Zeenius bowel movement displayed inside a transparent cube of resin hanging from the gallery ceiling, and a wineglass filled with Zee's own spit framed on a wall.

Zee's publicist describes his work as "an illuminating insight on the human condition. It reminds us that we are not the sum of our parts, but the parts of our sum."

I'm no expert on postmodern abstract art, but I have to admit that I found scraping mold from the grout between my bathroom tiles using an old toothbrush to be more illuminating than Zee's artwork, and a considerably more apt statement on the human condition.

Frank tosses the magazine onto his desk. "That's what I want in your year-end piece. That tone. That sarcasm."

"Frank, I wasn't being sarcastic. I was being sincere," I say, straight-faced.

"You cut him to shreds in a way that Naomi could never do. She's far too effusive to the artists she's trying to cultivate. Okay, get out of here, Liv. I have a budget meeting to prepare for."

Before returning to my desk, I stop at the office of our style editor, Sonya, and ask for her thoughts on Emily's handbag collection. I've given her the handbag samples that Emily gave me as well as a link to Emily's Instagram feed so she can see her other designs.

"At best, they looked like cheap and nasty knockoffs. At worst, well, let me suggest she finds a new hobby. I can't see how she can build a career as a serious designer if all she's doing is knocking off iconic designs."

She hands me back the handbag and purse that Emily gave me with the tips of her fingers as if they're contaminated.

I'm almost relieved at her candor. I can honestly tell Marco that I did my best to get Emily's collection written up in the magazine. Hopefully, if Dean has hard feelings, they won't be directed toward Marco. Remembering Dean's behavior at the restaurant, I have no doubt he's more than capable of petty acts of revenge.

When I return to my desk after a late lunch, I find a Post-it note on my keyboard. KEVIN ASKED YOU TO CALL, it reads. It includes his cell phone number.

Kevin is the waiter at the restaurant that I went to with Marco, Dean, and Emily. It's the third time he's called.

I returned his first message thinking I'd left something behind at the café. Of course I hadn't. He said he'd called to thank me for being so gracious by coming back to sort out the tip. Even though he was superpolite, the call creeped me out. As did his next call a few days later, which I didn't return.

I crumple up the note and toss it in the trash. Kevin's messages are starting to scare me.

Chapter
Fourteen

Detective Darcy Halliday's hair was damp from the quick shower she'd taken in the women's locker room as soon as they'd returned to the precinct. She'd changed into a navy suit with a teal shirt which she kept in her locker. Her detective badge was clipped to her waistband, her service weapon was strapped in a holster on her left hip. Handcuffs hung off the back of her pants.

She stood back and observed the photo she'd printed and taped to the office window near her desk of the *WAKE UP!* message at the crime scene.

Lavelle wandered over from his desk to take a look.

"What are you thinking?" he asked.

"Was the message intended for the victim?" Halliday asked. "Regret for killing him? Or was it written for someone else? And why write the message on the window and then lower the shades? Why not keep the shades up? Or write the message on the bedroom wall near the body?"

"Because the message wasn't intended for the victim," Lavelle said, cottoning on to her train of thought.

"Exactly. That's why the killer wrote it in reverse; to make sure it was read properly from outside the building. The killer was making a statement to the outside world, not to the victim."

The glass door behind them slammed loudly. They both turned around to see Detectives Rosco and Tran from Central Robbery walking toward them between a row of desks.

"Looks like the cavalry's arrived," said Lavelle, holding out his hand to greet the two detectives.

He'd cleared two tables near Halliday's desk by the window, where both loan detectives would sit for the duration they'd be helping out. They'd be on transfer for a couple of weeks. It might be shorter or longer depending on how quickly they got a break in the case.

Halliday's cell phone rang just as Lavelle brought the detectives over to her for an introduction. She quickly shook their hands before answering.

"Halliday," she said, moving to the window where she'd taped the photo.

On the line was Owen Jeffries, an old friend from the military who had been recruited to the CIA when he finished his last tour.

"So you got my voicemail," she said.

"Sure did. What's up?"

While Halliday briefed Jeffries on the murder, she texted him the photo of the ghoulish writing on the window. "Any thoughts?" she asked.

"It shows premeditation," he said, once he received the photo.

"Why do you say that?"

"It's not natural to sign-write the message so it could be read correctly from the outside. It involves reversing not just the words but the shape of the letters. In my opinion, achieving this type of complex writing without any mistake, especially during a high stress situation such as after committing a murder, would require a cool head and planning."

"What sort of planning?" Halliday asked.

"It could be as simple as writing the message in reverse on a piece of paper before the murder. Or even on the back of a hand. That way it could be copied letter by letter to avoid mistakes. There are no mistakes, or reversing errors in the photo you sent me. That suggests it was preplanned."

The captain motioned for everyone on the investigation team to assemble in his office. Halliday covered the phone receiver and asked Lavelle to start without her. His expression suggested it wasn't a smart move for her to be late to her own briefing.

She pulled a notepad across the desk and wrote: *Talking to an old friend from my unit who's in the CIA. Give me a couple of minutes.* He nodded and headed into the office with Rosco and Tran.

Halliday asked Jeffries if he could run the message through the CIA's handwriting analysis database to compare the writing sample from the window to the millions of samples in the CIA and law enforcement databases.

"I can also do one better. I can run it through a new algo we've developed that gives a pretty good profile of the probable characteristics of the writer."

"What sorts of characteristics?"

"It can tell us with a high degree of probability whether the message was written by a male or female. The rough height of the writer. Left- or right-handed. Native English speaker. A read on the writer's age since writing styles taught at schools have changed over time. That sort of thing," he said. "Normally you'd have to request permission, but since we're old friends, I can cut through the red tape and run it through for you today."

"I was hoping you'd say that," she said.

"Make sure the lab cuts off the glass pane and scans it," Jeffries instructed. "It's more accurate than relying on photos or a tracing outline of the message."

The squeaking wheels of the portable whiteboard Halliday pulled into Captain Ken Clarke's office brought the conversation she'd interrupted to an immediate halt.

The captain was propped on the edge of his desk as he listened to Jack Lavelle give an overview of the case. Lavelle was leaning against a filing cabinet with his arms crossed as he spoke. Rosco and Tran sat on a sofa in front of a large internal window that looked out at rows of detectives' cluttered desks. Detective Tran half rose to give Halliday his seat, but she motioned for him to stay put.

"The ME believes the victim was killed by a single stab wound," said Lavelle. "Death was immediate, or close to it. No hesitation wounds. The crime scene was neat and organized. No signs of a struggle. Forensic evidence at the scene suggests that a woman might have been involved."

"Why a woman?" the captain interrupted.

Lavelle looked at Halliday, the incline of his head inviting her to answer the question.

"We found a long strand of black hair, believed to be from a woman, on a pillow next to the victim," Halliday explained. "A neighbor saw a woman with long dark hair exit the elevator with a man yesterday morning. We believe that man may have been the victim."

Halliday handed around packets of printouts of several photos from the crime scene that she'd taken on her phone. Among them was a photo of the victim's bloodied feet and of the writing daubed in blood on the bedroom window.

"*WAKE UP!*" The captain read it out loud. "Is it a political statement?"

"We don't know yet," said Halliday.

"I think it was a hit," said Rosco. "How often do we ever find a stabbing victim with only one wound? I'll tell you how often. Never. There are always several. Sometimes dozens, or more. I don't think the slashes to the feet count."

"They don't. They were almost certainly done postmortem," Halliday noted. "As far as we know pending the autopsy results, the victim was killed by a single knife wound to the heart. The victim died almost instantly. Blood spatter was minimal. You're right. It's rare, almost unheard of, for there to be a single stab wound in a homicide. There's usually defense wounds, overkill wounds, and sometimes hesitation wounds."

"Exactly," said Rosco. "Not too many people can kill a man with one slash of a knife. Not unless they have skills. Ex–special forces. Once we get an ID on the vic, we should look into whether he has any connections to organized crime. We should hone in on the Russians. The Russian mafia recruits former Russian special forces soldiers. Those guys sure like using knives."

"Knives and poison," said the captain. "Both seem to have played a role in this case." He tapped his finger on a photo of the wine bottle that Lavelle said might have been spiked with a sedative. "Do we know what kind of knife was used?"

"The perp took the murder weapon," Lavelle said.

"Well, there you go!" Rosco added. "A perp so attached to his blade that he can't bring himself to leave it behind. It adds fuel to the theory that it was a killer for hire."

"It wasn't a mob hit." Halliday's tone was so emphatic that everyone went silent.

"How do you know?" the captain asked.

"If it was a mob hit, the killer would have used a gun. Two bullets in the head is faster and more accurate than a knife."

Halliday swapped to a detached tone now that she had their attention. She knew from experience never to show that she was emotionally invested in a theory. It was the sign of a cop with tunnel vision, and a cop with tunnel vision was a lousy investigator. She wasn't blinkered. She just happened to have more information than they did.

"Even contract killers have preferences," said Lavelle.

"Contract killers do their job and leave. They don't get sidetracked with art projects," said Halliday. To emphasize her point, she slapped a photo of the *WAKE UP!* message under a magnet on the whiteboard.

Lavelle liked the way Halliday stood her ground. He hated when detectives, especially new ones, buckled at the first sign of an opposing opinion and embraced groupthink.

"The writing on the window could have been deliberate. A bum steer," Rosco remarked. "I've seen contract killers fixing crime scenes before to give the impression it's the work of a serial killer. A slogan in blood on a wall. A mutilated body that looks like it was cut up by a sicko to send everyone on a wild goose chase."

"I don't chase geese." Halliday was firm.

"So what's your theory?" Lavelle asked.

He agreed with Halliday that it wasn't a contract killing. There was nothing specific that jumped out at him when he was at the scene. His judgment was based on pure instinct honed by almost two decades working homicides.

"I won't speculate. It's too soon to have a theory. We don't even know the victim's identity," she pointed out. Halliday wouldn't be drawn on theories when there were no witnesses and the forensics information was still being worked on.

She knew about confirmation bias and how airing a theory led some detectives to inadvertently look for evidence that supported their hunch, while ignoring evidence that undermined it.

"Let's focus on the nuts and bolts of this investigation. Fingerprints, CCTV footage, and identifying the victim," said the captain. "Follow the evidence."

He rose to his feet to indicate the briefing was over. "Keep me updated. I don't want to find out anything on the evening news that I should have found out first here in this office. Detective Lavelle, stay back."

The captain waited until the last person left his office and shut the door.

"Jack, what's your impression of Halliday?" The captain sat back down behind his desk as he asked the question.

"She has good instincts and a real eye for detail. You don't see that combination too often," Lavelle said.

"Yup, she has a good reputation," agreed the captain. As he spoke, he sorted through a pile of files on his desk.

"You don't sound convinced?" Lavelle asked, noticing a file with Halliday's name on it.

"Between you and me, I'm being pushed to consider changing Halliday's status from temporary replacement for Al to his permanent replacement." Noticing Lavelle's raised eyebrow, the captain added, "Al's putting in his papers. We'll have a permanent opening next month." "I want your input on Halliday. I don't want to be arm-twisted into taking her just to meet a gender quota."

"Is there a reason why you have reservations about her?" Lavelle asked.

"Her military records are sealed."

"So?"

"I don't like sealed records. They make me nervous."

"I bet her records are sealed because she served in an intel unit," Lavelle said.

"How do you know that she worked in military intelligence?" The captain sat forward, his interest piqued.

"She was on the phone earlier to a buddy from her old unit. He's now in the CIA. I don't think you have anything to worry about when it comes to her military record. Her record's sealed because it's classified."

"Maybe." The captain shrugged. "Still, I need to know who's join-ing my team. Since the military won't tell me, I need you to find out. I won't risk hiring a detective who turns out to be a liability just to help boost the department's percentage of female detectives on the job."

"You're asking me to spy on her? It's not my style. You know that."

"Not spy, Jack. I want you to observe Halliday in the field and tell me whether you'd put your life in her hands. That'll be good enough for me."

Chapter
Fifteen

Lunch is a crustless cheese sandwich with soggy alfalfa taken from an oversized platter ordered in for the design meeting. I have little appetite. I feel antsy, like I'm craving caffeine. I push a flavored coffee capsule into the coffee machine.

While the machine hisses and splutters noisily, I tune in to a whispered conversation going on somewhere behind me.

"I'm not surprised she seems so . . . lost and confused, with everything she's been through."

The conversation stops midsentence when they realize it's me standing with my back to them. They quickly launch into a contrived discussion about weekend plans. Apparently, I'm supposed to believe that's what they were discussing all along.

I take my coffee mug to the office window and drink, looking down at the street while trying to figure out what I should do. I tried to call Amy after the design meeting. Her phone wasn't on, which usually means she's at work. Marco's phone is also turned off. I suppose I should leave the office and go down to the police precinct in person to ask for their help, but I don't trust the police and I'm afraid of what I might find out.

A noise explodes behind me and I whirl around. Someone has unmuted the office TV to listen to the noon news break without realizing the volume was on the highest setting.

As the newsreader talks, footage appears on the TV screen from outside an apartment building where the anchor says a murder took place. I recognize the building from the article I read earlier.

Crimson writing on an apartment window appears on the TV screen. The camera settles on the words WAKE UP! I stifle a sudden desire to check my wrist, where the same message is written in blue ballpoint letters.

"Police will be trying to determine what the message means and why the killer wrote it as they investigate the brutal murder of an as yet unidentified male," the newsreader says.

Fresh footage flashes on the TV screen. This time it shows a close-up of two detectives quickly going down the stairs of the building to the street. One is an attractive woman with chestnut shoulder-length hair wearing a navy police jacket. The second detective has tightly cropped dark brown hair, stubble, and deep-set ink-blue eyes. They both ignore reporters shoving microphones in their direction and shouting out questions about the murder as they walk away.

The footage cuts to video of a stretcher with a black body bag being pushed into a van.

"Police aren't divulging the name of the victim or saying whether they have any suspects at this point," the newsreader says.

She calls the murderer "The Sleepless Killer." Almost immediately a graphic appears at the bottom of the TV screen saying the same thing. The news program crosses to a reporter at the scene standing in front of the police tape.

"Not surprisingly, the building's residents are afraid they might be next," the reporter says. "The good news is they might not need to worry for much longer. A police source told me that evidence has been found at the scene that could help identify the killer within hours."

The newsreader moves on to another story. I turn away and accidentally bump into a young woman holding a mug of coffee. It spills all over my clothes.

"I am soooo sorry," she says, looking mortified. "That was totally my fault. I was watching the TV instead of looking where I was going."

"It's not just your fault. I wasn't looking where I was going either," I reassure her, dabbing my wet clothes with a napkin to get rid of the stains. My clothes are ruined.

"Coffee stains are the worst," calls out Claudine, the magazine stylist, who has just finished eating her lunch. "Come with me, Liv. We'll find something in the closet for you to wear."

The closet is where the magazine keeps all the clothes and accessories we use for photo shoots. Most of the garments have been given to the magazine as freebies from brands hoping to get a plug in one of our issues.

I follow Claudine into a large rectangular room with huge windows. In the middle is an enormous table covered with bolts of fabric and color swatches. It's surrounded by long chrome racks of clothes pressed against the walls. The mood boards of color palettes presented at the meeting earlier are propped up against a window.

Claudine slides hangers along the rack noisily as she pulls out a few pants and tops and tells me to choose an outfit. I opt for a pair of dark skinny jeans and a loose navy cashmere sweater.

The changing room is little more than a booth with a black curtain for privacy. Inside are a stool and a full-length mirror. I pull off my coffee-stained clothes and drop them on the floor.

I'm about to put on the clothes that Claudine brought me when I catch sight of the reflection of my near-naked body in the mirror. My forearms are covered with scribbles in ballpoint pen that reach up to my elbows. There's so much writing that it looks as if I have tattoo sleeves. Some of the messages are washed out and illegible. Others are incomprehensible rants that strike me as paranoid and delusional. DON'T TRUST ANYONE and DON'T ANSWER THE PHONE are some of the more comprehensible ones.

Claudine reaches into the changing room to hang another garment on a wall hook for me to try on. "This will look great with that outfit. How are you going in there?"

"Good," I say absently, staring at myself.

My gaze moves down my bra and rib cage to the top of my abdomen. It stops abruptly at what I presume is a lipstick smudge on the mirror. I lean forward to wipe the red mark off the mirror. The stain remains. That's when I realize the red mark isn't on the mirror, it's on my skin, just below my rib cage.

I look down curiously to examine it with my fingers. It's not a mark. It's an ugly clump of puckered red scar tissue that I've never seen before.

Chapter
Sixteen

Wednesday 12:08 P.M.

When Detective Darcy Halliday came out of the meeting with the captain, she found a padded envelope lying on her desk. Inside was a black hard drive that had been couriered over by the surveillance company responsible for the CCTV cameras in the apartment building where the murder had taken place.

Halliday plugged the hard drive into her computer. There were dozens of files. Each file contained footage from a different security camera. The building was wired up with surveillance cameras on each floor, as well as in all the elevators and at all the entrances and exits.

Halliday clicked on the footage from the camera on the floor of the murder scene. The camera angle that appeared on her computer screen showed the corridor leading to the elevator doors. The video was in color, but the hues were washed out. Halliday wasn't looking for Hollywood production quality. All she wanted was a clear photo of the suspect's face.

The medical examiner had said the victim was likely murdered six to nine hours before he'd examined the body. That gave Halliday a rough band of time to focus on.

Halliday rewound the footage until she found the time code of the video taken before midnight. The corridor lights were off. Nothing was visible in the darkness. Halliday fast-forwarded through the dark footage. Eventually, a few minutes after two A.M., Halliday noticed a change in the dim light in the vicinity of the apartment doorway. The teenage neighbor had told her he'd heard a door banging shut at around that time.

A hint of movement was noticeable as the front door opened and then closed. Halliday re-played the video on slo-mo, pausing to freeze the frame every few seconds. Someone had surreptitiously left the apartment and gone into the stairwell in the middle of the night.

"You think that's the killer?" asked Lavelle, looking over Halliday's shoulder at a freeze-framed shot of a silhouette on her computer screen.

"It's very likely," Halliday said, trying to enhance the silhouette. "I can't get it clearer than this," she said in frustration. "We need to go through footage of all the exits. There has to be a clearer visual of this person leaving the building. Right now, all we can see is a shadowy blob."

"Rosco and Tran will follow up," Lavelle said. "We need to get going soon. Forensics called. They're ready to walk us through the crime scene."

Halliday was about to unplug the hard drive to give to Rosco when she remembered something important. "Give me a second. I want to see if we have a visual of that couple coming out of the elevator yesterday morning."

She quickly found the footage she was looking for, at 10:08 A.M. the previous morning.

Halliday recognized the older woman with short hair walking toward the elevator. That was the neighbor she'd talked with earlier. When she reached the elevator, the neighbor pressed a button and waited. Twenty seconds later, the elevator doors opened and a man and a woman stepped out.

Halliday paused the video. She was certain the man was the victim. He was roughly the same height and build as the stiff she'd found in bed at the crime scene that morning. The man in the video also had tawny hair, just like the victim, and he had the same distinctive dimples permanently indented into his cheeks.

The man's hand rested on the long-haired woman's lower back as they came out of the elevator, but it wasn't a romantic gesture. It looked as if he was propping her up. She wore jeans and a long cable-knit sweater. All Halliday could see was a curtain of hair obscuring her face.

The man unlocked the front door of the apartment, and they both went inside. Perhaps for the last time. Within twenty-four hours, the man was brutally murdered in that same apartment, and the woman had disappeared.

As she looked at the blurry security camera footage of the long-haired woman, Halliday couldn't help but think that they'd found their prime suspect. She rewound the video back to the moment the couple came out of the elevator. She pressed Play to watch it again.

"Look up," Halliday pleaded, but the woman continued to stare down at her feet.

"She's not looking up," said Lavelle, disgusted by their bad luck. "It's almost as if she's deliberately hiding her identity from the CCTV cameras."

Halliday took a screenshot of the best photo they had of the woman. Her face was largely obscured, but there was a chance that someone who knew her might recognize her anyway. Halliday printed off a hundred copies of the photo to give to the cops going door-to-door in the vicinity of the crime scene. From the photo, it looked as if the suspect was a slender Caucasian woman of average height with waist-long coffee-colored hair.

"We might get lucky. Maybe someone will recognize her," Halliday told Lavelle, as she scooped up the pages from the printer and followed him downstairs to the car.

Chapter
Seventeen

Two Years Earlier

I'm taking the subway home from work when my phone vibrates in my handbag. It's Amy. She texts that she's going on a mini vacation over the three-day gap before her next shift at the hospital. Early birthday present. Plus I need to work on my tan! A string of sunshine and beach emojis follow the message.

You deserve it, hon, I write back.

She does deserve it. Amy's in the final stretch of her internship. I've never seen anyone work so hard. Last week she worked six night shifts in a row. Other times she's up at five in the morning for an early morning shift that often drags on well into the evening. Her dedication to her patients is incredible.

Amy and I were introduced at a party by a mutual friend who knew we were both looking for a roommate. We immediately clicked. We come from different worlds, with different life experiences. Yet after sharing our apartment for almost five years, our bond is much deeper than just that of roommates, or even close friends. Amy's the sister I never had.

She's the only person I've ever told about my nomadic childhood, moving to different towns and schools every time Mom got a new man in her life, during which time she'd all but ignore me while she devoted herself to the relationship. Not to mention her meltdowns when her marriages broke up, and the way she'd guilt-trip me for being the cause of all her heartache. "Men don't want women with baggage," she'd tell me. Amy knows it all.

I know all her secrets, too, like how she began her affair with Brett months before he split with his wife, and her lifelong dream of going to Africa to work as a doctor with a humanitarian organization. There's very little we don't tell each other.

When I get home, I unlock the front door tentatively and push it open with a creak. "It's just you and me, kid," I tell Shawna as she rubs herself against my legs in greeting.

I pour her food into a bowl while I text-message Marco to suggest he come over and stay the night. He doesn't text back. I dial his cell phone. The call goes straight to voicemail.

When I examine the contents of the fridge, I decide it's a good thing Marco didn't respond. We're out of everything, other than eggs and cheese. I should go to the supermarket to pick up groceries, but I'm too beat. Instead I head to the bathroom, where I fill the tub with hot water and a splash of lavender oil.

I wish I'd joined Amy on her mini vacation. I'm also feeling burnt out. Work has been stressful. There has been more sniping than usual among the staff writers. Naomi's still furious that I've been assigned the arts roundup. Her only communication with me all week has been to take subtle potshots during editorial meetings. It's been exhausting.

I slide into the hot water and put a wet terry towel over my face. The water is so warm that I drift to sleep. When I wake, the bath water is getting cold and there's an intermittent thumping noise nearby. At first I think that someone is hitting a nail with a hammer somewhere in the building. After listening to more thumps, I realize the noise is coming from inside my apartment.

Amy's away so it can't be her. I think for a hopeful moment that Marco received my text and came here to take me up on my invitation. But Marco doesn't have keys to the apartment so it can't be him. The only possibility left is that there's an intruder in the apartment.

Cold fear slides through me like liquid mercury as I climb out of the bath, careful not to make any splashing noises. I throw my satin robe onto my wet body without toweling off and press my ear against the bathroom door. The thumping noise resumes.

Someone is definitely in the apartment. I haven't brought my phone into the bathroom so I can't call for help. Instead, I push down the bathroom door handle soundlessly and count to three before swinging it open and charging to the front door. My robe flaps behind me as I run. The lock opens quickly despite my slippery hands. I step out onto the landing dripping wet and feeling like a total idiot.

The building door opens downstairs. I tentatively move forward to the banister to see who's come in. It's a neighbor who lives on the fourth floor. She doesn't notice me as she strides up the stairs two at a time, her eyes peeled on her phone as she talks on FaceTime. When she reaches my landing, she glances up and makes eye contact before continuing to her floor.

Seeing the neighbor makes me feel more stupid than ever. Of course, there isn't an intruder. The banging must be from the new tenants assembling their flatpack furniture like they did the other night until late.

I return to my apartment and close the door behind me. Once inside, I call Marco.

"Is everything okay, Liv?" he asks.

The murmur of voices in the background and the clatter of cutlery scraping against plates tells me that he must be at a restaurant.

"Did you get my text about staying tonight?" I head down the corridor toward Amy's bedroom, where the banging noise came from. I feel more courageous knowing there's someone on the phone line who can call the cops if something goes wrong.

"I just saw your message. I wish I could come over, but I'm out of town."

"Where are you?"

A floorboard creaks behind me. I freeze.

"A tech conference. Chicago. I fly back on Friday night."

"I didn't know that you're away this week," I say, feeling incredibly alone and vulnerable as I realize there's no way Marco can come to my aid. I take another step forward.

"I thought I mentioned it," he says a little too sharply. Marco hates it when I pry. "You sound upset about something," he says, cottoning on to the fear in my voice. "Are you sure everything's okay, Liv?"

"I'm just disappointed that you can't come over. Amy's away and the apartment feels very . . . empty," I say, too embarrassed to tell him that I'm spooked being alone in my own home.

"I'll make it up to you." His voice is husky with promise.

"I'll hold you to it," I say haltingly before hanging up.

The banging resumes. It's definitely coming from Amy's room. I walk toward her bedroom door, holding the phone as if it's a weapon. When I reach her room, I gently kick the door fully open and turn on the bedroom light.

Amy forgot to latch the window. The wind must have blown it open and it's hitting the wall.

I close the window and turn around to examine the room. There's a walk-in closet and a desk in a nook by the window. When Amy was a medical student, the desk was always covered with books. Nowadays, it's empty other than a silver laptop.

On her bed is a small suitcase that she appears to have abandoned half-packed. I presume she opted for a bigger suitcase and more clothes. Amy always overpacks. It's not unknown for her to take two suitcases for a weekend trip. As I turn to leave the bedroom, I almost trip over Shawna's tail, which is sticking out from under Amy's bed.

"So that's where you are!" Shawna opens her one good eye and stares at me in disdain before returning to sleep.

I head to the kitchen to prepare something to eat, acutely aware that it will be slim pickings given the state of my fridge. Besides the eggs and cheese, I find a jar of asparagus in the cupboard. I cook a cheese and asparagus omelet, which I eat while watching TV in the living room.

My eyes get heavy and I fall asleep on the sofa in the middle of the show. I wake to the sound of banging. It's Amy's window again. I can't begin to fathom how it could have opened when I closed it firmly earlier. Once again I go in to turn on the lights and close the window. This time, I double-check to make sure it won't accidentally open again.

The alarm clock next to Amy's bed tells me it's getting close to midnight. I stumble to the bathroom and brush my teeth before opening my bedroom door.

I turn on the light and stand stunned at the entrance of my room. It was neat when I left for work this morning. It's not like that now. My bedroom's a mess. The bed is rumpled. The closet doors and some of my dresser drawers are partly open. It looks as if someone was rummaging through my stuff.

One of the photo frames lies on the floor amid a pile of smashed glass. It's a photo of Marco and me on a weekend trip to Maine. I pick up the frame and the broken glass and put it on the table next to my bed. My chest tightens with fear when I see my bedroom window. Someone has drawn a heart pierced by an arrow in the dust on the glass pane.

I call 9–1–1 even though it goes against the grain for me to turn to the police. I have a deep-seated distrust of the authorities ever since the night a cop pulled me out of Mom's arms when I was taken by child protection as a kid. That memory has never left me. It doesn't help that when I was in college, I was roughly handcuffed and arrested when I happened to be in the vicinity of a student protest. The cops let me go after reviewing footage that showed I wasn't involved, but the experience only deepened my distrust.

Two uniformed police officers arrive twenty minutes later. By then, I've changed into sweats and curled up on the armchair in the living room, taking deep breaths as I try to stay calm. The officers listen politely as I give them a blow-by-blow of what happened.

"So you didn't go into your bedroom at all when you came home?" a heavyset cop with a thin mustache asks while his much younger dark-haired partner checks the window latches in the kitchen and living room for signs of a break-in.

"The last time I was in my bedroom was this morning before I left for work. It was neat. My bed was made. It didn't look anything like this." I gesture toward the mess.

I follow the younger cop to Amy's room when he checks the window. "Looks like the window catch needs to be fixed. That's why it's swinging open when the wind is up," he says, as he plays around with the latch.

He tells me that nobody could have scaled the external wall of our building to get in through that window. "Not unless it was a cat burglar. Do you know whether your roommate is missing any valuables?"

"It's hard for me to say." I rest my eyes on Amy's silver laptop. "Amy's computer is still here."

"That would have gone in a second if the place had been robbed. So would that." He points at a gold necklace and some other jewelry in a crystal bowl on Amy's bedside table.

He twists the catch to make sure the window closes properly this time and tells me to get the super to fix it in the morning.

"I suggest you go to sleep and talk to your roommate tomorrow. Maybe she drew the heart on the window as a joke," the burly cop with the mustache tells me when we return to the living room.

"I really think someone was here," I say dubiously.

"There's no sign of a break-in. We checked thoroughly."

"Just because there's no sign of a break-in doesn't mean it didn't happen. Can't you at least take fingerprints?"

"Ma'am, there's no sign a crime took place here. Nothing's been stolen. We don't take fingerprints when there's no indication a crime was committed." He talks to me like I'm a child.

"So you're saying I trashed my own bedroom and I don't remember?"

"There's probably a perfectly good explanation for everything that happened. Cats can be vindictive when they're left alone. They're smarter than people think."

"My cat is smart, but even she can't open and close drawers and closet doors. Nor can she draw hearts on windows."

"Maybe your roommate did that before she went on vacation," the burly cop suggests, trying to shut me down. "Maybe she borrowed some of your clothes and she was in such a rush to pack that she left a mess behind."

"Amy wouldn't do that. She knows that I'm a neat freak. Someone else was here."

He sighs impatiently. "Look, we've checked your apartment. There's nobody here except for you." He opens the front door and gestures with his head for his partner to follow.

"Someone must have come into the apartment and messed up my bedroom. Even if that person didn't steal something, it's still a crime. Breaking and entering. Isn't it?" I'm annoyed that they're literally doing nothing to get to the bottom of this.

"It would be a crime. If it had happened," he says, turning around enough for me to see a judgmental glint in his eyes. "But there's no evidence there was a break-in. Nothing's missing. There's no forced entry. Is there someone you think might have broken into your apartment just to mess with you? Someone with a grudge? An ex-boyfriend? A neighbor?"

"Nobody I know would do something like this!"

"What about someone you don't know?" the junior cop chimes in, earning an irate glance from his partner.

"What do you mean?"

"Have you been harassed recently, ma'am? Anonymous messages? Calls? Threats of any type?"

"You're asking whether I've been stalked?"

"Yes, I am."

Kevin, the waiter from Café del Mar, left three more messages for me at work. I wouldn't define his calls as stalking. He's never done anything more than leave me innocuous messages. But I find it weird that a waiter, with whom I had a fleeting conversation, would track me down at my office and call me repeatedly.

I'm about to mention his name, when I change my mind. Some people are really bad at reading social cues. Kevin might be one of them, and that's why he keeps calling me at work. Plus, it might antagonize him if the police confront him about his calls to me. The fact is that bitter experience over many years has taught me not to trust cops. Things always go haywire when the police get involved.

"Nobody's stalking me," I say, with more conviction than I feel.

Chapter
Eighteen

Claudine holds her hands together in delight and tells me to spin around when I come out of the changing room dressed in the outfit she's styled for me.

She inclines her head at an angle, as if not quite sure about how I look, and then scrambles in a closet and removes an asymmetrical silver-blue cardigan so long that it reaches the top of my thighs. It suits my outfit of skinny jeans and a cashmere black scoop neck top.

"It's still missing something," says Claudine.

She disappears into a storeroom and returns with a necklace made of different shades of blue-and-clear quartz stones. Standing behind me, she clips on the hook of the necklace.

"One last thing and then you can go," she promises.

She pulls out a handful of cosmetics samples from a box and sorts through them until she finds shades that suit my coloring. "This will finish off your look."

As I apply the makeup, I see my reflection in the small mirror morph back into . . . me.

I almost fool myself into thinking that everything is back to normal until I remember the jagged scar on my body. No matter how hard I try, I can't remember what caused it. There's a gaping hole in my memory from the moment I answered the phone on my desk on what was definitely a blue-sky summer's day until the moment I woke on the park bench this morning to the biting chill of an approaching winter. I tell myself my memory loss is temporary, the aftereffects of a late night, or really bad jet lag. Clarity will return very soon.

The main office is deserted when I emerge in my new clothes and fresh makeup. I feel bereft as I watch everyone talking animatedly in glass-walled meeting rooms scattered around the office, probably planning the next issues of the magazine.

I don't belong here anymore. That thought pierces me with a visceral sense of irretrievable loss. I loved working at *Cultura*. Being here, doing this job was among the happiest times of my life. I don't know how I became an interloper in my own life. I could ask Josie or someone else to fill me in, but I'm embarrassed to reveal how confused I am.

I dial Amy again. She's a doctor. She'll tell me what to do. I can almost hear her faintly amused voice telling me to sleep it off, the way she has countless times when I was wooly-headed from a hangover, or a bad flu.

Unfortunately, Amy's phone is still turned off. I consider asking the hospital to page her, but I know that Amy hates getting personal calls at work. In the end I call Marco. Sheer relief runs through me when my call is answered.

"Marco!"

"Who is this?" a man snaps.

"Marco?" My voice lilts uncertainly.

"There's no Marco here."

"But . . . this is Marco's phone?"

"Listen, lady, for the millionth time, this is a wrong number. How many times do I have to tell you the same thing!"

A dejected click tells me he's hung up on me. I dial the number again. This time I double-check to make sure it's correct.

"Lady," says the same gruff voice as before. "I told you already. You've dialed the wrong number."

"It's definitely Marco's number." Hysteria rises inside of me.

"No, it's not. Just like I told you the last time you called. And the time before that. And the time before that. You get my drift."

I don't get it. I'm certain this is Marco's cell phone number. "Is Marco ghosting me?" I ask. "Tell him that Liv called. I'm his girl-friend. I need to speak to him. It's urgent."

"Trust me, lady. This is the wrong number. You need to stop call-ing," he shouts over a grinding truck engine before hanging up.

The conversation drains me. I put my head in my hands. Everything has changed beyond recognition. The office. Me. The scar, I think, as I absentmindedly rub it through my borrowed designer clothes.

On the office television set, a news report flashes again on the screen, with that shot of the words WAKE UP! written on an apartment building window.

I have the same message written on my skin. It must be more than a coincidence. I'm consumed by a powerful urge to go there. Maybe being there will bring back my memory and dissolve the confusion that has hung over me like a blinding fog ever since I woke on the park bench.

The article I'd read earlier mentioned the location of the building where the murder took place. I check the article again. It's near the corner of Fifty-Third and Lexington.

As I leave the office, the receptionist asks whether I spoke with the man whose call she transferred earlier. I shudder when I remember the frightening voice on the phone, his tone accusing and cajoling at the same time.

"I spoke with him."

"He called again. He said the first call was cut off. I transferred him to you but you didn't pick up."

"I was in a meeting."

"Oh. He said he'll swing by later. In fact, he asked me to tell you to stay in the office until he gets here. He says it's important."

"I have an appointment and I'm already late," I lie, rushing out of the office even faster.

Nine subway stops and five minutes' walk later, I'm standing outside the apartment building that I recognize from the news bulletin.

A police car and a forensics van are parked on the curb near police barricades. Uniformed cops stand on the sidewalk at the entrance. A few residents wait to be allowed inside, visibly annoyed at having to line up to get into their own building.

Onlookers loiter behind the barricade. I don't join them. I feel intimidated by the heavy police presence. Instead I go into a high-end shoe shop directly across the street. I pretend to look at the boots in the window display, while surreptitiously watching the police outside the building.

"Can I help?" I almost jump as a shop assistant comes from behind me.

"Sure," I say, pointing to a knee-high boot in the shop window display. "Do you have it in a size seven?"

She disappears into a back storeroom and returns carrying an oversized shoe box.

"What's going on out there?" I ask.

"Someone was murdered in the building across the street." She whispers discreetly even though there're no other customers in the store.

She lifts up the shoebox lid and removes the boots, extolling the virtues of the Italian-made leather soles and inner lining.

She stops in the middle of her explanation as a police officer comes inside. "Why don't you try on the boots and see for yourself how comfortable they are," she suggests, before rushing over to the police officer and leading him to a corner near the cash register.

I listen intently to their hushed conversation as I put on the boots. He tells her the police are collecting security camera footage from the stores along the street.

"We think the killer might have been filmed leaving the scene of the murder," he says. "We're talking to all the stores along this block to get surveillance footage from early this morning."

The saleswoman noticeably lowers her voice. "We have cameras facing the street. You'll need to speak with my manager to get copies. Do you have any idea who might have done it?" she asks. "The murder, I mean."

"A woman with long dark hair down to her waist was seen with the victim. Have you seen anyone answering that description in the vicinity over the past few days?" he asks.

"Not that I recall," she says.

Self-consciously, I touch my short hair as creeping panic runs through me. My hair was long when I woke up in the park this morning, just as the cop described. The words WAKE UP! are written on my wrist. It's more than a coincidence. I have a terrible feeling that I'm connected to this crime.

I pace around the store in the boots, making what I hope is a convincing show of pretending to deliberate whether to buy them. By the time the police officer leaves the store, I've taken off the boots and slipped into my own shoes.

"Aren't those boots just to die for?" the saleswoman says.

"They're lovely, but I have very wide feet and they just don't feel right. I'll come again to try on another style when I have more time," I say, before hastily rushing out.

I barge straight into a throng of people craning their necks on the sidewalk as they look up at the apartment building across the street.

"Someone was killed there today. Murdered." A man in jeans and a khaki windbreaker points up at the sixth-floor window. "The killer wrote a message on the window. Can you see it?"

I look up, squinting. I can't see the writing from this distance.

"I heard on the news that the message is written in the victim's own blood. That's why I came down here. I wanted to see it for myself," says someone in the crowd as he holds out an iPhone and tries to zoom in on the window in question.

"What do you think it means?" a woman asks nobody in particular.

"The murderer is sending us a message," a man responds.

"It's a warning," says someone else, his voice rising hysterically. "We must wake up and repent for our sins before it's too late."

Chapter
Nineteen

The crime scene was transformed by the time Darcy Halliday and Jack Lavelle signed their names on the log sheet and ducked under the yellow crime scene tape strung across the entrance of the apartment.

Kneeling on the floor in the living room, a forensic technician carefully removed fingerprints from the arm of a leather sofa. Another technician was painstakingly brushing black dust across the stainless steel fridge door to look for prints.

In the bedroom, numbered cards were scattered across the room to indicate where trace evidence had been found. The mattress was stripped bare. The sheets had been bagged as evidence. Bloodstains were evident on the mattress.

In the corner, Detective James Bowen was drawing a plan of the bedroom with precise measurements. Bowen was a bear of a man with a furrowed brow and a full beard that was a mix of brown and gray.

"Tell me you found something to help us ID the victim? A dry cleaning ticket? A cell phone? Better yet, his missing wallet?" Halliday asked.

She'd worked closely with Bowen when she'd done a stint in the forensics unit after she'd received her detective's badge. When it came to working a crime scene, nobody was more thorough.

"We've been through everything in the apartment with a fine-tooth comb. There's no ID, no wallets or credit cards or anything else that will enable a quick identification of the victim, or the woman who was with him."

"You're sure it was a woman?" Lavelle asked.

In answer, Bowen slid open the bedroom closet door to show a selection of women's clothes neatly hung on cedar hangers. Halliday pushed the hangers across the rack to take a better look. The clothes were largely fashion items from mass market brands. She noticed they all had the faintest whiff of mildew.

The odor was so subtle that most people wouldn't have noticed it, but Halliday smelled it immediately. She'd lived in a basement apartment in her last year of college and her nose had been sensitive to the smell of mildewed clothes ever since.

She handed Bowen the flyer she'd printed, showing the security camera image of the mystery woman with long hair exiting the elevator along with a man the previous morning. The date and time code were stamped on the image.

"The man, who we believe is the victim, entered this apartment with this woman yesterday morning," said Lavelle.

Bowen lifted up his glasses to take a closer look. "Long dark hair. It sure looks like she's our gal. Shame we can't see her face."

"She's awfully shy in front of the cameras," agreed Halliday.

Bowen rummaged in a metal case filled with evidence bags and retrieved several small sealed bags. Each contained a human hair. "Based on the unusual length of the hairs, I'd say it's likely these hairs put the woman in your photo in the bedroom with the victim around the time he died."

"How do you know the woman was here at around the time of the murder?" Halliday asked.

"One of the long hairs was found on the victim's body. With blood on it," he said. "I suspect she was leaning over him when the hair fell. I'd say the woman in the photo is your prime suspect. Unfortunately, there's no root sheath on any of the hairs we collected. We won't be able to run them for DNA without intact roots."

"That's a real pity," said Halliday, deflated.

Detective Bowen walked them through the bedroom pointing to different evidence cards and explaining what had been found in each location.

"There was a partial print on a lipstick applicator we found wedged behind a leg of the bed. We're testing the lipstick for DNA," he said.

"You think the lipstick belongs to our suspect?" Lavelle asked.

"Who knows. It might have been here for months," said Bowen.

In the bathroom, Bowen pointed out where they'd found finger-prints on the sink, faucets, light switch, and cupboard doors. They'd bagged the long black hair that Halliday had seen near the sink, and found a matching hair on the floor.

"We found some interesting items in the bedroom that we'll get the lab to do a rush job on," Bowen said.

"Like what?" Halliday asked.

"We found foreign matter on the pillow where the victim's head was." He showed them a small evidence bag containing tiny granules of a black substance.

"Any idea what it is?" Halliday held the evidence bag up to the light to get a better look.

"My guess is that it's flecks of paint. Black," Bowen responded.

He held up another handful of evidence bags with a single strand of hair in each. "I don't think these hairs are from the victim or the long-haired woman," Bowen said. "They're shorter in length and the color is different. It's a few shades lighter."

"You think there might have been a third person in the apartment?" Halliday asked.

"Could be," he said. "It's also possible the hairs are from someone who stayed here in the past. The owner or another short-stay guest. We need to get the owner's prints and hair samples for matching purposes."

"Can't," said Lavelle. "The owner's in Hong Kong until next week."

"That'll slow things down."

After they'd gone through the apartment, Halliday and Lavelle went down to show the doorman the photo of the long-haired woman.

"I don't think I've seen her before," the doorman said, after taking a close look. "But I wouldn't bet my house on it. There are people coming and going all the time. There are at least eight apartments in the building that are rented out on short-term rental sites. The night doorman regularly gives guests the keys to their rentals when they check in late. He might remember them."

"Yeah, I've been trying to get hold of him," said Lavelle. "His phone is off."

"He's probably still sleeping," said the doorman. "He starts work at six. Come again tonight. He'll be here," he said, before rushing to the door to help a woman arriving with an armful of shopping bags.

After talking to the doorman, Halliday and Lavelle split up. He went to talk to the officer supervising the door knocking and murder weapon search, while Halliday went down to the basement to check out the building's rear exits.

There were two service exits from the basement. Both came out into a narrow lane behind the apartment building. The first exit was where the garbage Dumpsters were located. There was also a rear exit at the bottom of the fire escape stairs. Black-fingerprint residue coated the metal door handles and light switches at both exits where the forensics team had taken prints.

Halliday pushed open the fire exit doors and stepped into an alley behind the building. Ten yards away was a street. On that street, directly facing the end of the lane was a liquor store. Halliday crossed the side street and went inside.

An elderly man with a drooping gray mustache hunched on a stool behind the counter manually checking an order book with a blue ballpoint pen. He looked up when Halliday approached, holding out her badge.

"How can I help you, Detective?"

"Do you have security cameras pointing out to the street?"

"We sure do. Had a robbery a few years back. They threw a brick into the store window, grabbed whatever they could, and drove off. We put up cameras after that."

He motioned toward a bank of small screens behind the counter. They showed footage from different angles in and outside the store. One of the camera angles showed a clear shot of the end of the alley across the street. That was the killer's likely exit route.

"Can I get a copy of the footage from that camera?" Halliday asked.

"My son knows how to do that. I barely know how to turn on a computer. He's out right now. Leave me your number and I'll get him to get right onto it as soon as he gets back."

Halliday left her business card and then walked back to the main entrance of the building, where she waited for Lavelle. Across the street, people were milling around on the sidewalk, craning their necks to look up at the apartment where the murder took place.

"What's going on over there?" Halliday asked a cop outside the building.

"The TV news ran pictures of the message on the apartment window. People are coming to take a look like it's a tourist attraction."

"Some tourist attraction!"

Halliday crossed the street and joined the group looking up at the window. Seeing it from this angle cemented Halliday's view the message was intended for the outside world. That's why the killer had written it on the apartment window instead of on a wall near the body, or on the body itself.

A glazier was due to arrive shortly to cut out the entire pane of glass for analysis at the lab as Owen Jeffries had requested. It would be replaced with new glass. Within a day, the police barriers would be gone, along with the gawkers. Halliday knew from experience that in all likelihood the murder would be quickly forgotten in the shuffle of fresh news headlines.

While Halliday waited for Lavelle to return, she showed the onlookers the flyer of the female suspect leaving the elevator with the victim. Most shrugged blankly when she asked if they recognized anyone in the photo.

"Ma'am, have you seen this woman before?" Halliday handed a flyer to a fashionably dressed woman with a short asymmetrical hairstyle who'd joined the crowd after coming out of a high-end shoe store.

The woman took the flyer and studied it. Halliday noticed black-and-blue writing on the back of her hands. It struck her as strange that an otherwise smartly dressed woman would write on her hands like a schoolgirl.

Before Halliday could read any of the writing on the woman's hands, the woman moved them away self-consciously and handed back the flyer.

"I haven't seen her before," she said. "I'm sorry that I can't help you." She turned abruptly and disappeared into a throng of pedestrians.

Chapter
Twenty

My gaze moves from the apartment window down to a female detective standing in front of me on the busy sidewalk. She's the detective I saw earlier on the TV news.

She holds out a flyer and asks whether I recognize the long-haired woman in the photograph. I freeze when I see the photo. Even though the woman's face is downcast, her long waist-length hair is distinctive. My hair was that long before I had it cut short this morning. The woman's clothes look a lot like the ones I threw away after I was splashed with coffee at the *Cultura* office.

Running through my mind is the horrible thought that I'm the woman the police are looking for. I hand the flyer back to the detective, mumbling something about how I don't know who it is, before I walk away as calmly as possible.

Once I've put some distance between us, I push up my sleeve and stare at the writing on my wrist. Just because the words *WAKE UP!* are written both at the murder scene and on my skin doesn't mean I have anything to do with what happened. Does it?

Then I remember the man who'd called the office earlier. He asked if I'd taken a knife. Fear rushes through me at the terrifying thought that there's yet another link connecting me to this crime.

"Liv?"

I flinch at the sound of my name.

"Liv?"

I walk faster, pretending not to hear. I'm afraid it's the detective coming after me. Ahead of me is a green traffic light. I stride ahead, willing myself to make it across the street before it changes to red.

It's too late. The light flashes amber and then red before I reach the curb. I'm cornered. I move deep into the knot of people waiting to cross the street, desperate to disappear into the crowd.

"Liv. Liv Reese."

Just as I'm about to bolt across the street against the lights, a hand squeezes my shoulder.

Reluctantly, I turn around. I'm both shocked and relieved to see it's Dean, Marco's investor. He wears jeans and a white shirt. His craggy face seems genuinely happy to see me.

Before I can say a word, he leans in and kisses me on both cheeks before stepping back to admire me, still holding my hands. "It's been a long time. How have you been?"

"Great. Really good."

"That's terrific. I heard you moved abroad? London, right? I guess you wanted a clean break."

His words ring ominously in my head. A clean break from what?

Before I can ask him, the traffic light turns green. We cross together, pushed by the tide of pedestrians behind us.

"How about we grab some lunch?" he suggests. "You're a foodie, right? Boy, do I know a place that will knock your socks off!"

Without waiting for my answer, Dean raises his arm to hail a cab. As the cab changes lanes to pull up by the curb, my heart drops when I glimpse a ballpoint pen message scribbled on the side of my hand.

DON'T TRUST ANYONE, it says.

Chapter
Twenty-One

Two Years Earlier

I'm on the train heading home when Frank, my editor, texts me with a request to attend an art show preview.

Now? I text back with one hand, clutching the overhead rail with my other hand to steady myself when the train brakes suddenly to stop at the next station. I have plans tonight.

Are you in or out? It's a huge deal. It's Q!!

What's Q???

I immediately regret it the second I press Send. Note to self, never show ignorance about the arts scene when you're working at a culture magazine. Frank texts me an eye-roll emoji. A moment later my phone rings.

"Liv," Frank says, without any preliminaries. "Q is a guerrilla artist. He's one of the hottest new names in performance art." The background noise gets louder as the train speeds up. "Q doesn't just test boundaries, Q takes them to a new constellation. Like Banksy, nobody knows Q's real name. Q could be the art gallery guard, or a waiter carrying a tray of champagne at the opening. Or Q could be someone in the audience. Nobody ever knows."

"Sounds intriguing," I respond, even though I'm not intrigued at all.

"You have no idea how lucky we are to get this invitation, and it was addressed to you. Will you go?"

Amy's arranged a dinner for her birthday at her favorite restaurant and I can't be late. "The thing is that I actually have another . . ."

"To be clear, Liv." Frank's voice is clipped. "If I have to ask someone else to do it then I won't ask you the next time an opportunity this good lands on my desk. I need to know that my reporters will drop anything for a good story."

"Text me the details and I'll be there."

In truth, I'm kicking myself. I would never say this at the office, but I've never been to a performance art event that didn't make me want to barf. Maybe I'm cynical, or maybe I've seen too much in my life, but I find these sorts of things fatuous and self-indulgent.

Also, I can't bear the thought of letting Amy down tonight by not turning up for her birthday celebration. I certainly can't stand up Marco. He's coming as my plus-one. It wouldn't be fair to him if I came late, especially since Amy is one of his least favorite people in the world. As Marco says, my boyfriend and my best friend don't actually need to like each other.

I text Marco on the way to the gallery to tell him that I have to cancel the predinner drinks we'd arranged. I have to stop off at an art show for the magazine. I'll meet you at the restaurant.

Fine, he responds. I can tell he's pissed.

The gallery is in a renovated red-brick warehouse by the Manhattan Bridge. A bronze plaque by the entrance says it used to store cotton at the turn of the twentieth century. The address that Frank sent takes me to an entrance at the rear of the building.

I go around the block into a narrow back alley alongside a wire fence until I find a doorway between two lots of Dumpsters that smell of rotting garbage. The door is turquoise. It has a sign on it that says: Q: ADVANCE VIEWING. ENTRY BY INVITATION ONLY.

I'm surprised such a well-known artist would have his preview in such an awful location. Maybe that's the point; Q is a guerrilla artist. Perhaps walking past Dumpsters to get into the exhibition is part of the "guerrilla experience."

I swallow my apprehension as I push open the turquoise door. There's no public relations person armed with glossy brochures to meet me at the entrance. I presume that's because I'm late. A hum of chatter and clinking glasses deep inside the gallery tells me the art show is in full swing.

Walking across a polished concrete floor, I reach a door with a sign that says: ENTER HERE. The door leads me into a dark room. Tiny fairy lights on the floor delineate a path in the dark. I can just make out a wall of lockers and another sign saying: CONDITION OF ENTRY: ALL BAGS, PHONES AND OTHER POSSESSIONS ARE TO BE LEFT IN A SECURE LOCKER.

It's inconvenient since there's no way to take notes or record interviews without using my phone, but I play by the rules. I lock my purse in a locker and put the key, which is on a multicolored elastic band, over my wrist like a bracelet. I'll take notes in my head and write them all down when I get out of here.

The ambient sounds of people talking and a string quartet moving into Vivaldi's *Four Seasons* gets louder as I move past the lockers toward a partly open door. Through the gap, I glimpse a bold red canvas on a wall.

Someone taps a wineglass with a knife to get everyone's attention. It's followed by an announcement by an MC asking everyone to gather for speeches.

I rush through the open door into the gallery, keen not to miss the speeches. When I'm inside, I halt midstep. The red canvas is not real.

It's a projection on a white wall. All the other walls are empty. There's no artwork on the walls at all. No paintings. No people. No waiters wandering around with trays of glasses filled with red and white wine. No MC.

The door behind me slams shut. The ambient sounds of the gallery show continue on the other side of a wall. I feel trapped and disoriented, like I've taken a wrong turn in a maze. I'm trying to figure out how to reach the art show when the lights go off.

I stand still, blind and helpless in the dark. I focus all my senses on the hum of the art show behind the wall, until suddenly that sound disappears as well. It's replaced by a hollow silence. The only sounds are my own heartbeat and quickening breath.

A frisson of terror runs through me as I recognize how vulnerable I am, alone in a warehouse. A spotlight turns on. Its beam moves along the floor playfully as if urging me to join it. I follow the beam into another room, equally dark and silent.

Another spotlight turns on and settles on an exhibit surrounded by red velvet ropes. A woman sits on a wooden chair. Frayed sailing rope is wrapped around her torso. I can't see her face. There's a burlap sack over her head. Her ankles are tied to the legs of the chair. Her arms are tied behind her back.

A museum sign says: WOMAN ON CHAIR.

That's when I realize the woman is the display.

She groans and contorts her body as if trying to break the bonds that tie her to the chair. Her dress is ripped open, revealing a lace bra and smooth pale flesh.

Performance art has never been to my taste, but I'm here to write about it, so I walk closer to get a better look. A whispered chant gets louder the closer I get to the red velvet barrier, until it becomes deafening: *"Kill. Kill. Kill."*

The woman emits an animal groan as the chanting roars louder. It sounds as if she's gagged under the burlap sack. The sounds she makes are barely human. On a table next to her is a glass box. Inside are a knife and a pair of scissors. Next to it is a hammer. A sign on the table says: DO NOT TOUCH.

"Kill. Kill. Kill," the chanting continues.

As the chanting reaches a fever pitch, I reach the velvet ropes cordoning off the "exhibit." I'm close enough to the woman to see a tattoo of tiny, brightly colored butterflies on her shoulder.

Black-and-white footage appears on the stark white walls of the room. The footage is badly scratched like an old-fashioned movie film reel.

On one wall is footage of a woman undressing until she is naked. She slides into a bath and fully immerses herself under water. All that can be seen are bubbles of various sizes at the top of the water until they, too, disappear and there is nothing.

On another screen is a young woman leaving an apartment building. It's filmed from the perspective of a voyeur watching the woman from the bushes.

On the third and largest screen, a woman walks across an empty parking lot to her car late at night. The heels of her shoes click with each step that she takes. Heavy breathing in the background gets louder and louder, mocking the woman's lack of awareness that she's being watched. She presses her electronic key to open her car. It beeps twice.

High-pitched violin notes rise deafeningly as the camera gets closer and closer, zooming in on her eyes widening as she realizes she's in danger. As the violin hits the highest note, the footage on all the screens disappears in a tide of spilt red.

The spotlight turns off and the room is cast into pitch darkness again. My heart beats rapidly, mimicking the terror of the woman in the video. I'm filled with a desperate urge to get out of here. Just as I'm about to turn and run, a light appears in a far corner of the room. Someone is sitting on a stool, backlit. I see only their silhouette.

"We're honored to have you here today, Liv. You can play with the display in any way you like," says the disembodied voice of a man who I assume is the famous Q.

"What about the signs saying not to touch the display?" I ask.

"It's like life." He shrugs. "Some people obey the rules. Others break them. We all have free will. You could have broken the glass box and freed the woman. That would have been a reasonable choice. Or you could have left her there, as you did. Another reasonable choice."

"Does she want to be free?"

"You're asking the wrong question. You should ask whether you wanted to free her. Whether you felt constrained by the rules, or whether ignoring her plight was your natural inclination. Did you want to break the glass box?"

"Yes."

"So why didn't you?"

"Because the sign said not to touch the display."

"I see." Silence follows. "There are no right or wrong answers. You can do whatever you like. To her. To me. To yourself," he says.

"What I'd like to do is interview you," I say, trying to get in control of the conversation.

"Why?"

"To get a broader understanding of your work."

"My work speaks for itself."

The spotlight returns. "Leave your business card in the locker where you stored your belongings," Q instructs. "I'll contact you."

The spotlight guides me back to the locker room. I leave my business card in the locker as instructed before I collect my things and rush out of the building. The turquoise door slams shut behind me with an iron clang that echoes long after it's closed.

I lean against an alley wall near a Dumpster, taking a series of deep breaths to calm myself and stop my legs from trembling. It feels as if this exhibition was designed for the sole purpose of terrifying me.

Chapter
Twenty-Two

Detective Jack Lavelle was dubious about eating a vegetarian burger until he saw Darcy Halliday unwrap hers and take a bite.

"I'll have the same but with extra hot sauce," he told the waitress. "And hold the tomatoes."

"You won't regret it," Halliday said in between bites. She wiped a trickle of sauce dripping down her chin with a napkin and scooped up a handful of sweet potato fries.

Halliday had asked Lavelle to stop at the hole-in-the-wall vegan eatery on the way to the precinct so they could grab lunch. She hadn't eaten anything since the previous night, other than a couple of crackers from a box she kept in her desk drawer. There hadn't been time for breakfast in the crucial first hours of the homicide investigation.

"Not bad, right?" Halliday said, after he'd taken the first mouthful. His expression answered her question more succinctly than words.

They ate quickly, talking shop in between mouthfuls of food.

One of the most pressing issues was getting hold of the owner of the apartment. Lavelle was tracking the progress of his flight across the Pacific Ocean and would call him as soon as the plane landed in Hong Kong.

In Lavelle's car was an envelope with over a dozen evidence bags, each containing a USB drive with video footage from the security cameras of stores and apartment buildings. The police officers canvassing on their behalf were still in the process of collecting more footage. Lavelle expected there would be thousands of hours to go through by the time they were done.

After viewing the footage and following up on any information so far collected by the patrol cops canvassing the area, they'd go back to the crime scene in the late afternoon to question residents who'd been at work when they'd knocked on their doors in the morning. The night doorman would be on duty by then as well. They had plenty of questions for him, considering that the murder had taken place under his watch.

At a temporary lull in the conversation, Lavelle asked, "What made you want to work homicide?"

"I'm embarrassed to tell you. It sounds hokey."

"Try me." Lavelle stopped eating while he waited for her answer.

"When I was a kid, I guess around thirteen, I did a summer camp on law enforcement. One of the cops who mentored us was a homicide detective. He told us that homicide cops served a much more important purpose in society than just putting killers behind bars. 'Homicide detectives,' he said, 'are what keep us civilized. We are the last line of defense against the barbarians,'" she quoted, pausing to take a sip of her drink. "I guess it stuck with me."

"I'll bet you didn't expect the boring side of the job."

"Like what?"

"Like the paperwork."

It was a frequent gripe. They were required to record every aspect of their investigation in a log book. Nothing was too minor to be documented.

"To tell you the truth, there are days when I'm buried under so much paperwork that I wonder why I left the military."

"How long did you serve for?"

"Almost six years."

"What made you enlist?" Lavelle asked.

"It paid for my college education. I was in ROTC. Plus, I thought it would be a good way to get new experiences. You know. Make friends. Visit exotic places. The joke was on me. There is nothing exotic about three months on a military base in Helmand province."

"Why did you leave?"

She sighed. "Let's just say I did several tours of duty, the last couple in Afghanistan. I made friends. Some of them died. Others made it through, and then died. Like that friend I told you about who had his leg blown off and then decided there was nothing worth sticking around for. Not even his baby girl."

"Sounds like you went through a tough time."

Her jaw tightened. "At the end of my last tour, I decided not to push my luck, so I put in my papers. It turned out to be harder to adjust than I'd anticipated. It's not something a person can understand until they've done it."

"So you became a cop?" he asked.

"Not straightaway. There were job offers. Due to the nature of my service," she said cryptically.

"CIA?" he asked.

"I can't go into details. I turned them down. I wanted to be stateside and I wanted to be a civilian. No more taking orders," she said.

"If you didn't want to take orders, then how did you end up in this job?"

"Civilian life turned out to be harder than I thought. Starting from scratch. Building a network out of nothing. Getting recruiters to recognize that I wasn't a traditional candidate but that I had plenty of other skills. Coming to terms with the idea that most of the jobs I applied for were about money, nothing more. No sense of service, or community. No greater good. To cut a long story short, a friend suggested I join the NYPD. I did and I've never looked back. I guess I like being in uniform."

"Detectives don't wear uniforms!"

"Sure we do. This is as much a uniform as any other." She tugged at the lapel of her navy jacket. "Believe me, I wouldn't wear a suit if I didn't have to. I bet you wouldn't either." She smiled. "Enough about me. What brought you into this line of work, Detective?"

"Third-generation homicide detective," Lavelle said. "My dad used to say working homicide is like malaria. Once it gets in your blood, you can't get rid of it."

"My dad sold insurance. I'm grateful that didn't get into my blood!" Halliday scrunched up her wrapper and threw it in the trash. Her phone rang as they rose from the table.

"Detective Halliday," she said.

"Darcy, this is Grace from the lab. I have preliminary results from the wine bottle you dropped off earlier as a rush job."

Halliday followed Lavelle toward his car. "Go ahead."

"We have a fourteen-point match to a print in the IAFIS database."

The IAFIS was the FBI's national fingerprint database. A fourteen-point match was good enough to be presented as evidence in court.

"The fingerprint on the wine bottle matched the prints of a perp in the database?" Halliday asked, with barely contained excitement.

"The prints on the wine bottle don't match a perp," said Grace.

"Then who do they match?"

"They match the prints of a crime victim."

The FBI database contained every print ever put into the system. Many of them were those of criminals, or suspected criminals. But there were other prints, too, belonging to upstanding citizens. Among them were prints of victims whose fingerprints and DNA were taken as part of an investigation. It was always necessary to take prints of everyone who'd been at the crime scene, from first responders to cops and even the victims, so their prints could be ruled out from the evidence. The prints were almost always kept on file.

Halliday took out a notepad and a pen as she climbed into Lavelle's car. "What's the name?"

"Her name is Liv Reese. That's R-E-E-S-E," Grace spelled out. "I have a social security number and her last known address on file from two years ago."

Halliday wrote down the details. Liv Reese's last known address was in Brooklyn. "Grace, do you have any information about the crime in which this woman, Liv Reese, was a victim? I assume her prints were taken to eliminate them from the forensics at the crime scene?"

"There's no additional information in the system," the lab technician said. "Jerry Krause handled the case. Talk to him. He'll know more."

Halliday updated Lavelle after she'd hung up. "Do you know Jerry Krause?"

"Oh yeah. Jerry and I go way back." Lavelle's lackluster tone suggested he was no fan of the other detective. "I'll call him when we get to the precinct."

When they arrived, Lavelle gave Rosco and Tran the USB drives with CCTV footage to add to their growing pile of security camera footage to review.

"We haven't found any more visuals of the woman with long hair. It's like she disappeared into thin air," said Rosco.

"Nobody disappears into thin air," said Lavelle. "Take a closer look at people coming and going. Look for people wearing baseball hats, beanies, or hoodies. Even high-collared jackets. Anything that covers their hair. We estimate her height at around five foot six, so pay special attention to people of a similar stature."

Halliday opened her laptop to find out more about Liv Reese, but before she could run a search, Lavelle signaled to her to join him in an interview room. He wanted her with him when he called Jerry Krause in case Halliday had any questions for the detective.

The interview room was bland and windowless. It was used to talk to potential witnesses and informants. The table in the room was round rather than rectangular, to encourage collaboration.

In the middle of the table was a telephone. Lavelle pulled it over to the edge so they could both be near the speaker while they spoke with Krause.

There was no love lost between the two detectives. Lavelle had partnered with Krause when he first became a detective. Their partnership had been mercifully brief, and they hadn't had much to do with each other since. Over the years they'd drifted to different units at different precincts.

"Don't expect too much," Lavelle warned Halliday. "When I worked with Krause, he had lousy instincts and he always looked for shortcuts. I doubt he'd pass if he did the detective exam today."

He punched in Krause's number.

"Krause." The detective's crusty voice was tinged with a mixture of irritation and apathy.

"This is Jack Lavelle. I have my partner with me here, Darcy Halliday."

"I feel like I've won the sweepstakes. Two homicide detectives for the price of one!" What's up?"

"Does the name Liv Reese ring any bells for you?" Lavelle asked.

Krause paused. Halliday could sense him trying to figure out the lay of the land before he answered. "What about her?" he asked cautiously.

"Her name came up in connection with a case you were investigating. We wanted to get the lowdown from you."

"I'm strapped for time here, folks. The case is an old unsolved. I can't recall all the specifics. Call my old precinct and they'll get you the file. It'll all be in there. Now if you'll both excuse me, I really need to . . ."

"Detective, we're not quite done yet. I have a few questions," Halliday interrupted. "The records say Liv Reese was a crime victim. They don't give details but . . ."

"She was never a crime victim," Krause thundered. Halliday had hit a nerve.

"What do you mean?" she asked.

"Liv Reese was a suspect. A murder suspect."

"Was she charged?"

"The DA never charged her," Krause acknowledged.

"Why not?" Lavelle asked.

"He claimed there wasn't enough evidence for a conviction." There was palpable derision in Krause's voice.

"Maybe that's because she didn't do it?" Halliday suggested.

"Detective Halliday, I'll give you a word of advice from an old-timer who has clearly done this job for a heck of a lot longer than you; absence of evidence is not vindication," Krause said, pausing to let it sink in. "I'll tell you something else, Detective. If Liv Reese didn't do it, then I feel damn sorry for her."

"Why?"

"Because that would mean she's the only witness to one of the most cold-blooded murders that I've ever investigated."

Chapter
Twenty-Three

Wednesday 1:45 P.M.

Dean presses his hand on the small of my back as he guides me toward the cab that's pulled up on the curb ahead of us.

"You're going to love it. The food's terrific," he says.

The closer we get to the car, the more my body resists. DON'T TRUST ANYONE, says the message on my hand. I don't trust Dean, but I very much want to talk to him. His is the only familiar face that I've encountered since I woke up in the park this morning. I'm bursting with questions, but I don't like the idea of being bundled off in a cab with him.

"On second thought, I'm kind of in a hurry. Can we go somewhere nearby?" I ask. "There's a place over there that looks good." I point in desperation toward a retro-looking deli farther along the street.

"Sure. If that's what you want."

Dean waves off the cab and walks with me to the deli. It turns out to be an old-school deli that does lunches and coffees on cheap Formica tables. The place is noisy and very crowded. A waitress shows us to a table in the middle of a crush of lunchtime diners. She hands us each a laminated menu and runs through the specials so quickly I barely catch them before she's moved away to take an order at another table.

I bury my face in the menu, but I have no appetite. A restless nervous energy has been racing through my body since the detective showed me the flyer with the photo of a long-haired woman linked to last night's murder. I'm starting to believe that woman may be me.

"What can I get you?" The waitress's wrinkled hands and stooped shoulders suggest she's spent most of her sixty-plus years leaning over tables asking diners that question.

"I'll have lemonade," I tell her.

Dean orders a Reuben on toasted rye. "Bring me sauerkraut and pickles on the side. Oh, and I'll take a bottle of Coke and a separate glass of ice. Ice chips if you have them. Ice blocks are okay, too, so long as they're not too big." The waitress takes his order with a blank expression.

"You're very specific about your food," I say once she's gone.

"I'm a very detail-oriented person. That's why I've been such a successful entrepreneur. It's the tiny details that make all the difference," he says, flashing bleached teeth that contrast sharply with his fake tan and dyed hair. Despite his obvious efforts to hold back the tide of time, Dean's aged since that lunch with Marco and Emily. For one thing, he's packing a lot more pounds.

I remember how he stiffed our waiter on his tip when we ate at Café del Mar that day. What was the waiter's name? Kevin. He's the one who started calling me at work. For days in a row, I'd come into the office to find a fresh Post-it note slapped on my computer screen. KEVIN CALLED. AGAIN.

It feels as if it happened yesterday. I shake the thought away. I know now that it happened more than two years ago. Two years that I inexplicably can't remember. That's why I'm here. This lunch is my chance to get Dean to tell me everything he knows.

I try to build a rapport by asking about Emily's handbag design business. He immediately shuts that conversation down.

"We broke up last year. Turns out the marriage game isn't for me," he says. "Tell me about you. How are you managing?"

"Fine. Fine," I say, dwelling on his use of the word "managing." It strikes me as an odd phrase, filled with a meaning that I don't grasp. "What about you?"

"I've been keeping myself busy with a new venture," says Dean, veering into a monologue about an organic vegan oatmeal latte company that he's invested in. "We've given baskets of the product to celebrities. They love how it fits in with their eco values. Hey, are you still writing about food at that magazine, *Cultura*? I heard you were working for them in London."

"Actually, I'm not there anymore," I say, remembering the alien feeling of not belonging when I visited the office earlier.

He visibly deflates and his eyes wander restlessly around the deli as if he's looking for an escape route. That's when I realize why he was so keen to have lunch with me. He brought me here to butter me up so I'd do a write-up on his oatmeal latte venture.

Dean glances at his gold Rolex and taps his fingers on the table impatiently as he looks longingly toward the waitress, almost beseeching her to hurry up and bring his food. When the silence gets too heavy, and he realizes he has no choice but to kill time with me until the food arrives, he asks what brought me to this neighborhood.

"Shoe shopping. I need boots for winter." I'm surprised at how easily I lie. "I went into a store that was having a sale on Italian boots. While I was there, the shop assistant told me someone was murdered in the building across the street."

"So that's why there were police everywhere!" he says. "The world is going back to the bad old days. You probably weren't even born in the eighties, Liv. Trust me, in those days a person couldn't walk down the block without getting mugged. Not to mention murdered. There were murders all the time. You can't imagine how crazy . . ."

He stops midsentence as if he's spoken out of turn. Then he breaks off a bit of breadstick from the complimentary bread basket on the table and pops it into his mouth, chewing it deliberately slowly as he stares at me with an intensity that fills me with trepidation.

The waitress puts a tall glass of freshly squeezed lemonade in front of me and places a Coke bottle and a glass of crushed ice in front of Dean.

"Your order will be ready shortly," she tells him.

He straightens his cutlery until the silverware is arranged with military precision. He moves the Coke can so that it's exactly above the tip of the knife. He puts the glass next to the Coke can, but not so close that it's touching. The salt shaker goes to the left. The pepper shaker to the right. The hot sauce goes just behind the salt. He puts the ketchup right behind the pepper. He does all of this with laser-sharp focus.

When he's done, he looks up as if he's just remembered I'm here. His eyes land on my hands as I sip my lemonade. I can tell he's noticed the messages scribbled all over them.

I lower the glass and put my hands in my lap so the writing is out of sight, but Dean's seen enough of it that I feel I need to acknowledge it.

"Bad habit. My mom used to make me scrub it off with soap and water when I did it as a kid."

"So why do you still do it?"

I instinctively shrug and then immediately regret it. This is the opportunity I've been looking for to segue into asking him to tell me what he knows about my life over the past two years. It's blindingly clear from his comments that he knows more than I do. I pluck up my courage. "I have issues remembering things . . ."

"Memory problems! Tell me about it," he cuts in. "I'm not sure if they're a blessing or a curse. There are some things I'd rather forget. Like my ex," he says, laughing at his own joke. "I mean, what was I thinking, marrying Emily? She sure wasn't the sharpest tool in the shed. All my kids said so, but I was in love. Lust. Whatever."

The waitress leans across and puts his sandwich and a bowl of pickles on the table. "How about you, Liv?" he asks, as he unfolds a napkin and puts it on his lap. "Tell me about your life since we last saw each other."

His question hits me like a sucker punch. I have no answer to give him because I don't know myself what my life has been like for the past two years.

For a moment I can't breathe or move at all. When I can, I scramble up and mutter something about needing the restroom. In the ladies', I lean over the sink to hold myself up as my body trembles violently. I'm having a panic attack. I splash my face and take in a series of deep breaths until I've calmed down. Then I lift up my top and stare at the scar below my rib cage in the restroom mirror. It's a horrible feeling, knowing that my body has been disfigured and I don't remember what happened.

Dean's eating when I come out of the restroom. I stand out of his line of vision and watch him add mustard and mayo to his sandwich. Two spoons of each. Three shakes of salt. Two of pepper. His obsessiveness chills me.

I steel myself before returning to the table, uncertain how much to confide in Dean.

As I move toward the table, a phone rings. I freeze midstep. The old-fashioned ringtone cuts through all the noise. It feels as if everyone in the restaurant has frozen, and time is standing still. The only sound in the deli is the insistent ring of the phone. Each successive shrill ring makes me more tense until I'm as taut as a high wire.

I feel I'll snap if the phone doesn't stop ringing.

Numbly, I walk to our table. "I'm sorry," I tell Dean, as he bites into his sandwich. He stares back at me, his beady eyes blinking rapidly. "I really need to go."

Before he can do anything, I run out of the deli and down a nearby set of stairs into the subway.

Chapter
Twenty-Four

Two Years Earlier

A saxophonist plays a solo that sounds like a jazzed-up version of *Boléro* as I walk into Café Lisbon. Winding my way around tables in the crowded fusion restaurant, I catch sight of Amy and Marco. They're sitting next to each other at a long table that Amy reserved for the evening.

They're the only people at the crowded table not looking at the band. For once they're talking in a civilized manner. I'm relieved they're getting along.

On the way here, I worried that without me to act as a buffer, they'd get into another argument and it would ruin the evening. It saddens me that my best friend and my boyfriend can't stand each other. Those two have gone from barely tolerating each other when I first started dating Marco, to pretty much detesting each other. Things are at a point where Marco rarely visits my place at all if there's any chance that Amy will be there.

It started shortly after I began dating Marco. He and Amy got into an argument over politics. It became more than a little heated. She's progressive. Marco says he's a moderate. Amy insists he's actually a conservative in disguise.

It's true they have radically different views of the world. Marco's a lawyer turned entrepreneur who worships at the shrine of capitalism. Amy's an idealistic doctor who considers money to be a dirty word. Although, as Marco has cynically pointed out more than once, that might be because her family had so much of it.

I listen to the rising notes of the sax as I watch Amy put her hand on Marco's arm and hold it there as she makes a point. The gesture is typical of Amy. She's warm and incredibly tactile. She's always hugging, rubbing arms, or massaging shoulders. It's part of her charm, along with the way she bats her eyes like a femme fatale in a cartoon to get anything she wants.

And I do mean anything. Amy gets freebies wherever she goes. At restaurants, it's free meals. Bartenders always give her free drinks at bars. When she travels she gets flight upgrades. One time on a girls' trip to Aruba, she complained to the hotel manager that her assigned room stank of stale cigarettes. She was offered a free upgrade to a beach villa along with a complimentary massage at the hotel spa.

It doesn't hurt that she's drop-dead gorgeous. She has delicate features and long flaxen hair that she inherited from her Swedish grandma. But it's not just her looks that make her stand out. Amy has bucketloads of charisma. She's one of those rare people who instantly lights up a room just by walking into it.

Neither Amy nor Marco has seen me yet. Their seats are pressed back against a wall, which forces them to sit unnaturally close to each other.

I feel a twinge of unease when Amy flicks her hair—one of her go-to flirty gestures that I've seen a thousand times before when she sets her sights on someone. Amy falls in love so frequently that I honestly lose track of all her boyfriends, and she falls out of love even faster. Except with Brett, the surgeon she's been dating since last year.

It's the first time I've seen her so in love that it's the guy who has the upper hand in the relationship. Luckily for Amy, Brett is besotted with her, too.

Unlike Amy, I'm always the heartbroken one who cries on her shoulder, while she consoles me with hilarious, and largely made-up, stories about being dumped by various boyfriends over the years. I know they're made up because Amy instigates all her breakups. It's one of many secrets she's shared with me over the years.

It's thanks to Amy that I met Marco in the first place. She was asked on a blind date; a friend of a friend's brother. She only agreed to the date if they could each bring a friend and make it a blind double date. Marco turned out to be that friend.

It was at a Japanese restaurant. We bonded over our terrible chopstick skills. Marco and Amy argued over whether sushi should be eaten with chopsticks or fingers. Amy insisted the correct way was using fingers. She lived in Japan for a semester when she was a sophomore and claimed to have survived on a diet of sushi and sake.

By the time the evening was over, I was head over heels. Marco, apparently, not so much. It took him three weeks to call me. He said it was because he was snowed under with work, although I later gathered, by joining a few dots, there had been another girl in the interim.

"There she is," Amy screeches when she sees me approaching the table. "Marco and I were wondering what happened to you."

Amy stands up and wraps her slender arms around me in a clingy hug. Compared to Amy in her sleeveless figure-hugging rose silk dress, I feel positively grimy. Since I had to come straight from Q's creepy preview, I didn't have time to go home and change into the sexy midnight-blue dress I was going to wear tonight. I put on makeup in the cab over here and opened up the collar of my wine-colored satin shirt to display a striking black pearl pendant that belonged to my mom.

Amy takes her seat at the head of the table. I sit where she was sitting next to Marco, surrounded by a cloud of jasmine that Amy left behind like a scent marker.

"You look stunning, Liv," Marco says, kissing me.

He puts his arm possessively around the back of my chair and caresses the nape of my neck as we talk. I explain that I didn't have time to go home and change.

"Liv, honestly, it doesn't matter. You look amazing in anything. Or in nothing," he whispers, laughing softly at the faint blush that runs across my cheeks. I lean my head against his muscular chest for a moment, reveling in the security of being with Marco after the unsettling experience at Q's art preview.

"What were you and Amy talking about when I arrived?" I ask eventually.

"You. It's the only topic Amy and I agree on."

"Really? What about me?" I say, amused, because he's right; I'm all they have in common.

"We talked about how you're never on time. You'd be late to your own wedding."

"It's funeral," I correct playfully, smiling at his inside joke. "I'd be late to my own funeral." Marco mixes up his idioms on purpose to amuse me, rather than because English is his second language. He speaks it as flawlessly as his Italian.

"Well, either way, you really are never on time, Liv!"

"You two can criticize my lack of punctuality all you want just as long as Amy wasn't discussing plans for my birthday. I have an awful feeling that she's planning a surprise party. I've told her so many times that I hate surprises, especially surprise parties. Everyone always tries to act so . . ."

"Surprised," Marco finishes my sentence.

"Exactly."

"Well, we were talking about you, but I promise that surprise parties didn't come up. I was telling Amy how lucky I am that I broke my ironclad rule against blind dates the night we met," he says. "If I hadn't gone that night then I'd never have met you." He kisses the back of my hand and squeezes it tightly.

A waiter comes by the table and fills my wineglass with Rioja.

The other dinner guests are mostly Amy's work friends from the hospital. The hospital crowd inevitably talk shop whenever they're together, which can get boring for the rest of us who have no interest in hospital politics.

The empty seat to Amy's right, opposite mine, is for Brett. He's always running late whenever he's working, or on call. Brett is a cardiothoracic surgeon, older than Amy by over a decade. He turns forty next year, but he looks years younger. He's a fitness fanatic with a wiry frame and a great physique. He broke up with his wife shortly after meeting Amy. Apparently, it had been in the cards for a while.

Amy has dated Brett for almost eight months. It's her personal best. Sometimes I think the secret to their successful relationship is that they barely see each other. Their schedules at the hospital always seem to clash. And when Brett's off from work, he has family responsibilities. He has two kids from his broken marriage. Amy confided in me once that she both admires and resents Brett's dedication to his children because it cuts into the time they spend together, although she admits that he's an amazing dad.

The waiter brings me a menu and I order a grilled salmon dish with chili and lime. As I hand back the menu, my eyes flick to the bar where a man sitting on a barstool watches our table over a glass of bourbon.

Our eyes lock. His smile is so engaging that I unwittingly smile back for a fraction of a second. I look away to see that Brett's finally arrived. He strides toward our table holding an extravagant floral bouquet of pastel flowers wrapped in brown paper. He hands it to Amy, along with a Tiffany jewelry box. A smile spreads across Amy's face when she lifts the lid.

Brett mouths "thank you" to me as Amy puts on her new earrings. They're white gold with a stunning diamond and aquamarine setting that matches the color of her eyes. She's over the moon, as I knew she would be.

"I can't take all the credit," Brett laughs, after Amy kisses him. "Liv chose the earrings. She has wonderful taste. The second she saw them she knew they'd be perfect for you."

Brett doesn't tell Amy that the earrings came with a price tag that almost made me swoon. I was about to ask the saleswoman to show me something cheaper, assuming that Brett would balk at the cost. But he didn't blink an eye as he produced his platinum credit card.

He'd told me that he wanted to spoil Amy with something very special. For his birthday, Amy bought him a thousand-dollar pair of shoes for his custom-made shoe collection. He happily paid ten times that amount for her earrings.

We had coffee after we left the jewelry store, and all we talked about was Amy. Brett asked me to convince her to drop the idea of going to Africa to work for a medical aid group. He said it was a waste of her remarkable talent. He thinks Amy should specialize in pediatrics first and then they could both go together to Africa to do humanitarian work for a year.

"I've always intended to give back. Amy and I would make an incredible team," he told me.

It sounded like Brett had their lives all planned out. He even confided that he'd pull strings to get Amy into the pediatrics program at the hospital once she finishes her internship. When there was nothing more to say about Amy, he started talking about his kids and all the prep schools where they were being registered years in advance. He didn't once express the slightest interest in me. Marco was right. Brett is self-obsessed.

He orders a medium-rare steak without looking at the menu. It arrives after most people have finished their meals. When he's almost done eating, he gets a text message on his phone. He whispers something to Amy and kisses her before rising from the table and sprinting out.

"Brett's been called to the hospital," Amy tells me. "A three-car pileup at the turnpike. He says it sounds ugly. It's going to be a long night."

Amy does not appear upset at her boyfriend's fleeting appearance at her birthday dinner. I suppose she knew the drill when she became involved with a surgeon. Brett's soon-to-be ex-wife obviously did not. From what Amy's told me, one of the prime reasons behind their breakup was his ex's resentment at the way that Brett always prioritized his patients before his family. It's not something that troubles Amy. She's equally dedicated to her career. In that respect, they're a perfect match.

"Are you a doctor, too?" one of Amy's doctor friends asks.

"Hardly," I laugh. "I'm a staff writer at *Cultura Magazine*."

"Really? What do you write about?"

"All things food. The making of it. The eating of it. Celebrity chefs. I sometimes write about the arts scene as well when our art reviewer isn't available. In fact, I came here from an advance viewing of a performance art show."

"I've always wondered about performance art. What is it exactly?" he asks.

"Have you heard of Marina Abramović?"

"Is she a Russian scientist?"

"She's a performance artist. She's very famous. She did a performance at the Museum of Modern Art a few years ago where she sat at a table all day and stared at members of the public brave enough to sit opposite her. There was a documentary made about it."

"Are you telling me that sitting on a chair and staring at people for hours upon end is considered to be art?"

"It is for some people. Performance art is a type of conceptual art in which the public interacts with the artist's vision."

Through the corner of my eye, I notice the man sitting at the bar turning around again and unabashedly listening to our conversation.

"It sounds like pretentious, self-indulgent crap," the doctor says.

"It's all a matter of perspective," I say, trying to be diplomatic. "The show I went to earlier contained violent themes. It seemed very personal, and vaguely threatening. I'm not sure I'll do a write-up, at least not before I interview the artist to find out more about his motivation and inspirations."

A waitress arrives with a birthday cake for Amy. Through the bright flames of the birthday candles, I notice the man at the bar has disappeared.

When we leave the restaurant an hour later, I'm slightly tipsy. Marco ruefully declines my invitation to stay over. He tells me he's flying to Houston early in the morning and still has to pack.

"It's a last-minute trip. I managed to get a meeting with an investor who I've been trying to connect with for months," he tells me. That explains why he didn't mention it before. "I'll make it up to you, hon. We'll do something extra special on the weekend."

He kisses me before getting into a cab. As he closes the door, I realize that Marco will be going in the same direction as Amy. She's heading to Brett's place so she can be there when he gets back from work.

"Marco." I tap on the cab window. "Can you drop Amy at Brett's apartment?"

"Sure," he says. It's obvious that Marco's not crazy about the idea, but he knows it makes sense since they really are going in the same direction.

I hustle Amy over from where she's standing by the curb trying to book an Uber. We hug and she gets into the backseat.

Marco's cab drives off. I watch it disappear around the corner before I turn and walk away, encouraged by the thought that maybe the two people closest to me in the world have finally reached a point where they can be civil.

In truth, I wish Amy had come home with me rather than head over to Brett's place. I'm still rattled by that incident at the apartment the other night and I'd rather not sleep there alone.

Even though it's midweek, the streets are busy as people leave restaurants and stroll home in the refreshing night air, or head somewhere for a nightcap or dessert.

I get so lost in my thoughts that I don't notice the streets have emptied until I'm walking alongside a park on a dark stretch of street. I walk faster. After what happened at the apartment the other night, I want to get out of this lonely area as quickly as possible.

As I walk, I hear myself breathing. Heavily.

Too heavily.

My stomach drops like I'm plunging down a roller coaster. That's not my breathing I'm hearing. It's coming from someone walking behind me.

Chapter
Twenty-Five

"We have a problem."

Detective Tran signaled to Detective Halliday to come over to the desk where he was trawling through CCTV footage.

"What's wrong with your screen?" Halliday asked as she leaned over Tran's desk and looked at his computer screen. It was filled with static.

"There's nothing wrong with my screen," said Tran. "The static you're seeing is the footage from the security cameras at the rear basement exits of the building."

"You're telling me those cameras didn't film anything last night?"

"That's exactly what I'm telling you. They were both offline."

"Do we know if someone tampered with them?"

"The security company supervisor won't know until his technicians have physically checked the cameras this afternoon. I just got off the phone with him," said Tran. "He thinks it's more likely it was a technical fault rather than sabotage."

On the whiteboard, Halliday had taped a screenshot of the CCTV footage taken just after 2 A.M. in the hallway outside the apartment where the murder had taken place. The murky shadow of a person could be seen leaving the apartment and going into the stairwell. The investigative team were all working on the assumption that the figure was the killer. An innocent person would have taken the elevator rather than try to leave surreptitiously.

Tran had gone through the CCTV footage from all the other entry and exit points in the building trying to track the mystery person's escape route, but the figure hadn't appeared in any of the footage from the other cameras at the relevant time period.

He'd had high hopes of getting a visual of the killer in the CCTV footage of the basement exits. Instead, all he got was static.

"What's going on?" asked Lavelle, who had just finished taking a phone call at his cluttered desk.

"We've hit a brick wall," Halliday said. "It appears the security cameras filming the basement exits weren't functioning properly last night. Tran believes the killer used one of those exits to leave the building. He's already checked CCTV footage from the other exits."

Tran turned his laptop so that Lavelle could see the static on the screen.

"Unless the killer never left the building," Lavelle theorized.

"We won't know for sure because we're missing key footage that could tell us definitively if the killer left the building or not," Tran said.

"I think we might have a backup option," said Halliday. "The liquor store facing the end of the lane behind the apartment building is all wired up with security cameras. They would have captured anyone who came out of the lane."

Halliday called the liquor store again. This time the manager answered the phone. He told her he'd received the message she'd left with his elderly dad and they could come over anytime to download whatever footage they needed.

She would have left straightaway to collect the footage, but Lavelle had disappeared into the captain's office.

While Halliday waited for Lavelle, she ran a series of checks on the name Liv Reese, the woman whose prints were on the wine bottle found next to the bed at the murder scene.

First she tried the DMV's driver's license database. Four people by the name of Liv Reese had a New York driver's license, but they didn't fit their profile: a newly qualified sixteen-year-old driver and three women ranging from their sixties upward. There were no outstanding warrants in the name Liv Reese. She had no criminal record either.

Halliday searched for "Liv Reese" on Facebook and Instagram. She hoped to find photos on a social media feed that would resemble the long-haired woman who was seen getting out of the elevator with the male victim less than twenty-four hours before he was murdered.

The search results were extensive, and Halliday didn't have time to go through it systematically. She made a note to do it later.

She did a quick general internet search instead, not expecting much. She certainly didn't expect to find an Interpol alert near the top of the search results. Halliday read the Interpol yellow notice, which was an international missing person report posted the previous day, for a woman by the name of Liv Reese who had last been seen in London a month earlier.

The missing person alert was accompanied by an ID photo of the woman taken from a London public transport travel card that bore her name. The woman in the overexposed photo had dark brown hair of indeterminate length. Her eyes were wide and surprised, as if the photo had been taken before she was ready.

It wasn't possible for Halliday to determine categorically whether the woman in the photo was the same woman they had seen in the footage. But there were enough similarities between the two women to make Halliday think it could be the same person.

Halliday dialed Interpol to get more information and was directed to a desk officer at Scotland Yard, who in turn gave Halliday the number of the detective sergeant who'd filed the missing person report. London was five hours ahead, and it was well into the evening when she called. From the loud background music blaring over the phone line, she could tell she'd caught him at a bad time.

"Hold on. I'll move somewhere quiet so I can hear you," he shouted over the thumping beat of music.

Halliday could hear the British detective's footsteps and the hum of passing cars as he moved away from the raucous noise.

"I'm outside now. We should be able to hear each other properly," he said. "Sorry about that. I was having a pint with the lads when you called. Who did you say you are?"

"My name is Darcy Halliday. I'm a New York City Police detective and I'm calling about a yellow notice alert you gave to Interpol for a woman by the name of Liv Reese."

"Have you located her?" he asked.

"Not exactly," said Halliday. "Her name came up in connection with another case. When I ran a search, I found the Interpol missing person report. I need to determine whether it's the same Liv Reese. Can you tell me when your person went missing and why a yellow notice was issued?"

"We believe she went missing about three weeks ago. We only found out a couple of days ago when her social worker filed a missing person report. Apparently, she'd missed several hospital appointments and wasn't responding to repeated calls. When we went to Liv Reese's flat, it was apparent she'd packed in a hurry and left. Her credit card records indicated that she'd bought a train ticket to Paris. After that, I'm afraid we lost all trace of her."

"How old is she?"

"Thirty-one, I believe," he said. "She's a dual US–British citizen. I have a pending request with your Department of Homeland Security to find out if she entered the United States."

"Why is there so much concern about this woman skipping town?"

Halliday asked. "People pack up and move all the time. Without Scotland Yard or Interpol launching international manhunts, I might add."

"This case is different."

"How?"

"Liv Reese has a serious medical condition."

"What's her condition?" Halliday asked.

"She suffers from memory blackouts."

"So she's an amnesiac who doesn't know who she is?"

"Oh, she knows who she is," he hedged. "It's complicated. She gets intermittent blackouts during which time she can't retain memories."

"You think she's currently suffering from a memory blackout?"

"Yes, we do. The blackout appears to have begun a few weeks ago. We believe she's still in the throes of it. She took almost four thousand pounds out of her UK bank account before she disappeared. She told the bank teller that she was going to Paris on holiday. She hasn't withdrawn any more money since then, nor has she used her credit card. That suggests she's either suffering a blackout, or . . ." His voice dropped off meaningfully.

"Or what?"

"Or she's dead."

"Tell me about the blackouts." Halliday opted against mentioning that she believed Liv Reese was alive and well, and that she had been seen one day earlier in the company of a man who was subsequently murdered hours later. "How exactly do these memory blackouts manifest themselves?"

"According to her doctors, every time she goes to sleep, she wakes up with no memory of anything that has happened in her life, going back to when she was still living in New York two years ago."

"That seems very specific. Why two years?"

"What do you mean?" he asked.

"Why not five years, or ten? Why does she forget everything going back two years?"

"It's two years and three months, actually," he clarified. "You don't know anything about the case, do you, Detective Halliday?"

"Not a lot. That's why I contacted you."

"Liv Reese was almost murdered two years ago. I gather that's why she moved to London. For her own safety. Her assailant was never caught. By all accounts, she was doing well, establishing a life for herself in Britain, until a few weeks ago, when she apparently woke in her London flat suffering a memory blackout. She didn't remember a single thing that had transpired going back more than two years to the day when she was almost killed."

"So she's living in the past," said Halliday.

"Something like that. Only worse," he said, "because every time she goes to sleep, she forgets everything all over again. The poor woman is absolutely helpless. In fact, she's a sitting duck, really. That's why we enlisted Interpol to help us find her."

"What do you mean, she's a sitting duck?"

"Well, if the person who tried to kill her two years ago finds her before we do, we're terribly worried that she'd have no idea this individual was a threat to her."

Chapter
Twenty-Six

Wednesday 2:28 P.M.

The rattle of a jackhammer drilling at a construction site gets louder as I climb the subway station stairs to street level. I emerge into daylight only to get body-slammed by a woman rushing past in a whirl of shopping bags.

"Hey, lady! Watch where you're going," the woman calls out.

Farther ahead, a tourist in a puffer jacket drags an oversized suitcase out of a budget hotel directly into my path. I step out of the way to let him pass. His wife and daughters, dressed in matching puffer jackets, walk behind him wheeling their own suitcases.

The family walks slowly, like their bodies are weighed down by fatigue, until I realize it's me who's exhausted. All I want to do is sleep. I walk into the narrow lobby of the hotel and ask a receptionist how much it costs to get a room.

While I wait for her to check the rates and vacancies on her computer screen, I look down at the knuckles of my hands resting on the counter. STAY AWAKE, they read.

The message immediately revives me. I can't get a room. I can't go to sleep. By the time the reception clerk looks up from her screen, I'm heading out through the smoked-glass lobby door.

"Stay awake," I repeat to myself until a constant hum in my head takes on the rhythm of those words. "Stay awake. Stay awake."

There's a Starbucks on the corner. I order two double expressos to go. The coffee is so strong I wince as I drink every drop of it. I swig the second expresso like it's a shot.

It doesn't take long until the caffeine kicks in, surging through me. After that everything moves in hyperspeed. Traffic rushes past and my mind races ahead at a thousand miles a minute. All I can think about is being with Marco. I ache to lie against his chest with his arms wrapped protectively around me and his scent on my lips. The thought overwhelms me, like I'm an addict needing a fix. I raise my hand abruptly to hail a cab. It pulls over and I scramble inside.

The scenery zips by through the windows of the cab. I talk so fast that the cab driver asks me to repeat myself. Twice. I hop out a block before my destination because the traffic is jammed. I can walk faster than the traffic can move.

At Marco's building, the doorman is signing for a delivery when I walk in. "Hi Bill," I say without stopping. I walk straight into an open elevator just before the doors close.

There's only me in the elevator, along with a woman in her seventies with champagne hair. She's holding a Whole Foods bag to her chest like it's a shield.

Nervously, I tidy my hair as the elevator rises. The woman in the elevator slowly edges away to the farthest corner as if hoping I won't notice. I do notice, but I don't care.

The woman looks at me strangely when she gets out at her floor. I realize that I've been muttering "Stay awake" under my breath the whole time.

I want to explain, but the doors have already shut and the elevator is pummeling up again at full speed. When the elevator stops on Marco's floor, I step out and walk toward his apartment at the end of the corridor. I freeze when I see his front door.

Someone is coming out. It's not Marco. It's a woman with shiny hair. She wraps a red scarf around her neck and buttons her navy overcoat as she walks toward me. Her cheeks are flushed and her mouth is swollen as if she's just been kissed.

There's something about her that reminds me of me. I stumble toward the apartment. The woman brushes past me without stopping. I feel an icy breeze as if I've passed a ghost.

I press my eye to the peephole of Marco's front door and stare at the concave reflection of my pupil.

"Marco. It's me, Liv. Can we talk?" I bang on the door with my fist and ring the doorbell at the same time.

A clatter of metal startles me. I turn around to see a cleaner pushing a metal bucket with a mop near the elevators. The cleaner stares at me as if she's telling me something. Her mouth opens and shuts. I don't hear any words. All I hear is buzzing.

"You've got to leave."

I'm not sure who says it. Either way I'm in the elevator again. The doorman yells out as I pass him. "Lady, every few days you turn up here. I've told you plenty of times not to come back. Next time I see you, I'll call the cops."

His threats are drowned out by the traffic as I come out onto the street and wait for a bus to pull up. Soon, I'm on the bus looking down as pedestrians stride along the sidewalk while we're stuck in traffic. My mind churns so many confused thoughts that I feel like I'm spinning on an out-of-control amusement park ride. I lean my head against the window and close my eyes for a moment of respite. I'm lulled by the hydraulic bus doors opening and closing as we move through snarling traffic.

I get off the bus and walk along the river to Bellevue Hospital. In the distance are the rectangular towers of the United Nations headquarters. I'm walking so fast it feels as if I am flying.

There's a long line at the ER reception desk so I head over to general reception and ask if they can page Dr. Amy Decker.

"I'm sorry, ma'am," the woman says after checking her computer. "There's no doctor by that name working here. Are you sure you're at the right hospital?"

"Yes. Amy definitely works here."

The woman shrinks away at my vehemence. "It's my first week here. Maybe I'm not looking in the right place," she explains. She taps the shoulder of a colleague sitting next to her to enlist her help. Her colleague has dark hair that curves against her neck and suspicious eyes.

"Why are you asking for Dr. Decker?" she asks.

"Amy's a friend. A close friend."

I rub my temples to soothe the painful throb in my head as the woman looks at me strangely. She picks up a phone and makes a call, swiveling around on her chair so that I can't hear her hushed conversation.

"Dr. Graham is coming to see you," she tells me once she's hung up.

"Brett?" My eyes widen in surprise. I want to talk to Amy, not Brett.

Brett turns up a couple of minutes later dressed in blue surgical scrubs that match his eyes. He beelines across the waiting area toward me. When he reaches me, he gently takes both my hands and helps me sit on an upholstered chair near the reception desk.

"Are you okay, Liv?" he asks, squatting down, as the receptionist watches curiously from her desk.

"Yes. No. Sort of." Tears well in my eyes, making everything look blurry. I self-consciously wipe them away with my fingers, but they keep coming back. "Brett. I don't understand what's going on. Everything's very confusing."

"I know it is," he says gently.

Brett's so close to me that I can smell a mixture of aftershave and antiseptic.

"I'm in the middle of ward rounds. I still have two more patients to see, but I promise that as soon as I'm done I'll be back to explain everything. Wait here for me, Liv. It's important. It's not safe for you out there. Do you understand?"

"Yes, of course."

"Good. I'll be back very soon and then we'll talk."

He takes a few magazines off a table and hands them to me to read. Then he has a quiet word with the woman behind the reception desk. She nods her head vigorously. I get the impression that Brett's asked her to keep an eye on me.

Live electricity crackles in my head like a warning signal as he walks away. It gets louder and louder until I can't bear it anymore. I feel restless and suddenly terrified of what Brett's going to tell me.

I notice the secretary is distracted by a call. I slip out of my seat and head toward the exit, bursting out of the glass lobby door into a buffeting draft. It feels as if the wind is blowing me along against my will. Eventually, I stop and lean against a rail overlooking the East River, gasping for air and wondering why I can't stop crying.

Chapter
Twenty-Seven

Two Years Earlier

I was an idiot not to ask Marco to give me a ride home when he left the restaurant last night. I should never have walked home by myself. It was false bravado from drinking too much wine at Amy's party.

Now I'm hemmed in between the iron railings of a park on my left and a deserted trade school shut for the night on the other side.

The labored breathing and footsteps behind me make me acutely aware that I'm on a dark and isolated stretch of street. Nobody is around other than me and the stranger following me.

I deliberate whether it's tactically best to run and risk my pursuer catching up and overpowering me, or whether it's smarter to pretend I'm unaware I'm being followed while walking through this lonely stretch as quickly as possible. I decide it's safest to maintain the pretense since I'm unlikely to outrun him.

The headlights of an approaching car cut through the darkness enough for me to see a residential side street coming up after the trade school. I dash across the street as the car passes and then run full speed toward the side street, almost bumping into a couple getting out of a car near the corner.

"Sorry," I say, as I slalom past them.

The end of the street hits a well-lit intersection that connects to the street where I live. My lungs burn as I approach my street. Breathlessly, I slow to a fast walk as I tell myself I'm being paranoid and that I was just imagining being followed.

It was the product of alcohol and fear stoked by that awful avant-garde performance art show. That art show has probably spooked me for life.

Flashing through my head like a warning is the image of the bound and gagged woman writhing on the chair behind the red velvet exhibit ropes, and the black-and-white footage beamed on the gallery walls around her of a woman being watched by an unseen predator. I tell myself that it was only art. Bad art.

The thick foliage of the trees diffuses the streetlights, casting the street into a dark gloom. When I'm halfway down my street I hear footsteps again. They echo my own. I don't turn around to check who's behind me. Instead I assume it's my pursuer.

My building is very close. As I approach the stoop, I pretend to walk straight ahead. At the last second I bolt up the stairs and open the door with a well-practiced single turn of my key. I clamber inside and shut the door behind me. Once it's closed, I lean against it and gasp for breath until my racing heart slows.

Shawna meows insistently when I let myself into the apartment. I lock the front door behind me and hover near the kitchen window to look down at the street. I make sure to stand far enough away from the window so that nobody will see me watching. There's nobody there. Just rows of parked cars on either side. I feel like an idiot.

Thunder rumbles and Shawna rubs herself nervously against my legs at the sound of an impending summer storm. My terror from the other night returns even though there's no more banging windows and my bedroom looks exactly as it did when I left home this morning. I wish Amy had come back with me instead of going to Brett's apartment.

I'm still rattled by what happened the other night in the apartment, even though there's no logical reason for it to bother me. Amy admitted to borrowing a sarong from my closet and looking for a couple of other clothes she wanted to take with her on her vacation. That's why my drawers and closet doors were partly open.

She agrees with the police that Shawna might have accidentally knocked over my photo frame. I still don't have an explanation for how a heart was drawn in the dust on my bedroom window. Amy thinks it might have been there for a while and I just noticed it. She said one of her hometown friends who was camping out in our living room a few weeks ago used to do things like that when they were teenagers. There's probably a logical explanation for everything, but the fear I felt that night hasn't quite left me, especially now that I'm once again alone in the nighttime stillness of the apartment.

I open the fridge to take out milk for Shawna as a treat. The milk carton is empty, which means there's also no milk for my morning coffee. I close my bedroom door when I go to sleep, and push a chair up against the door handle, more to calm my nerves than because I think it will stop an intruder from bursting in while I sleep. I hear the storm overnight in my dreams. Pouring rain angrily hits the concrete outside.

When I wake in the morning, the alarm clock next to my bed is turned off. I've woken an hour later than usual. Exhausted, I go to the kitchen and robotically make myself coffee.

It's only when I'm taking an unopened carton of milk from the fridge door to pour into my coffee mug that I remember there was no milk in the fridge last night. I assume Amy came back early this morning and brought milk.

But when I go to the bathroom to clean my teeth, I notice that Amy's bedroom door is wide open, as it was when I came home last night, and her room is filled with daylight. I tentatively stick my head through her doorway. Amy's bed hasn't been slept in. Her window shades are up. I'm certain that she didn't come back last night.

How on earth did the carton of milk get into the fridge if Amy didn't bring it? There's obviously a rational explanation. I must have been so distracted from being followed home last night that I didn't notice there was already milk in the fridge door.

I turn on my phone and check my updates as I stir my coffee. I drink it standing against the kitchen counter, basking in sunlight shining through the window above the sink. A message notification from an anonymous number comes up on my phone screen.

Enjoy your coffee. I know how much you like it milky.

The message terrifies me so much that I instinctively toss the contents of the mug into the sink and peer surreptitiously out the window. Is someone watching me? How else would the sender know that I was drinking coffee? Or my preference for extra milk.

Even more terrifying is the realization that I was right the first time; there was no milk in the fridge last night. The implications of that make my blood run cold. Someone must have come into the apartment while I slept and put a carton of milk in the fridge, which means someone is watching me and has a key to my apartment. It's the final straw.

I grab my purse and head to the local police precinct, where I show the text message to the duty officer. Since this is the second incident, the officer calls a detective downstairs to talk to me.

The detective comes down five minutes later. He's a heavyset man in a creased suit, balding, with squinty eyes and an expression that exudes boredom. He tells me his name is Detective Krause.

"How much did you drink last night?" Detective Krause asks a few minutes later when we're in a cramped interview room and I'm sitting on the other side of a small desk facing his hulking frame. He scribbles my answers in a notebook.

"Two glasses of wine. Actually, three." I remember that I finished the meal with a Madeira port.

"After drinking three glasses of wine, you walked home thinking that someone followed you. You didn't see this person and you didn't report it. In addition, you are certain there was no milk in the kitchen fridge before you went to sleep, but you found a full carton this morning when you woke. Is that what happened?"

"Yes, that's right. That text message I received this morning telling me to enjoy my coffee suggests that whoever sent the text left the milk for me."

"But you said there was no sign of a break-in. So how did this intruder put the milk carton in your fridge?"

"Maybe he picked the lock while I was sleeping."

The detective stares at me, openmouthed, like I'm crazy.

"You're telling me that someone came into your apartment, put a carton of milk in your fridge, and then left without stealing a single thing?"

"What I'm saying," I say tersely, "is that the incident last night, in addition to what happened the other night, suggests a pattern. The officers who came to my apartment last time told me to look out for a pattern."

"I don't see any pattern," Detective Krause says, dropping his pen abruptly onto the table. "The police report from the other night says there were no signs of a break-in and there's no history of harassment. There was also nothing stolen. The officer who signed the report indicated the mess in your bedroom might have been caused by a domestic pet."

"My cat didn't do it. And, incidentally, my cat doesn't generally put milk cartons in the fridge or send me text messages either. It wasn't my cat," I sigh with frustration. "There must be something you can do, Detective!" I'm getting upset now. "Please, surely you can find out who sent me that text? I bet it's the same person who broke into my apartment the other night."

"You want me," he points to himself, "to get a federal warrant to access private phone records and use them to arrest whoever sent you this text message on suspicion that this individual broke into your apartment to put a carton of milk in your fridge? Miss Reese, no judge would sign off on a warrant based on the information you've given me."

"This message is implicitly threatening." I hold up my cell phone so he can see the text I was sent. "The person who sent it implies that he knows what I'm doing as well as my likes and dislikes. I *was* followed last night, Detective Krause. I'm certain of it. What more do you need in order to investigate?"

"A heck of a lot more."

"Such as?"

"Keep a journal. If you're being followed, write it down. When. What time. What happened. Keep any messages you get. Most importantly, never communicate with a stalker."

"How can I communicate with a stalker if I honestly don't know who's stalking me?" I'm horrified at the thought that someone in my orbit might be harassing me. "Nobody I know would do something like this."

"I've had cases where someone nursing a grudge acts months or even years later," he says.

George's bearded face flashes in my head. The veteran *Cultura* photographer lost his job when I complained about him deliberately putting his hand up my thigh on a work trip. When the HR manager called me into her office to tell me he'd been fired, she made it clear that I should let her know if he caused any trouble for me. I immediately knew that I'd made an enemy by reporting him. But that was ages ago. Surely George has moved on since then. Hasn't he?

"It could be someone from your past, or it could be, as I said earlier, simply a mistake. Maybe things have been stressful for you at work. Maybe you drank too much last night. There might be a perfectly innocent explanation."

"Detective," I insist, "I did not imagine it. I just don't know who'd do this to me."

"Okay." He holds up his hands defensively. "Don't assume it's someone you know."

"What do you mean?"

"Oftentimes, a stalker is completely unknown to the victim. Maybe the victim did something nice, like hold open an elevator door. The stalker creates a fantasy world about that person and becomes obsessed."

My stomach gets queasy as I consider the possibility that it was the waiter, Kevin, who followed me home last night and put the milk in the fridge. I tell myself that's ridiculous. I have not a scrap of evidence that Kevin has done anything other than try to call me at my office a handful of times, which is creepy but not illegal.

"What happens if I only have a hunch as to who might be doing this? No evidence, just a hunch. What do you do in that scenario, Detective?"

"Probably nothing." He shifts his big frame in his chair. "Without evidence, we'd watch and wait until the individual crossed a line."

"Detective, are you actually telling me you can't do anything to help me until this person hurts me?" I ask.

His silence is pretty much my answer.

Chapter
Twenty-Eight

Wednesday 2:52 P.M.

Detective Halliday immediately dialed Homeland Security after ending the call with the Scotland Yard detective.

"I need to know whether a woman by the name of Liv Reese entered the United States over the past month," Halliday told the clerk.

She tapped her pen on her desk impatiently while the clerk performed a data search. Through the internal window of the captain's office, she saw Jack Lavelle stand up. His meeting with the captain was wrapping up. She'd heard on the precinct rumor mill that they'd been partners for years, and that it was Jack whom everyone had expected to rise through the ranks.

"Are you there, Detective?"

"Yes." Halliday shifted her attention back to the call.

"Liv Catherine Reese arrived at JFK on a flight from Paris." The clerk gave the flight number and a date three weeks earlier. "According to our records, she arrived on a US passport. She holds joint US–British citizenship via her father. Do you need any other information?"

"What address did she write on her arrival card?" Halliday asked.

"It's an address in Brooklyn." The clerk hesitated. "Her handwriting is hard to read. I'll email it to you."

The scanned copy of the arrival card was already in Halliday's inbox when she ended the call. She opened it up and magnified the image so she could decipher the cramped handwriting.

"Bingo," she said under her breath.

The address Liv Reese had written in block letters on her airport immigration card was the same address as the one listed for her in the fingerprint database.

It proved that the Liv Reese who was the subject of an Interpol missing person search was the Liv Reese whose fingerprints were at the crime scene, and who in turn was the same woman whose prints were put into the system more than two years earlier when she was almost murdered. They were one and the same person.

"We have a Brooklyn address for the woman whose prints were found at the murder scene," Halliday told Lavelle as he came out of the captain's office.

"Let's head over there. You drive." Lavelle tossed her his car keys and Halliday snatched them in the air. "I'll meet you out front in two minutes."

Liv Reese's address was on the second floor of an old brownstone in Brooklyn, which had been remodeled into a modern four-floor building with a rooftop.

Fall leaves in the gutter swirled from the wind on the narrow tree-lined street as Halliday and Lavelle walked to the apartment. They took the stairs in unison up to the top of the stoop.

Lavelle pressed the intercom buzzer. There was no answer. He did it again. This time they both heard an angry thud of footsteps rushing down the stairs. The door swung open only enough for them to glimpse a woman with dark blond hair, who looked nothing like the Interpol photo of Liv Reese.

"You need to leave or I'll call the police," said the woman through the gap.

"We *are* the police." Halliday held up her detective's badge. "My name is Detective Darcy Halliday. This is Detective Jack Lavelle. We're looking for this woman. Have you seen her?" She pushed the Interpol photo of Liv Reese through the crack in the door.

"You'd better come in," the woman said, opening the door. She introduced herself as Angela as she led them up the stairs.

"I don't have much time to talk. I'm between Zoom meetings," Angela said, swinging open her apartment door to let them in.

On the dinner table were a laptop and a pile of files. Hanging over a chair was a tailored jacket, which Angela obviously wore to look professional from the waist up for her Zoom meetings. Below the waist, she wore gray yoga pants and fluffy slippers.

"I have fifteen minutes until my next meeting. Let's get straight to the point," Angela said. "The woman in the photo you showed me downstairs rang our doorbell early this morning. She looked a bit different, but I'm certain it was the same person. I'm very good with faces."

"Run us through what happened last night," Halliday said.

"Our doorbell rings in the middle of the night. It rings and rings. Wakes us up. I had an early conference call with Shanghai. Let me tell you, I did not appreciate being woken at three in the morning."

"I can imagine," Halliday sympathized.

"I went downstairs to answer the door. Grant followed me. He knew I'd be furious. There's a woman standing on the stoop. She acts as if she lives in our apartment. She actually asks us if we're out-of-town guests staying the night! She seems to think her roommate invited us. Total nut job."

"What's her roommate's name?" Halliday asked.

"I don't remember. Wait! We sometimes get mail for her."

She jumped up from the sofa and removed a couple of unopened envelopes from a basket on a white oak bookshelf. "Dr. Amy Decker," she said, passing them the envelope.

"Go on," said Halliday.

"It was very weird. When we told the woman to leave, she got all teary and told us that she'd lost her purse and phone and she had nowhere to go. Grant felt bad. He's a pushover. He let her come up to use the phone. Next thing, she's in our apartment accusing me of killing her cat and acting as if she owns the place. I was furious. She even went into our bedroom. We threatened to call the cops and she left."

"Has this happened before?"

"Grant and I just came back from vacation a couple of days ago. Our neighbor mentioned hearing our doorbell ringing in the middle of the night while we were away. He said it happened more than once. Maybe it was the same woman. Maybe last night wasn't the first time she came here. I couldn't say for sure."

"Any idea where she went, or what direction she took after she left your apartment?" Halliday asked.

"Grant went to sleep. I waited by the kitchen sink, which faces the street, to make sure she left. She was hanging around our stoop. Then she sat down on the stairs. I said to myself that if she was still there in five minutes I was definitely calling the cops."

"Did you?" Halliday asked.

"No. She waved down a cab coming down our street."

"Did you notice the name of the cab company or get a plate number?"

"It was too dark out for me to see the plates," said Angela with a shrug. "I'm pretty sure the cab picked her up at about three in the morning, if that helps.

"She's not dangerous, is she?" Angela asked, suddenly wary.

"You never can tell," said Lavelle. "Call us if she comes back or if you think of anything else." He handed her a card with his contact details.

Halliday called Tran as they walked back to the car. She asked him to call every cab company in the city and find out if they'd had a car at the Williamsburg address at around three that morning.

In the old days, that sort of job would wear holes in the soles of a cop's shoes. It would mean going into the depots of every cab company in the city and looking through their log books. These days, cab companies worked with a GPS system. It would be a relatively quick and painless task for them to review their GPS data to see whether any vehicles had been there that morning.

"I need the cab driver's name and phone number. I especially want to know where he dropped her off. The cab GPS should have that information even if the driver doesn't remember," Halliday told Tran. "We're heading over to the liquor store now to look at the CCTV footage. I'm still waiting to get hold of Detective Krause's file. Did his old precinct call?"

"No," said Tran. "Do you want me to go over there and get the files?"

"We'll take care of it. Can you run a name for us, in the meantime?" she asked.

"Sure. What's the name?"

"Dr. Amy Decker." Halliday read the name off the unopened letter. "Apparently she and Liv Reese shared an apartment a few years back."

Chapter
Twenty-Nine

The beep of a delivery truck reversing to offload goods cuts through the hiss of white noise in my head. Someone is talking to me. I turn around.

"I already told you, it's not open," calls out a stocky man with a bushy gray mustache wearing a white apron covered in flour dust. He stands outside the pizza place across the street, smoking a cigarette. I get the impression I've been standing here for a while, staring into space.

"Lady," he says, dropping cigarette ash onto the sidewalk. "The bar doesn't open for hours."

I look up. Above my head is a sign that reads NOCTURNAL. The bar looks seedy, as most bars do in the cold, hard light of day. Pressing my face to the stippled art deco glass doors, I look inside. The lights are off. From what little I can see there's nobody here.

"It opens at five. The place next door sells liquor if you can't wait until then," the man calls out. He gestures toward a bodega next to his pizza shop before stubbing out his cigarette with the bottom of his shoe and going back inside.

My mouth is dry and I feel woozy like I've just been roused from a deep sleep. I've felt this way since I woke on the E train, my head pounding like the beat of a war drum. I have no recollection of getting onto the subway and no idea where I was going. It feels as if time has skipped ahead without me noticing.

The last thing I remember before waking on the train was the sudden ring of my desk phone in the office. It was so loud and insistent that it startled me. "This is Liv," I said into the receiver.

Everything after that is a blank until I opened my eyes, my body swaying with the movements of the train as it shot through a subway tunnel.

My hands were covered with ballpoint writing. Amid the scribble was an underlined message with the name and address of a place called Nocturnal. Something about the name struck a chord. It drew me here like a magnet.

I cross the street to the bodega. My body's working on autopilot and my mind is a blank as I enter the store. A man with a wide friendly face beams at me from behind the counter; his smile is filled with warm recognition. I smile back stiffly. I've never seen this shopkeeper before in my life.

I stop at a wall of refrigerators to check out the assortment of drinks arranged neatly on shelves. Stifling an exhausted yawn, I remove a can of iced coffee espresso from the fridge. It contains enough caffeine to keep an elephant awake for the next twelve hours.

"How much do I owe?" I ask the man at the counter as I put the coffee can down with a thump.

He stares at me tight-lipped, his jaw protruding slightly. Hurt shines in his thickly lashed brown eyes. I get the impression that I've offended him in some way. Perhaps by not saying hello.

"I'll put it on your tab," he says.

I'm about to tell him I don't have a tab when he continues. "Every day it's the same, Liv. You never sleep. You're up all night. You walk around like a zombie during the day. Two, three caffeine drinks a day. It's good for business. My business. Not good for you," he says, shaking his head sadly.

He puts my purchase into a plastic bag and hands it to me by the handles. "You should take better care of yourself. You've lost more weight. Soon there won't be anything left of you."

I'm stunned into silence at the familiar way this stranger talks to me, like we know each other. I look down at myself. He's right. I've never been so thin, nor felt so fragile.

"Go home and rest," he tells me. "You look as if you haven't slept for days."

Standing on the sidewalk outside the bodega, I wonder if he's right. I'm utterly exhausted. I look up at the sky. It's overcast and steely gray. Even that confuses me. It's supposed to be the middle of summer. Yet it looks and feels like a blustery fall day. The buildings whirl around me with dizzying speed. I close my eyes and wait for everything to stop spinning.

"Are you all right, Liv?"

A man holding a box of groceries stands in front of me, his wide, pleasant face creased with concern. He looks like a younger version of the shopkeeper. He has the same strong, slightly protruding jaw and he speaks with the same Middle Eastern accent.

"Are you having another migraine attack? Do you want me to get you some water so you can take your medicine?"

"I'm fine," I insist, even though it's far from the truth.

"I'm delivering this order to a customer on your street. Come with me. I'll see you home."

I follow behind him like he's a pied piper. I'm too dazed and exhausted to explain that I don't actually live anywhere near here. Two streets later, he stops by a flight of stairs leading to the entrance of a light brick apartment building. He rests the box of groceries on a ledge.

"We're here," he announces.

I look around, blinking in confusion. He's brought me to someone else's street, and he's waiting outside someone else's apartment building for me to go inside.

I take a tentative step up the stairs. I figure I'll take a cab out of here once he's gone. It seems less awkward than explaining that he's mixed me up with someone else.

"That's not your building!" he tells me, as I take another step up the stairs. "You live across the street, Liv." He points to a dark brick building on the other side of the street. I stare at it, bewildered.

"You don't remember. Do you?"

"Remember what?"

"Your address."

"Of course, I know my address. I live in Brooklyn," I say.

"That's where you used to live." His voice oozes compassion. "You've moved, Liv. You live in the building across the street now."

His certainty leaves me baffled. "I know where I live and it's not here."

"Come with me. The doorman will explain."

He picks up the box of groceries and crosses the street, herding me along with him, until we're standing by a counter tiled with old-fashioned brown ceramic tiles.

"Good afternoon, Miss Reese," says the doorman, standing up from behind the counter to greet me. "I have your key here for you."

He hands me a key ring. My name and an apartment number are written on the tag in my own handwriting. The doorman gestures for me to enter a waiting elevator. It feels as if I'm being sucked into a vacuum as I step into the dimly lit elevator. I turn and stare helplessly at the doorman. I don't know which floor number to press.

He leans in and presses the button for the basement, unfazed by my confusion. It's almost as if he expects me not to know where to go. The doors slide shut and the elevator heaves down with a sudden jolt, taking me with it.

When the doors slide open with a rattle, I step out into a long poorly lit corridor. The ceiling is low and the walls are yellowing with age. A rancid smell of cooking fumes hangs in the air mixed with a faint tinge of mildew. I walk down the long corridor looking for the apartment that corresponds with the number on the key ring.

I find the apartment at the end of the hall. There's an envelope on the doorstep. It's an electricity bill and it's addressed to me.

Chapter
Thirty

Two Years Earlier

My red boxing gloves are tied together and slung over my shoulders like a necklace as Amy and I walk home after kickboxing class. I have never been so exhausted in all my life. Amy might have a great bedside manner when she's seeing patients at the hospital, but when she puts on her boxing gloves she gives a heck of a wallop.

I was so beat after class that I slumped on a bench in the locker room with a wet towel over my head and told Amy I wasn't physically capable of moving. She jokingly offered to order an Uber for the five-minute ride home. In the end, it was Amy's lighthearted mockery that gave me the push I needed to get up and walk back with her in the stifling morning heat.

When we reach the landing, we both see a special delivery outside our front door. Amy picks up an enormous bundle of blood-red roses wrapped in frothy paper. A gold box of expensive chocolate truffles is tied to the flowers with an enormous matching gold bow. It's the sort of grand romantic gesture that's typical of Brett. He loves spoiling Amy.

"Brett said he was arranging a surprise for me because he had to leave the restaurant early the other night. This must have cost him a fortune." Amy cradles the bouquet in her arms as we go inside.

Amy's cell phone rings. From the muffled conversation that ensues, I gather it's a call from the hospital. When Amy finishes the call, she asks me to put the roses in a vase for her.

"They've called me into work. I have to get changed quickly. My Uber will be here in ten minutes."

While Amy takes a quick shower, I go over to the dinner table where she's left the flower arrangement. The gold ribbon tied around the roses is tightly knotted. Shawna jumps onto the table and meows furiously as I ease the knot open with my nails.

Something sharp pricks my finger. I screech "Ouch" so loudly that the cat jumps down in panic and glares at me with her pale green eyes as if to say: "I told you so." A trickle of blood runs down my hand.

"Are you all right?" Amy rushes out of her bedroom, freshly showered and dressed for work. She grabs her purse and keys.

"I must have cut it on something." I clutch my finger tightly. It's throbbing like mad.

"There's a bottle of disinfectant in the bathroom medicine cabinet. Put some on. I'll take a look when I get back." The front door closes behind her as she leaves.

I wrap a Kleenex around my finger and then open the bouquet and spill the roses into a pile. There's a small envelope among the stems. I tear open the envelope and read the gift card inside. The flowers weren't sent anonymously. I'm surprised to discover the name on the envelope is not Amy's name. It's mine.

Tearing open the envelope, I pull out a generic florist's card with a brief message.

"To L." It's followed by a heart.

I'm moved by Marco's sweet gesture. I take the gold lid off the chocolate box. Inside are a dozen truffles, each individually decorated with swirls of contrasting colored chocolate drizzle. I call Marco to thank him for the thoughtful gift, but there's no answer, so I text him instead.

Roses AND chocolates! You're spoiling me!!

I pop a truffle into my mouth and savor the heady taste of chocolate and liqueur as I lie on the sofa and relax with a magazine. As I flick through the glossy pages, my eyes get heavy and I drift off, the magazine falling onto my lap.

I'm woken by a beep from my cell phone lying on a sofa cushion next to me. My eyes are so blurred I struggle to read the hazy message on the screen. It's from Marco.

I can't take the credit for your flowers. You must have a secret admirer!

A stab of fear pierces me as I remember my discussion with the police about stalking. I try to get up, but I'm overcome by a paralyzing exhaustion. The front door opens. Through the drowsiness that envelops me, I wonder what brought Amy back so quickly. I try to ask her but my tongue is too thick to form words.

A shadow appears on the living room wall. It's too tall to be Amy. It's someone else. I try to lift my head to see who it is, but my muscles don't cooperate. Sleep overwhelms me. The shadow disappears into a black mist.

I'm stretched out on the sofa when I wake again. The apartment is cast in a twilight glow that suggests I've slept the day away. Keys rattle in the front door.

"Liv?"

I peek through my lashes. Amy looks down at me with concern.

"Is everything all right?"

"I was sleeping so deeply. Such strange dreams . . ." I mumble.

I gather enough strength to move into a sitting position on the sofa cushion. I cradle my throbbing head in my hands as I listen to Amy's chatter.

"I don't know who called me into work," she says. "Not only did they *not* need me, they were actually overstaffed. Since I was already in the city, I went shopping. Like I need an excuse to buy more clothes I don't need. Right!"

Amy puts her shopping bags on the floor next to the sofa and takes out an assortment of packages wrapped in reams of tissue paper. She tears open the paper and holds the various garments she bought against her slim figure while I gush approvingly.

The cobwebs of sleep disappear as I look away from Amy and her impromptu fashion show to the roses beautifully arranged in a glass vase on the coffee table.

"Thanks for putting the roses in water. I dozed off before I had a chance to do it."

"Liv, I didn't put the flowers in the vase," Amy says. "I was in a rush to get to work. You arranged the flowers. Don't you remember?"

Chapter
Thirty-One

Detective Jack Lavelle checked the list of flights arriving at Hong Kong International Airport while Halliday drove them to the liquor store to collect copies of the store's CCTV footage.

The apartment owner's flight was due to land at any moment. "If we can find out the victim's identity then we can blow this case wide open by working backward," Lavelle said, refreshing the arrivals screen on his phone for the dozenth time.

"What do you mean by 'working backward'?" Halliday asked.

"We get an ID on the victim. After that, we figure out who his enemies were."

"What if he didn't have enemies?"

"Everyone has enemies. Ninety percent of homicides are about figuring out who the victim pissed off enough to kill."

"What if the victim didn't piss someone off at all? Maybe this murder had nothing to do with settling scores. What if the killer was trying to make a statement?"

"You're saying this because of the writing on the bedroom window?"

"Yes," said Halliday. "The murderer spent considerable time writing a message on the window with the victim's blood. Think about what it took to write that sign. The killer would have gone backward and forward from the window to the body to get more blood. It was a statement. This murder wasn't about the victim. It wasn't about revenge, or acting out a fantasy. This murder was about getting attention."

"Is it possible you're overthinking it?"

"In what way?" Halliday asked.

Lavelle shrugged. "Most homicides I've dealt with over the past two decades had one thing in common."

"Let me guess. Greed? Jealousy?"

"Not even close," Lavelle said.

"Then what?"

"Getting even."

"Getting even?"

"Yes. You can't imagine what some people will do to settle a score."

His voice trailed off as the word "Landed" appeared on his screen. He immediately dialed the owner's number.

Halliday listened to Lavelle's side of the conversation as she drove. The owner of the apartment was obviously shocked at first to hear that a murder had been committed in his apartment. His shock was quickly followed by concern. He wanted to know how much damage had been caused.

Lavelle told him the police department had arranged for the windowpane to be replaced since it was needed as evidence.

"Otherwise there's no damage and not much blood. You could get a cleaning service to steam-clean the mattress and carpet," he said. "Or you might want to replace them both given what happened in there.

Either way, you'll probably need someone to clean up the place. For one thing, the fingerprint powder leaves a residue on all the surfaces it's brushed on," Lavelle told him.

"He sounded more worried about the state of his apartment than that a man was murdered in his bed," Halliday remarked when the call was over, flicking a sideways glance at Lavelle as she drove. "Did he tell you what you wanted to know?"

"The apartment was booked via a short-stay bookings website. The name of the guy who booked it is James E. Carter Jr. He put down his home address as 1600 Pennsylvania Avenue."

"That's the address of the White House," said Halliday.

"Yes, it is. The owner didn't notice he'd been given a fake address and the name of our thirty-ninth president. His main concern was that the payment went through. It did. He charges three hundred dollars a night plus tax. His guest paid for a week up front."

"How did the guest pay?"

"Visa," said Lavelle.

"We should be able to get a name for him from the credit card company. Hopefully, the card wasn't stolen along with the fake address and Jimmy Carter's name," Halliday said.

An international call with a UK country code flashed on her phone screen. Halliday answered it on the hands-free system.

"Is this Detective Halliday?" asked a woman with a clipped British accent.

"Yes, it is."

"Detective Halliday, this is Marcia Nichols. I'm calling from London. I heard via Scotland Yard that you might have found Liv Reese?"

"We haven't found her yet," Halliday clarified. "We saw the Interpol missing person alert and I contacted Scotland Yard for more information. What is your involvement in this?"

"I'm Liv's social worker," Marcia said. "I was the one who asked the police to file a missing person report when we couldn't locate her.

We've been awfully worried about her. I'm not sure if you're aware, but Liv has a condition that makes her quite vulnerable."

"What can you tell me about her condition?" Halliday asked.

"Well, it's rather complicated. Maybe I should start at the beginning."

"Go ahead," said Halliday, signaling to take a left turn.

"Liv moved to London about two years ago after she was almost killed. Attempted murder, I believe. The killer got away."

"Do you know the specifics of what happened?" Halliday asked.

"I'm afraid I don't," said the social worker. "Neither did Liv."

"What do you mean?"

"Liv was in a coma after the incident. She never remembered what happened. She moved to London afterward to start afresh. As far as I know, her life here was relatively normal. In fact, from what we can tell, she had no memory problems other than being unable to remember the incident in which she was almost killed. That's perfectly normal given that she'd been unconscious for days afterward. In fact, it was probably a blessing in disguise."

"The Scotland Yard detective told me that she's suffering from a memory blackout," Halliday said, pulling to a stop at a red traffic light. "When did that start?"

"As best we can tell, it began five weeks ago."

"Can you tell me what happened?"

"Liv woke up one morning in her flat in Clapham. According to her neighbor, she was very confused. She didn't know where she was, or how she'd gotten there. Liv panicked and ran downstairs. When she attempted to cross the street, she was almost hit by a double-decker. She must have thought she was in New York because she apparently looked the wrong way when she tried to cross. Fortunately, someone pushed her out of the way just in time. She fell onto the pavement. An ambulance was called and she was brought to the hospital where I work. Saint Vincent's."

"Was she badly hurt?" Halliday asked.

"She had a few bruises. No head injuries or concussion. Usually she'd have been discharged straightaway but due to her obvious confusion, she was reviewed by a psychiatrist."

"What did the psychiatrist find?"

"That she had no idea how she happened to be in London. No idea whatsoever. She had no memory of moving to the UK, or of her life in London. In fact, she had no memory of anything going back two years. He diagnosed her as suffering from some sort of repetitive memory blackout."

"What do you mean by repetitive?" Halliday asked, pressing on the gas as the traffic light turned green.

"Liv was kept overnight at the hospital for observation. Her doctor discovered that every time Liv fell asleep, her memory reset back to two years earlier."

"How did they know that?" Halliday asked.

"Because each time she woke up in her hospital bed, she didn't have the faintest idea that she was in London. She consistently told her medical team that her last memory before waking up in hospital was working at her desk in her office in New York. She remembered answering her phone, but she couldn't remember anything that happened after that until she woke up in a London hospital. And what's more, whatever new memories she'd formed when she was awake disappeared once she went to sleep, and the whole process started all over again."

"Why would somebody suddenly lose their memory like that, out of the blue?" Halliday asked.

"Dr. Stanhope, her psychiatrist, says her condition may have been induced by insomnia. Apparently, Liv hadn't been sleeping properly for weeks before her sudden memory loss," the social worker said. "In fact, when I took her back to her flat after she was discharged, I found piles of medications. All sorts of pills to help her stay awake. NoDoz.

Alert. She drinks a dozen cups of coffee a day. Dr. Stanhope thinks it's all connected. The insomnia and her blackouts."

"She must be high as a kite on caffeine if she's drinking so much of it," said Halliday, turning onto a street near the liquor store.

"It's a stimulant. It makes her very nervous and erratic."

"Enough to be violent?"

"Oh, Liv's not violent," said the social worker. "She's lovely. She's had a very hard time of it. She has nobody to look out for her, which is very difficult for someone who wakes up each morning without any memory. Usually when these things happen there's a family to support the patient. In Liv's case, it's just her."

"She doesn't have any family at all?" Halliday asked, backing into a parking spot.

"Her parents are both dead. There's an aunt who lives in Southampton. She's the one who told me that Liv moved to the UK after the attempt on her life. Her aunt also confirmed that Liv didn't appear to have any memory troubles when she first moved to London. She knows that Liv had a man in her life for a while, but she never met him and she doesn't know who he was. They're not particularly close, Liv and her aunt. Apparently, Liv grew up estranged from her father's family. Her parents' divorce was acrimonious."

"What is your role then? Are you a liaison between Liv and the hospital?"

"In a manner of speaking," Marcia said. "I taught Liv strategies so she could manage her day-to-day life somewhat normally, despite the memory loss."

"How does someone who can't retain memories live a normal life?" Halliday asked. "I understand that she may have gone to France, and there's a possibility that she's back in the US now? How would she travel like that without being able to remember anything?"

"Well, it's really about writing everything down. Keeping dynamic documents that become a surrogate for her missing memory."

"What does that involve exactly?"

"Simple things. I taught Liv to stick Post-it notes with reminders on her front door. I encouraged her to write the key things she needs to remember each day on her hands so that it's visible when she wakes up. Due to the insomnia, Liv sometimes nods off in the middle of the day in all sorts of places; trains, park benches. Each time she wakes with no memory, so the notes on her hands are often the first things she sees. They tell her what's going on," she said. "The most important tool is her journal."

Halliday turned off the engine.

"When I settled Liv back home at her flat in Clapham after she was discharged from the hospital, we put up a message in big letters on the wall opposite her bed telling her to read her journal. The message was supposed to be the first thing that she saw when she woke up. I wanted her to start her day reading her journal so she'd know about her condition and she wouldn't get anxious when she realized she didn't know where she was or how she'd gotten there. Her journal fills in all the missing pieces of her memory so she can function somewhat normally."

"What sorts of things does she write in her journal?"

"Everything. The journal is her surrogate memory," the social worker said. "She writes what happens each day so that when she wakes, she can read her journal posts and resume her life where she left off. The journal contains a detailed explanation about her condition. It has her address and her doctors' contact details, as well as other basic information that we all take for granted. Bank accounts. Her landlord's contact details. All sorts of mundane things that are crucial for a person to live a normal life."

"So it's fair to say the journal is her lifeline?" Halliday asked.

"Very much so," said the social worker. "I dread to think what would happen if Liv lost it."

Chapter
Thirty-Two

The bill from the electricity company lying by the front door might have my name on it, but there's no way I actually live here, I think as I unlock the door with a loud rattle of the keys and step into a grim apartment.

The yellowing drapes covering the windows cast a mustard gloom. The apartment is furnished with a badly worn brown vinyl sofa and a cluttered coffee table. Rays of dust particles hang in the air.

This place couldn't be more different from my cute two-bedroom in Brooklyn. The view from my bedroom window is of my neighbor's brightly decorated flower box which overflows with vibrant blooms in spring and summer. It's most certainly not the ugly sight of Dumpsters in an alley that I can see through the grille windows set high up on the walls of this basement apartment with its claustrophobically low ceilings.

Dust chokes my lungs, already burning from the noxious smell of wet paint that fills the place. The delivery guy who escorted me here said I have problems with my memory and that I don't always remember this apartment is my home. He's wrong. Never in a million years would I live in such a dump.

I reach blindly for the front door handle to let myself out and come face-to-face with a black-and-white photograph stuck on the back of the front door.

What's Marco's photo doing here?

There are other photographs stuck on the door. There's a photo of Amy in a swimsuit, her sunglasses pushed to the top of her head. That photo was taken on the girls' trip to Cancun when Amy charmed the manager into upgrading us to a luxury seaside villa. There's a group photo taken at the staff Christmas party at *Cultura* when I first started working at the magazine. I've circled the face of the staff photographer, George, standing in the crowd. There's also a photo taken by the waiter of everyone raising a glass to celebrate Amy's birthday at Café Lisbon.

A sudden mechanical noise startles me. I swing around to see what's caused it. It's the motor of a clunky refrigerator. I head across the small living area to a narrow galley kitchen that's about three decades out of date.

A window lets in meager light from the rear alley. Underneath it, an overflowing bag of trash is slumped in the corner, swarmed by tiny flies. Some of the trash has spilled to the floor. Among it are blister packs of pills with names such as NoDoz and Alert. In the bag are piles of empty cans of caffeine drinks.

Colorful magnets in the shape of letters are arranged on the dented white fridge door. They're the type preschool kids use to practice spelling.

The magnets are arranged into colorful words and phrases. STAY AWAKE, it says across the freezer door. I look at the back of my hands. Under each of my knuckles is a letter spelling the same thing: S-T-A-Y A-W-A-K-E. Under one of the magnets is a doctor's appointment card with my name on it, along with an appointment date and time. I slip the card into my pocket.

Seeing another link between me and this hovel makes me light-headed. I open the fridge. Every shelf is stacked with caffeine drinks and individual bottles of store-bought coffee. Extra strong.

The sink is filled with a pile of black ash. It's the burnt remnants of paper. Among the ash are yellow bits of charred Post-it notes. There's also a badly burned book. The word "Journal" is embossed on the scorched remnants of a blue cover. The burned pages turn to ash when I touch them. Whatever was written in this book has been destroyed.

I rush away from the kitchen to the living room. It's filled with a headache-inducing odor of wet paint. I pull open the dusty curtains to get some light in here. The longest wall has been partly painted black with a roller brush. On the floor is an empty can of black paint. Alongside it are a roller brush and a paint tray stained black. It looks as if someone left in a hurry, perhaps to get more paint to finish the wall.

The white, as yet unpainted, part of the wall is graffitied with an array of random sentences. Most are written in pen. A couple are in marker. One appears to be written by a finger dipped in black coffee.

Memories lie.
Don't trust anyone.
He's coming for me.

The writing strikes a chord. I pick up a dusty pen lying on the floor and neatly copy the messages onto my arm. When I'm done, I move through a doorway into what must be a bedroom, although it looks more like a prison cell, perhaps because all the walls are covered with fresh coats of black paint.

A single barred window is set high up on the wall. A ray of light captures dust hanging in the air as if defying gravity. The only furniture in the bedroom is a bare camping mattress on the floor with a crumpled pillow and a half-open sleeping bag on top of it.

Across the room is a closet. I open the door to see what's inside. Empty wire hangers sit at odd angles on the metal rod, giving the impression that someone packed in a hurry. A couple of garments and a few socks are scattered on the floor.

Whoever painted the bedroom walls black also painted over several newspaper clippings stuck to the wall. A newspaper article in the far corner of the wall appears to have sections that weren't painted over, probably because the paint roller couldn't get into the corner. I peel the newspaper clipping off the wall and read the bits of text that aren't covered in paint.

"Police are hoping to question a comatose woman who they believe witnessed . . . Doctors are bringing the woman out of the medically-induced coma . . . Police hope she will be well enough to undergo questioning later this week. . . . Mystery continues to swirl around the brutal . . ." The rest of the article is painted over and indecipherable.

An old-fashioned telephone rings so loudly that I drop the clipping to the ground. The phone is ringing somewhere in the apartment. It makes my blood run cold.

Chapter
Thirty-Three

Detective Darcy Halliday watched a live feed of CCTV footage on a screen behind the counter in the liquor store as the owner gave change to a customer buying a bottle of malt.

On the screen, she could see Detective Jack Lavelle walking out of a narrow lane behind the apartment building where the murder had taken place. He walked about eight yards down the lane to an intersecting street and stood in full view of the liquor store's security cameras, where he reached into his jacket pocket and answered his phone. It was Halliday on the line.

"It's a perfect angle," she said. "If the killer came out that way, then it's almost certain we'll get a visual. I have the USB stick with the CCTV footage from overnight. Let's watch it in the car."

Sitting in the Ford a few minutes later, Halliday plugged the memory stick into her iPad. They were silent as they watched the recorded footage.

Given that the CCTV cameras at the building's rear doors weren't working, the liquor store's footage might be their only chance of seeing the killer.

The time code–stamped footage was drained of color due to the low quality of the camera lenses and the poor light. They didn't need bells and whistles. All they needed was for the suspect to come out of the lane and look up so they could get a clear view of a face.

Halliday fast-forwarded the footage until she reached the section with a time stamp after two in the morning.

At seven minutes past two, they saw a movement in the lane.

"Here it is," Halliday said.

In the CCTV footage, someone was walking down the lane toward the liquor store. They both leaned forward in anticipation.

It was only when the suspect approached the curb that the detectives were able to see the suspect's face thanks to a nearby streetlight. Halliday froze the video.

"It's a woman," said Lavelle.

They stared at the hazy image. The woman's long hair was tied in a plait that was starting to unravel.

"Not just any woman. That's Liv Reese," Halliday said.

"I'm not so sure," said Lavelle dubiously. "The image is too murky. We can't see her face properly."

"Trust me. It's her," said Halliday, comparing the Interpol photo of Liv Reese to the woman in the CCTV footage. "I'll ask the social worker in London if she can give us an ID based on the footage. Otherwise we'll need to use facial recognition software."

Halliday messaged a screenshot of the woman's face to the social worker. Marcia, do you recognize her? she texted.

Halliday's phone rang seconds later. "You've found Liv!" Marcia called out. "I'm delighted. How is she?"

"We haven't found her," said Halliday. "She appears on some CCTV footage so we know she's here in New York City. We just don't know where. But we will find her."

Halliday tried to keep her tone light. She wasn't ready to tell the social worker that Liv Reese appeared to have fled the scene of a murder early that morning. That put her at the top of their list of suspects.

Not only did they have Liv Reese's prints at the scene, they now had visuals putting her in the apartment building at the time of the murder. That was more than enough to bring her in for questioning.

"Marcia, I know it's late there but I have a couple more questions," said Halliday, thinking ahead. They would need more to build a case against Liv Reese.

"Of course, anything I can do to help."

"You mentioned that you've encouraged Liv to write notes and messages as reminders. Has Liv ever written the words WAKE UP on her hands, or anywhere else?"

The social worker sighed. "I tried to get Liv to write practical messages on her hands, such as her address and emergency contact numbers. But when I last saw her several weeks ago, she'd written messages that came across as delusional. So in answer to your question, yes, I've seen handwriting on Liv's hands saying things like DON'T SLEEP, STAY AWAKE, and WAKE UP."

"Do you know why she chooses to write those particular messages?" Halliday asked.

"Liv tries her very best not to fall asleep. Perhaps deep down she knows that she'll forget everything once she sleeps. Dr. Stanhope, her psychiatrist, says her self-induced insomnia actually exacerbates her condition. She falls asleep all the time out of sheer exhaustion."

"It sounds like a terrible way to live," said Halliday.

"Lack of sleep does horrible things to a person's mind," said the social worker. "It can make some people psychotic."

Chapter
Thirty-Four

Wednesday 3:51 P.M.

The telephone rings and my nerves shatter. It traps me in an indecisive limbo. I'm desperate to leave this apartment, but the ring of the phone erodes my willpower. I'm powerless to resist its pull.

I find the phone plugged into a socket on the floor next to the sofa. It would be so easy to pull the plug from the wall and break the hypnotic hold the phone has over me, but I resist the urge. Instead I hover my hand over the receiver as it continues to ring.

DON'T ANSWER THE PHONE, says a Post-it note stuck to the phone.

It rings again. This time I snatch up the receiver and press it hard against my ear.

"Hello?"

Silence.

"Hello? Who's there?"

More silence, followed by a *click*. The line has been cut. It must have been a wrong number. I put the phone back on the console.

It rings again. I answer it immediately.

"Liv. I've been looking for you everywhere."

The man's voice is so muffled that I have to strain to hear properly.

"I knew you'd eventually return home, Liv."

"What do you want?" I ask, my voice tight with fear.

"I need to know where you left the knife." His muffled voice is drowned out by the roar of traffic.

"What knife?" I ask blankly. I have no idea what he's talking about.

"Don't tell me that you fell asleep again! Did you, Liv? Did you fall asleep?" he rasps.

I don't respond.

"Where did you wake up this time? Tell me, Liv."

"I woke up on the subway," I concede.

"You don't remember what happened last night, do you?"

"No."

"I thought so. You forget everything every time you fall asleep."

"How do you know all of this about me? Who are you?" I clutch the phone receiver tightly.

He ignores my question. "You try to stay awake all the time. You even write it on your hands as a reminder. It's taking a toll on you, Liv. The insomnia. It's taking a toll on your sanity."

I look at the back of my hands and read the letters across the knuckles. STAY AWAKE.

"How do you know about the writing on my hands?"

"Honey, I know more about you than you know about yourself," he rasps again. There's something about his muffled voice that's vaguely familiar, but I can't place it.

A car horn blasts. I hear it in stereo, over the phone line and through the apartment windows. The long aggressive blast goes on for seconds. A truck driver leans out of his window and shouts: "What the hell is wrong with you!"

A series of expletives follows. Once again, I hear it all unfold in stereo. It tells me what I intuitively know. The man on the phone is outside this building.

There's a pause as he talks to somebody. My heart skips a beat when I realize he must be talking to a doorman. I hear a door slam shut over the phone line, and then the tap of footsteps quickly going down stairs. He's in the building. He must be on his way down to this apartment.

I glance at the white unpainted section of living room wall. Pulsating on the wall is a scribble: HE'S COMING FOR ME.

It's too late to leave through the front door. I look around for another exit. The living room and bedroom windows are high off the ground. They're all barred. The only way out is through the kitchen window. It's lower and appears to have a hinged grille that can be opened in case of a fire.

"You've done something terrible, Liv."

I almost jump at the voice coming through the phone again. I struggle to hear as I run my hands over the kitchen window bars looking for a latch to open the grille.

"What have I done?" I force myself to hide my fear. I can't let him realize I know he's here.

"You haven't seen the news?" he asks.

"What's on the news?"

"The murder. Your fingerprints are all over the apartment. The police will eventually piece things together and determine that it was you."

"I didn't kill anyone," I say, climbing onto a stool to reach the latch, which is at the top of the window grille.

"How could you possibly know what you've done? You don't remember."

"I know I'm not a murderer. It's not in me to kill someone." I prod and pull at the window bar latch. It's unyielding. I break into a sweat as I wrestle to get it open.

"Everyone is capable of murder," he says. His footsteps thud as he walks down the stairs. "Given the right provocation."

"Not me."

"All the evidence points to you, Liv. Even the words WAKE UP! written on the window link back to you. The same slogan is written on your wrist."

A door bangs down the hallway. It's the stairwell door slamming behind him. He's on my floor. His footsteps echo as he walks down the corridor.

"The evidence ties you directly to the murder," he rasps.

"I didn't kill anyone," I insist.

"I know that. And you know that. But the evidence suggests otherwise. The police might think differently."

"What do you want from me?" My voice is barely above a whisper.

"I want to help you, Liv. All I need to know is where you put the knife. Is it in the apartment with you, Liv?"

I finally release the stubborn catch on the window bars. The security grille swings open.

"They'll find you, Liv. When they do, they'll put you away for the rest of your life. It's only a matter of time. I'm the only person who can help you clear your name."

"What do you mean it's only a matter of time?"

The window's stuck. I grit my teeth and use all my strength to lift it up.

"Every time you fall asleep, you forget everything. You'll forget this conversation, too, within hours. By the time the police track you down, you won't be able to say a single word in your own defense."

The footsteps pause in the corridor. There's a rattle of keys. He's outside the apartment. Using every ounce of strength, I push the window up enough to create a gap. It's too narrow for me to squeeze through. I try again, forcing up the window with my shoulder until there's enough space for me to crawl through.

A key enters the front door lock. The lock clicks.

He's here.

I wriggle through the narrow opening. My legs are still dangling in the kitchen when the apartment door swings wide open. I pull my legs through the gap and run out of the alley and into the street.

Chapter
Thirty-Five

Two Years Earlier

Amy's hand hovers over the box of truffles as she decides which chocolate to take. She settles on a milk chocolate truffle with white chocolate drizzle.

"Don't eat it!" I call out as she's about to put the chocolate ball in her mouth.

"What?"

"Don't eat the chocolate."

"Why not?"

"It's spiked."

Amy looks dumbfounded. "What makes you think it's spiked?"

"I ate one earlier. I couldn't keep my eyes open afterward. It felt as if I'd been drugged."

"Liv, none of the chocolates have been eaten yet. Take a look."

Amy hands the gold foil box to me to inspect. "See! All the truffles are in the box. Nobody's eaten any of them."

Amy's right. The box is full. None of the chocolates are missing.

"I guess I must have dreamed it," I say, mortified.

"Liv, what has gotten into you lately?"

Amy sits next to me on the sofa and inspects the finger I hurt earlier when I opened the bouquet of roses.

"What do you mean?" I ask as she opens her first aid kit.

"You're paranoid about everything," she says, taking a sterile needle from the kit to remove what she says is a thorn in my finger.

"Like what?" I wince as she teases the thorn loose with the tip of the needle.

"Well, let's start off with the fact that you called the police because you thought someone had ransacked your bedroom when all I did was borrow a few clothes for my vacation," she says. "And then you wanted them to do a full-blown criminal investigation into how a carton of milk got into our fridge. Now this drama about the chocolates being spiked. Liv, I'm worried about you. Your paranoia is off the charts."

The way Amy puts it, I have to admit that my behavior does sound deranged. "It must be stress," I say, defensively. "Work has been intense lately."

I grit my teeth as Amy pokes the needle deeper into my skin and then takes out a set of tweezers from the first aid kit.

"You should take a few days off work, Liv. Go somewhere relaxing."

"I wish it was that easy."

"It is that easy. Tell that boss of yours, Frank, that you're taking a couple of personal days. You work long enough hours that he should cut you some slack."

"I need all my leave for my vacation with Marco in October."

"Vacation? Where are you going?" Amy hovers the tweezers over my fingers before pulling out the thorn.

"France. We're thinking about doing a cycling trip in the Loire Valley."

Amy doesn't respond as she cleans my finger again with antiseptic lotion and puts on a bandage.

"Your finger should be fine now," she says in a thin voice when she's done.

She gets up abruptly and takes her assortment of shopping bags to her bedroom. I rise from the sofa and follow the delicious aroma of food cooking in the kitchen. Looking through the oven glass, I see a delicious casserole bubbling in a ceramic dish on the oven rack.

"It smells amazing," I tell Amy, when she comes into the kitchen. "Where did you get the recipe?"

"Recipe? What are you talking about?"

"The casserole in the oven! And here I thought you couldn't boil an egg."

"Liv, you know I don't cook."

"Then who made the casserole?"

"You, of course," she says, looking at me weirdly again. "You're the only one of us who cooks."

I'm speechless. I'd know if I cooked dinner. Wouldn't I? Everything feels so out of place. That's when I realize that I haven't seen the cat since I woke up.

"Where's Shawna?"

"Probably prowling around the neighborhood," says Amy.

"She's usually back by this time."

I tap a can of cat food with a spoon by the kitchen window. The noise always brings her home. We both hear a faint sound in the hall closet. Amy opens the closet door and Shawna runs out, skittish and visibly distressed.

"How on earth did you get locked in the closet you silly thing?" Amy asks the cat as she picks her up.

Hanging in the closet is my dry cleaning. A receipt stapled to the front of the clear plastic garment bag indicates it was collected today. Payment was in cash.

"Did you pick up my dry cleaning? I'll transfer the money I owe to your account."

Amy doesn't hear me. She's deep in concentration, typing a text on her phone.

"What did you just say?" She looks up after she's sent the message.

"I thanked you for picking up my dry cleaning."

"What dry cleaning?" Amy looks at me strangely. "I didn't pick anything up today."

Her denial makes me wobble. I put my hand against the door frame to support myself. If I didn't collect the dry cleaning, and Amy didn't collect it, then who did? First, milk appearing in the fridge, and then a casserole in the oven. Now my dry cleaning miraculously turning up in the hall closet. Someone *was* here while I was sleeping. It's the only explanation. The question is who, and why.

"Are you all right, Liv? No offense, but you're acting really strange."

"I'm feeling a bit dizzy," I say, to explain my weird behavior.

Amy will think I've gone nuts if I tell her that I believe someone came into the apartment while I was asleep to heat up a casserole and bring in my dry cleaning. It's ridiculous. Even I think I'm crazy. Yet I can't think of any other explanation.

When I go into my bedroom, I find another bunch of flowers in a vase next to my bed. This bouquet is a combination of white and pale pink gardenias. They fill my bedroom with an intoxicating floral aroma.

My cell phone beeps with a message on my Snapchat app. I open it to see a photograph of the gardenias next to my bed along with a message. This is how a boyfriend is supposed to treat the woman he is dating, Liv.

Who is this? I write back.

By the time I press Send, the original message has disappeared, as if it never existed. I kick myself for not taking a screenshot of it.

I call the police. This time two detectives arrive half an hour later. The first is the surly detective I talked with a few days ago when I made the report about the milk carton. His partner, Detective Larry

Regan, is around my age. He has rich chocolate-colored hair and matching velvet eyes.

"I remember you," says Krause, the surly detective. "Did someone leave you eggs this time? Or maybe a loaf of bread?" He laughs at his own joke. It makes me instantly regret calling the police, and reminds me why I've never trusted cops.

"A bouquet of flowers was left next to my bed. I didn't put it there and neither did my roommate." I tell them about all the other strange things that happened today.

"And you think what? That a stranger brought your dry cleaning to your apartment and cooked dinner for you?" Detective Krause scoffs. "I wouldn't mind a stalker like that. Do you think he irons shirts and starches collars, too? He'd be worth his weight in gold."

His shoulders shake with stifled laugher at his own joke. The younger detective doesn't laugh. If anything, he looks visibly discomforted by his partner's rudeness as he dutifully writes down the details that I've provided in his notebook. He tells me to come to the police station to sign the statement the next morning.

Amy shows the detectives out and stays on the stoop to make a call. I distinctly hear her say: "This has gotten out of hand."

A floorboard creaks when I step onto the landing to hear better. Amy must have heard it, too, because she leaves the building and continues her phone conversation down the street, where she stands with her back to me on the corner, talking intensely on the phone.

Repulsed by the thought that a stalker left me gifts while I slept, I grab the bouquets of flowers, the casserole dish, and the box of chocolate truffles and I throw the whole lot in a trash can by the street as the detectives drive away in their gray Ford. I go upstairs with a horrible feeling that my life is spinning out of my control.

Chapter
Thirty-Six

Darcy Halliday could see that Jack Lavelle was getting increasingly frustrated as he paced the sidewalk alongside his parked car, where she sat in the front passenger seat.

So far everyone he'd spoken with at the credit card company had demanded a warrant in order to divulge the name of the credit card holder who'd booked the apartment where the murder had taken place. Lavelle could arrange a warrant, but it would take a while. In the meantime, his entire investigation was being held up by pedants, obsessed with dotting the i's and crossing the t's for the sake of it.

While Lavelle waited on hold for the fourth time, he bent down and spoke to Halliday through the open passenger window. "Call in a BOLO on the Reese woman while I deal with these idiots," he said. His jaw was tense. A BOLO was a "be on the lookout" alert that would be distributed across the NYPD.

"I think we should wait," said Halliday. "If it leaks to the media or Liv Reese gets wind of it, then she might run."

"It wasn't a request, Detective," he snapped.

"What happens if she didn't do it?" Halliday pushed. "A BOLO puts her in the sights of every trigger-happy cop in New York. And if the media gets hold of it, she'll be on the front page of every tabloid. Imagine waking with no memory and seeing your face on the front page of all the newspapers. It will freak her out," she said. "Who knows what she'll do?"

"It would make my job a hell of a lot easier if you would do as you're asked." Lavelle enunciated each word.

A senior manager came on the line and he stepped away from the car to explain the situation. Halliday dictated the BOLO over the phone to Detective Tran.

"Be on the lookout for a woman by the name of Liv Reese," Halliday said. "She is wanted in connection with a murder. She is described as approximately five foot six, around one hundred twenty to one hundred thirty pounds. She has long dark hair reaching almost to her waist. The suspect has a severe memory impairment that makes her erratic and disoriented. It is not known if she is armed. Officers should approach with caution."

To accompany the BOLO, Halliday messaged Tran a still photo of the security camera footage of Liv Reese in the alley behind the apartment building in the early hours of the morning, her long plait unraveling. She asked him to also include the photo from the Interpol missing person report.

"I shouldn't have lashed out at you. I was out of line," Lavelle apologized when he'd finished his call and climbed back into the driver's seat. "I bet those idiots had the information on the computer screens in front of them. They just wanted written requests to cover their collective asses. Stupid pencil pushers. The body was found nine hours ago and we still don't know the victim's name."

"The BOLO will be broadcast as soon as the captain signs off on it.

The night shift will get hard copies at their briefing," Halliday replied, making no effort to hide her annoyance. She was used to taking orders in the military. That didn't mean she had to agree with them.

"Good," he said, turning on the car engine.

"I hope we don't regret it, Jack."

"We won't. If the Reese woman did it then we'll have our suspect. If she didn't, then she'll be safer with us than she is wandering the streets in a state of confusion. Especially if whoever tried to kill her two years ago finds out that she's returned."

"I don't know how safe she'll be with every cop in New York thinking she's a dangerous killer."

"Much as I hate to say that Krause was right, the odds are that she is a dangerous killer."

"Based on what?" asked Halliday, mostly to be contrary. It was true that Liv Reese was emerging as their prime suspect.

"Based on the laws of probability," Lavelle said. "The fact is that until we have an ID on the victim, this whole case rests on supposition. In fact, screw it. I'm going to call in the big guns. I'm cutting through this bullshit red tape. We're this close to knowing the victim's identity. I am not going to allow some credit card company to give us the runaround."

Halliday knew they couldn't begin to make a case against Liv Reese if they didn't have a pretty good idea of her motive to commit murder. Her potential motive and the victim's identity were indelibly connected. Knowing one of those unknowns would help them figure out the other. At the moment, they knew neither.

Lavelle called an old friend who worked financial crimes for the FBI on speakerphone as he drove through heavy traffic. He asked his buddy to use his contacts to get an ID on the credit card holder.

Minutes later, Lavelle's friend called back and relayed the credit card holder's details over the speakerphone.

"His name is Edward Cole. He's an executive at a magazine. Age thirty-nine."

"What magazine does he work at?" Jack asked, stopping at a red light.

"*Cultura*. Heard of it?"

"No," said Jack.

"I have," Halliday chimed in. "It's a high-end glossy magazine that claims to be the last word on music, arts, theater, style. Basically, any-thing cultural. Hence the name."

"That must be why Jack and I haven't heard of it. Our idea of cul-ture is watching the Knicks. Isn't it, Jack?"

"Something like that," said Lavelle. "Hey, thanks, buddy. I definitely owe you one."

"Let's find out more about Edward Cole," Halliday said, dialing Tran.

"It's me again," she said when the detective answered. "Can you run a name through the DMV. We want a driver's license for a thirty-nine-year-old male by the name of Edward Cole. That's C-O-L-E. We need the name and contact details for him and his next of kin."

"Stay on the line and I'll take a look now," said Tran.

A moment later, he said, "Edward Cole received a driver's license . . . four months ago."

"That's weird. Who gets a driver's license at the grand old age of thirty-nine?" Halliday pondered out loud.

"Gimme a minute and I'll find out," said Tran, pausing as he ran another search. "Cole is not a US citizen. He's only been in the coun-try for five months."

"Let me guess where he's from," Halliday said. "Britain."

"How did you know?"

"Shot in the dark," said Halliday, glancing at Lavelle.

"There's no next of kin listed in the database," said Tran. "There is an address for him. It's a few blocks from the murder scene."

"Why would Cole rent a second apartment near the apartment where he lives?" Halliday asked Lavelle after the call.

"Maybe his relationship broke up. He needed somewhere to stay for a few nights," Lavelle suggested.

"Sounds as if you're speaking from experience," Halliday said.

"Oh, yeah. Bitter experience."

Lavelle had done the same thing when his relationship with his girlfriend broke up a few months earlier. He'd rented an Airbnb for a few days and then extended it for a few days longer. Two weeks later, the penny finally dropped. He and Ingrid weren't getting back together.

"That doesn't explain why Cole booked the apartment using a fake name and a fake address," Halliday pointed out.

"Maybe he didn't want someone to find out he was staying there. Like a wife, or a girlfriend."

"You think he was having an affair with Liv Reese?"

"That would certainly explain all that sneaking around," Lavelle said. He did a quick U-turn and drove in the direction of Edward Cole's apartment.

Chapter
Thirty-Seven

Outside a subway entrance, a man with a scraggly beard and a knitted orange beanie strums a guitar as he sings a 1970s pop song about a Californian hotel where you can check out but never leave. His twangy voice competes with the deafening clatter of construction across the street.

I throw money onto the torn red lining of his guitar case. I'm across town now, having jumped into a passing cab after I ran from the basement apartment. My heart is still racing after my terrifying escape.

I won't report it to the police. They'll treat me with derision, just like that awful Detective Krause did when he mocked me for making a complaint about the break-ins at Amy's and my apartment. As if to emphasize the point, just above my wrist is a handwritten message that says DON'T TALK TO THE COPS EVER!!

It's wise advice. The last thing I need right now is to explain a situation to the police that I don't understand myself. How does one explain the inexplicable? One moment I was answering the phone at my desk in the office, the next I woke on a train howling through the subway. Those two moments are like bookends. Everything in between is missing.

It's not just my memory that's gone. My phone and wallet are also missing. I don't recognize the clothes that I'm wearing, or the pretty beaded necklace around my neck. Or the writing on the back of my hands, so much writing saying so many strange things. It terrifies me to read it all. Mom would hate that I still scribble on my hands. She always said it was so unladylike.

A huge yellow sales sign in the window of an electronics store catches my attention. I go inside and beeline to a row of display computers arranged on a long white counter.

I choose a laptop in the middle of the row and immediately open a web browser to run a search. I want to see if there are reports about a murder last night. The man who called me at that apartment said it was in the news.

It turns out there was a murder. I click on the first article I see, which is accompanied by a photograph of an apartment window. The words WAKE UP! are written in red on the window.

There's not much information in the article. It says that an as-yet unidentified man was found dead in a midtown apartment and police are investigating. The article says the killer is believed to have used the victim's blood to write that message on the window. It's a chilling thought.

Lower down is another photograph. The caption says it was taken from a security camera near the murder scene. It's a grainy photo of a woman with long dark hair exiting an elevator with a man. The woman's face isn't visible because she's looking down at the floor. The face of the man accompanying her is obscured by a black square, obviously intended to block out his features. I assume he's the murder victim.

Through the corner of my eye, I notice a salesman heading toward me. I click the mouse to close the browser and it disappears just as he reaches me.

"Can I help you?" he asks.

"I'm looking for a lightweight laptop that's reliable and very fast," I tell him because I can hardly admit that I only came into the store for the free computer access.

He takes my query as an invitation to go into an excruciatingly long sales pitch that involves demonstrating all sorts of features on the laptop. I wish he'd leave. There are so many more important things that I want to find out about, such as this murder, and how the world went from midsummer to late fall without me noticing.

I mutter my thanks to the salesman and quickly leave the store. I'm more confused than ever from the scraps of information I've gleaned from my web search. All I have are more questions.

I stop to look at a pile of newspapers at a newsstand farther up the street. The date on the masthead says it's November, not July. The year is two years into the future. That makes no sense. But then neither do the headlines. They describe a chaotic, pestilent world I barely recognize.

The date on the masthead prompts me to take out the medical appointment card that I found on the fridge at the basement apartment. My appointment was today, almost three hours ago. I'll go anyway. Maybe the doctor will know what's happened to me.

As I make my way to the subway, I notice a public phone by an escalator. I pull loose coins out of my pocket and shove a couple of them into the coin slot.

Marco's phone rings and rings and then goes to voicemail. He's obviously rejected my call. He must be in a meeting. I hang up without leaving a message.

I dial Amy's number next. Her phone rings repeatedly until an automated message says the number is invalid. In a panic, I call her mom, whose number is the same as Amy's with a one-digit difference. Amy once told me with some embarrassment that her entire family has cell phones with consecutive numbers under a family plan.

Amy's mom answers on the second ring. "Hello?"

"Is this Margaret Decker?"

"Yes, this is Margaret," Amy's mom sings down the line.

"This is Liv Reese." I wait for an indication of recognition. There is none. Just a deafening silence that makes me squirm. "I'm Amy's roommate."

"I know who you are. What do you want?" Her voice is icy.

"I'm trying to get ahold of Amy. Her phone isn't working."

"Are you serious?" Her voice lashes me into silence.

"I really need to talk to Amy." I pause, confused by her belligerence. "It's kind of an emergency."

"You have some nerve."

Her tone stings like a slap across the face. "I'm sorry if I've called at a bad time, Mrs. Decker. It's just that I need to speak to Amy urgently."

"You, of all people, should know why you can't get ahold of Amy," she says.

My throat is paralyzed. I don't know what to say so I say nothing as she goes into a furious rant. Her voice comes and goes in between angry crackles of electricity inside my head.

"How could you! You are sick. Sick!! Calling me like this. Don't you have any decency, any . . ." She hangs up.

I shudder at the silence on the dead phone line. I walk numbly against a tide of pedestrians streaming toward the subway entrance. I'm surrounded by people jostling me, but I've never felt more alone in my life.

Chapter
Thirty-Eight

The front door of the apartment opened as far as the latch chain would allow. Halliday flashed her detective's badge toward a woman peering through the gap.

"What is it that you want?" the woman asked, making no attempt to unlatch the door.

"It would be easier if we came inside to talk," Halliday responded, noncommittally.

The woman released the latch chain and swung the door open to let them in. She wore jeans and a cream cashmere sweater. Her honey-colored hair was arranged in a loose chignon. She told them her name was Elisabeth.

Halliday and Lavelle glanced at each other to silently decide who'd do the talking. Halliday nodded slightly. She'd do it.

"We're actually here about Edward Cole. What is your relationship to him?" Halliday asked when they were all seated.

"Nobody calls him Edward. We all call him Ted," said Elisabeth. "Ted is my fiancé. Why are you asking about Ted?"

"Edward Cole—Ted," Halliday corrected herself, "rented a short-stay apartment for a week. We found the body of a man in that apartment early this morning. We believe that man might be Ted."

"You're wrong." Elisabeth was emphatic. "Ted was here last night. You've made a mistake."

"Very possibly," said Halliday. "But we need to know for sure. I'd like to show you a photo, if you don't mind."

"Go ahead," said Elisabeth, steeling herself as Halliday turned on her iPad and found a crime scene photo that clearly showed the victim's face.

Halliday turned the screen around. Elisabeth inhaled sharply. Her complexion turned to ash. She put her hand over her mouth as sobs racked her body.

Ten minutes later, Elisabeth sat with a blanket over her shoulders, her body trembling as she cupped a mug of sweetened coffee that Lavelle had made for her. Despite her grief, she insisted on answering their questions.

"I met Ted at a dinner party. There was an instant chemistry. Within a couple of months, Ted and I had moved in together and he'd proposed to me."

"Sounds like a whirlwind romance," said Halliday.

"We didn't want to waste time dating when we both knew we wanted to be with each other for the rest of our lives. We were going to start a family straight after the wedding. Ted would have been an amazing dad." Elisabeth put her fist against her mouth to gain control of her emotions.

"Do you know why Ted rented the apartment nearby?"

Elisabeth nodded. "He was helping a friend who was in trouble."

"Which friend?" Halliday asked.

"It was more than a friend," Elisabeth admitted. "It was his ex."

"So he rented the apartment to help his ex-girlfriend?"

Elisabeth nodded. "Ted came here last night and told me everything. He said he didn't want to keep secrets from me."

"Do you know his ex's name?"

"Her name's Liv. Liv Reese."

Halliday and Lavelle kept their expressions blank. The dots were connecting.

"Are you aware that he rented the apartment using a fake name?"

"Yes," she said. "He didn't want anyone to know that she was hiding there."

"Did Ted give a reason for the secrecy?"

"He was worried she might be in danger."

"What danger?"

"She was almost murdered a few years ago. Ted was worried the killer was after her again. He wanted to protect her. Ted felt responsible for her."

"Did he ever tell you why he broke off their relationship?"

"Ted said their relationship had been rocky for a long time," Elisabeth said. "She suffered from severe insomnia. She wouldn't sleep for days. She was constantly popping pills to stay awake. Her condition was getting worse, not better, and she refused to get help. But what bothered Ted most was that she wouldn't let go."

"Let go of what?"

"Of her past," said Elisabeth. "Ted told me once that she was haunted by her inability to remember what happened the day she was almost murdered. It consumed her. It dominated her life, to the exclusion of everything else. All she ever talked about was finding out who did it and getting justice."

"Is that the reason why Ted moved to New York?"

"He took the job because it was a promotion, but mostly because he couldn't take it anymore," Elisabeth said. "He said he couldn't build a future with a woman who was trapped in the past. Deep down he must have known she wouldn't come with him to New York. She suffered night terrors that the killer would find her again. The thought of returning back here, to the place where it happened, terrified her. To cut a long story short, their relationship died a natural death once he moved here. And now Ted is dead. Because of her. It had to be because of her." Elisabeth broke down.

"Have you ever met Liv Reese?" Halliday asked, once Elisabeth was able to talk again.

"I met her for the first time two weeks ago when she turned up at our engagement party at my parents' house in Scarsdale," Elisabeth said, wiping her eyes. "She was dressed inappropriately for the occasion, in a white scrunched dress and bare feet. She'd walked across the waterlogged lawn. Her feet were splattered with mud and loose grass. Her hair was very long," she said. "Ted was shocked when he saw her. He took her aside to talk privately in the garden."

"Do you know what they discussed?"

"He asked her to leave."

"How did she take it?"

"She claimed to have no idea who he was. She told him she'd come to the party because she'd found the invitation that morning stuck to the front door of the place where she was staying with a Post-it note telling her she had to come. Her behavior was so bizarre that we honestly thought she was drunk, or on drugs. My mom called for a town car to take her home. Ted contacted the driver afterward to get her address. He wanted to see her."

"Do you know why?"

"He told me last night that he wanted to make sure she was okay. When he arrived at her apartment, she had no idea who he was. Ted realized she was suffering from amnesia."

"Did Ted mention whether Liv had suffered from memory problems when they were dating in London?"

"That's why Ted was so worried about her. She'd never had memory problems when she lived in London. Other than not remembering the stabbing incident, which Ted said was probably due to her being in a coma afterward."

"Do you have any idea how she found out about the engagement party?" Halliday asked.

"I sent her an invitation," Elisabeth said, color returning to her cheeks as she flushed with shame. "She brought the invitation with her that day."

"I don't get it," said Lavelle, who'd been standing by the window and letting Halliday ask most of the questions. "Why invite your fiancé's ex to your engagement party?"

"I didn't expect her to actually turn up. She was living in London," Elisabeth said defensively.

She paused for a moment as if unsure how much to divulge, then took a deep breath and explained in a rush of words, "Liv would call Ted constantly from London. Several times a week. I hoped the invitation would drive home the fact that Ted wasn't hers anymore."

"What did she say in these phone calls?" Halliday asked. "Did she ever threaten Ted?"

"Sometimes she'd call and tell Ted that she couldn't sleep and that she missed him. Other times, she'd cry and ask him to give her another chance. It tore him up. She'd been through a terrible ordeal. She was emotionally fragile. Ted felt guilty," Elisabeth said. "That's why we were so relieved when the calls stopped. We assumed she'd finally come to terms with the breakup."

"Then why did you send her the invitation to your engagement party?" Lavelle asked.

"Actually, I'd already mailed her the invitation a week before the calls stopped," Elisabeth said, her cheeks flushing again. "I sent it because I wanted her to know that our marriage was real. I wanted her to realize it was time for her to let go of Ted. When she suddenly stopped calling, I thought it had worked. That the invitation had given her closure. I was as surprised as Ted when she turned up at the party."

Halliday jotted down a quick timeline in her notebook. Liv's calls to Ted had stopped abruptly five weeks ago, around the time she'd received the invitation to his engagement party. That coincided with the time of Liv's first known memory blackout, according to the social worker. Halliday wondered if Liv Reese stopped calling Ted because she had a memory blackout. Perhaps she simply didn't remember him anymore.

It was possible that the invitation had been the catalyst that sparked Liv Reese's amnesia. Maybe the shock of learning that she'd lost Ted for good caused her psyche to block out everything that had transpired in the last two years, all the trauma and all the heartbreak. Without her recent memories, it was as if her life was back to how it had been before she'd met Ted and before she'd been stabbed. It was the ultimate form of denial.

"Was she violent when she came to the engagement party? Did she make any threats?" Lavelle asked.

"No," said Elisabeth. "Her presence alone was ruining our party. I should never have sent her the invitation. Ted was furious when he found out."

Her shoulders shook again with sobs. Halliday and Lavelle exchanged glances. It was entirely possible that Ted Cole might still be alive if his fiancée hadn't sent the invitation to his ex.

"Ted felt obliged to help her." Elisabeth kept talking through her tears. "He told me last night that he'd found a doctor who was a world expert at treating memory problems. Normally there's a long wait to see him, but Ted pulled strings to get her seen quickly."

"Do you know the doctor's name?" Halliday asked.

"Ted didn't say. Do you think Ted's ex is responsible? Did Liv Reese kill Ted?" Elisabeth looked up at them, waiting for their answer.

"Our investigation has just begun," Halliday responded. "Did Ted do or say anything when he came here last night that you think might help us figure out what happened?"

"Not really," Elisabeth said, after a moment's thought. "Except for maybe one thing." She stood up and went to her bedroom, returning a moment later with a piece of paper. It contained a photocopy of a sketch made from small dots that formed the shape of a lily. At the top was a phone number.

"What is that?" Halliday asked.

"A drawing of some sort," said Elisabeth. "Ted received a call while he was here. It was Lou, a menswear designer we both know. I gathered that Ted had asked him about this design and he was calling Ted back with information."

"Did you hear their conversation?"

"Only the start. Ted took the phone into our bedroom where he continued the call. It struck me as strange because he'd come here to tell me the truth about his ex and then he gets a call and he's being secretive again. He left in a rush straight after the call. He must have accidentally dropped the paper with the sketch. I found it this morning on the carpet next to the bed."

Halliday and Lavelle left the apartment carrying an evidence bag with the sketch, as well as evidence bags containing Ted Cole's toothbrush, hairbrush, and wristwatch. The lab would, hopefully, match the DNA and any fingerprints on his personal belongings to the body they'd found in the apartment.

Halliday drove through heavy afternoon traffic toward the forensics lab to hand in the evidence bags as Lavelle updated the captain on the phone. Even as she listened to his side of the conversation, she couldn't stop thinking of Elisabeth, Ted Cole's heartbroken fiancée.

"Worst part of the job, telling people they've lost a loved one," remarked Halliday when Lavelle was off the phone. "Worse even than the mountain of paperwork they bury us in."

"Tell me about it," said Lavelle. "I've done more of these than I care to count."

She double-parked and waited at the wheel, while Lavelle took the evidence bags up to forensics. Halliday called the phone number that had been scrawled on the sketch, which she'd photographed on her phone before Lavelle had taken it up to the lab. Her call went straight to voicemail. She hung up without leaving a message.

Since Lavelle was taking longer than he'd anticipated, Halliday turned on the radio to distract herself with music. She'd been in plenty of tense situations. She'd driven in military convoys along roads mined with bombs disguised as rocks. She'd been shot at more times than she remembered. Since she'd joined the NYPD, she'd been involved in drug busts and undercover operations. Halliday could deal with danger. It was grief that tore her apart.

The click of the driver's door opening interrupted her thoughts. Lavelle explained as he put on his safety belt that the lab technician had taken prints off Cole's toothbrush while he'd waited. She'd then done a quick comparison with prints taken from the victim at the crime scene.

"It's not an official ID, but it's just as good for our purposes. Ted Cole is definitely the victim," he said. "Oh, and there's another update. They found traces of sedatives in the wine bottle, just as you'd suspected. The wine was spiked. That's why Cole didn't fight back when he was stabbed. He was fast asleep."

"At least that's a small mercy for him," she said quietly.

As Halliday turned on the engine, Lavelle's phone rang. He took it on speaker. It was a detective at the Ninetieth Precinct in Brooklyn, Detective Krause's old precinct. His name was Larry Regan.

"We have the files you wanted," Regan said.

"Any chance you could have them scanned and sent over?" Lavelle asked.

"They're huge files," said Regan. "There's way too much to scan. I could send you the originals, but it might only get to you in the morning. Or you could send someone to collect them."

"We'll drive over and take a look in person," said Lavelle.

He and Halliday were eager to find out exactly what had happened to Liv Reese two years earlier. Krause had made it pretty clear he thought she was the perpetrator, not the victim. He'd been scant with details and deliberately cagey. Knowing Krause the way he did, Lavelle guessed that he resented other cops looking into his old case.

"What's the connection between the two cases?" Regan asked.

"We don't know," said Lavelle. "All we know is that Liv Reese's fingerprints have turned up at the scene of another homicide."

"Who was the victim?" Regan asked.

"Her ex-boyfriend," said Lavelle.

Regan was silent as he absorbed that information. "In that case it sounds as if we'll have plenty to discuss when you get here."

Chapter
Thirty-Nine

Two Years Earlier

Amy's lying on her back in a bikini on the rooftop of our building when I come up and arrange my beach towel alongside hers. Her oversized sunglasses reflect the pristine blue sky and a snippet of street art graffiti on the rustic brick wall behind us.

I hike up my mint-green sundress with spaghetti straps to avoid tan lines before relaxing on my towel. It's a rare treat for us to be here alone. Usually the rooftop is crowded on weekends. Judging by the pile of crushed beer cans and empty tequila bottles in the trash, I'm guessing everyone else is sleeping off hangovers.

I sit with my back against the brick wall and read my novel. Two chapters into my book, I glance up when the rooftop door creaks open. Someone watches us from the shadows of the stairwell before turning away. Footsteps clatter down the metal stairs and the door slams shut.

It's probably nothing, just another resident checking to see if the deck area is available. Still, it creeps me out. I've been getting that feeling a lot lately. Too many weird things have been happening. Each time, my anxiety builds to a boiling point. I'm constantly looking over my shoulder.

Amy thinks I'm being paranoid, but it's not just me. Shawna's skittish, which is totally out-of-character. She was a pretty chill cat, until recently.

This morning, I received a Snapchat message as I pushed my shopping cart along the canned food aisle at our local supermarket.

Mint really is your color, the message said, referencing the color of my sundress.

Looking up from the phone, I scrutinized the shoppers in the aisle around me. They were too busy taking products off the shelves or pushing their carts to show the slightest interest in me. Within seconds, the message disappeared and I was left wondering if I'd imagined it.

This time I took a screenshot of the text before it disappeared. It's exactly the sort of evidence of harassment the cops told me to bring them so they can investigate further, although I still haven't decided whether to show it to the police.

What's that expression: "Once bitten, twice shy"? I haven't contacted the cops since I fell asleep on the sofa and woke to find signs that someone had been in the apartment. My face burns as I remember Detective Krause joking about whether my stalker will leave a loaf of bread in the fridge next time instead of milk. I'm not inclined to risk being mocked again by showing the cops a screenshot of another ambiguous message. They'll only explain it away, like the last time.

Thinking about the text message I received at the supermarket makes me look nervously around the empty rooftop. I feel like I'm being watched again, which is silly because it's just me here, and Amy. She looks dead to the world as she lies tanning in her coral bikini with her sunglasses covering her eyes.

I assume Amy's asleep until she reaches for her phone, which is ringing on silent mode. She rejects the call without even looking at it.

"Who is it?"

"Brett," she mutters. It's the first sound out of her in an hour.

"You don't want to speak to him?"

"I'm not talking to Brett right now."

I've shared an apartment with Amy for years. Usually I'm blasé about the ups and downs of her roller-coaster relationships. But Brett has lasted longer than any of Amy's other boyfriends. He wines and dines her. He showers her with exorbitant gifts, and takes her on luxury weekend breaks. He indulges her every whim and Amy laps it up. For the first time, I've wondered whether she might settle down.

"Why aren't you talking to Brett?" I ask, unable to hide my surprise.

"It's a long story. Let's just say that our relationship is getting close to its 'use by date.' It's been heading in this direction for a while. I haven't told Brett that it's over, so don't say anything." She changes the subject. "How's everything with you and Marco?"

"Pretty good," I say, still shocked Amy's thinking of dumping Brett. "I'm crazy about Marco. You know that! The thing is . . ." My voice drops off.

"What?"

"I'm not sure that he's as into me. Sometimes I think that he slots me into his life when it's convenient for him. Other times, I feel frozen out. And . . ."

"And? What?" Amy turns to her side, reclining on her elbow. She pushes her sunglasses onto the top of her head and stares at me, waiting for me to elaborate.

"He wanted me to get free publicity for his investor's wife, who's a handbag designer. The style team refused to do a write-up, and I don't blame them. Emily is not a great designer. She's not even a good designer. Marco was upset when I told him. He really wanted to keep

Dean, his investor, happy. At first I felt guilty about it, but now I'm sort of annoyed."

"Why?"

"I'm annoyed that Marco expected me to help him in the first place. It makes me feel . . . used," I tell her. "I'm seeing him this afternoon. Do you think I should say something?"

Amy slides her sunglasses off her head back onto her face, hiding the expression in her eyes. "Liv, I wasn't going to say anything, but here goes. You're wasting your time on Marco. That relationship will never go anywhere. Break up with him. Go meet someone new."

"Aren't you a little biased because you two don't like each other?"

"I'm only biased against him because I think he's wrong for you. You need someone stable and reliable after your messed-up gypsy childhood. All your mother's marriages, going from having money to being dirt poor every time she had a breakup, being taken by child services when she went on drinking binges. Not to mention all the other crap that you've told me about. All that takes a toll."

"What toll?"

"Well," says Amy, choosing her words carefully. "For one thing, I don't think you're good at telling the good apples from the bad ones."

"You think Marco is bad?"

"He's an asshole. Don't get me wrong. That's okay. As long as a girl knows what she's getting into. You don't," she says pointedly. "Look, everything with Marco is a means to an end. He's a wheeler and dealer. That's literally his profession; a salesman." She pauses, seeing my hurt expression. "Liv, you deserve someone who loves you for who you are, not for what you can do for him."

"Does such a person even exist, Amy? Because if he does, then I sure haven't come across this paragon of virtue yet."

"You will," she says. "But not if you keep wasting your time on the Marcos of this world."

"I know you only want what's best for me, Amy. But I'm in love with Marco, flaws and all. He's awesome in so many ways. I'm not going to break up with him in the hope that I'll meet someone better."

"Then there's nothing more to say," she says, before turning around and lying on her stomach. She unclips her bikini top to prevent tan lines and falls asleep.

After a while longer, I'm getting thirsty from lying in the sun. I collect my things and go down to the apartment to get ready for my cycling trip with Marco. I don't wake Amy. She'll come down when she's ready. I'm halfway down the stairs when I realize I left my straw sun hat on the roof.

I go all the way back up the metal stairs and push open the rooftop door. I'm immediately hit by a sweltering blast of heat. Amy's standing by a rooftop wall, looking at the view of the East River, her back to me as she talks on the phone. She doesn't notice me retrieving my hat from under the ledge where I was lying earlier.

"You have to tell her."

Amy pauses midsentence as she realizes she's not alone. She turns around and sees me standing on the roof, holding my hat awkwardly to my stomach.

"I forgot my sun hat," I say meekly.

My cell phone rings with a blocked number as I open the front door of our apartment.

"Who is this?" I ask.

"Your partner in crime."

"Tell me who you are or I'm going to end this call. Now." I'm rude for a reason. I assume the voice on the phone is the stalker that the police don't believe exists.

"I'm Q. You were at the special advance showing of my exhibition. You asked me to contact you for an interview," he says, amused by my hostile tone.

It's the artist whose disturbing exhibition I went to last week. He's caught me unprepared. I grapple around for a pen and a notebook in a kitchen drawer. I was expecting a sit-down interview at a prearranged time. Instead he's called me unexpectedly and caught me off balance. I wonder if it was deliberate.

"Did you enjoy the performance?" he asks.

"It was certainly unique," I respond, thinking back to the bizarre exhibit in the warehouse. "Does it have a title?" I'm standing by the kitchen sink looking into the street as I talk.

"Mirror Four," he says. "That's the title of the show."

The name throws me. I don't recall seeing a mirror at the exhibition. All I saw was a gagged woman with a burlap sack over her head, bound to a chair. I remember that her clothes were almost shredded. It was more a macabre horror show than anything to do with mirrors.

"What's the significance of the name?"

"The exhibition is what I call a four-dimensional mirror," he says quietly. "It signifies a metaphorical mirror that shows my audience for what they really are."

"Which is?"

"Good. Evil. Banal. Maybe all three."

"Usually in performance art, the artist is part of the experience. What's your role in the exhibit?"

"I'm a voyeur," he answers. "I arrange the experience and then I step back and watch. What happens next is in the hands of the audience. They can do whatever they like. Free the woman with the scissors. Cut her with the knife. Or walk away as you did, Liv."

"I didn't walk away. I observed and then I left," I say defensively.

"There's no such thing as being an observer. Doing nothing is doing something. Being passive has consequences."

I roll my eyes, grateful we're only talking on the phone and he can't see me. As far as I'm concerned, Q's experimental sensory experience is nothing more than heavy-handed social commentary. It's fatuous, and it leaves me cold. Of course, I'm too polite to tell him that. Instead I ask him to tell me about his inspiration for the work.

"The Bible."

"In what way?"

"What's the greatest gift God gave humankind?"

I run through my lax religious education. "The Ten Commandments?"

Through the kitchen window, I see a white minivan stopping outside. Its engine idles noisily as the driver gets out and disappears into the entrance of the building across the street.

"Free will, Liv," he chastises. "Genesis Two. God told Adam not to eat the apple. Adam had a choice. He could obey God's order not to eat the apple, or he could exercise free will and eat it anyway. He chose the second option."

I check the time. I really need to get ready or I'll be late to meet Marco for our cycling trip this afternoon.

"How does the story of Adam relate to your exhibit?" I ask somewhat impatiently as I walk to my bedroom and take out a T-shirt and Lycra shorts.

"You had choices, Liv. You had free will. You could have rescued the woman in my exhibit. Instead you walked away. Why?"

"There were signs on the exhibit that said 'Do Not Touch.' I didn't want to interfere or break any rules."

"So you left? Because of a stupid rule?" he asks.

"Yes."

"Bystanders can be just as culpable as perpetrators."

"Perhaps in real life," I say. "In this case, it was an art exhibition. It wasn't real."

"The ropes. The duct tape. The gag. All were real." He sounds offended. "The woman. She was a real woman bound to a real chair. With real blood in her veins. The hammer was real. So was the rope. You could have smashed the glass box with the hammer and taken out the scissors to cut her bonds and free her. Instead you abandoned her there and left."

He's right. I should have cut the woman free. His accusation chills me. I want to tell him that his exhibition frightened me with its realism.

"I thought that was part of the performance. I didn't know I had a role to play."

"Everyone has roles to play. Sometimes we don't know it until it's too late. You were given a choice, Liv. Every choice has a consequence."

I walk to my bedroom and glance out the window. The minivan driver comes out of the building across the street carrying a large box. He slides open the van door and puts the box on a rear seat before slamming the door shut and going around to the driver's seat.

The van's engine pops and whines as it drives off. It sounds as if the same noise is coming over the phone line. As if Q is on my street. I look out the window, expecting to see a man on the street below. There's nobody's around except for a young couple walking a French bulldog on a leash.

When the call with Q is over, a text message comes up on my screen. It's from Marco.

Something's come up. I can't go cycling today. I'll be in touch.

It's the sort of brusque message someone might send a business acquaintance, not a girlfriend.

I remember what Amy told me about Marco being a bad apple, and I wonder if she's right.

Chapter
Forty

"Your appointment was for this morning," says the doctor's reception-ist when I give her my name. Before I can apologize for being late, she adds: "Nevertheless, Dr. Brenner left instructions to squeeze you in no matter when you turned up. He'll see you as soon as he's finished with his current patient."

She tells me to take a seat in the clinic waiting area, where several aqua chairs are pushed in a tight row by a frosted-glass wall. I take a corner seat opposite a wall clock. The slow movement of time lulls me into a semitrance. It's broken when the receptionist's phone rings with a loud and sudden peal.

"You can go in," she tells me.

Dr. Brenner's eyes are magnified by the lenses of his silver-framed glasses. He asks me how I'm feeling. I shift uneasily on the uphol-stered chair next to his desk and answer that I'm fine. That's a lie, but it doesn't matter, because I look fine on the outside. And that's what counts.

Isn't it?

"Ted couldn't make it today?" he asks. "I'd really hoped he'd join you so we could discuss your treatment plan." He stares at me without blinking as he patiently waits for me to answer.

"Something came up at work. He sends his apologies," I lie.

I'm too embarrassed to admit I don't know anyone named Ted. I only came here because I found the appointment card at that awful basement apartment. I figured that if I went to the appointment with this neurologist then he'd be able to tell me why everything has felt like a fractured dream since I woke on the subway.

Dr. Brenner is talking again. I stare at his mouth, trying to focus.

"Do you have your journal or any of the notes you showed me last time?" he asks.

"I didn't bring anything with me," I fib, once again not knowing what he's talking about.

He's about to say something else, but obviously thinks better of it because he clears his throat awkwardly and picks up a pen from the ink blotter on his desk.

"Let's begin. I'd like you to remember the following three things," he says. "Red flower, blue car, and a tennis ball. Can you remember that?"

"Of course," I respond. My eyes focus on the glint of the doctor's wedding ring as I memorize those words.

Dr. Brenner has my patient file open on his computer. I shift in my chair to get a better look, but I'm still too far away to see anything other than a blur of words on the screen.

"I have the results of the MRI," he says.

He twists his laptop in my direction so that I can see the image of my brain filling the screen. "There's no indication of any organic brain damage. Certainly nothing that comes up in the scan. That's good news. Great news, in fact," he emphasizes.

Dr. Brenner leads me to an examination table. I sit with my legs hanging over the edge as he examines me, running through a battery of tests to check my motor skills and reflexes as well as my muscular strength. When he's done, he shines a penlight into one eye at a time and asks me to follow the light.

"What's today's date?" he asks, turning off the silver penlight with a click.

I tell him the date. I remember it from the newspaper I saw earlier at the newsstand. He asks me to name the five most recent presidents. I do better and go all the way back to Nixon.

"Can you tell me what were those four things I asked you to remember early on?" he asks when I'm back on the chair next to his desk.

"There were three things. Red flower, blue car, and a tennis ball."

"Very good." He turns his swivel chair to face his desk and types something, then turns back to me. "Are you still taking caffeine tablets and anti-narcolepsy drugs to stop yourself from falling asleep?"

I squirm under his steady gaze as I remember the piles of NoDoz tablets I saw in the trash at the basement apartment where I've apparently been living.

"Not anymore."

"Excellent. I'm pleased you followed my advice." He nods encouragingly.

I press my hands to my side so he won't notice the messages on my skin telling me not to sleep. Although I suspect he already saw them.

"Do you remember the reason why you came to see me?"

"Yes," I answer confidently, even though I don't have the slightest idea. He is silent as he waits for me to elaborate. The faint tug of a headache gives me an idea. "I came to see you because of my migraines." My voice rises hopefully.

"Just your migraines?"

"Sure." I try to inject conviction into my voice. It comes out as a falsetto.

Both of us know I'm lying.

"What about memory issues?" he prompts.

"My memory is fine, as you just saw. I answered all your questions perfectly," I respond.

His eyes widen through the lenses of his glasses. He clicks his pen and leans forward in his black swivel chair.

"Liv, you came to see me not because of migraines but because of problems with your memory."

"What kind of problems?" I'm terrified to hear the answer.

I remember the phone call at the basement apartment earlier. The caller said I forget things when I fall asleep. Is it possible that he was telling the truth? And if he was right about that, then maybe he was right about all the other things he said.

"You appear to be in what I'd call a repetitive dissociative fugue. It's a rare form of amnesia," the doctor tells me. The word "amnesia" hangs in the air. It fits in with all the strange occurrences that have happened today.

"How long have I had it for?"

"I'm not sure. This is only your second appointment with me. We're still trying to get to the bottom of it."

"How could I possibly have amnesia? I remember so much about my life going back to my childhood."

"What things do you remember?"

"Well, for instance, I was cast in the role of Ophelia in a high school play. That was more than a decade ago, and I can still recite the lines, almost word for word."

"I don't doubt it," he says. "Our brains are highly complex. It's a different mechanism in your brain that appears to be blocked. You might remember dialogue from *Hamlet*, but unless you keep a written record of this conversation, you won't remember what we've discussed when you next wake up. You won't remember me. You won't remember being here. You won't remember anything that happened to you today. None of it."

"What happened to cause this?"

"I don't know exactly. Ted was going to make some inquiries in London to figure it out. What I do know is that it appears to be connected to your sleep patterns. Whenever you fall asleep, you wake up without any memory of events in your recent past."

I look out into the bright sunlight coming through his office window and lose myself in my thoughts. I've lost such a big chunk of my memory. It makes me feel bereft, like I've lost a limb, or an eye.

"Liv? Liv?" Dr. Brenner must have been talking to me. I didn't hear any of it. "Do you have any questions?"

"Is that why I drink so much caffeine and take NoDoz tablets?" I ask, thinking of the energy drinks filling the fridge at that horrible apartment. "Am I forcing myself to stay awake so I won't forget?"

"I believe so," he says. "Deep down you must know that you're going to forget everything when you sleep, so you try to fight it for as long as possible. Narcolepsy drugs, caffeine pills. Triple-strength coffee. You take whatever will keep you awake. It's a sort of self-induced insomnia. Sometimes you stay up for a full twenty-four hours. Or longer," he says. "I suspect it's affecting the levels of serotonin in your brain. The lower levels of serotonin, which controls moods, might be one of the causes of the fugues you're experiencing."

"It sounds like a vicious cycle. The longer I stay awake, the more it takes a toll on my memory."

"It is a vicious cycle. You need to break it if you're to get better."

He writes something on what looks like a prescription pad and hands it to me. I'm expecting it to be a script for drugs. Instead, he's written the name of another doctor.

"A psychiatrist?" I look up in surprise.

"Dr. Rosen specializes in memory problems. Due to the circumstances of your condition and the fact that we can't find any indication of damage to your brain in the scans, I believe this problem is most likely psychological. Dr. Rosen and I often work together with complex cases such as yours."

He holds up a palm as if he knows I'm going to push back. "We need to work out what triggered your memory disorder. Fugues with no organic cause are usually the result of trauma, extreme psychological trauma. Dr. Rosen can help you identify and work through that trauma."

"Trauma? What trauma?" I ask blankly.

He pauses as if contemplating how best to answer. "It's best you discuss that with Dr. Rosen."

I can barely hear him over an electrical crackle, rising in my head until it gets so explosive I want to put my hands over my ears and scream. When it stops, I realize I'm crying.

Dr. Brenner tries to comfort me. He tells me that his secretary will call Ted to come and get me. He says that he doesn't want me to be alone.

"But I don't know Ted," I say so softly that only I can hear.

His reassuring voice washes over me until I find myself on an aqua chair listening to a baby screaming in a pediatrician's examination room down the hall. Dr. Brenner's secretary squats next to me, holding out a box of Kleenex.

"I've left a message for Ted," she says. "I'm sure he'll call back very soon. Meanwhile, Dr. Brenner has asked Dr. Rosen to come down and talk to you when he's done with his next patient."

The minute hand of the waiting room clock looks as if it's frozen in time. I can't take waiting anymore. I get up from my seat and lean across the receptionist's desk to ask her what's going on.

"I've just left another message for Ted. His voicemail says if he doesn't answer then he's probably in a meeting. I'm sure he'll call back soon."

"Maybe you don't have the correct contact details for him? Can I check?" I'm curious to find out more about this mysterious Ted who is apparently listed as my next of kin.

"Is this his phone number?" she asks, rotating her computer screen so I can read it.

I don't recognize the phone number. The address, on the other hand, is a whole different story.

Chapter
Forty-One

Detective Jack Lavelle navigated afternoon traffic to Brooklyn as he and Detective Halliday went over the shards of information they'd picked up so far on the case.

According to his fiancée, Elisabeth, Ted Cole had rented an apartment for his ex-girlfriend as a safe house because he was worried she might be in danger. It was in that apartment that he had been found stabbed to death early that morning.

"It seems straightforward," Lavelle said. "Liv Reese snapped. She stabbed her ex, Ted Cole, and fled."

"I think it's too early for us to focus on her to the exclusion of all other suspects," argued Halliday. "Ted believed that Liv Reese was in danger. That's why he moved her to a safe house. Maybe the person he was trying to protect her from confronted them both and murdered Ted."

"If that's the case then why wasn't she murdered as well?" Lavelle asked.

"I don't know," said Halliday after a moment's thought. "I still think we need to find out why Ted thought Liv was in danger."

"Maybe he made it up," said Lavelle.

"Why would he do that?"

"Maybe Ted told his fiancée that his ex was in danger to hide the fact that he'd rented an apartment to conduct an affair with her behind Elisabeth's back."

"If Ted and Liv were having an affair, then why would Ted tell Elisabeth anything at all?" said Halliday. "Why not cover his tracks by telling her that he was late at work, or on a business trip? No." She shook her head. "Ted told Elisabeth the truth. He had no reason to lie. He was genuinely worried about Liv's welfare. We need to find out why."

"We don't have limitless resources," Lavelle said. "Right now we have a likely suspect, and that suspect is Liv Reese. She found out that her ex was getting married. It upset her enough to pack up her life in London and travel back to New York. We know that for sure. Anger and betrayal. Liv Reese had one heck of a motive for murder."

"Not everyone with a motive kills," Halliday pointed out.

"True, but she had more than motive," said Lavelle.

Motive was the final piece in the trifecta. Liv Reese had opportunity, they both agreed on that. Security camera footage showed her leaving the scene of the crime. She also had means. Ted Cole was stabbed while he was sleeping, possibly after drinking wine laced with sedatives. Liv's fingerprints were on the bottle.

"You saw the long dark hairs on the pillow next to Cole. Liv Reese was most likely in bed with him on the night of the murder," Lavelle said, sounding exasperated by Halliday's refusal to be swayed. "And we know she was having mental health issues in London. She'd seen a psychiatrist. Even her social worker agreed that her insomnia might make her psychotic."

"I'll admit that it doesn't look good for Liv Reese," Halliday conceded. "Call me contrary, but I'm still keeping an open mind."

The facts all lined up to support Lavelle's theory. Liv Reese looked as guilty as sin. Still, Halliday felt in her gut they were missing something.

She looked through the windshield as they drove, trying to figure out what it was that bothered her enough to seriously consider the remote possibility that someone else had done it.

"You're very quiet," Lavelle commented after a while.

"That's because we're missing something."

"What makes you think that?" Lavelle asked, flashing her a sideways glance.

"I don't think any of this is as straightforward as it appears. It's true all the evidence points to Liv Reese. She's rightly our prime suspect," Halliday admitted.

"Yes, she is. So why aren't you convinced?"

"I worry it may be an optical illusion," Halliday said. "We have only some of the pieces of the puzzle. It's made us think the emerging pattern is something other than what it actually is."

Halliday knew a thing or two about puzzles. When she'd left the military and was dealing with the emotional withdrawal of being alone after spending years with a tight-knit group of military buddies, she'd taken up doing complex jigsaw puzzles to keep her mind preoccupied.

The veterans' counselor had recommended it as a strategy to eliminate stress and give her a sense of achievement. It helped lift her out of the depressive hole that so many veterans fell into during their transition into civilian life, especially those like her who'd spent so much of their service in combat zones.

Halliday took out her phone and Googled a phone number for Saint Vincent's Hospital in London.

It was well after 11:00 P.M. London time when the switchboard operator answered. Halliday asked for a phone number for Dr. Stanhope, Liv Reese's psychiatrist.

"I'm a police detective in New York," she explained. "I need to speak to Dr. Stanhope urgently. It's about one of his patients. She may be in serious trouble."

The operator gave her a cell phone number for the doctor. Halliday dialed it immediately, hoping that he kept his phone on after hours. He did.

"Stanhope." His voice was husky from being woken.

"I'm sorry for disturbing you so late in your night, Doctor. I'm a detective in New York and I'm investigating a case involving a patient of yours, Liv Reese," Halliday said.

His bedsheets rustled over the phone line as he climbed out of bed.

"Liv Reese has turned up here in New York. I'm one of the detectives looking for her."

"The hospital social worker told me earlier that you might get in touch," he said. "I hope you understand that I'm quite limited in what I can tell you. There are certain things about my patient that I am not at liberty to discuss. Patient confidentiality. You understand."

"I believe she may be in danger. I hope that gives you some leeway to talk to me about her. Incidentally, I know she has some sort of amnesia and I'd be interested in your take on it."

"It's a very rare condition. It's a type of dissociative fugue. Except instead of one fugue episode, Liv is experiencing a series of repetitive fugue episodes. They begin every time Liv wakes and end every time she falls asleep."

"Help me out here, Doctor. I'm not great with medical jargon," Halliday said. "What do you mean by dissociative fugue?"

"It's a type of amnesia that has a psychological cause. It's often sparked by trauma and it presents with quite unusual characteristics."

"Such as?"

"A person tries to resume his or her old life after suffering a trauma. They don't realize that time has passed. We've had cases of people with dissociative fugue who have taken on new names, started new lives. There are even cases of people who have begun speaking in different accents, or languages." He paused to let his words sink in. "You must have heard of the crime writer Agatha Christie?"

"Of course," said Halliday.

"In 1926, after she discovered her husband was having an affair, Christie disappeared. The police dredged the local lake, believing she might have drowned. Thousands of volunteers searched for her in the countryside. Meanwhile, a woman claiming to be a grieving mother from Cape Town checked in at a health spa under a name very similar to the name of the mistress of Agatha Christie's unfaithful husband. Eventually, one of the guests recognized her as the famous crime writer and alerted the authorities. Christie regained her memory, but she never remembered anything that happened to her during her time at the health spa."

"You believe the same thing happened to Liv Reese?"

"It's very possible. If anything, her situation is significantly more dire."

"In what way?"

"Her fugue incidents are repetitive. They happen every time she wakes up," he says. "That puts her in a constant state of confusion and makes her extremely vulnerable. It's very rare. In fact, I don't recall ever seeing another case with that presentation."

"Do you know what might have prompted her to leave England and return to New York?"

"I'm afraid I haven't seen Liv for a while. My wife and I have just returned from a visit to Australia for the birth of our first grandchild. Liv was supposed to see a colleague while I was away. It appears she didn't attend her appointments. We only found out she'd disappeared when I returned to work a few days ago. I asked the social worker to contact the missing person department at Scotland Yard when she couldn't get hold of Liv," he said. "From what you're telling me, she's in New York again. Her old stomping ground."

"That's correct," said Halliday.

"That's very interesting. Very interesting indeed."

"Why is that?"

"I suspect Liv's subconsciously trying to find out the source of the trauma that caused these fugue states," he said. "Killing her monster, as it were, may be her way to assert control. To break the cycle and get her memory back."

Chapter
Forty-Two

Two Years Earlier

I stare at myself in the window as the train roars through a subway tunnel with a deafening howl. I wonder if the silk scarf tied jauntily around my neck is over the top, especially on such a sweltering summer day. Marco gave me the scarf as a gift. I thought it would be nice to wear it when I see him later tonight.

We've arranged to meet for dinner at Stefanie. There's a two-month wait to get into the restaurant, but Marco pulled strings to get us a table. I'm impressed. I'm a food writer and even I couldn't get a table at Stefanie on short notice. Marco hinted he's taking me there because he wants to discuss something important. I'm filled with a nervous anticipation.

I sway in tandem with the passengers in the train car. It's like we're a single seething organism, moving to the familiar rhythmic ritual of the morning commute.

When the train reaches my stop, I push my way out of the car and through the mass of passengers waiting on the platform. My phone rings as I climb the stairs to street level. I answer it as I walk into my office.

"Liv? Where are you?" Amy sounds sleepy.

"I'm almost at work," I respond, pressing the elevator button. "Why? Is something wrong?"

"No," she yawns. "I just woke and heard creaking floorboards. You didn't answer when I called out your name so I figured I'd call and see what's going on." She yawns again.

"It wasn't me. I've just arrived at work."

"It must be the new people in the apartment upstairs. They make such a racket when they leave in the morning. Listen, Liv, since I have you on the line, I think Shawna needs to see the vet."

"Why?"

"She's limping. She won't put pressure on her right front paw. I think she might have been injured. Maybe she was in a fight or something. She seems spooked . . ." The rest of her sentence is swallowed up by the noise of the elevator doors opening.

"Amy? I can't hear you."

Her voice has been replaced by crackling silence as the call drops out. I take the elevator up to the office. Once I get out, I dial Amy's cell phone again.

Her phone's engaged so I leave her a message. "Amy, your call dropped out. Bad reception. I'm in the office now. Call me on my cell or my desk phone when you're free."

I push open the glass office doors and walk past the reception desk, turning my head to smile at the dimple-cheeked receptionist. "Good morning, Natalie."

She mouths a greeting before answering a call.

It's late morning when Marco's number flashes on my screen. It's unusual for him to call me at work and I'm afraid he's calling to cancel our dinner. He canceled our bike ride, and now this. My body tenses as I wonder whether he's planning on breaking up with me tonight.

Maybe that's why he's taking me to such a smart restaurant: it guarantees him a cordial breakup without any histrionics. I could always tell when Mom's relationships were about to explode. Canceled dates. A sudden coldness. I can't believe it's happening to me, too. The more I think about it, the more convinced I am that he's going to break up with me tonight.

Marco's call eventually goes to voicemail. I quickly turn off my cell phone so he can't get through. It's childish and counterproductive. All it does is make me anxious to find out why Marco was calling me in the first place. I'm about to ring him back when Frank calls me into his office.

"Where's the draft of your story on the Q preview show?"

"It was horrible. Gratuitous violence and pop philosophy. It was the performance art equivalent of a snuff film. I don't think *Cultura* should deign that sort of thing a write-up."

"That's my job to decide, and it's your job to write," he tells me. "I want your copy on my desk tomorrow. Once I get it, then we can talk it through." Before I can respond, we're both called into a meeting on the January issue of the magazine.

When the meeting finally breaks up, I return to my desk and start working on my write-up of the Q exhibition. I do preliminary stuff first, transcribing my notes and going over Q's quotes from the phone interview before I get started on writing the actual article.

Outside, it's a perfect summer day. The sky is a canvas of unblemished blue. I bask in the sunshine streaking across my desk, typing rapidly on my laptop. I'm startled by my desk phone ringing abruptly.

"This is Liv," I say into the receiver.

"Liv?" It's Amy. There's a strange inflection in her tone that sends a shiver down my spine. "Liv, can you come home?" I can tell she's been crying.

"Now?"

"Yes."

"Is it Shawna?"

"Yeah." Her voice wobbles. It sounds as if she's swallowing back tears. "Please come quickly. There's been a . . . I'm . . . sorry. Just come. Please. As soon as you can. . . ." The phone line clicks. She's hung up.

I grab my purse and rush out of the office, muttering something about an emergency to Natalie as I race past the reception desk. I try to call Amy again on my way home in the back of a cab. She's not answering the phone. I stare out the window, sick with worry, as the cab navigates through midday traffic. When the driver finally drops me off on my street, I don't bother to wait for my change. Instead, I stride to the building and race up the stairs to my apartment.

"Amy?" I call out once I'm inside. "Amy?"

There's no response. Her bedroom door is slightly open.

"Amy, is everything all right?"

I push open her door and step into her dimly lit bedroom.

Amy and Marco are in her bed. Naked, with the sheet down to their waists, their heads propped up against the headboard.

"What's going on? The two of you . . ."

I'm so shocked at their betrayal that I don't immediately notice the terrible details. Their eyes are unblinking and there are holes in their chests. Blood trails down to their navels, pooling on the sheets like crimson inkblots.

"They've been sleeping together behind your back for weeks."

I'm about to turn toward the chilling voice behind me when powerful arms restrain me, pulling me into a macabre bear hug. His arms are like steel clamps around my body. I open my mouth to scream, but only a terrified whisper comes out.

"What have you done?" I ask.

"Not me. What have *you* done, Liv?" His breath hits the nape of my neck as he whispers in my ear. "The police will conclude that you were so devastated to find your best friend and your boyfriend in bed that, in the heat of the moment, you went to the kitchen and took out a chef's knife. A nice touch, I might add, given that you're a food writer. You took the knife and came in here, killing them and then yourself," he says. "A double murder and suicide. Tragic but neat, at least from my perspective."

Before I can speak, he takes my hand and forces me to grip the smooth metal handle of a kitchen knife. I look down and see his shoes, which are the color of blood with a unique dotted pattern by the toes.

As I try to squirm out of his arms, he lifts up my hand and forces me to thrust the blade deep into my torso. The pain is excruciating. I crumple onto my knees and collapse on my side. He turns and walks out of the room as I lie on the carpet and stare at Amy's pink kimono rocking on the hook behind her door.

I slide toward Amy's desk and desperately tug the cord of her land-line phone until it tumbles onto the carpet next to me. I grab the receiver and dial clumsily. My hands are slippery with blood as I try to apply pressure on my own wound. I'm vaguely aware of the front door closing.

"Nine-one-one," a woman says. "What is your emergency?"

"I've been stabbed," I gasp into the receiver.

I whisper my address to her, panting heavily as I choke on my own blood.

"What's your name?" the dispatcher asks.

"Liv," I murmur. I can feel myself drifting into unconsciousness.

"Liv, there's an ambulance nearby. It's going to be there real soon. I'll stay with you on the line until it arrives. Okay?"

"I'm so tired," I slur.

"I know you are, honey. But you can't go to sleep. Try to stay awake. . . . Liv, honey," she says. "I need you to stay awake. Okay?"

I don't have enough strength to answer her. I lie with my head on the carpet and stare at Amy's kimono. It turns from pink to black and I pass out.

The dispatcher's strained voice calls out: "Liv, are you awake?"

I snap my eyes open, focusing on the kimono like it's a beacon. "Yeah," I rasp. My voices fades away as darkness engulfs me again.

"Wake up, Liv." Her voice is loud and urgent. "I need you to wake up. Can you do that for me? The ambulance is almost there. Stay with me."

"I'm trying," I gasp.

"You need to stay awake, Liv," she orders. "The ambulance is downstairs. The paramedics are on their way up. Stay awake. You have to do that. Liv? You have to stay awake."

Chapter
Forty-Three

Wednesday 5:29 P.M.

The white bricks of the Ninetieth in Williamsburg had dulled over time, giving the Brooklyn precinct with the second-highest murder rate in the borough the grim air of a military-style bunker.

Detectives Lavelle and Halliday were met by their counterpart, Larry Regan, at the top of the stairs. Regan wore a thin black tie with a white business shirt, his sleeves rolled up to his elbows. He was a gangly young detective with chocolate-brown eyes and a crop of dark hair. In his arms was a huge document box with the files they'd come to collect.

"I'm going to need you to sign for it," he said, handing over a clipboard.

Lavelle leaned the clipboard onto the stair railing and signed the forms before taking the box. The hefty weight was unexpected.

"There's a lot of paperwork in there. It'll take a lot of time for you to go through it all," said Regan. "I worked on the case early on. I can give you a quick overview if you have a few minutes."

"Sure. We can make time," said Lavelle.

Regan fed coins into a vending machine and bought them each a can of soda. Drinks in hand, he led them to a "soft room" at the end of the corridor.

"We won't be disturbed here," he said, turning on the overhead fluorescent lights.

It was called a soft room because it was used for the families of victims and traumatized witnesses. Hard rooms were the hard-core interrogation rooms for suspects, often painted in sickly colors, with minimal furniture and no windows other than a one-way mirror.

The soft room had a table and chairs, a couple of sofas and a bookshelf with scuffed toys and magazines. At the far end was a square window that looked out onto the precinct parking lot, where squad cars and unmarked police vehicles were parked in untidy rows.

Regan unpacked three bulging files from the document box. Each file had several strategically placed elastic bands around it to stop documents from falling out.

"That's a lot of material," said Lavelle.

"The investigation was extensive." Regan tapped the document box. "This case happened almost two and a half years ago. It officially remains 'unsolved.' Right now, it might as well be a cold case."

"Why?"

"It's been open season around here lately. We're getting homicides every day. There's no time to deal with unsolveds right now. Plus, it was Krause's case. When he moved to Queens, it was given to another senior detective. He's on leave right now, which is why you're talking to me."

"You were Krause's partner?" Lavelle asked.

"Briefly. We didn't see eye to eye."

"I bet you didn't," Lavelle said. "Why the interest in this case?"

"Because I think we screwed it up," said Regan, not mincing words.

"Why?"

He let Lavelle and Halliday flick through the pages of the files while he recounted the basic facts of the case and the investigation.

"It was a double murder," he said. "Liv Reese's boyfriend, Marco Reggio, and her best friend, Amy Decker, were killed. Liv Reese was the only survivor. She suffered a near-fatal knife wound. Amy Decker was a doctor finishing her internship at Bellevue. Originally from Wisconsin. She was killed a couple of weeks after her twenty-seventh birthday. Reggio was an ex-finance guy turned entrepreneur. Age thirty-four. They were having an affair behind Liv Reese's back. In fact they were in bed together when they were killed."

"Do you think Liv Reese killed them?" Halliday asked, looking up from the file.

"The way Krause saw it, Liv Reese caught them in bed together. Killed them both and then stabbed herself. Murder-suicide. She covered it up by calling nine-one-one and pretending she'd been attacked."

"Why would she call nine-one-one if it was a murder-suicide? She didn't need to worry about covering it up if she was dead," Halliday pointed out.

"Exactly," said Regan. "There are other inconsistencies, as you'll see in the files. It didn't help that her recollections of the murders were almost nonexistent."

"She didn't remember anything at all?"

"She barely had a pulse when the paramedics reached her. She was in a coma for almost two weeks. When she came out of it, she remembered almost nothing about the murder. She did have flashbacks months later, but her recollections weren't consistent with the evidence."

"How so?"

"For example, she had a flashback about shoes covered in blood, except there was no blood trail on the carpet."

Halliday shuffled through the crime scene photos. She paused to look at a ghoulish photo of Amy Decker and Marco Reggio. They were sitting in bed, naked, with a bloodied sheet at their waists. Both had been stabbed in their torsos, much the way that Ted Cole had been stabbed.

She handed the photo to Lavelle. He nodded. It was uncanny. A single stab wound. Same location. Similar MO to the Ted Cole killing.

"It sounds as if you didn't agree with Krause that Reese did it?" Lavelle asked.

"Krause believed it was an open-shut case; jealous girlfriend stabs cheating boyfriend and his lover who happened to be her best friend. Jealousy and betrayal, prime motives for murder."

"It is a convincing scenario," said Lavelle.

"I agree. Amy Decker's family thought so, too. But the anomalies bothered me. I carried out my own inquiries after hours. The more I learned, the less sure I was that Liv Reese had done it."

"Why?" Halliday asked.

"I consulted with a top forensic expert on knife wounds. He told me there was no way the stab wound in Liv Reese's torso was self-inflicted. She's left-handed. The wound would have been made by someone who was right-handed due to the angle the blade penetrated the body."

"Forensic experts can be wrong," said Halliday.

"There were other leads that we never followed up on. Potential suspects."

"Like who?"

"An artist whose exhibition Liv Reese reviewed. Have you ever heard of Zee?"

Halliday nodded. Lavelle shook his head.

"Zee's an avant-garde artist who was accused of beating up his pregnant girlfriend," Regan said. "He was outed on social media, and his career was basically over. He reinvented himself as a guerrilla performance artist known as Q. At least, that's what a recent exposé in *The New York Times* suggests."

"What does Zee have to do with Liv Reese?" she asked.

"She wrote a scathing review of Zee's last exhibition before he went underground. Her review was the beginning of the end of his career," Regan said. "Shortly before the Decker-Reggio murders, Liv was invited to a preview exhibition by Q. She found it violent and disturbing. She didn't want to write about it, but her editor insisted. She was working on the article on the afternoon of the murders."

"So you're saying that if Zee and Q were one and the same person, then it's possible he was trying to get back at her for ruining his career."

"Yes," said Regan. "I went through her notebook after the murders. The Q exhibition was creepy as hell. It was almost as if he brought her there to scare her."

"Why do you say that?"

"Because the exhibition that she described in her reporter's notebook contained themes of violence, misogyny, and bondage that were completely different to the actual exhibition that ran months later."

"Were there other suspects?"

"A photographer, George Yanis."

"What's his story?"

"He was fired after Liv Reese filed a sexual harassment complaint against him at the magazine where she worked. She wasn't the first, but he blamed her. He told people he'd get even with her. Krause flatly refused to look into him as a possible suspect. Then there were the stalking complaints she made in the weeks before the murders."

"Stalking? She was stalked?" Lavelle asked, snapping to attention.

"The police reports are in the files." Regan flicked through the folders until he found several reports, which he handed to Halliday and Lavelle.

"You're telling us that Krause didn't look into the stalking when he was investigating the Decker-Reggio murders?" Halliday asked, surprised.

"He thought it was bogus. He thought she'd made up the stalking incidents because she'd intended to kill Amy and Marco and wanted to create an alternate suspect. He said it showed premeditation. He believed Liv knew Amy and Marco were sleeping together. According to some of the neighbors, they were hardly discreet."

"What did you think?" Lavelle asked.

"I went with Krause to her apartment after one of her stalking complaints. This was a few days before the double murder. She was terrified. It wasn't acting. Krause thought it was a big joke. When we left, he told me she was a nut job. Maybe he was right. But her fear, it was real."

"Why did Krause think it was a joke?" Halliday asked.

"She claimed a stranger put a casserole in her oven and brought her dry cleaning back home. She said he left flowers next to her bed. A week or so earlier, she said someone had put a carton of milk in her fridge while she slept."

"That all sounds . . . insane," said Halliday.

"Yup, but some stalkers will do things that are bat-shit crazy," said Regan. "You can't imagine what these people will do to insert themselves into someone's life. I had a case once where the stalker got a job as a window cleaner so he could see into his victim's apartment. The night I was there I saw something that made me think Liv Reese was telling the truth."

"What was it?"

"While I was in her bedroom on the night Krause and I were called over there, I had a prickly feeling we were being watched. When everyone left the room, I turned off the lights and stayed behind. I saw a man holding binoculars in an apartment across the street," he said. "Liv Reese was definitely being watched. I know for sure because I saw him watching her."

"You told Krause?"

"He dismissed it as a creepy neighbor. Maybe if he'd taken her stalking complaints seriously then the murders wouldn't have happened."

Regan said that he'd seen Liv throw the flowers and chocolates in a trash can on the street after they drove away from her apartment. He'd driven around the block and gone back to collect them.

"The box of chocolates sent with the roses was an exclusive Belgian brand. Eight bucks a chocolate. All handmade. I took the box to the store hoping they could tell me who'd bought them. They insisted that someone had replaced their truffles with cheap imitations."

"Why would someone do that?"

Regan shrugged. "No idea, but Liv Reese claimed to have been drugged after eating one of the truffles. It was while she was drugged that she claimed someone came into her apartment. If the truffles delivered to her were laced with sedatives, then it would make sense for whoever sent them to switch them over when he was in the apartment to cover his tracks."

Halliday skimmed the forensics report from the double murder two years earlier.

"None of what you said, even if true, contradicts the possibility that she murdered her friends," she said, looking up from the report.

"True," said Regan. "But we never did get to the bottom of some of the other creepy things that went on before the murders."

"Such as?" Halliday asked.

"The dry cleaner said her clothes were collected by her boyfriend. When I asked him to describe the boyfriend, he said it was a man with light brown hair, tall and thin with a bump on his nose and a gap between his teeth," he said. "Marco Reggio didn't look a bit like that."

"Did you ever speak to the neighbor across the street? The one you thought was spying on the apartment?" Halliday asked.

"Krause chewed me out when I admitted that I'd looked into her stalking claims and that I thought there might be something to it. He insisted there was no stalker. He was certain Liv Reese had committed the murders. She was still unconscious in the hospital at that point, and he was biding his time for her to come out of the coma so he could interrogate her. He planned to get her to confess and charge her with the Decker-Reggio murders."

Regan added that he'd just earned his shield. It was his first gig in homicide and he had been told to defer to Krause as the more experienced detective.

"We had a big argument. Krause said that by looking into other lines of investigation, I was helping the defense build a case that Liv Reese didn't murder her friends."

A future defense team would get all the information gathered during the discovery process, including everything that Regan had turned up in his after-hours investigation.

"Krause said the defense would twist the information that I'd found to make the jury think there were other possible suspects. To create reasonable doubt," said Regan. "That's why we had a blowup, Krause and me. I resented his accusation that I was screwing up the case just because I wanted to make sure we arrested the right person. Krause stopped me from investigating further. He said it was our job to find the evidence to prove the Reese woman's guilt. Period. He didn't want any time wasted looking for other suspects."

"Yet Liv Reese was never charged," Halliday pointed out.

"The prosecutor refused to move forward with an indictment," said Regan. "She said Krause's case was all supposition, with little evidence. Meanwhile, I found out the neighbor who'd been watching her apartment with binoculars moved out the day before the murder. It was a short-term rental. He'd paid for a week of rent that he didn't use, and let me tell you, the rent didn't come cheap."

"Sounds like he wanted to get out in a hurry," said Halliday.

"Fortunately, he was a slob. He didn't bother to take out the trash. I found a dozen empty beer cans and a pile of take-out containers in the apartment when the janitor let me in. I took the beer cans and gave them to a friend at the forensics lab."

Regan took out a second file. He went through the papers one by one until he found the one he needed. It was a fingerprint report. He held it up in the air so they could both see it.

"His name's Joe Chalmers," he said. "Long record. Breaking and entering. Car theft. One assault years ago. He was cashing welfare checks at the time of the murder. So how could he afford to rent the apartment opposite Liv Reese's place?"

"Someone else paid for it," said Halliday.

"I believe so."

"Did you track down Joe Chalmers?"

"He skipped town. Nobody knew where he'd gone."

"Maybe we should look for him again," Halliday suggested to Lavelle.

"Actually, when I heard you were interested in seeing the Decker-Reggio murder file, I looked him up," Regan said. "He's back in town. Living in public housing. I thought I'd check in on him sometime."

"Why wait?" said Lavelle, grabbing his jacket from the back of his chair as he stood up.

Chapter
Forty-Four

Wednesday 5:34 P.M.

Dr. Brenner's secretary leaves the reception desk to print an insurance form for a patient who's just arrived. I take advantage of her absence to slip out of the clinic and head to the nearest subway station, where I rush into a train car a moment before the doors close.

The late afternoon light is subdued and the street smells of fresh rain when I emerge from the subway steps onto the street and walk along the slick sidewalk toward my office.

This mysterious Ted was listed as my emergency contact in my file at Dr. Brenner's office. Incredibly, the address listed for him is the *Cultura* office.

Natalie's not sitting behind the reception desk when I go in. Instead there's a temp with cropped hair and platinum bangs. Her mascara has run and black stains have formed dark pools under her eyes. Track marks of tears run down her cheeks.

"Are you all right?" I ask.

She nods and shakes her head at the same time. Then she bursts into tears. "You'd better go in."

The office has been redecorated from understated classy neutrals to a brash color scheme of urban grays with touches of electric blue and lime green. The place looks more like a hotel lobby than an office.

Despite the upbeat decor, a sense of despair hangs over the place. In the middle of the office, a woman with corkscrew curls hugs another woman with long red hair. Their eyes are puffy. They've both been crying.

"I can't believe it," says the woman with red hair.

"Neither can I," says her friend as they embrace.

"What happened?" I ask.

Both women swallow hard like they're about to deliver bad news.

"Liv, you should sit down," says the woman with the curls.

"Why? What's wrong?"

My mind races as I try to think what could have happened to cause such despair. I look across the office into an expansive glass-walled meeting room, where staff sit around a boardroom table looking shell-shocked. Some hold their hands to their mouths. Others openly sob.

"What's happened?" Panic laces my voice.

"I can't put it into words because if I do, then it will be real . . . and I don't want it to be real," says the woman with the corkscrew hair.

Her friend with red hair takes my hand and lowers me onto a backless round sofa, like I'm an invalid. "This is so hard, Liv," she says, sitting next to me and resting our interlocked hands on her tartan skirt. I look into her despondent eyes in confusion and try to figure out how she knows my name.

"Ted is dead," she says, finally. Her freckled face puckers in sorrow. Fresh tears well in her eyes.

"Dead?" I respond weakly. They both burst into tears.

Their sadness is infectious. Tears stream down my cheeks and my chest is heavy with grief.

I don't know why I'm so emotional. After all, I don't actually know who Ted is, other than that Dr. Brenner seems to think he's my friend. I came to the office to find him.

My voice trembles. "Everyone must be in shock."

"We're devastated. We can't even imagine what you're going through. You've been through so much already, Liv. And now this . . ." Her voice drops off.

I'm hit by a sudden dizziness as her words reverberate in my head. Dr. Brenner also alluded to a trauma in my past. My body sways. Both women grab hold of me as if they're afraid I'll collapse.

"We should get her something to drink," one of them says to the other.

They help me to the office pantry, where someone pulls out a white chair for me at a matching table and someone else brings me a Coke.

"For the sugar," she says, pulling the aluminum tab with a hiss and handing me the cold can.

I take a few sips and set the can aside, watching colleagues console each other with drawn-out comforting hugs. Someone turns on an enormous television hanging on a wall in the pantry area. The electronic theme music of the afternoon news program blasts across the office.

"Police have released the name of the man who was murdered while he slept in a midtown apartment last night," says the newsreader. "He is Edward 'Ted' Cole, an executive at *Cultura Magazine*. Police say they have opened an investigation into his . . ."

The name echoes in my head as the TV blares. Ted is dead. That's why he didn't come with me to my appointment with Dr. Brenner.

Footage runs on the screen showing the words *WAKE UP!* written in blood on a window.

I have the same message on my wrist, just like the man who called me at that grim basement apartment earlier said when he made those vile accusations. He suggested that I murdered someone this morning. I gasp as I realize that "someone" must be Ted. Is it possible that I killed the very man that everyone in this office is mourning?

There's no way I could have killed him. I'm not violent. I faint at the sight of blood. It's ridiculous to even think I might have been responsible. But Ted is dead, and I have a big black hole in my memory and a slogan written on my skin that matches the one daubed at the crime scene.

Looking out the window, I try to absorb everything that's happened since I arrived at my office. Down on the street below, pedestrians crowd the sidewalks like pesky ants as they head home from work. It's a scene I've seen thousands of times before. This time it feels as if I'm watching it from another dimension.

The reflection of the red-haired woman in the tartan skirt appears in the window. "I'm so sorry for your loss, Liv," she says, standing behind me.

"Thank you," I answer without turning around.

"Even though you and Ted ended your engagement, it must be unbelievably painful. He always raved about how much talent you had, and how you worked your way up the ladder at the magazine," she stutters. "I guess I just want you to know that I'm here for you. We all are."

I'm shocked to learn that Ted and I were engaged. How could I not remember the man I was going to marry? "Why would someone kill him?" I ask.

She swings around to face the reception area.

"Looks like the police are here to find out," she says.

Chapter
Forty-Five

Wednesday 6:14 P.M.

Joe Chalmers was carrying home a six-pack of beer from the bus stop when the three detectives beelined toward him on the concrete expanse outside the public housing building where he lived with his girlfriend.

Lavelle and Halliday followed Regan toward Chalmers, striding in unison, their badges displayed on the waistbands of their suits. It was obvious that Chalmers immediately knew they were law enforcement. He was visibly torn between dropping the cans of Bud and bolting off, or staying put and talking to the police.

"He's going to run," Halliday said, reading his body language.

Chalmers's flight instinct, honed by years of being on the wrong side of the law, took over from his common sense. He dropped the beer with a thud and bolted toward the street, where a bus was pulling up.

Halliday, who was on the side closest to his escape route, sprinted after him. She chased him onto the grass, where he tripped over an exposed tree root and went flying.

"You okay there?" She approached the patch of grass where he was lying splayed on the ground and held out a hand to help him up. He looked at her outstretched hand skeptically.

"We can talk here or we can talk at the precinct," she said. "If we take you to the precinct, then we might as well charge you with failing to stop when requested by a police officer. I'm sure we'll think up a few other charges while we're at it. What's your preference?"

"I'll talk." He scrambled to his feet without her help. He had a gap between his two front teeth just the way the dry cleaner had described to Detective Regan two years earlier.

"What do you want to know?" he asked.

"Two years ago, you were living in an apartment that you couldn't possibly afford in Williamsburg," Halliday said. She recited the address. "What were you doing there?"

Halliday's eyes fixed on Lavelle for a second as she waited for Chalmers to answer. She didn't want the other detectives joining them and changing the dynamics. Lavelle nodded to let her know they'd give her space.

"I don't got to justify where I live," Chalmers said.

"Sure you do," said Halliday. "Especially when the neighbor you'd been spying on with binoculars turns up dead."

"I didn't have anything to do with that. I wasn't even living there when it happened. Left town a couple of days before." He slapped his hands together to wipe off the dirt from his fall.

"How did you know about the murders?" Halliday asked.

"Read it in the papers."

"I don't believe you," said Halliday. She reached for her handcuffs and snapped them open.

"Okay, okay. I'll tell you what I know," he said. "A dude paid me to live in that apartment for a couple of weeks. In return I had to do chores."

"What chores?"

"I had to drop off laundry. One time, I had to buy food from some fancy restaurant and heat it up in their oven. Another time I had to go inside in the middle of the night and put a carton of milk in the fridge. I didn't hurt anyone. I just did things to mess with the women living there."

"What was the point of messing with them?"

"Dunno. He never said. He just messaged me things to do. It was harmless stuff. Easiest money I ever made," he said. "I only went into the apartment a couple of times. I didn't break any laws."

"Other than breaking and entering. It wasn't your apartment," Halliday pointed out.

"Yeah, okay. But I didn't hurt anyone, or steal anything. He said if I did, I wouldn't get the rest of the money."

"How much were you paid?"

"Two grand up front. I was supposed to get another three at the end. Never got it."

"Because you skipped town?" Halliday asked.

"Yeah."

"Who hired you?"

"Some guy. Met him at a bar. He gave me a burner phone. We communicated by text after that," he said. "He messaged me tasks. Instructions. I texted him back when they were completed."

"What instructions did he give you?"

"The things I already told you. One time I had to leave flowers and chocolates by the front door. Then he texted me half an hour later and told me to go into the apartment and leave more flowers by her bed and replace the chocolates in the box with new ones. He'd put something in the chocolates to make her fall asleep and he wanted them all replaced."

"Did he explain why he wanted you to do these things?" Halliday asked.

"He said he wanted to scare her." Chalmers laughed nervously.

"Well, he scared her all right. I'd watch her looking out the windows, trying to figure out whether she was going nuts."

"How did you get in and out of the apartment?" Halliday asked.

"He gave me keys. Told me to dress like a plumber and act like I belonged. That way nobody would be the wiser. It worked perfectly."

"If you didn't do anything violent, like you claim, why did you skip town?"

"He called me with one final task."

"What was it?" Halliday asked.

"He wanted me to kill them."

"Kill who?"

"The hot blonde who lived in the apartment and the guy she was sleeping with when her roommate was at work. Dark-haired guy. Looked Italian. He wanted them both dead. Promised to pay me another five grand."

"What did you tell him?"

"I said no," Chalmers said. "Murder is hard-core. I don't do stuff like that. He said he'd find someone else. A few days later he told me to meet at a warehouse at Hunts Point to get the rest of my cash. I didn't turn up."

"Why not?"

"It stunk. I worried he'd try to make sure I kept my mouth shut. Permanently. So I did a disappearing act."

"Who set you up with this guy?"

"Dude I knew used to give me jobs. Debt collection, mostly. He set up the meet. Turned out to be a bad move on his part."

"Why?"

"Because he's dead."

"How did he die?"

He shrugged. "Heard he was stabbed. Body was found floating in the East River. When I found out, I figured it was the man at the bar who did it, or someone he paid to cover his tracks for him. I made a good decision to get out of town. I've kept a low profile ever since. More than two years now on the straight and narrow."

"What did the man who hired you look like?"

He shrugged. "No idea. He sat next to me in a crowded bar. Told me to keep looking straight ahead while he slid over the phone. All I saw were his hands. No tattoos. No wedding ring. Nicely trimmed nails. Looked like he took care of himself. Dude didn't drink either," he said. "I thought that was weird. Who asks to meet at a bar and doesn't order a drink?"

When Halliday indicated she was done, Lavelle approached, holding the pack of beer that Chalmers had ditched. A couple of cans were dented, but they were otherwise intact.

"Not sure if I did you a favor by rescuing your beer," Lavelle said, tossing the box to Chalmers. "So here's what happens next. Detective Regan will take you to the precinct where you'll provide him with a sworn statement."

Chalmers breathed hard with a mixture of fear and relief as he nodded. He stepped forward to follow Regan when Lavelle slammed his palm hard against Chalmers's chest.

"If you disappear again, then me and Detective Halliday over here will personally look for you. We'll haul your ass back and we'll throw the book at you so hard your hair will be snow-white when you get out of the slammer."

As they climbed back into their car, Lavelle asked Halliday if she believed Chalmers's story.

"Why lie about something like that?" asked Halliday, starting the engine. "He has nothing to gain and everything to lose."

She pulled the car out into steady traffic. They drove in silence for a while, contemplating how Chalmers's information potentially changed the complexion of the case.

Halliday finally spoke. "Ted Cole's fiancée, Elisabeth, told us that he rented that apartment as a safe house for Liv Reese. He believed Amy and Marco's killer was coming after her."

"Why would the killer bother getting rid of Liv Reese, two years later?" Lavelle said. "Especially since she never remembered what happened."

"The killer might not know that," said Halliday, looking over her shoulder as she changed lanes. "Even if the killer knew she'd never remembered what happened that day, imagine the stress of knowing an eyewitness's memory could return any time. Now that really is a motive for murder."

"Where are you going with this, Halliday?"

"Jack, I think the killer is looking for Liv Reese. I think this whole thing is about tying off loose ends from the Decker-Reggio murders. Liv Reese is the biggest loose end of all. We need to find her before he does."

Chapter
Forty-Six

Wednesday 6:37 P.M.

The *Cultura Magazine* meeting room is like a fishbowl for all the privacy it offers. The police officers must quickly realize that everyone in the office is surreptitiously watching them through the glass walls because somebody lowers the internal privacy shade so we can't see inside.

An HR manager emerges from the meeting room and walks to the middle of the office as if she's about to make an announcement. Everyone drifts over to listen.

"The police are here, as you've all no doubt noticed. They've asked for everyone to stay back to be questioned. Detectives will be here shortly. Once they arrive, they'll split up and talk to us individually. They've asked that nobody leave until they've been questioned."

Everyone scatters as they wait to be summoned for their interview with the police. A telephone rings somewhere near me. My heart rate goes up with each successive ring. I grip my hands into fists until my knuckles are white and my nails cut into my palms.

The phone stops ringing as abruptly as it began.

"Liv. Liv."

My name is being called out by a disembodied voice behind a white partition.

"Liv, there's a call for you," says a man with John Lennon glasses, holding up a desk phone.

"Hello?" I press the phone receiver hard against my ear.

"Liv, it's me," says the same muffled voice I heard on the phone at the basement apartment.

"What do you want?"

"The cops in your office are going to arrest you once they know you're there. The net is tightening around you. I can help you, Liv."

"How?" I ask suspiciously.

"Your memory lapses. I'll tell you what happened last night. I'll tell you what you've forgotten."

"Why should I trust you?"

"Because Ted asked me to take care of you. I'm outside your building. Come down now and I'll explain everything."

"I need to think about it."

"You don't have time." His voice fades in and out as a police siren wails over the phone line. "Come down and I'll tell you what happened. I'll help you clear your name."

Car doors slam in the background.

"That noise you just heard are more cops," he tells me. "They're coming up to your office to look for you. Come down now, Liv. I'll wait for you outside the coffee place on the corner."

"I don't know." I'm torn between fear of this stranger and an overwhelming desire to hear what he knows about me.

He senses my desperation to find out the truth. "Write my phone number on your hand in case you can't find me," he orders. He dictates a cell phone number and tells me to write above it the words "Call for help."

"I'm waiting for you downstairs," he says. "Come down now. You don't have much time left until they come for you, Liv. Hurry." The call disconnects with a click.

Two police officers stand near the reception desk. Their casual stance doesn't fool anyone. It's obvious they've been posted to guard the office entrance.

Someone turns up the volume of the TV. Synthesized theme music blares, drawing everyone to the TV like moths to a flame. The evening news is about to begin.

"Police are investigating the brutal murder of a magazine executive, who was found stabbed to death this morning," the anchor says.

A photo of a smiling man with tawny hair and crinkled eyes appears on the screen. Everyone around me lets out an audible cry of shock at the sight of their colleague's photo on the news.

"Police are asking the public to call the hotline if they have details of the victim's whereabouts in the hours before he died. Police are particularly interested in finding a woman with long hair who was seen with the victim before his death."

The anchor pauses for a moment. "We've just obtained CCTV footage taken outside the building where the murder occurred. Our sources tell us the woman seen fleeing the scene is the prime suspect in this morning's murder."

Grainy security camera footage shows a woman with long hair in a loose plait emerging from a dark lane. I stare dumbfounded at the TV screen. The only difference between me and the woman on the TV is that her hair is incredibly long, whereas mine is cropped short. That woman is me. I was there last night when Ted Cole was murdered. I'm the police's prime suspect.

"Anyone who has seen this woman, or who has information on her whereabouts, should contact NYPD at the hotline . . ."

I'm barely conscious of the news anchor's voice reading out the hotline phone number as I glance furtively at the huddle of horrified magazine staff. Someone is bound to notice the resemblance between me and the police's prime suspect, despite our vastly different haircuts and the haziness of the image.

I need to get out of here. I can't go through the main doors. The cops standing near the reception desk will stop me.

Everyone returns to their desks when the news program moves to another story. I pick up a file and go into the photocopy room near the back of the office where the emergency door to the fire escape stairs is located. I turn on the copier and print off a ream of blank pages to cover the sound of me pushing open the fire escape door and shutting it behind me.

I race down the stairs, taking them two at a time, until I'm in a rear alley, trying to decide where to go now that I know I'm wanted for murder.

Chapter
Forty-Seven

Two Days Earlier

Bang! Bang! Violent pounding rouses me from a deep sleep. There are three short bursts followed by a long knock that seems to go on for seconds after it's finished. *Baaaaang!!!*

I bolt upright, confused. Instead of my usual view of the flower-box window in the apartment across the street, I'm facing a cracked wall covered with writing.

The banging resumes, louder than before. This time the person knocking rattles a door handle and calls out my name.

I scramble up from the camping mattress. It's on the floor, which explains the ache in my lower back as I rise to my feet, disoriented and confused. Everything about this place is unfamiliar; the mattress, the odor of mildew seeping through the apartment. The newspaper clippings and paranoid writing slapped across the walls.

The apartment reverberates with another bang on the door. This time it's more of an open palm slap than a pounding fist. It sounds as if whoever is on the other side is about to give up.

"Liv. Please. Let me in," pleads a man with a British accent.

I'm wearing a sleeveless tight camisole and bikini underwear. Unsure of where my clothes are, I grab an oversized sweatshirt hanging off the closet handle and charge toward the front door.

"Who are you and what do you want?" I call out.

"Liv." His relief is audible. "I've been so worried about you. Please let me in. It's Ted."

I step toward the peephole. A man in jeans and a brown bomber jacket is on the other side, looking furtively over his shoulder.

"I don't know anyone called Ted." I clutch the collar of the sweatshirt.

"Yes, you do. You don't remember me, Liv, just like you don't remember the apartment where you woke up. There are a lot of things you don't remember. It's too complicated to explain through a door. Let me come in and I'll tell you everything."

I'm about to unlock the bolt when I see a Post-it note taped to the doorframe. It says: DON'T OPEN THE DOOR TO ANYONE!!! Underneath I've written: EXCEPT TED.

I look through the peephole again. He rubs the back of his neck anxiously. Something tells me I can trust this man with rumpled tawny hair and dimples denting his handsome cheeks.

I turn the bolt and let him into the apartment. He comes in and immediately locks the door behind him, looking through the peephole to make sure he wasn't followed.

"Liv, there's not a lot of time to explain," he says. "You're in danger. I've rented an apartment where you can stay until we figure out what to do. Grab some clothes. We need to leave quickly."

I barely hear him as my gaze takes in the dim mustard light of the apartment where I apparently slept last night. The old cracked leather sofa has stuffing coming out of the upholstery and the coffee table is covered with clutter and empty take-out cups of coffee. There are blister packs of medication strewn everywhere. I'm disgusted I spent the night in such a grimy place.

"Where am I? And who are you?" I ask.

The man puts his right hand into his jacket as if he's taking out a weapon. I instinctively flinch, afraid he's going to hurt me. He removes his hand slowly and produces a photo. It's the two of us with our arms around each other, laughing into the camera. I'm showing off a sparkling diamond ring on my finger.

"This was taken the day I proposed to you, Liv."

I'm speechless, transfixed by the expression of bliss on our faces. "Why don't I remember you?"

"It's a long story. I'll tell you everything. But first, I have to get you out of here, Liv."

He goes into the bedroom and pulls clothes off hangers, tossing them into a duffel bag. He throws jeans and a top in my direction and I dress quickly as he packs. Next to the camping mattress is a phone with a cracked screen. I stick it in the back pocket of my jeans and cover it with a long cardigan with big pockets.

He's in the living room, frantically rummaging through the clutter on the coffee table, when I come out of the bedroom, fully dressed in black-heeled ankle boots.

"Your journal, Liv. Where is it?"

"What journal?"

I stare in shock at the living room wall. "What the . . ."

The wall is covered with photos of Amy and Marco and a garbled mess of newspaper clippings. Arrows point in multiple directions between notes written directly on the wall.

"What is this?"

"I'll explain later. We need to get out of here. You're not safe. I'll come back tomorrow to get your journal and anything else you need."

He unlocks the door and opens it a fraction, sticking his head out to look down the corridor. We hurry down a dingy, airless corridor that smells of damp and greasy cooking fumes. Instead of taking the elevator, we sprint up the emergency stairs to ground level, where we come out into an alley at the rear of the building. I move toward the street, but he blocks my way with his arm.

"Wait." He steps out of the alley to check that the coast is clear.

He takes my arm and escorts me to a silver car parked farther down the street, which he unlocks with a remote-controlled key. He throws the duffel bag in the trunk and tells me to get into the backseat and lie low. He fires up the ignition before he even buckles up.

"Stay down, Liv." He glances back at me. "I'll explain everything at the safe house."

Chapter
Forty-Eight

Wednesday 7:21 P.M.

Streetlights cast a warm glow as Jack Lavelle parked his car opposite the Brooklyn building where Liv Reese and Amy Decker used to live.

Lavelle and Halliday leaned back in their car seats and watched the backlit silhouettes of the couple who now lived in the apartment move across the drawn window shades like shadow puppets as they cooked dinner. Below the kitchen windows, the street door to the building was shut and still in the evening gloom.

Liv Reese had arrived at that entrance in the early hours of the morning, firmly believing she still lived there. There was a good chance she'd return again if she fell asleep and woke without any memory of what had transpired over the past two years.

"It's as if she's living the same day over and over again," said Halliday. "She wakes every morning thinking her life is the way it was two years ago, before she was almost murdered."

"I'd feel bad for her if I didn't think she killed Ted Cole," Lavelle commented.

"Despite what Joe Chalmers told us?"

"I thought about it on the drive over," Lavelle said. "We're not investigating the Decker-Reggio murders. We're investigating the Ted Cole murder. We can't ignore that the evidence points to Liv Reese as Cole's killer."

"Maybe it only looks that way because we still know so little," Halliday said. Outside, a bearded hipster carrying a guitar case scrambled into a van that had stopped for him in the narrow car-lined street.

"It more than looks that way," said Lavelle. "Liv Reese's prints were found at the murder scene. The WAKE UP! sign on the window is exactly the type of message she writes to herself, according to the British social worker who taught her to write reminders on her hands as memory aids. Let's not forget the victim was Liv Reese's former fiancé. And he was about to get married."

"Not everyone murders their ex-fiancé just because they're getting married," said Halliday. "I didn't kill mine. In fact, I went to his wedding, danced with him and his bride. I even gave one of the speeches. The groom was blushing more than the bride by the time I was done!"

"You're not erratic, sleep deprived to the point of being psychotic, and your fingerprints aren't all over a murder scene," Lavelle pointed out.

After a tense moment of silence, he turned toward Halliday. "You don't really think that someone else murdered Ted Cole, do you?"

"All I'm saying is this case is like an iceberg. The more we find out, the more I realize that we're only seeing a fraction of what's there," she answered. "I'd like to know a heck of a lot more before I slap cuffs on anyone."

Time dragged on. Lavelle tapped his fingers restlessly on the steering wheel as they watched Liv Reese's old apartment building.

"It's the waiting that kills me," Halliday muttered, stifling a yawn.

"It comes with the job. Along with the two P's."

"What's the two P's?" Halliday asked.

"Patience and persistence."

"It was the same when I was in the military. We'd wait for days, even weeks, for a Taliban cell to break cover. When they did, half the time another unit would get the action, or everything would be over in minutes."

"Sounds like you miss it?"

"We all hated it while we were there. Couldn't wait to get home. We literally counted the days. But once we were home, we all felt a loss. We missed being around each other. I guess we missed the military life as well. I even missed the damn reveille. Imagine missing being woken by a bugle at dawn each morning!" She laughed dryly.

"It must have been tough to return to civilian life."

"Others had it worse."

"Like your friend. The one who died?" Lavelle asked.

"Him among others. Veterans have a suicide rate more than twice that of civilians."

"How did you get yourself on track?"

"I joined the NYPD," answered Halliday, hoping that would end that line of discussion. She was loath to talk about the dark days she'd experienced when she was first discharged. Regret mixed with relief was a potent combination. There was guilt, too, at leaving behind local translators and assets whose lives would always be at risk if the Taliban ever so much as suspected they'd helped the US military.

Halliday had fought hard for one of her informants in particular to be moved stateside. He was Emad, a medical student whose brother was in the Taliban. Emad had risked his life to bring her valuable intel on plans to bomb a humanitarian convoy. Her efforts to get Emad out had come to nothing other than her being ordered to redeploy two weeks ahead of schedule. It had taken a long time for her to come to terms with her abrupt departure from Afghanistan, leaving Emad and others in the lurch without being able to tell them that she'd failed them. For a while, the guilt had eaten into her so deep that it had almost overwhelmed her.

"Being a cop gave me purpose. It's the ones who can't find a purpose that get into trouble."

Halliday quickly changed the subject. "I'll let you in on a secret. I'm a little afraid of you, Jack," she joked. "In fact, I think most of the detectives at the precinct feel the same way."

"You don't strike me as the kind of person who's afraid of anything."

"Okay. Let's say I'm intimidated by you, not afraid," she clarified. "You have the highest solve rate of any detective in the city. You prefer to work alone. You turn down promotions routinely. It's considered a monumental feat to get you to attend Thursday night drinks."

"I signed up to be a homicide detective. Not a pencil pusher with a fancy title, even if they do get more money. As for the rest, I'm picky when it comes to partners. Eventually, the captain gave up and allowed me to work alone."

"You didn't answer my question about drinks night."

"My son sleeps over most Thursday nights. I get little enough time with him as it is." Lavelle turned on the car radio.

They listened in silence as Alicia Keys sang about dreams being made in concrete jungles to the faint orchestra of clattering pots and pans and cutlery scraping against plates drifting down from apartments along the street. Halliday felt a stab of hunger. Dinner, she told herself, would have to wait until later.

"I'm betting Al's not coming back," she said.

"That's the rumor."

"The precinct rumor mill is more accurate than the evening news," Halliday observed. "I'm guessing the captain partnered us up on this case because he wants you to vet me?"

"The captain wants to know how you think, and most importantly how you act under pressure. He also wants to know if you're a team player. Al's a great detective. His will be big shoes to fill."

"What are you going to tell the captain about me?" Halliday asked.

"It's too early to say, although so far I'm impressed."

"Even though we disagree over whether Liv Reese should be our prime suspect in this case?"

"Especially because we disagree," he said. "I prefer to work with people who aren't afraid to speak up. There are too many people who self-censor because they're afraid they'll rile people up or say something that goes against the consensus. I'm not like that. I value open, well-reasoned debate. I think it makes us better detectives."

Farther down the street, a man arriving home from work pushed a garbage can to the curb. Lavelle watched him with rapt attention.

"Look at both sides of the street," he told Halliday. "What does it tell you?"

Halliday looked around. Cans lined the curbs on both sides of the street.

"Tomorrow must be trash day."

"Now ask yourself, what were the two things missing from the Ted Cole murder scene?" Lavelle asked.

"The murder weapon and . . . Liv Reese."

"Exactly," said Lavelle. "Rosco messaged me while we were heading over here to say the search team still hasn't found the murder weapon near the crime scene. It occurs to me there's a possibility that Liv Reese might have tossed the weapon when she was here early this morning. The garbage cans along this street are going to be collected first thing tomorrow morning. I'd feel a heck of a lot better if I knew what was in them."

"You want to search every can on the street?"

"Not the whole street. But I sure would like to poke about in the trash over there." Lavelle pointed to a row of cans near the entrance to Liv Reese's old building.

He unclipped his seat belt. "Come on, Detective," he said, swinging open his car door. "It'll be fun. This is the glamorous part of detective work they don't show on TV."

Chapter
Forty-Nine

Lavelle popped the trunk and removed a package containing disposable overalls, masks, and gloves, as well as a roll of giant extra-thick
trash bags in case they needed to transport trash to the precinct to sort
through.

"Are you seriously telling me you keep a trash collection kit in your
car, just in case?" Halliday asked in amazement. "You must have been
a boy scout as a kid."

"If you've ever had to stand in a Dumpster with garbage up to your
neck, ruining a brand-new five-hundred-dollar suit, then you'll understand the value of being prepared."

"So you do this a lot?" Halliday asked dryly.

"Garbage is a window to a person's soul. A bit like their internet
browsing history, but a whole lot smellier," he said, ripping open the
packaging and removing a white plastic set of coveralls. "It's not the
first time I've gone through trash and it won't be the last. In fact, I'd
say it's an occupational hazard."

He took off his shoes before stepping into the coveralls and pulling them up over his charcoal suit. He put his shoes back on and donned a pair of thick rubber gloves. Halliday was ripping open her plastic pouch to get changed when they both heard high heels tapping purposefully along the street behind them.

A woman in an overcoat with extremely long dark hair was walking nonchalantly toward Liv Reese's building. The woman bore more than a passing resemblance to their suspect.

"It's not her. She's too tall," whispered Halliday, as the woman came closer. The woman took the stairs to the top of the stoop and rifled around in her purse for her keys to open the street door of the building.

"Follow behind her and go inside. Interview the neighbors. Ask if anyone saw anything. Tell them to call nine-one-one if Liv Reese turns up again."

There were fourteen apartments on four floors. Halliday took the stairs down to the basement and worked her way up to each apartment floor by floor.

Only half the people living in the building were home. None recognized the photo she showed them of Liv Reese leaving the crime scene early that morning.

On her way back down the stairs, Halliday stopped at an apartment on the third floor where she'd heard a baby crying earlier. Nobody had answered when she'd knocked on her way up. She knocked again, three loud taps.

A woman carrying a sleeping infant in a baby sling opened the door. She held a spatula in her right hand. Halliday introduced herself and showed the woman the photo of Liv Reese.

"Have you seen this woman around recently?" she asked.

"Not recently," said the woman.

"But you do know her?" Halliday pressed.

"Sure, she lived here with Amy a few years back. Her name's Viv, or Liv. Something like that."

"It's Liv," Halliday said. "You actually knew her?"

"I knew Amy better," said the woman, inviting Halliday into her apartment. She returned to the stove and flipped an omelet she was in the middle of cooking.

"We used to have a block party once a year on the rooftop. Amy and I were on the committee. She was a great gal. Her roommate was more introspective. Don't get me wrong, she seemed nice enough. I never thought it was right, all that stuff people said about her afterward."

"What did people say about her?"

"That she killed Amy and that boyfriend of hers and then pretended she'd been attacked."

"You don't think that's what happened?"

"I never thought she did it."

"Why?" Halliday asked.

"She didn't strike me as a killer."

"Lots of killers don't strike people as killers. Until they kill," Halliday countered.

"Maybe." She shrugged. "But I never thought she did it."

"Have you seen Liv around lately?"

"No," she said. "You're not the first person to ask either."

"What do you mean?"

"I took the baby and Lance for a long walk last week. Lance's our rescue dog." She gestured toward a dog with German shepherd coloring and floppy Labrador ears sleeping in a basket. "When we went out, I noticed a man sitting in a car. He was still there when we got back. I was struggling to get the stroller up the stairs. He got out of the car and carried the stroller up to the top of the stoop. Then he asked me if I'd seen his cousin. He showed me a photo of Liv."

"Are you sure it was her?"

"Absolutely. I recognized her instantly."

"What did you tell him?"

"I said I didn't know who she was."

"Why did you lie?"

"I didn't buy the cousin business."

"You didn't happen to get his plate number? Or remember the model of his car, or the color?" Halliday asked.

The woman closed her eyes as if trying to remember. "I'd like to say it was dark blue. It was a standard four-door sedan, that I remember. Not sure of the make."

"What about the man? Did he give you a name? Do you remember how he looked?"

"I was too busy with the baby and the dog to get a good look at him."

"Would you remember him if you saw him again?"

"I doubt it." She shrugged. "I'm pretty awful with faces."

When Halliday returned to the car, Lavelle was stepping out of the disposable coveralls.

"How did it go?" she asked.

"Better than expected."

He lifted up his trunk. Halliday expected to find it filled with garbage for sorting at the precinct. Instead, lying on the carpeted floor of the trunk were two clear plastic evidence bags. Both were neatly labeled. Lavelle held up the first bag. It contained a white T-shirt stained with blood.

"But that's not all," he said, as if he was a late-night TV salesman. He handed Halliday the second bag. Inside was a stainless steel knife coated in blood.

"The murder weapon?"

"I'd say so. The lab will tell us for sure. It was wrapped in the T-shirt and tossed into the trash. I've asked for a warrant for Liv Reese's arrest."

"Looks like you were right. She did do it after all," said Halliday, opening the passenger door and getting in.

"It's confirmation bias, Darcy," he said, sliding into the driver's seat.

"What do you mean?"

"People naturally look for evidence to support their preconceived views. You thought Liv Reese might not have done it. You were looking for reasons to prove your point."

"Not at all," said Halliday. "I simply hadn't made up my mind yet. Unlike you, Jack."

"I was just following the evidence," he said, turning on the engine. "We're out of here. We'll drop off the knife at forensics. Then we have to head straight to the precinct to put out a wildfire."

"What wildfire?"

Lavelle told Halliday that while she was going door-to-door, Rosco called to tell him the captain had leaked the CCTV footage showing Liv Reese leaving the crime scene.

"He figured that if the media ran the surveillance footage it would speed things up. The footage ran on the evening news. Now the phones are running off the hook at the precinct. We're getting hundreds of calls with supposed sightings of Liv Reese all over the city. She's like the new Yeti."

"Ninety-nine percent of them will be bogus," Halliday groaned. "We'll spend the next week chasing dead ends."

"That's not the worst of it," said Lavelle. "Liv Reese was at the *Cultura* offices when our people turned up to search Ted Cole's office and question the staff. She must have seen herself in the CCTV footage on the news. She bolted out of there like she was being chased by the devil. Liv Reese is on the run."

Chapter
Fifty

Wednesday 7:58 P.M.

Escalators go up and down in endless loops as I join the back of a line at the Amtrak ticket office at Penn Station. It's impossible to hear myself think over the noisy announcements on the sound system.

I find myself weighing the pros and cons of each route. Deciding which train I'll take feels like the most important decision of my life now that I know I'm a fugitive.

I killed a man last night. At least that's what the police think. Not without reason, I might add. Millions of people will have seen the same news report showing CCTV footage of me fleeing the scene of Ted Cole's murder. It's only a matter of time until someone realizes that woman is me and alerts the cops.

I overheard enough whispered conversations during my visit to the *Cultura* offices to collect scraps of information on Ted Cole. I gather he worked at *Cultura*'s sister magazine in London before he was transferred to New York earlier in the year to lead the commercial team.

The redheaded woman in the tartan skirt at the office said that I was once engaged to marry him.

I can hardly believe that I was in love with a man I can't remember. Ted Cole is as unfamiliar to me as the random stranger standing in front of me in the Amtrak ticket line.

"I'd like an economy seat on tonight's train to Miami," I say when I reach the front of the line.

I pay with cash. I have no idea why I'm carrying so much cash, but I guess I'm lucky I have it. Without this money, I'd be destitute. My phone and wallet are missing, but it doesn't seem to matter much now that I'm on the run.

"The train leaves in an hour and fifteen," the man says, printing my ticket and pushing it toward me. "We recommend you head over to the platform at least forty-five minutes before the train is due to roll in."

Ticket in hand, I pause as Ted Cole's pixelated face flashes on a giant screen hanging on a pillar in the concourse. I take a moment to watch the news break flashing on the screen. Until a few hours ago, I didn't know Ted existed, let alone that we were once in love. A deep sadness washes over me as I stare at his crinkling eyes. Mom always told me to marry a man who smiles with his eyes.

A high-pitched squeak breaks into my thoughts. A cleaner in a blue coverall stops his cleaning cart to empty a trash bag and replace it. He works quickly with a practiced air, like he's been doing this all his life.

The nightly ritual of the station winding down for the night provides a mundane normalcy to this otherwise surreal day. I'm still coming to grips with everything that has happened since I woke on the subway train this afternoon.

I stifle an exhausted yawn. Dr. Brenner told me I forget things whenever I go to sleep. I can't allow myself to sleep no matter how tired I feel right now.

Since I have nothing else to do, I head to the assigned platform for my train, where I lean against a vending machine and watch a procession of people feed coins into a slot to select snacks. I distract myself trying to guess what snack each person will choose.

After a while, a woman gets up from a bench and I take her seat. An announcement tells us the Miami train is running ten minutes behind schedule. Everyone groans.

My body feels drained and my eyes are heavy. I force myself to stay alert by focusing on the rhythm of a train departing on a platform somewhere behind me. The clatter as it builds up speed morphs into a chant: *Stay Awake. Stay Awake. Stay Awake. Stay Awake.* I repeat it to myself as I stare at the tracks, waiting for my train to pull in.

The train tracks hypnotize me with their perfect symmetry. Exhaustion overwhelms me. My eyes close and I drift off.

A loud voice startles me awake.

"Excuse me, ma'am."

I snap open my eyes and stare into the concerned face of a train conductor leaning toward me.

"Ma'am, this platform is closed."

"Platform? Closed?"

I look down in confusion. I'm clutching a train ticket to Miami.

The conductor peers at the ticket. "Ma'am, the Miami train left a half hour ago. You slept through it."

I look at him blankly. I have no idea why I'd be taking a train to Miami. I close my eyes again, convinced I must be dreaming.

"Ma'am, I have to ask you to leave."

I flinch at his booming voice and immediately snap open my eyes again. I'm not dreaming. It's late at night and I'm on an empty train platform. I don't have the faintest idea how I got here. The last thing I remember is answering the phone at my desk in the office. It was daytime then.

"Did I black out or something?"

"You missed your train. You must have fallen asleep. The next train to Miami doesn't leave until morning. You'll have to find somewhere to stay for the night."

"Somewhere to stay . . . for the night?"

"Yes, ma'am. You can't stay here. We're closing the platform. You have to leave."

I stumble to my feet and take the escalator up to the concourse. I'm so woozy and confused that it feels as if the ground under my feet is turning to quicksand as I walk. Nothing makes sense. I'm about to head to the subway to go home to my apartment in Brooklyn when I notice writing covering my hands and arms. It looks as if I've been vandalized while I slept.

Letters written under each knuckle spell out the words STAY AWAKE. Another message says: DON'T SLEEP! I FORGET EVERYTHING WHEN I FALL ASLEEP. A phone number under the words CALL FOR HELP is circled on my palm. It feels like a lifeline.

Near the escalators is a public phone. I feed coins from my pockets into the slot and dial the number written on my palm.

"Hello?"

"Liv! Where are you?" I strain to hear the muffled voice as a round of train departure announcements blare.

"I'm at Penn Station. I don't know what's going on." My voice rises in panic.

"Did you just wake up?" he asks, his voice barely audible under the deafening loudspeaker announcements.

"Yes. I must have fallen asleep waiting for a train." I yawn. The train station loudspeaker reverberates through my head. I shouldn't be here. "I need to go home."

"Liv, you can't go home. You're in danger."

"What danger?"

"It's a long story. I'll explain when I see you. Meet me at a bar called Nocturnal."

Chapter
Fifty-One

Two Days Earlier

Ted swings open the front door and stands back to let me into the apartment. It's a modern one-bedroom with the sterile atmosphere of a hotel. It has an open-plan kitchen with stainless steel appliances and a white stone counter. The bedroom is furnished in blue-grays. There are satin sheets on the mattress and a sliding-door closet.

"Liv, I can't stress enough that you can't go out and you can't contact anyone. Do you understand?" Ted's tone is deadly serious as he locks and bolts the front door. "It's for your own protection. Nobody knows you're here. We have to keep it that way."

"Sure." I say it with conviction so he'll believe me. The cell phone that I slipped into my rear pocket presses into my flesh. It's my escape plan if I decide I don't trust him after all.

Ted opens the fridge and tells me to help myself to anything I need. He has filled the shelves with salads, yogurts, and fresh fruit. "You've been living off coffee for too long," he says, pouring orange juice into tall glasses and tossing in ice cubes.

He picks up our glasses and moves them to a coffee table in the living area. I curl up in the corner of a gray L-shaped leather sofa, sipping my drink while he paces nervously.

"Now would be a good time to tell me what's going on," I suggest.

He runs a hand through his tawny hair as if bracing himself for a difficult conversation. "I'll start at the beginning. Two years ago, Amy and Marco were murdered."

"You're lying." Nausea rises in my throat until rage takes over. "Actually, I'm not listening to this."

I get up and storm past him to the front door. It's locked. I turn around to demand he unlock the door when I see the headline of the newspaper clipping he's holding up in the air to show me. I snatch the newspaper from his hand and read in silent horror. The article says Amy and Marco were killed in a double homicide.

"This article says a third person was taken to the hospital with critical injuries. Who was it?" I ask quietly, still holding onto the clipping.

"It was you, Liv. You're lucky to be alive. There's a scar on your torso from the stab wound."

I lift up my top and am confronted by a jagged scar under my rib cage. Seeing the scar drives home the truth of what I've just read. Amy and Marco really are dead. I lower myself back onto the sofa, my body trembling with shock.

Ted sits next to me. He leans my head against his chest and puts his arms around me. His warm comforting embrace tugs at my heart. I feel as if I've come home.

"I'm so sorry, Liv. I hate having to tell you the same terrible news over and over again," he murmurs. "Each time it devastates you as if it's the first time you've heard it."

"Who killed them?"

"Nobody knows."

"I was there. I must have seen something?"

"You were almost killed yourself. When you woke from the coma, you didn't remember anything about the murder," he says. "Over time, snippets of images would flash in your head. You thought they were memories from the murder, but you were never sure."

Ted recounts how I once described a flashback of looking up from the floor and seeing Amy's pink kimono hanging on her bedroom door hook. Another time I woke in the middle of the night and immediately sketched a dotted medallion pattern that flashed in my head. I'd insisted that I'd seen it when I was stabbed.

"One time you had a memory of shoes covered in blood walking away from you. When you looked into it, you found out there were no bloody footprints at the scene. You must have imagined it," Ted tells me. "You also remembered a voice urging you to 'stay awake' and a siren in the background. Although those recollections came to you after you insisted on listening to a recording of the nine-one-one call in the hope that it would jog your memory."

Later, I think about the flashbacks Ted described as I hang my clothes in the closet in the bedroom and arrange my toiletries in a bathroom cupboard.

My last memory before waking this morning was answering my office phone. "This is Liv," I'd said into the receiver.

After that I remember nothing until Ted's pounding on the front door woke me this morning at that dingy basement apartment. I don't remember Amy and Marco's murders. I don't remember being stabbed, or being in the hospital. I don't remember Ted, or our engagement. Or any flashbacks of the murder. My life over the past two years is a blank.

"How did we meet?" I ask Ted later, sitting on a kitchen barstool as I watch him make sandwiches for lunch.

"We met when you moved to London," he says, cutting in half my lox and cream cheese bagel.

"I lived in London?"

"After Amy and Marco were killed, you moved to London and freelanced at *Cultura UK*. That's where I worked. We fell in love and got engaged."

I look at my hands. No rings. "Where's my engagement ring?"

"It didn't work out," he says, handing me a plate.

"Why? What happened to us?"

"I was offered a big promotion. It involved relocating to New York. You flatly refused to move back here. You were afraid the killer might come after you since you were the only witness. We tried to keep things going, but it gradually fizzled out," he says, pausing as if deliberating how much more to tell me. "To be fair, things weren't great before then."

"In what way?" I toy with my sandwich. My appetite has disappeared.

"You were consumed with finding out who killed Amy and Marco. It took over your life. You blamed yourself because you knew the killer was still free, and you believed that if you could only remember who it was, then the cops would arrest him, or her," he says.

"That's why we broke up?"

He lifts up my chin and looks deeply into my eyes. "I wanted to make a life with you, Liv. Get married. Have a family. You kept delaying it."

"Why?"

"Your obsession with the past. Constantly trying to piece together what happened. Listening to the nine-one-one recording over and over again. Papering the walls of our flat with newspaper clippings. Amy and Marco's murders were all you ever talked about. It consumed you. Ultimately it consumed our relationship. It destroyed us."

He reaches for my hand and squeezes it gently. "Marco cheated on you, Liv. With your best friend. They betrayed you, and yet you couldn't let go. You blamed yourself for their deaths. You kept letting the past come between us." His voice is laced with raw pain. "You never gave us a chance."

"I wish I could go back and change things," I say, my eyes wet. "I feel like you and I could have been happy together."

"Yes," he says, shaking his head as if to break a spell. "It's too late now to turn back the clock. But it's not too late to help you. Something happened to you after we broke up, which has caused you to lose your memory. You never had any memory problems when we were together in London, but now you forget things on a daily basis. It makes you vulnerable, and it puts you in danger. That's why I arranged for you to see a doctor who specializes in amnesia. I want to help you get your life back on track."

He releases my hand. It makes me feel lost and alone, a reminder that whatever we had together is gone.

He notices that I've only taken a single bite of the bagel sandwich. "Eat up, Liv. You need to take care of yourself. Proper nutrition, and sleep. Lots of sleep."

He watches with grim satisfaction as I eat. "For as long as I've known you, you've suffered from severe insomnia. It gave you wild mood swings and made you paranoid and fatigued. Dr. Brenner says the insomnia may be a cause of your memory problems. That's why I want to make sure you get back into a healthy routine."

"Why are you helping me, Ted? If we've broken up?" I ask later, as we wash the dishes.

"Because I still care about you. I worry about you, Liv," he says, handing me a plate to dry with a dish towel.

He tells me that when he tracked me down at the basement apartment a couple of weeks ago, he saw that I'd put up all sorts of information about Amy and Marco's murders on the walls. Apparently when we were together in London, I kept files and drew diagrams on the wall where I listed leads and unanswered questions. In the past, he'd resented it. When he saw I was still doing it, he was more sympathetic.

"God knows how you'd come that far with your investigation, let alone managed to get from London to New York and rent an apartment all by yourself with your memory issues," he says. "It made me realize that finding out what happened to Amy and Marco might be a compulsion because deep down you want closure. You *want* to move on with your life. So I helped you with your investigation." He rubs the back of his neck. "Helping you turned out to be a mistake."

"Why?"

"We poked at a hornets' nest," he says. "That's why you're here."

"I don't understand."

"I asked the night doorman at your apartment building to keep an eye on you. He called me early this morning because he saw someone following you home in the middle of the night, and then hovering around on the street. I'm worried that my inquiries into Amy and Marco's murders might have alerted their killer that you're back. That's why I moved you here. To keep you safe."

Ted hands me another wet plate to wipe and checks the peephole in the front door. His nervousness astonishes me. He truly believes I'm in danger. I wonder how all the things he described could have happened without me remembering any of it.

"It feels as if I've woken from a deep sleep and the world has changed, except for me," I say sadly. "How long do I have to stay here for, Ted?"

"A few days. You saw Dr. Brenner almost two weeks ago. He's the medical expert I arranged for you to see. I took you to get scans at the hospital the other day. We have an appointment with Brenner tomorrow to get the results and a treatment plan. It's all written in your journal."

"My what?"

"You have a journal. We left it behind at your old apartment, along with your purse, in our rush to leave," he says. "I'll get it all tomorrow. You write everything that happens to you in your journal. It's become a proxy for your missing memory. It allows you to function somewhat normally, which is probably how you were able to get to New York from London. You write the key events of the day as they happen."

He hands me a piece of paper and a pen and suggests I write everything he's told me in longhand so I can add it to my journal when he brings it back tomorrow. "It's important you have a written history of what we've discussed in your own handwriting in case you fall asleep and wake in a panic."

He hands me a roll of cash that he said he found amid the clutter on the coffee table when he came to get me this morning. I put it in my jeans pocket. He makes me write his cell phone number on both palms so I'll notice it.

"In case of an emergency," he says.

Later, I'm staring at my long hair in the bathroom, wondering whether I should ask Ted to book me a haircut with my stylist, Stevie, when I hear a hushed phone conversation in the kitchen. He's talking to a woman.

From his side of the conversation, I can tell she's upset he's here with me. He placates her by promising to come over soon. I feel a twinge of jealousy.

"Liv, I need to go out for a while," he tells me. "Lock the door behind me."

Next to the door are Post-it notes with instructions like DON'T OPEN THE DOOR and DON'T TALK TO STRANGERS. He made me write the notes after I wrote the journal entry. He said it's better if the warning notes are in my own writing as I'll be more likely to obey the instructions.

I look through the peephole as I bolt the door shut. He hovers near the door until he hears the final click of the lock, then turns toward the elevator.

Picking up the remote control, I turn on the television and lie on the sofa. I drift off to the canned applause of a game show.

I'm woken by a phone ringing. I open my eyes to discover that I'm lying curled up on a sofa in a dark apartment that I don't recognize, looking out at a nighttime view I've never seen before.

Fluorescent lights blink at me from the living room windows as the phone rings. Through my dazed confusion, I gradually realize the ringing is coming from a phone in my back pocket.

"Hello?"

"Liv?" The voice is almost drowned out by the raucous noise of a bar in the background.

"Yes?"

"Amy needs your help."

"Where is she?"

"She's at a bar called Nocturnal. Write down the address." There's no paper, so I write it on the back of my hand.

Chapter
Fifty-Two

Wednesday 8:40 P.M.

Halliday and Lavelle walked into a deafening hive of activity at the precinct. Half a dozen cops sat at a row of desks that had been pushed together to form a long line across the back wall of the Detective Bureau.

They'd been rounded up to take calls from the general public. The phones had been running hot ever since the security camera footage had been broadcast on the nightly news. That, along with the message written in the victim's blood on the window, had turned the murder into the biggest story on a slow news day.

Halliday slipped off her jacket and checked the messages on her desk. A thick package of crime scene photos had been sent by special delivery along with an initial report on the forensics that had already been processed. She gave it a cursory inspection. There wasn't anything there that she didn't already know.

Someone turned up the volume of the television on the wall. Halliday looked up, curious to see what the media was reporting.

"Police are looking for a woman who they suspect may have killed a British magazine executive during a romantic tryst," the anchor's voice blasted across the office. "The murderer is believed to have used the victim's own blood to write a chilling message on a window. Police have not yet released the name of the suspect. Our sources tell us that she may be the former fiancée of the murdered businessman, Ted Cole, who was stabbed to death last night. . . ."

Lavelle muted the television and turned to the staff manning the hotline. "Any leads?"

"We have one guy who thinks the suspect is his long-lost sister who was abducted by aliens forty-nine years ago and kept in a cryogenic freezer on a spaceship," said one of the officers. "He says that's why her hair is so long."

"I just finished with a caller who's convinced the woman is a vampire. He claims to be a vampire slayer. He's offering his services at a discount."

"What's his rate?" asked Lavelle.

"Twenty bucks an hour. Plus tax," said the officer, shaking his head with disbelief.

"That is the going rate," said Lavelle dryly. "Did we get any tips that are actually worth chasing?"

"A hairdresser called earlier." A uniformed officer leaned back in his chair and handed a note to Halliday. "She said a woman with long hair arrived this morning without an appointment. The woman insisted on having her hair cut very short."

Halliday looked at the note. The hairdresser worked at a salon near the *Cultura* offices. Halliday called the hairdresser from her desk.

"She had very long dark hair down to her waist just like in the picture on the news," said the hairdresser, once Halliday had gone through the preliminaries. "Her behavior was weird, like she was zoned out. I thought she was drugged or on sedatives."

"What did she talk about while you were cutting her hair?"

"Nothing," said the hairdresser. "She daydreamed, mostly. When she came to the cash register to settle her bill, she panicked like she didn't know how she was going to pay. Then she patted down her clothes and found a big wad of cash in her jeans pocket. I mean a *huge* wad of cash. At least a thousand dollars. Probably more."

"Did she say or do anything else that seemed odd?"

"She had writing all over the back of her hands. Weird stuff. I remember seeing the words STAY AWAKE written on her knuckles. It reminded me of the *WAKE UP!* sign I saw on the news. That's why I called the hotline."

Based on the hairdresser's description, Halliday was sure the woman in question was Liv Reese. By the time she was done talking to the hairdresser, Lavelle was on the phone taking another tip.

"Who was that?" Halliday asked Lavelle as she passed his desk after he hung up.

"It was Liv Reese's doctor. His name is Brenner," he answered. "He said she turned up hours late for her appointment this afternoon."

"That's not exactly a crime," Halliday said.

"Ted Cole was supposed to have come *with her* to the appointment," said Lavelle. "Dr. Brenner was shocked when he saw on the news that Ted Cole had been murdered. He immediately called us."

"How does he know that Ted Cole was supposed to have accompanied her?"

"Because Cole set it up. He contacted Brenner through a mutual friend a couple of weeks ago to beg him to help an ex-girlfriend who was suffering from memory loss," Lavelle told her. "Ted Cole brought Liv Reese to Brenner for an initial appointment, and took her to the hospital to get brain scans. He was supposed to be there with her today to get the results."

"What kind of doctor is Brenner?"

"He's a neurologist. Apparently, he's a world leader at helping amnesiacs get their memories back," said Lavelle. "He said Liv Reese was very upset after her appointment this afternoon. He said she's likely very confused and disoriented. He thinks there's a good chance she'll reach out to a friend for help the next time she wakes without any memory."

"I'll go through the Decker-Reggio murder files and put together a list of people she might contact," Halliday offered.

"Good. By the way, the captain wants us to brief him as soon as he gets in."

The captain's interest in the case was at a fever pitch. It had risen over the course of the day along with the storm of media coverage.

Halliday went back to her desk to go through the files. The ringing of the hotline phones was so loud that eventually she took the document box to a vacant interview room so she could concentrate.

She spread the contents of the files in small piles along the table and wrote key names on the whiteboard. Halliday's phone rang while she was adding another name to the list.

"Detective Halliday," she said.

"It's Gene Tawalski here, from Eastern Island Cabs. We got a request to go over our GPS data. Turns out we had a car on the street in question a few minutes after three this morning. I just got off the phone with the driver. He picked up a woman."

"Did he describe her?"

"Long hair. He told me that she was out of it, but not in an addict-on-a-high sort of way. He said that she reminded him of his mom who has Alzheimer's. The woman was confused. She couldn't decide where she wanted to go. Halfway into the ride, she changed her mind. Asked to be dropped somewhere else."

"Where did he drop her off?"

"At a bar. It's called Nocturnal."

Chapter
Fifty-Three

Wednesday 9:35 P.M.

Laughter spills onto the street as the glass doors of Nocturnal are pushed open. A man and a woman step unsteadily onto the sidewalk, their arms drunkenly entangled. Their voices are decibels too loud for the hushed street. I slip past them into the riotous roar of the crowded bar.

I squeeze past a table of men in dress shirts and loosened ties as they raise their glasses and toss down their drinks in unison. The thud of empty glasses slamming onto a table hits me like an aftershock. I head toward the bar where I was instructed to wait.

"Hey, honey. I like your new look." The warm drunken voice in my ear is quickly followed by a hand snaking around my waist, pulling me in. "Come here." A ruddy-faced man leans in to kiss me with foul whiskey breath. Instead he kisses air as I evade his grasp and disappear into the crowd.

Hoots of laughter and shouted conversations assault me as I push through a tight crush of people. I'm hit by an eerie sense of déjà vu when I glimpse my flushed face in a triple paneled mirror behind the bar. It's as if I'm looking at an alternate version of myself in a parallel universe.

A bartender with dark hair and a goatee pours drinks from a beer tap nozzle. His shirt sleeves are pushed to his elbows, displaying a tattoo on his forearm.

I slide onto an empty barstool near the black-painted window facing the street. Looking into the mirror, I check to see if anyone is beelining toward me through the sea of drinkers. So far nobody seems to have noticed me, except the bartender.

He looks up and winks as he pours tequila into shot glasses, barely spilling a drop before adding a plate of lime wedges and crushed salt to the tray. A waitress picks up the tray and takes it to the table of businessmen.

"You're looking great tonight, Liv," the bartender says. "What can I get you?"

"I don't suppose you serve coffee!" I stifle a yawn, certain I must have imagined the bartender saying my name. "I need something to wake me up."

"How about an espresso martini?"

"Is it any good?"

"It must be. You drink a couple of them a night."

I'm about to tell him that's not possible, since I've never been here before, when he turns around and takes a bottle of vodka off a shelf. He pours a generous amount into a cocktail shaker before adding vermouth and other ingredients I can't identify in the murky light.

I stare into the swirling colors reflected on the stainless steel of the cocktail maker as he shakes it and pours the icy mixture into a frosted martini glass. He tosses on a couple of roasted coffee beans as decoration before sliding the glass across the bar to me.

"I know this is a weird question," I say, after paying him and taking a tentative sip. "I wanted to ask you if . . ."

"You've been here before?"

"How did you know I was going to ask you that?"

"Because every time you come here, you ask me the same question."

"I don't remember ever coming here before."

"That's because you have a problem with your memory." He gestures toward the writing on the backs of my hands. "That's why you write reminders on your hands."

The bartender abandons me midsentence to serve a customer farther along the bar. My eyes dart toward a large-screen television broadcasting the news.

When he's back, the bartender takes something from a drawer under the bar and hands it to me. It's a cell phone with a cracked screen.

"Why are you giving this to me?"

"It's your phone. Someone found it last night and handed it in to the cloakroom attendant. It eventually found its way to me."

"This phone isn't mine." I hold out the phone so he can take it back. "I've never seen it before in my life."

"Trust me, Liv. It's your phone. You just don't remember," the bartender says, making no effort to take it.

A silver-haired man gestures to the bartender that he wants a drink. "Turn it on. You'll see it's your phone. You use your thumbprint to unlock it instead of a code," the bartender says, moving away to pour the man a single malt.

I fiddle with the phone button to turn it on. As I do, my eyes catch sight of the TV again. A grainy photo of a woman is on the screen. I blink, certain I imagined it. When I look again, I know it's real. The woman on the TV screen is me.

Chapter
Fifty-Four

Wednesday 9:48 P.M.

I stare in astonishment at my face plastered on the evening news. "Police searching for woman suspected of murdering magazine executive," says a graphic below my photo.

I'm convincing myself the vodka must have been spiked to induce this hallucination when I glance in the mirror behind the bar and see the reflection of a patrol cop pushing open the art deco glass doors at the entrance. My stomach free-falls as more cops enter.

"Is there a nearby exit?" I ask the bartender, who has just finished serving his customer. I fan my hand in front of my face as if I'm about to faint. "I'm feeling claustrophobic. I need fresh air."

"I'll let you out through the back. Come with me."

I slip off the barstool and join the bartender at a STAFF ONLY door at the end of the timber counter. He pushes open the door with his shoulder and we enter a narrow dimly-lit corridor. It's much quieter than the bar, but I can still feel the vibrations of the music. The bartender unlocks a storeroom with a key from his pocket. He swings the door open to a small windowless room filled with supply boxes.

The door slams shut behind us after we enter. I swallow nervously as I realize that I'm trapped in here with him. The bartender rummages around in a metal locker, seemingly unaware of my sudden trepidation. He turns and throws something in my direction. I catch it in midair. It's a black leather jacket infused with men's aftershave.

"It's freezing outside. Put it on. You can give it back to me some other time," he tells me.

He unlocks another door, which he pushes wide open, letting in a cold draft of air. I step out into the night chill, shoving my hands in the pockets of the borrowed jacket to stay warm as he closes the door behind me.

Parked near the rear door is a white van with a navy Nocturnal logo on its side. I walk past the van and come out onto a street around the block from the bar. Curious to see what's happening with the police, I backtrack to the entrance.

Three police squad cars are parked on the curb; their siren lights rotate. I merge into a crowd of drinkers who are talking loudly on the sidewalk, speculating about why the police are there. The prevailing theory appears to be a drug bust.

"What's going on?" I ask someone who's just finished talking to a cop near the entrance.

"The police are looking for a murder suspect." He shoves a flyer at me. "Take it. I don't need it."

I read the notice as I shuffle through the crowd of bar patrons spilling across the sidewalk. It contains the same grainy photo I saw on the TV of a woman who looks just like me. It's impossible to read the writing under the photo until I'm near a streetlight.

"Police are asking the public to call the hotline number below if they have any information on the whereabouts of the woman in the photograph. Her name is Liv Reese. Her height is five foot six and she is described as . . ."

Electricity crackles inside my head. It goes faster and faster, mimicking my racing heartbeat. The police really are looking for me in connection to a murder.

It's ludicrous to think that I'd kill anyone. On the other hand, I know that I blacked out for a period of time because I have no recollection of anything that happened between the time I answered a phone call at my office on a sunny summer's day and the moment I woke on the Amtrak platform clutching a train ticket to Miami. There's obviously a missing gap of time that I can't account for. And if there's a missing gap of time then how can I be certain of anything?

I slip into the doorway of a Korean restaurant and scan my thumbprint on the cell phone the bartender gave me earlier. The phone unlocks. A series of voicemails and text message alerts immediately pops up on the screen.

They're from someone called Ted. I don't know anyone by that name. But when I listen to the first voicemail, it's apparent that Ted knows me.

"Liv, it's Ted. Where are you? You were supposed to stay in the apartment."

"Liv, it's Ted again. Please call me. It's urgent." He recites a cell phone number.

His messages get increasingly frantic.

Liv. I'm heading back to the apartment to see if you're there, reads one of his texts.

In the last voice message, he sounds almost resigned. "Liv, it's Ted. I'm guessing you fell asleep and don't remember me. You're probably asking yourself why some guy called Ted is calling you. Please check your emails. It will explain who I am and why you urgently need to call me. You are in danger, Liv. Read the email. Do it now and then call me!"

I follow his instructions and tap the email icon. The top message in my inbox is an email from Ted containing a photo of a journal entry written in my own handwriting.

A man called Ted woke me this morning. He pounded on the door of a basement apartment where I was sleeping on a camping mattress on the floor. I didn't know why I was in that apartment. I also didn't know who Ted was, even though he claimed to know me. It felt as if I'd woken to discover that I was living someone else's life.

Ted explained that I'm suffering from memory problems. I forget everything going back almost two and a half years, when Amy and Marco were murdered.

Yes, they were murdered.

I didn't believe it until Ted showed me a news article. He's since shown me other articles explaining what happened in horrifying detail. One article was illustrated with a photo of me on a stretcher with an oxygen mask over my face as paramedics lifted me into an ambulance. The article said I was taken to the hospital with life-threatening injuries. There's a scar on my torso from where I was stabbed. Ted says I've never remembered what happened because I was in a coma afterward. Once I recovered, I moved to London where we met and fell in love.

Things didn't work out. Ted moved to New York for work. I stayed behind. Apparently I was fine for a while, going about my life without any memory problems, although Ted says the underlying trauma of the murder left me with insomnia, and what he calls an unhealthy obsession with finding out what happened the day Amy and Marco were killed.

Sometime over the past few weeks, I began having memory problems. Ted only found out a couple of weeks ago when I turned up at a function out of the blue without remembering him. He said he's since taken me to a specialist who believes that my memory resets every time I wake up, taking me back to the day of the murder.

That's why I didn't recognize Ted this morning. That's why I didn't recognize the basement apartment where I was sleeping, even though I've apparently lived there for several weeks after renting it when I left London. That's why everything Ted tells me about the past two years feels as if it's happened to someone else.

Ted's moved me to this apartment to keep me safe. He made me write warnings on Post-it notes that he stuck next to the front door. They're to remind me not to go out. Ted's worried that Amy and Marco's murderer may come for me.

The letter goes on to explain the intricacies of my condition, Ted's and my rocky relationship, and the reasons for our breakup.

If the journal entry hadn't been written in my own handwriting, I wouldn't have believed a word of it.

I look up from my phone. Several cops are standing in a huddle by a patrol car down the street near the bar. I consider approaching them and telling them that I'm the woman they're looking for.

I take a step forward and then withdraw back into the shadowed doorway of the restaurant. I can't bring myself to do it. A crowd of bar-goers take videos of each other while they wait to be allowed back into Nocturnal. The last thing I want is to be handcuffed and shunted into a police car while dozens of people post videos of my arrest on social media. The public humiliation would be excruciating.

I do the next best thing. I dial the number of the police hotline printed on the flyer that I'm holding.

Chapter
Fifty-Five

The siren lights from the patrol cars parked outside Nocturnal shone through the stippled glass, casting a purple haze across the sea of revelers as Darcy Halliday and Jack Lavelle pushed open the doors and entered the loud and stifling bar.

"She's changed her hairstyle." Halliday shouted to be heard over the explosion of noise as she spoke to a cop standing near a velvet rope inside the entrance.

"What do you mean?"

"We're not looking for a female suspect with long dark hair anymore. The photo on this notice and in the media is out of date. She cut her hair. We're looking for a woman with short hair. Tell your people."

Lavelle and Halliday split up. They moved through the crowds, showing patrons a digitally enhanced photo of what Liv Reese would look like with short hair.

"Have you seen this woman?" Halliday showed the photograph on her phone screen to a waitress clearing empty beer bottles from a ledge.

"Sure. She comes here a lot," the waitress yelled back.

"Has she been here tonight?"

"Beats me. Ask Harry. She always gravitates to his end of the bar. We think she has a crush on him."

Halliday waded into a tight knot of drinkers to get to the bar. "Watch it," she said when she was jostled by a drunk man passing her.

A bartender with a nose ring told her that Harry had gone to the storage room and would be back shortly. While she waited, Halliday talked to a few customers hunching over their drinks. They all shook their heads when she showed them the updated photograph of Liv Reese. Some of them appeared so drunk that Halliday doubted whether they'd have recognized photos of their own grandmothers.

A bartender with sleeves rolled up to his elbows came out of a STAFF ONLY door, carrying a cardboard box of chilled juices. He squatted down and packed the bottles into a fridge under the bar.

"What can I get you?" he asked Halliday when he stood up.

She held up her detective's shield and her phone with the photo of Liv Reese. "We're looking for this woman."

"Yeah, I know her. What do you want with her?"

"She's suspected of murder."

The bartender's head snapped up. "Liv? No way. She wouldn't hurt a fly. Sure, she has issues. She comes in here every night like it's the first time she's ever seen the place. I don't know how many times I've had the same conversation with her. But murder. Man, that's nuts."

"Ever seen her here with this guy?" Halliday swiped her phone to a photograph of Ted Cole.

"Sure. Liv was here with him a couple of nights ago. Nice guy. British. We had a long talk."

"About what?"

"Liv, of course."

"What about Liv?"

"He was worried people could take advantage of her because of her memory issues. Exploit her or lure her away. He said it would be like taking candy from a baby." He poured a whiskey sour and slid the glass over to a customer.

"When was she last here?" Halliday asked, gesturing to Lavelle to come over.

"She left a few minutes ago," said the bartender. "She was feeling claustrophobic and asked me to let her out through the back."

"So she's gone?"

Halliday looked at Lavelle incredulously as he joined her at the bar.

"Yeah," the bartender admitted.

"Any idea where she went?" Halliday asked.

"Maybe she went back to her apartment. She lives near here."

"Do you know where?"

His shrug was her answer. "There's a bodega across the street. Liv's a regular there. The delivery guy sometimes walks her home when she gets disoriented. They might know where you can find her."

Lavelle handed the bartender his card. "If you remember anything else, call us." He and Halliday turned to leave.

"Hang on," the bartender called out. He scrambled around in his wallet, searching for something. After a moment, he took out a business card and handed it victoriously to Halliday.

"Liv's friend Ted gave it to me," he said. "He'll help you find her."

"Thanks," said Halliday, looking down at Ted Cole's name and contact number embossed on the glossy *Cultura Magazine* business card. "Unfortunately, it's not much use to us."

"Why not?" asked the bartender, wiping a spill on the bar.

"Because Ted's the man who was killed overnight. Liv Reese is wanted for his murder."

Chapter
Fifty-Six

I move deeper into the doorway as my call to the police hotline is answered.

"I'm calling with information on Liv Reese," I whisper nervously.

"Go ahead. What information do you have?" a man asks.

"I know where she is."

"How do you know where she is?" From his skeptical tone, he thinks I'm a crank caller.

"Because I *am* Liv Reese."

Silence follows as he digests my comment. "I'll transfer you to someone. Stay right there."

Hold music blasts for a few seconds. It cuts out when a woman's voice comes on the line. "This is Detective Halliday." It's hard to hear her over the background noise.

"My name is Liv Reese. I think you're looking for me."

"Liv?" she says after a pregnant pause. "We've been so worried about you." She sounds like she cares. My eyes prick with tears. "Are you okay?"

"I'm not sure. I don't remember things. Lots of things. It's very confusing."

"You must be feeling very alone."

"I am." My mouth trembles, this time from emotion more than the cold. "I saw on the TV that the police are looking for me. Why?"

"It's hard to explain on the phone. It's better if we talk in person."

I can see the entrance to Nocturnal clearly from the doorway of the Korean restaurant. Near the patrol cars, a slim woman with shoulder-length hair talks on the phone amid a huddle of police She's dressed in a dark suit with a teal shirt. I'm certain that she's Detective Halliday.

"Where are you, Liv?"

"I'm near a bar called Nocturnal," I say, watching closely for a reaction from the woman on the phone to confirm my suspicion.

The woman taps the shoulder of a man in a charcoal suit and gestures to him. Within seconds, there's a flurry of activity. Police spread out along the street. I enter the Korean restaurant in a panic and wait behind a bamboo partition near the cash register, pretending to study a take-out menu. I feel sick to my stomach with fear. I should hang up, but I stay on the line.

"There are a lot of police out here tonight," I comment.

"They're looking for you. Liv, tell me where you are. I'll come to you," Detective Halliday says. "We'll talk. Just the two of us."

"I need to think."

I'm about to hang up when she calls out urgently. "Liv, take down my personal phone number. Call me directly."

She dictates a cell phone number. I write it on the top of a take-out menu and stuff it in my jeans pocket.

"Liv, are you still there?"

I can tell that she's trying to keep me on the phone. Through the gaps in the bamboo partition, I see cops jogging along the street, looking for me. I hang up without saying anything.

A waitress comes out of the swinging doors of the kitchen to the front counter where I'm standing.

"Are you here to collect a take-out order?" she asks.

"No, I'm here to eat in."

The waitress escorts me to a row of empty tables. I opt for a table behind a rowdy party of twelve celebrating a birthday. I sit there, hunched over a bowl of beef short rib soup, as I go through more messages on my phone.

I pay special attention to a voicemail and a text message that Ted sent me along with an attached photo of a sketch of a lily drawn out of tiny dots. In an accompanying message, Ted explains it's a fleur-de-lis, a symbol of French royalty, and a favorite of designers.

Ted says I drew the dotted picture after waking up one night when we were still together in London. I'd believed it was a flashback from the murder, although I had no idea what it meant. Ted says he made his own inquiries over the past few days to help me figure it out.

"The friend I contacted about the sketch just called me back," Ted says. "He's asked around and he has information on the design. I'm coming back now so we can discuss it. I think I know who killed Amy and Marco. It's time to involve the police."

Chapter
Fifty-Seven

Wednesday 10:35 P.M.

The night manager was deep-frying a fresh batch of jelly donuts for the late-night crowd when Halliday and Lavelle entered the bodega.

"Gimme a minute," he called out over the high-pitched spit of sizzling oil.

Halliday moved to the corner of the store to take a call coming through. She hoped it would be Liv Reese calling her back. It wasn't. It was her old army buddy Owen Jeffries.

"Darcy," said Jeffries. "I have the results of the writing analysis."

"What did you find?"

"It doesn't match any writing in our database at Langley."

Halliday deflated. It was another dead end.

"All that means," he added, "is that it wasn't written by a known terrorist, a convicted criminal, or anyone on our watch list. Our algorithm did provide some interesting insights, though."

"Like what?"

"The Post-it notes were not written by the person who wrote the message on the window. The Post-it notes were written by a left-hander. The words on the crime scene window were written by a right-hander."

"Liv Reese is left-handed," Halliday pointed out.

"Are you sure she's left-handed?"

"The forensics report in the Decker-Reggio murder files said the stab wounds were inflicted by a right-hander. It states categorically that Liv Reese was left-handed. Apparently, that discrepancy was a key reason why the prosecutors decided not to charge her, even though the investigating detective, a guy called Krause, was hell-bent on locking her up."

"Well, that is interesting." Jeffries was silent for a moment. "How tall is she?"

"About five six."

"In that case, it's very unlikely she wrote it," he said definitively.

"Why are you so certain?"

"According to the CIA algo, the person who wrote WAKE UP! on the window was somewhere between five foot nine and six foot three in height."

"How does your algorithm determine that?"

"It's based on machine learning," he said. "The angles of the letters, their shape, and the amount of ink, or in this case, blood, in specific areas of each letter indicate the direction where the hand pressure was coming from. That gives us a pretty good read of the person's height and hand preference."

The bodega manager lifted a metal drainer with the donuts out of the deep fryer as Halliday finished the call. She wondered how she'd break the news to Lavelle. His discovery of the likely murder weapon in the trash outside Liv Reese's old apartment had convinced her that Liv Reese had murdered Ted Cole. Jeffries's call turned that theory on its head.

"Sorry about the wait," said the manager.

Lavelle showed the manager his detective's shield and introduced Halliday, who'd joined him at the counter.

"We need an address for a customer. Her name is Liv Reese," he said, showing a couple of photos of her on his phone.

"That's the lady with the writing on her hands? I know her," the manager said. "She sure likes to drink caffeine drinks. Orders them by the box. Her address is in the delivery book."

He pulled a book out from under the cash register and flipped through the pages until he found her address. Liv Reese lived a couple of blocks away.

"Who was that on the phone?" Lavelle asked Halliday as they left the bodega.

"It was Owen, my buddy from the CIA. He ran the writing from the crime scene through their AI handwriting analysis system. It's one of the most sophisticated in the world. Their system says that Liv Reese did not write that slogan on the bedroom window." Halliday recounted everything that Jeffries told her.

Lavelle didn't look convinced. "I don't know how much stock I put in computer algorithms when there's so much hard and compelling evidence against her. She even disposed of the murder weapon," he said, opening the car door. "I have the warrant for Liv Reese's arrest. It was just emailed to me. Let's bring her in."

"We're going to arrest her?" Halliday asked, stopping in the middle of the sidewalk. "Despite what I just told you?"

"If she's innocent then she has nothing to worry about. I don't throw people into jail just to keep up my solve rates. But I'm not going to let her go on the say-so of a CIA algorithm."

"I'm not suggesting we let her go," said Halliday.

"Then what are you suggesting, Darcy?"

"We treat her as what she is. A potential witness. A possible suspect. But mostly a person going through a crisis. She doesn't have a memory anymore, Jack," said Halliday. "She must be terrified. We shouldn't amplify the terror by treating her like a criminal when the evidence is ambiguous, and now apparently contradictory."

"We'll bring her in for questioning and then we'll take it from there. You drive. I'll update the captain on the way." He threw Halliday the car keys.

Halliday parked halfway down the street from the building where Liv Reese now lived. When the backup team arrived, they all put on flak jackets and checked their weapons. Lavelle posted a few cops at the rear of the building. The other two came in with him and Halliday. They took the stairs down to the basement level.

Liv Reese's apartment was near the end of the corridor. Halliday and Lavelle both drew their weapons, pointing the barrels toward the ground as they each took a side of the front door.

"Police. Open up." Lavelle knocked on the door.

They pressed their backs to the wall and waited. There was no suggestion that Liv Reese had a gun, but the arrest operation would be carried out by the book. She didn't answer the first knock. Lavelle knocked again. There was still no response.

Rather than wait for a battering ram to be brought down, Lavelle took a small piece of wire from his pocket and jimmied the lock.

"Where did you learn how to do that?" Halliday whispered.

"An informant. Taught me everything he knew about breaking and entering." He pushed down the handle and swung open the door. Halliday went in first.

It took them less than half a minute to reach the conclusion that Liv Reese wasn't there. Someone turned on the living room light switch so they could see properly. The naked bulb dangling from the low ceiling was too weak to light up the room properly.

"It's because the walls are all painted black," said Halliday.

A noxious smell of wet paint indicated the walls had been painted recently. She stepped over an empty can of black paint and a roller brush on the floor. "Why paint the walls black?"

"So that nobody can see what's written on them," Lavelle said, picking up a loose piece of paper lying on the floor. It was a photograph of Marco Reggio. Tape on the corners of the page indicated it had originally been stuck to a wall.

Halliday found a pile of unused blister packs of NoDoz tablets on the coffee table. The British social worker hadn't been kidding when she said Liv Reese did anything she could to stop herself from falling asleep.

Halliday went into the galley kitchen and closed a partly open window with a loud thud. A bag of garbage slumped in the corner of the kitchen was filled with empty cans of caffeine drinks and a few used blister packs of medication to prevent sleep. On the fridge, the words STAY AWAKE were spelled out with colorful preschool letter magnets.

She swung open the fridge door. If trash was a window into a soul, as Lavelle had claimed, then refrigerators were equally revealing. Halliday had once found a packet of diamonds stuffed in a cabbage in a vegetable drawer, and an Uzi submachine gun in aluminum wrap under a frozen turkey in a freezer. She whistled in shock when she saw the contents of this fridge.

"Jack, take a look at this."

There was no food inside the fridge. It contained shelves of unopened caffeine drinks and cans of espresso coffee.

"She must be permanently wired if she's drinking this much caffeine all the time," Lavelle said. "No wonder she can't remember anything."

Halliday didn't respond. She was examining a stack of burned paper piled up in the kitchen sink. Among the scorched documents was the hard cover of a book embossed with the word "Journal." The social worker had told her that Liv Reese's journal was her lifeline. It appeared that lifeline was now a pile of ash.

"I'll get the crime scene team to come and process this place," Lavelle said, once they'd looked around properly. "Go home and get some sleep, Darcy."

"It's okay. I need to be up in case Liv Reese calls again," she said, stifling a yawn.

"You need to sleep. We both do. I'll head home as soon as the crime scene team arrives. Keep your phone on."

"I suppose she won't go far without any memory," Halliday said, making no effort to leave.

"She can't. The whole of NYPD is looking for her."

Patrol cars near the bus and train terminals were told to be on alert in case Liv Reese tried to skip town. There was also a car staking out her old apartment, and one outside the *Cultura* office building.

"We're waiting for a warrant to track her phone signal. It will be signed by a judge first thing in the morning. Once we have that, it should be easy to find her. Now go home and get some shut-eye, Darcy. In fact, take the car." Lavelle tossed Halliday the keys. "I'll take a cab home."

Chapter
Fifty-Eight

Twenty-Four Hours Earlier

The stippled glass doors of the bar swing open as a couple drunkenly stumbles out. I step into the warmth, glad to be out of the cold. Loud music vibrates through my body as I push through crowds of drinkers, some bopping to music as they watch a live band perform a Lady Gaga cover.

Everything has passed in a haze since I was woken by a phone call from a stranger telling me that Amy was in trouble and needed me to meet her here. I came right away. I'd walk over burning coals for Amy.

Amy always sticks out in a crowd, but I don't see her anywhere. My eyes settle on a blond woman watching the band. She turns to talk to the man next to her. I see her face and rule her out. She's definitely not Amy. Behind the bar, a bartender with a dark goatee in a white shirt rolled to his elbows pours a tray full of beers. I head over to ask if he's seen Amy. She lights up rooms. Everyone notices her.

"How are you, Liv?" the bartender asks when he sees me.

I do a double take. I don't know how he knows my name since I'm pretty sure that I've never been here before. Amy and I have barhopped together plenty of times, but not here. This place is memorable with its distinctive atmospheric decor; it's both modern and vintage, with the triple-paneled art deco mirror behind the bar that harkens back to the prohibition era.

"What can I get you?"

"I'm looking for my friend Amy." I describe her. "Have you seen her?"

He hesitates uncertainly and then sadly shakes his head.

"Did she leave already?"

"Not exactly," he says awkwardly. "Er, does Ted know you're here?"

I ignore his question, assuming he's mixed me up with someone else. Instead I twist around to look for Amy, scrambling off the barstool when I notice another tall blond woman in the crowd listening to the band. "Actually, I think I see her."

I push through the crowd looking for the woman, who seems to have disappeared. I move in and out of knots of people dancing to the music until I'm dizzy from looking at so many faces. The room begins to spin. Afraid I might faint, I head into the restroom, its walls painted midnight blue. I put my phone on a ledge above a sink and splash my face with water to revive myself.

After I've turned off the tap, I realize I've washed off writing on my palm. All that's left are remnants of a phone number and a faded word that says "Ted." There's still writing on the back of my hands. Weird messages that say things like STAY AWAKE and DON'T TRUST ANYONE, as well as the address of this bar.

The restroom door opens, letting in a blast of loud music as several women trail inside and begin to fix their makeup in the mirrors. I leave abruptly. As I come out, I'm enveloped in a warm embrace.

"Liv. Thank God I found you."

Chapter
Fifty-Nine

Wednesday 10:40 P.M.

A waitress clears away my empty bowl. The Korean restaurant is emptying out. The police cars parked outside Nocturnal have disappeared. I have to assume the cops left when they didn't find me. It's time that I left, too.

Even though Detective Halliday pretended to empathize with me earlier on the phone, I don't trust cops. Now that I know they suspect me of murder, I trust them even less. I'm afraid they'll frame me for a crime I didn't commit. I have no way to prove my innocence. I know that I blacked out for an unknown period of time until the moment I woke on the train platform holding a ticket to Miami. I also know from the messages from Ted that I forget things every time I wake up.

Once I've paid my bill, I head into the street, uncertain where to go. A couple of cops stand near the entrance of Nocturnal. Thankfully, neither of them see me. I glance back over my shoulder for a split second and collide into someone with such force that the wind is knocked out of me.

"Oh, my gosh, Liv. Are you okay?"

The bright glare of a streetlight burns my eyes as I look up at the first familiar face I've seen since I woke on the Amtrak platform earlier tonight without any memory of how I got there. "Brett, what are you doing here?"

"I had dinner with some colleagues at a place down the street. Are you sure you're okay, Liv?" he asks. "You're shivering."

"It's freezing tonight." I rub my arms.

"My car is down the street. I'll give you a ride," he offers.

"I don't want to take you out of your way." I hesitate.

"It's my pleasure. You'll freeze to death if you stay out here. Look at you, your teeth are chattering," he says. "Come on. Let's get you out of here."

I lower my gaze to the ground and watch our feet step in unison as we walk toward his car. My short black boots and his custom-made gray shoes move in an identical rhythm. A police car slowly approaches, its rotating siren lights reflecting on our faces.

Something niggles at me as we walk. Something important. It must be my nerves rattled by the police car cruising past.

"Almost there," Brett reassures me.

His car beeps twice as he unlocks it. I get into the front passenger seat and clip in the seat belt. Halos hover around the streetlights as we drive to the end of the street and make a right turn.

"You look tired, Liv." He glances at me with concern.

"I'm exhausted. It feels as if I haven't slept for days."

I'm so drained that I lean my head against the window and close my eyes, trying to figure out what was nagging at me before. An image pops into my head of the unusual sketch Ted had texted me. It was a dotted fleur-de-lis pattern, a symbol of the French monarchy.

Ted said I drew the sketch one night, insisting it was connected to Amy and Marco's murder. I realize that I saw that dotted pattern again just now as we walked to the car. His expensive leather shoes had the same unique fleur-de-lis dotted medallion pattern by the toes.

I glance at Brett uncertainly as he steers the car through nighttime traffic. Someone calls his phone. He lets it go to voicemail, telling me ruefully that it's the hospital calling him by mistake. Irritation inflects his voice as he tells me they've yet again forgotten that he's not on call tonight.

I stare out the window, looking into the dark as I visualize that dotted lily pattern again. This time an image comes into my head like a flashback. I'm looking down at a dotted pattern on the toes of expensive oxblood-colored shoes a moment before a man standing behind me plunges a knife into me. I fall to my knees and collapse on the carpet watching those oxblood shoes walk away from me, out of Amy's bedroom. Her pink kimono on the hook of the bedroom door sways as the front door slams shut.

Fear surges through me as realization dawns. I'm too scared to move, too scared even to breathe as I register just how perilous my situation is. I'm in a car with Amy and Marco's killer.

Perhaps sensing that something is wrong, he turns his head to look at me as he drives. "Are you okay, Liv? You look very pale."

"Yeah. Just tired." It takes every ounce of self-control for me to pretend that I still don't know what's going on.

"Why don't you close your eyes and go to sleep. I'll wake you when we get there," he suggests, his voice tinged with concern. He presses his foot on the gas as we accelerate through an intersection.

I don't fall for his kindness. I know who he really is. I know that he killed Amy and Marco, and that he probably intends to kill me.

I stare at the words STAY AWAKE written on the backs of my hands under my knuckles. From Ted's phone messages that I went through at the Korean restaurant, I know that every time I fall asleep I forget everything that has happened since the day Amy and Marco were killed. I close my eyes and pretend to sleep, repeating *Stay Awake, Stay Awake, Stay Awake* over and over in my head like a primal scream.

Sometime later, the car engine falls silent. He unclips his seat belt and gets out, locking me inside. I hear his footsteps recede, followed by murmured voices interlaced with the rush of cars speeding past. I take the risk of opening my eyes to sneak a peek. He's a few yards from the car, his back is to me as he talks on the phone. I assume he's returning the call that came while we were driving.

Keeping an eye on his back, I take the cell phone and the Korean take-out menu from the pocket of my jeans. I quickly type in the phone number of the female detective that I scribbled on the take-out menu and share my location with her.

Help me, I text her.

I press Send, then turn the phone to silent and slip it back into my pocket. The take-out menu has fallen to the floor of the car, but it's too risky to retrieve it. I kick it under my seat and pretend to sleep with my forehead against the passenger window. The driver's door opens and the car heaves as he gets in.

He fires up the ignition and pulls the car back into traffic. I feel his eyes boring into me. He must be trying to figure out if I really am sleeping. I force myself to breathe slowly and steadily as he watches me. He gently pushes my bangs off my face.

"It's a damn shame you and that friend of yours had to start poking around in the past," he says to himself.

A while later, he puts on instrumental jazz. The mellow music contrasts starkly with the cold terror gripping me so tightly that every nerve is on edge. I open my eyes for a millisecond to see we're driving through an unlit industrial area lined with warehouses. Gravel crunches under the car tires. We bounce over several deep potholes. Then we stop.

Chapter
Sixty

Wednesday 11:14 P.M.

I stay frozen, pretending to sleep, after he stops the car. All my senses are focused on trying to figure out what's going on and where we are. I'm too afraid to open my eyes to see our location. I sense that he is watching me. I need him to think that I'm still asleep.

He leans toward me, his breath warm against my skin. I force myself to stay still. This time he doesn't touch my hair. He flips open the glove compartment and takes something out. I don't know what it is until I hear a series of metal clicks. It sounds like a gun being loaded with a magazine of bullets.

"Wake up, Liv." He shakes my shoulders roughly and unbuckles my seat belt.

If I have any chance of getting away from him, I have to let him believe that I've just woken and thus lost my memory again. I give an exaggerated yawn and rub my eyes with exhaustion. "Where are we?"

"We're here to meet Amy." It chills me to hear him say her name in light of everything I've learned tonight.

"Amy's here?" I play along.

"She's waiting for you." He glances at his wristwatch. "We're running late."

I scramble out of the car. My knees are so weak they almost buckle under me. He holds on to my upper arm with pretend solicitousness. His grip is tight. There's no way I can break free. I don't let on that it hurts. The longer I keep this charade going, the longer I'll stay alive.

A cold wind buffets us as we walk toward an abandoned warehouse. Our way forward is lit up by the beam of his flashlight.

"What are we doing here?"

"Remember, Amy got tickets to a new production of *Macbeth* set in a dystopian world. You know how much she loves avant-garde theater. Personally, I think it's a bore, but I don't like to disappoint her."

We step over puddles as we approach the derelict building. The windows are boarded up and defaced with spray-painted expletives and crude drawings.

"I hope the audience gets to sit this time," I say, going along with his charade. "Last time Amy took me to one of these avant-garde plays, it was at an old brewery. We had to stand the whole time. My feet were in agony by the end of the evening."

"I'm pretty sure this performance is seated," he says, escorting me around to the back of the building. "Amy will be annoyed that we're so late."

He kicks in a board on a basement window at the back of the building, ruining any pretense that we're here to watch a play. He shoves me roughly through the window opening. I groan as I land hard on a concrete floor in a dark storeroom.

Hundreds of plastic bucket chairs are piled in stacks of varying heights. Old metal filing cabinets litter the floor, some tipped on their sides. Others stand upright. Boxes are stacked in unstable towers. A mass of desks is shoved against a wall. There are swivel chairs, too, dozens of them arranged in untidy rows.

High-pitched squeaking startles me. Rats. He points the flashlight at a rodent scampering along a window frame. Picking up a dusty folder from a desk, he throws it like a Frisbee at the rat. It hits its mark. The animals scatter. It makes my skin crawl. He eases his grip on my upper arm as he throws another folder.

I take my chance. I pull away from him and dive behind a desk. From there I slide on my belly under stacks of chairs until I'm far away from him. A flashlight beam moves across the concrete floor as he looks for me. I stay where I am, crouching in a ball under a stack of chairs. I watch his legs move through the gaps between the piled-up furniture as he searches for me.

There's a box of old staplers on the floor next to me. I pick one up and throw it as hard as I can across the room. It bounces off a wall with a thump and he goes after the noise to look for me. I push a swivel chair in his direction. Its wheels clatter as it rolls toward him. I use the noise as cover to hide behind a row of metal filing cabinets.

"Stop playing games, Liv. This place is dangerous," he says. When I don't respond, he adds: "We're running late. Amy will be annoyed."

"Amy's dead," I call out, unsure why he feels the need to keep up the pretense.

Through a narrow gap between the filing cabinets, I watch his custom-made shoes as he paces around looking for me. His shoes have a dotted fleur-de-lis design identical to the one in the drawing that Ted texted me along with a message suggesting it was a key clue to the identity of Amy and Marco's killer.

"I know that you killed Amy and Marco," I blurt out. My voice echoes around the room.

He pauses midstep and then freezes, like a cobra waiting to strike. When he realizes that I'm not saying anything else, he knocks over a stack of chairs as he intensifies his search for my hiding place.

"I always knew your memory would come back. That's why I had to kill your ex last night and frame you as the killer. I figured when you were found with his body, they'd pin Amy and Marco's murders on you, too. It would get me off the hook for good. It was sloppy of me to turn my back and let you disappear with the knife, but it ends here and now," he says. "You'll never get out of here."

He pauses to listen for a response so he can figure out where I'm hiding. I cover my mouth to stifle the sound of my breathing.

"I told you I was bringing you to Amy. And I am. Just not in the way that you thought." He laughs. "If you come to me now, I'll make sure it doesn't hurt. Just the way it didn't hurt your ex last night. An injection of pentazocine in his hairline with a fine needle. He fell onto the bed and was sleeping like a baby when he died.

"Make it easy on yourself, Liv. It's only a matter of time until I find you."

Chapter
Sixty-One

Twenty-Four Hours Earlier

It's the ceiling fan that wakes me, brushing my skin with a steady stream of cool air as it rattles above my head. I open my eyes and stare into a bluish haze that slowly morphs into someone else's bedroom.

The fan spins so fast I worry it might topple. The mattress is too firm. The satin sheets too slippery. The humming I heard in my sleep gets louder and more ominous until it crackles like a live electrical wire. The noise is coming from inside my head. It's my own private warning system and it's telling me that I'm in trouble. Big trouble.

I lie very still, my eyes shuttered by my lashes as I glance around the blue-gray bedroom trying to figure out where I am and how I got here. There's a bottle of white wine next to the bed. That surprises me. I don't like white wine and rarely drink it. On the carpet is a trail of women's clothes that I presume are mine. Just as I'm trying to figure out what's going on, the bedroom door is pushed open and someone comes into the room. His shadow reflects on the wall. It gets bigger as he gets closer until I recognize him.

"Brett?" I mutter, as if talking in my sleep.

"For fuck's sake, go to sleep," he says. "You're supposed to be se-dated."

The cruelness of his tone terrifies me almost as much as his words. Sedated? I think to myself. Why would I be sedated? And then I know through the most primal core of my being that he intends to hurt me. My survival instincts kick in. I feign sleep so well that I'm al-most dozing off as he squats down to check on me, touching me with a rubber-gloved hand.

He must be satisfied because he steps away and soon, I hear him humming in the kitchen as he opens a cabinet and takes something out. I turn my head to the side and gasp as I come face-to-face with a tawny-haired man sleeping next to me.

I pretend to sleep when Brett returns, letting out steady rhythmic breaths, all the while listening to the rustle of fabric as he strips clothes off the man next to me and drops them on the floor.

There's a squelching noise. The mattress shifts. I don't know what's going on until Brett puts the cold handle of a knife in my hand. It's wet and sticky. I smell blood. He arranges the sheets over both of us, practically tucking us in before disappearing into the bathroom.

Pipes groan and water splashes loudly. He's washing up. When I turn my head, I know instantly that the man next to me is dead.

Quickly, I get out of bed and pull on jeans and the woman's top lying on the carpet. I don't bother zipping up the jeans as I slide my feet into ankle boots, keeping one eye on the strip of light under the bathroom door to make sure he isn't coming out. The smell of bleach wafts into the bedroom through the crack under the bathroom door.

The knife has fallen off the bed onto a T-shirt lying on the floor. I grab the T-shirt, wrapping the knife in it, and head into the living area. With my free hand, I quietly unbolt the front door.

Hanging from a hook near the front door is a women's buttonless cardigan. I throw it over my arm as I creep out of the apartment and close the door softly behind me. A reflective light on the floor guides me to the stairwell in the dark. I take the stairs down to the basement, where I push open a door and find myself in an alley. I put on the cardigan and slide the T-shirt–wrapped knife into a pocket to save as evidence as I walk toward a liquor store on the corner. I'm so terrified and confused that all I can think about is warning Amy before he gets to her.

I wave down a taxi and give him the address of our apartment in Brooklyn. I stare out of the cab window as halos blink around street-lights like they're sharing a secret. Lulled by the hum of the radio, I feel my eyes get heavy, and I drift off.

Chapter
Sixty-Two

Wednesday 11:24 P.M.

Halliday was cruising around the block looking for a parking spot near her apartment building when a text message came through on her phone.

Help me, it said.

The phone number matched the number that Liv Reese had used to call the police information hotline earlier. She had also sent a tracking pin to allow Halliday to track her location. The tracking pin indicated that she was on the move, heading toward Queens.

Halliday called Lavelle's phone. There was no answer. She made a sharp turn and drove toward the location on the tracking map on her phone screen as she tried to get hold of Lavelle again. His phone went directly to voicemail. She assumed he was still waiting for the crime scene team at the basement apartment, where the phone signal was poor.

"Jack, it's Darcy. Liv Reese sent me a location tracking pin. I'm following it. She's heading to Queens. I think she's in trouble. Call me."

She called the precinct and spoke to Rosco, who was still going through CCTV footage, and told him the same thing.

"It could be a trap," he said dubiously.

"There's only one way to find out. I'm following her. Tell Jack. I'll keep you posted."

The location marker kept moving farther away on the navigation map as Halliday drove toward it. It moved along the grid to Queens and then headed toward Maspeth, where it turned into a labyrinth of side streets. Halliday estimated she was ten minutes away when Lavelle called.

She updated him on what had happened and her current location. As she spoke, the map showed that Liv Reese's car was driving through an industrial area of factories and warehouses.

"It's stopped," she said, when the tracker came to a sudden halt. "At an old storage warehouse. It's about five minutes away."

She gave him the address and asked him to get backup cars to meet her there. Halliday sped up. It was a bad sign that the tracking pin had stopped moving, especially in such a remote location. Nobody had any legitimate business in an old factory district so late at night.

Halliday turned into a narrow, unlit street lined with warehouses. The location marker for Liv Reese had stopped in a compound at the dead end of the street. She pulled to a stop while she was still out of view of the warehouse and radioed in her location. The dispatcher told her that backup was approximately ten minutes away.

She drew her weapon and entered the compound through a pedestrian gate that was bent and falling off its hinges. It rattled in the wind.

The asphalt parking area outside the warehouse was disintegrating and riddled with potholes. Most of the warehouse windows were boarded up. Some were defaced with graffiti.

A Lexus was parked in a delivery bay, the internal light still on. One of the car doors hadn't been closed properly. Halliday opened the door and looked around. A Korean restaurant menu with her phone number scribbled on top was on the floor under the front passenger's seat. Halliday moved behind a wall as she called in the plate number to Rosco.

"It's a leased car," he said after looking it up in the DMV database.

"Who does it belong to?"

"Don't know. It's a private company."

"Liv's location tracker is still on but it's not moving. She's somewhere in this compound. It doesn't look good," Halliday whispered.

"Hang tight. Backup will be there in under seven minutes."

Two loud bursts echoing from the warehouse drowned out his voice. "Shots fired," Halliday said. "I can't wait for backup."

Chapter
Sixty-Three

Brett pushes over a stack of chairs and they collapse on the floor with a deafening crash. "The police are looking for you, Liv. They think you killed Ted. There's strong evidence this time."

"What evidence?" I call out stupidly. He immediately moves toward my side of the room while he talks.

"The message on the bedroom window, for starters," he says, bending down to look for me under a desk. "I wrote it after you disappeared with the knife. Then I went upstairs and waited until daybreak in a utility room. The elevator was packed with people when I left. Nobody noticed me. The police saw you leave, though, in the middle of the night. The CCTV footage of you fleeing after the murder has been running on the news all evening. Everyone believes you killed Ted Cole, especially the police. There's only one thing that links me to his murder."

"What is it?" I ask, again despite my better judgment.

"The knife," he answers. "While I was cleaning up, I discovered

I nicked myself with the blade when I stabbed Ted. The knife has my blood on it. My DNA. When I came out of the bathroom after cleaning up with bleach, it was gone. You took the goddamn knife." He sighs impatiently. "I need to know where you put it, Liv. But, of course, you don't goddamn know what you did with it. Do you? You don't remember. Well, you're going to have to remember," he hisses.

Instead of responding, I crawl to a new hiding place, crouching under the legs of another stack of chairs. A filing cabinet hits the concrete floor with a loud crash. He pushes down another cabinet and kicks over a pile of boxes as he searches for me.

"Maybe I should leave you here and let you fall asleep," he calls out. "You'd wake up without knowing why you were here in the first place. That's if the rats don't gnaw you to death first."

I cover my mouth with my palm so he won't hear my shallow breathing as he stops talking and listens for a hint of where I'm hiding. He kicks a box like it's a hockey puck. It slides across the floor, hitting a brick wall. Rats squeal as they scatter. I grit my teeth as one of them runs over my leg.

"Liv, you have ten seconds to come out or I'm going to shoot," he calls out. "Ten, nine, eight . . ."

When he reaches the number four, he gives up counting and fires a gunshot into the wall. Another shot ricochets off a metal desk. I bite my lip to stop myself from screaming. I'm certain he fired the shot to elicit a scream so he'll know where I'm hiding.

He moves to the other side of the room, dragging desks out of the way. A shadow jumps into the basement through the window. It's so fast and so quiet that I decide that I imagined it.

He topples over a stack of chairs, slowly working his way across the basement toward me. I'm about to slide under a metal desk to hide somewhere else when a firm hand slaps over my mouth. I scream. No sound comes out. The hand presses against my mouth like a suction cup.

"I'm Detective Halliday," a voice whispers in my ear. "Liv, I need you to lie flat on the floor. Whatever happens, do not get up. Do not even move. No matter how scary it gets. Do you understand?"

I nod.

Chapter
Sixty-Four

Halliday left Liv lying flat on the ground as she crouched low and crept on her toes in the darkness. Any noise she made was drowned out by filing cabinets and piles of boxes hitting the floor as he tore up the place in his desperate search.

Halliday used the darkness and the noise to her advantage. She stayed down as she navigated around the overturned office furniture, sticking to the darkest edges of the room so he wouldn't notice any movement. She needed the advantage of surprise. When he turned his back to topple over another set of chairs, she rose and pointed her gun at his torso in a two-handed grip.

"Police. Drop your weapon."

He whirled around to face her, his gun hanging by his side.

"Drop your weapon. Or I will shoot," she repeated.

He held the gun by his thigh, making no attempt to drop it. Halliday sensed from his body language that he'd decided to go for broke.

As he lifted up his hand to fire at her, she fired two shots in quick succession. The first hit his hand gripping the gun. The force of the bullet flung the weapon out of his grasp onto the floor. The second shot hit him in the right shoulder, causing him to cry out in agony.

He'd collapsed onto the floor when Halliday reached him. She pushed him onto his stomach and cuffed his good hand to the leg of a desk. His other hand was bleeding profusely, but she was not going to leave him unrestrained while his gun was still lying around somewhere.

Halliday gave him first aid as she radioed for ambulances and additional police support. The beam of her flashlight found his weapon lying under a chair. She left it there. There would be an investigation into her use of live fire. It was better if his gun was found by someone else.

Liv was still huddled under the desk when Halliday found her. "Are you okay?" she asked, reaching out her hand to pull Liv from her hiding place. "It's all over."

"He was going to kill me," said Liv. Her face was pale, and she trembled violently. Halliday could see that she was in shock.

"It's over, Liv," said Halliday, putting her arm around her. "You're safe now."

The whine of sirens cut through the sudden silence that had descended on the basement storeroom once the echo of gunshots had faded.

"That must be the ambulances. The paramedics will take care of you."

"And then what?" Liv asked. "Are you going to arrest me for murder?"

Police lights lit up the darkness outside. A convoy of cop cars and two ambulances pulled to a stop outside the warehouse. Doors opened and slammed shut, followed by the thump of footsteps as police and medics ran toward them in the dark.

"You'll go to the hospital to make sure you're okay. While you're there, we'll look at the evidence with a new set of eyes. Remember, I was in here with you. I heard him talking to you before I came through the window. I heard him confess. All of that helps us build a case against him. Either way, he kidnapped and almost killed you. He's going to go away for a very long time."

Halliday helped Liv climb out of the basement window where a police officer waited with a thermal blanket. He threw it over her shivering body as he took her to the front ambulance, its whirring siren lights painting the warehouse crimson.

Chapter
Sixty-Five

Twelve Hours Later
Thursday 11:45 A.M.

"Halliday. Lavelle," the captain called out when he noticed the two detectives enter the office, single file. The glass Detective Bureau doors slammed shut behind them. "In my office. Now."

Lavelle leaned against the filing cabinet with his arms crossed. Halliday sat by the captain's desk while they waited for him to finish a phone call.

"Lavelle, you look like shit. Get rid of the stubble," the captain said when he'd hung up the phone. "That was the media team. They've scheduled a press briefing. You can't face TV cameras looking like a drunk, Jack."

"Not a drunk, just a hardworking detective too tired to shave this morning. We both had maybe two hours' sleep last night," Lavelle said, looking at Halliday for confirmation. "Anyway, I won't be addressing the media. Detective Halliday will do the talking."

The captain turned his attention to Halliday. She wore a dark blue suit with a pale pink shirt that matched her light makeup. Her chestnut hair was tied up in a tight ponytail. She looked fresh and focused.

"Jack says you did well."

"I held my own."

"You more than held your own," the captain said approvingly. "Now tell me. What evidence do we have against Brett Graham?"

Halliday handed him a preliminary report, which he flicked through as she spoke. "The lab's checking the Ted Cole murder weapon for Brett Graham's DNA. Apparently, he cut himself on the blade when he stabbed Cole."

Halliday's voice was hoarse. She'd been up most of the night fielding questions from internal investigators about the shooting. She'd been swabbed for gunshot residue and she'd had to write a detailed statement about what had happened at the warehouse. Her final statement was eight pages long.

Lavelle had stayed at the warehouse for most of the night while it was processed by investigators and the forensics team. He and Halliday had gone straight to the lab first thing in the morning to find out what evidence they had to build a case against Brett Graham.

"I see the Reese woman's prints are on the knife," the captain said, scanning the report. "That will complicate things in court."

They all knew it wouldn't be a cut-and-dry case, especially given Liv Reese's amnesia. It would be difficult to build a solid case on the testimony of a witness with documented memory problems.

"Any hard evidence that ties our suspect to the Cole murder?" the captain asked, handing the lab report back to Halliday.

"Microscopic chips of black paint were found at the murder scene," said Halliday. "The lab matched paint scraped from under Brett Graham's fingernails to the paint traces found at the murder scene. It also matches the black paint at Liv Reese's apartment, suggesting Brett Graham was at her apartment where he destroyed evidence by painting the walls and setting fire to her journal."

"He sure did everything he could to cover his tracks," the captain said. "That's a heck of a lot of effort to go to. He didn't even know Ted Cole. Why kill him?" the captain asked.

"To frame Liv Reese for the murder," said Lavelle. "He figured that once we charged Liv Reese for the Cole murder, we'd charge her with the Decker-Reggio murders as well, which had a similar MO. Then the case would be officially closed. He didn't want to live in fear that Liv Reese's memory might come back."

"Still, to kill a man just in case. I'm not sure if a jury would buy it," the captain said.

"Ted Cole was also helping Liv Reese find out who'd killed her friends," Halliday explained. "He was asking around about things that connected Graham to the Decker-Reggio murders. Graham found out and decided to remove Cole from the equation. Permanently. Framing Liv Reese was the cherry on top."

"What sorts of questions was Cole asking?"

Halliday told the captain how earlier that morning she had finally reached the designer who'd telephoned Cole when he was at the apartment of his fiancée, Elisabeth, on the night Cole was murdered. The designer said that Ted had asked him to make inquiries about a dotted fleur-de-lis sketch that Liv Reese had drawn after a flashback of Amy and Marco's murders.

"The designer reached out to an exclusive men's custom-made shoe store on Cole's behalf. The store is well-known for giving each client their own unique dotted medallion design. Brett Graham's design was a fleur-de-lis. It was on all his shoes."

Halliday showed the captain a copy of the sketch, as well as a photo of Graham's shoes from the previous night, which they'd taken into evidence. The captain whistled when she told him that the shoes cost over $1,500 a pair. Graham apparently owned more than a dozen pairs.

"When the owner of the shoe boutique heard that questions were being asked about Graham's unique shoe design, he contacted Graham as a curtesy to let him know," explained Halliday. "That's probably what tipped Graham off that Ted Cole, Liv Reese's ex, was asking questions about him."

On the way to brief the captain, the two detectives had stopped at the exclusive bespoke shoe store on Fifty-Seventh Street. The owner had shown Halliday and Lavelle photos of the shoes his artisans had made for Graham over the years. Among them was a pair of oxblood shoes that Amy had given Brett for his birthday before she died. Halliday suspected this was the pair he'd worn when he'd murdered Amy and Marco. That might explain Reese's flashback of shoes covered with blood that Detective Larry Regan had mentioned when they'd spoken to him earlier. At the time, Reese's recollection had been dismissed because there was no blood tracked on the carpet at the murder scene. Maybe the killer's shoes weren't covered in blood, they were simply the color of blood: oxblood, Halliday had suggested to Lavelle on the way back to the precinct.

"Liv Reese is awake again. Her doctors say she can talk to us," said Lavelle after checking a message on his phone. "We'd better head over to the hospital before she falls asleep again."

"Before you go, I'll need you to hand over your weapon, Detective Halliday," the captain told Halliday as she stood to leave. "It's only until the report on the shooting is submitted. You'll have plenty of time to catch up on paperwork over the next few days."

Halliday unclipped her service weapon from her holster, removed the ammunition clip, and put both down on his desk. She'd be on desk duty until the Internal Affairs investigation into the shooting was complete. From the way she'd been questioned the previous night, one of the key issues would be why she didn't shoot to kill. There had even been a suggestion that she might need extra sessions at the firing range to improve the accuracy of her shot.

Halliday told the investigators that she'd deliberately winged the suspect. They'd asked her why. She'd said she did it because she was a good enough shot to accurately disarm him without killing him. She preferred knowing he was in a prison cell rather than the grave.

"Being a desk jockey for a few days is actually good news," the captain said as he put her weapon and badge in a locked desk drawer.

"In what way?"

"It will give you time to prepare."

"Time to prepare for what?" Halliday asked.

"Your application. We have a permanent homicide detective position opening up. We're advertising it next week. You'd be our preferred candidate. That's if you decide to apply, of course. Maybe I'm being presumptuous, Detective Halliday. Maybe working homicides isn't your thing."

"I'll be putting in an application. Yes, I will," said Halliday before heading to the door.

"I'll need a referee to vouch for you," the captain called after her.

"You can put me down," said Lavelle, putting on his jacket and following Halliday out of the office.

Chapter
Sixty-Six

Liv Reese was dozing in a hospital bed when Halliday and Lavelle entered her room, waiting near the window as the nurse checked her vital signs.

She stirred from the noise of the beeping heart monitor machine and slowly opened her eyes. Liv had been up half the night giving a sworn videotaped statement to Detective Tran about what had happened at the warehouse. Lavelle had insisted Tran take her statement before Liv went to sleep because of the possibility that she might wake with no memory of the events of the previous night.

"How're you feeling today?" the nurse asked, half-opening the venetian blinds. Streaks of daylight covered the hospital bed linen.

"Exhausted," Liv answered. The hospital gown she wore emphasized the pallor of her skin. Her hair was rumpled from sleep and her eyes were bleary as she blinked to adjust to the light. "What's the time?"

"It's after two," the nurse said, wrapping a Velcro blood pressure sleeve around Liv's upper arm. "You've been asleep since the doctor woke you at ten this morning to check on you."

Liv noticed Halliday and Lavelle standing near the venetian window shades. When the nurse was done, she plumped up Liv's pillows and blankets and pulled over the uneaten food tray before leaving the room.

"You're the detective from last night." Liv's gaze fixed on Halliday.

"You remember me?" Halliday asked, pulling out the visitor's chair and sitting down so they were at the same eye level.

"I remember everything that happened after I woke on the train platform last night. I remember the warehouse, the shooting, and the ambulance ride to the hospital. I especially remember you. You saved my life."

Halliday colored slightly from the depth of Liv Reese's gratitude. "So you're cured? No more memory problems?" she asked.

"The doctors say that if I sleep properly and I don't take caffeine and other stimulants to stay awake, then it's unlikely to happen again. But there's no guarantee."

"Getting your memory back is a big step in the right direction," said Halliday.

Liv Reese's face was downcast. "I suppose," she said with a sad shrug. "The doctors don't think I'll ever remember the period that I've forgotten. That means I'll always be missing two years of my life. I guess it's something that I'll have to come to terms with."

Liv picked up the remote control for the bed and pressed a button to raise the bed so she could sit up properly. "I wouldn't be here if it wasn't for you, Detective. I'd be dead for sure. There are no words to thank you for what you did. Risking your own life to save mine."

"You should thank yourself. You were smart enough to alert me by sharing your location," Halliday said. "I dread to think what would have happened if you hadn't been so quick-thinking."

"I was taking a risk, trusting you," said Liv. "I knew you suspected me of murder. It was all over the TV. I figured that worst-case scenario you'd track me down to arrest me for murder. It seemed like my only hope."

"We're not pursuing any murder charges against you. We believe that Brett Graham drugged and killed Ted Cole. He wrote the WAKE UP! message on the window to make it look as if you'd done it because you have that same message written on your hand. It was another link that tied you to the Cole murder," said Halliday.

"Why would he kill Ted Cole?"

"Ted was asking uncomfortable questions that could connect Brett back to the Decker-Reggio murders. Brett decided to kill Ted and frame you for his murder," said Lavelle.

The pathologist had found a needle mark in Ted Cole's hairline. Their theory was that Brett Graham injected Ted with a sedative from behind, most likely in the bedroom. Ted collapsed on the bed where he was stripped of his clothes and stabbed. It was set up to look like an assignation. The idea was that Liv would be found holding the bloodied murder weapon while sleeping alongside Ted's lifeless body in the morning.

"Brett must have met you at the bar, Nocturnal, and taken you back to the apartment Ted rented for you. We don't know why you went with him. Perhaps, knowing you had no memory, he pretended to take you to Amy. Either way, at some point he gave you white wine from a bottle he'd laced with sedatives."

"I hate white wine. I never take more than a sip," said Liv.

"He probably didn't notice that you'd drunk very little. He must have left you alone, thinking you were fast asleep from the wine. That must have been when you escaped."

"I ran away?" Liv shook her head as if hoping it would help her remember.

"You more than ran away," said Lavelle. "You ran away with the murder weapon."

"Why would I have done that?" Liv asked.

"Maybe it was to save an important piece of evidence. The knife may help us convict him."

At the precinct, Rosco and Tran were trawling through CCTV footage to find footage of Brett Graham sneaking out of the apartment building after spending the night in the utility room. Halliday was sure something would come up in the hundreds of hours of surveillance footage if they looked hard enough.

The crime scene team would go back to the apartment building that afternoon to look for fingerprints in the utility room where he'd hidden. Once the search warrant was signed, Halliday and Lavelle would lead a team searching Brett Graham's apartment. They intended to take his custom-made fleur-de-lis shoe collection as evidence so that the lab could test the shoes for blood splatter that connected to the Decker-Reggio murders. They hoped to charge him for the double murder as well.

"How did Brett track me down?" Liv asked.

"He must have seen you at the hospital when you came to get your brain scans," said Halliday, explaining that Ted had arranged for Liv to see a neurologist about her amnesia. "We know that Brett accessed your medical file on the day you had the scan. His hospital ID number appears in the data history. That's what the hospital administrator told us when we spoke to her earlier. That's probably how Brett got hold of your address."

"Is that how he knew that my memory was erased each time I went to sleep?"

"We believe so. That information was detailed in your medical records he accessed."

There was a fine line between answering Liv's questions and giving her an information overload that might traumatize her further. They'd spoken to Liv's doctor before they came in and he'd asked them to go gentle on her. She was still emotionally fragile.

"It's my fault that Ted Cole was killed," said Liv. "He died because he was helping me. I'm incredibly sad that I don't remember him."

Halliday was sorry that Liv's journal had been destroyed. The social worker had said the journal was a written account of Liv's life since she'd been treated for unexplained memory loss at the hospital in London. Brett had burned the journal, turning it into a pile of ashes. With the journal destroyed and Ted gone, there was nobody to fill in Liv's memory.

Halliday and Lavelle had theorized how the murder had gone down on the way over to the hospital. The way they figured it, in the hours before the Cole murder and possibly afterward as well, Brett Graham had gone to Liv's basement apartment and destroyed everything she and Ted Cole had found out about Amy and Marco's murders. He burned her journal and the newspaper clippings she'd collected. He painted the apartment walls black so that nobody would be able to decipher the theories and clues Liv had scribbled on the walls.

Liv's cell phone number had probably been written in her journal. He'd called her up and lured her to Nocturnal, which he knew from reading her journal was her regular haunt. He'd somehow tricked her into taking him back to the safe-house apartment. That's where he drugged her with wine and hid while waiting for Cole to return. It appeared from phone records that while he waited, he'd used the apartment phone to contact the cleaning service to send a cleaner in the morning. The phone number for the cleaning service was on the fridge. He must have intended for the cleaner to find Liv fast asleep with Ted's body in the morning.

"What happens to me now?" Liv asked.

"You'll be free to resume your life once you're discharged in a couple of days," said Lavelle.

"What life? Either I go back to London to live a life I don't remember, or I stay here in a life that has changed beyond recognition," she said, despondently.

"Or maybe you start fresh," said Halliday, rising from her seat. "Transitions are never easy. You'll get through this, Liv. Trust me."

"We'd better get going," said Lavelle, checking his phone messages. "The doctor says we can talk to Brett Graham."

"Brett's here? At the hospital?" Liv asked, visibly distressed at the thought they were under the same roof.

"He's in a different wing, handcuffed to a bed with a police guard," said Halliday. "I hear he finds it humiliating to be treated like a criminal at the hospital where he used to throw around his weight as a big-time surgeon. He'll have to get used to it. It'll be a lot worse when he's in prison."

She paused as a good-looking man with dark hair and a goatee entered the hospital room carrying a stunning gift basket of flowers and a large foil GET WELL balloon.

"I know you," said Liv, as the man reticently approached her hospital bed. Liv furrowed her brow as she tried to place him. "You're the bartender from last night."

"Yes. I'd like to think that we're also good friends, even though this is the first time you've actually remembered me," he said with a smile. He put the flower arrangement next to Liv's hospital bed.

"If we're friends, then you'd better tell me your name, so I remember it the next time we see each other," Liv said.

"I'm Harry," he said, reaching out to shake Liv's hand before sitting down on the chair next to her hospital bed.

Halliday and Lavelle left the room, closing the door gently behind them.

Acknowledgments

Stay Awake was written during the throes of the COVID-19 pandemic. That is to say that it was largely written in my car, which was the only quiet place I could find while homeschooling my kids during 270 days of lockdown in Melbourne, Australia. It was a structurally challenging novel to write for a variety of reasons, not least because it was written from the perspective of an amnesiac. So, in short, I chose the worst possible time to write it. Perhaps not surprisingly, I wrote myself into the occasional blind alley. I have my agent, David Gernert, and Ellen Coughtrey and Anna Worrall from the Gernert Company, to thank for helping me navigate myself out of those dead ends. I wish to extend my deepest appreciation to Charles Spicer for his invaluable advice and support, as well as to Jennifer Enderlin, Sarah Grill, and the rest of the fabulous team at St. Martin's and Macmillan.

To Ali Watts and Johannes Jakob at my Australian publisher, Penguin Random House Australia, as well as to my other international publishers and translators, I am enormously grateful for all your support. I'd like to extend my appreciation to Rebecca Gardner and the rights team at the Gernert Company, and all their co-agents, for getting my novels the widest possible audience across the world.

Stay Awake was also written during two deaths in the family: that of my husband's beloved mother and his older brother. May their memories be blessed.

To my husband and sons, thank you for all you do for me (and I am not just referring to the constant flow of cups of tea!). Thank you also to my parents and my sister and brother. After *The Night Swim* was published, I received many messages that moved me greatly. Somehow these messages always managed to arrive just at the right moment, usually when I was going through an existential crisis and about to rip up the current manuscript. So a very special thanks to all the readers who reached out to me.